T0196914

Abby's Birthright

JUDON GRAY

authorHOUSE®

AuthorHouse™
1663 Liberty Drive
Bloomington, IN 47403
www.authorhouse.com
Phone: 1 (800) 839-8640

Published by AuthorHouse 11/19/2015

ISBN: 978-1-5049-6205-6 (sc)
ISBN: 978-1-5049-6204-9 (e)

Library of Congress Control Number: 2015918929

Print information available on the last page.

Chapter One

Abigail Anderson stared in horror at the smug smiling girl in front of her. "*You horrible rotten little witch! You're nothing but a disgusting liar Elizabeth Whatley! I absolutely hate you! You are a horrible, mean nasty person and no one can stand the likes of your lying big mouth! I hate you! I hate you! I hate you!*"

Horrified, Abby's hand quickly covered her mouth as she heard the unbidden ugly words she'd just screamed non-stop at her adversary. Her vision quickly scanned the ballroom to see what damage she had done to herself. Immediately, her face turned beet red. It felt as if her cheeks were going to burst into flames at any moment. Total embarrassment assailed her as she realized many of the dancing guests had stopped to stare at her with their mouths hanging open in surprise.

But even her embarrassment could not stop her anger from rising. She focused her uncontrollable rage back upon the smug smiling girl standing in front of her. Absolutely livid Abby suddenly slapped the other girl soundly on the cheek using all the strength her small frame could muster.

"*Oh! Why you….*" Gasping from the pain, Elizabeth automatically covered her injured cheek with her lace gloved hand.

Surprised, Abby looked in disbelief down at her own hand, now red and burning. She hadn't realize she was going to slap the hateful woman until after her hand firmly connected against the offending girl's face.

But to have done so in front of the dancing ball patrons was totally reprehensible. Vaguely aware of the spectacle she was making of herself, she realized it was now too late to undo the harm she'd done to her social status among her peers. Let alone the damage done to her by Elizabeth Whatley's nasty hate filled message. That terrible message, whether true or not was harmful enough to completely destroy the perfectly happy life Abby Anderson currently enjoyed. She was ruined! There was no way out! No way at all to fix the damages publicly done to her social status. Her whole body shook as this realization shattered her confidence.

Staring at her hand in disbelief did not stop Abby's anger from accelerating. It actually did the opposite. Her confusion and anger accelerated so quickly she was unable to think coherently. She raised her disbelieving, angry green eyes away from her red swelling hand and stared deliberately into her adversary's smirking violet eyes only to see that the disgusting excuse of a girl was smugly mocking her in return. Elizabeth was relishing her victory over Abby and she was making certain that Abby knew it.

Realizing how excited and delighted Elizabeth was at Abby's unacceptable behavior paralyzed Abby. Frozen in place, she found she couldn't move a muscle. For what seemed to her to be an eternity, her eyes remained angrily focused on Elizabeth. She didn't dare look at anyone else in the room. But her ears did not spare her the knowledge that the music had stopped and she knew that everyone in the room was now focusing on her own unacceptable ugly behavior. She knew that no one had heard the horrific tale Elizabeth had spouted. But in her heart she was fully aware that it would matter not. She would never be able to save herself now. Almost immediately her face grew to an embarrassing shade of purple! She wanted to explode into a thousand pieces and never ever be heard of again! Then the absolute worst that could happen, did happen.

Appalled at herself, Abby heard herself begin to splutter confusing loud incoherent sounds directed at her accusing adversary.

As if that additional embarrassment wasn't enough, she was additionally mortified to feel hot tears begin streaming down her scarlet cheeks for everyone else to see.

Everything was closing in on her and there was no place in the huge brightly lit ballroom where she could seek comfort or a single person to whom she could look to for support. Unable to control herself and embarrassed beyond words, Abby's fingers unconsciously grabbed the voluminous skirts of her pink silk ball gown, her legs pivoted on their own without instructions from her horrified conscious mind. She was out of the ballroom and halfway down the long decorated hallway to the main entry of the mansion before she realized she was running away from her adversary, the dancing guests, and from all the pain that the last few minutes had bestowed upon her.

She couldn't leave the Harrison's elaborately decorated Mansion quickly enough. Her only thought was to get away, far away from everyone who had witnessed her ugly behavior but mostly to get away from the girl who had delivered the malicious message that had just brought Abby's happy life to an abrupt halt.

Everyone stared in amazement at the crying girl as she flew pass them. Immediately they began gossiping among themselves. Unkind vicious rumors were artfully created by the dancing guests. Many began sharing juicy tidbits of information of their own creations. The immediate desire was the prestige they would gain to be the first one among them to tell the others the juiciest facts regarding the spectacle Abby Anderson had just made of herself. Attention to themselves was much more important than worry for the overly distraught young woman. Many had no concern at all that the tidbits they shared were exaggerated or entirely made up expressly for the convenience of the moment. That no one actually knew the truth was of zero concern in the excited atmosphere.

The event in attendance was the annual spring ball held the end of April, each year in Savannah, Georgia. In the year of 1849, it was absolutely unheard of for a debutant to portray untoward physical behavior towards another person, much less to utter such ugly hateful comments against anyone publicly, regardless of how the person personally felt about the other person. To do so immediately guaranteed the bearer of such behavior to be excommunicated from the genteel social crowd. Abby realized instantly that her unchecked angry responses to Elizabeth Whatley's unexpected and horrific comments had helped to complete the damage that Elizabeth had sought. And running away like a scared chicken certainly wasn't helping her either. But at this point she no longer cared. Her blooming social life had just come to a complete halt and there was no fix for the situation. Absolutely no way to repair the damage at all! She was utterly and completely destroyed!

Elizabeth Whatley covered her face with both hands more to hide her delighted smile of satisfaction than to nurture the angry red streaks that Abby's palm had left on her rosy cheekbone. It was her intent to destroy Abby Anderson tonight, but she was absolutely delighted that Abby, herself, had helped her to accomplish her ugly task. She knew Abby's physical abuse to her was to her advantage. As much as she wanted to retaliate she made a mental note to take care of retribution for the slap from Abby at a later date. For the moment, her purpose required her to let it slide.

In fact Things were going much better for Elizabeth than she could have ever hoped for. Abby's ugly un-lady like comments directed at her and then slapping her publicly was simply icing on the cake for Elizabeth. She smothered her delighted smile of satisfaction and feigned an injured look filled with surprise in front of the dancing guests now quickly gathering around her.

"Well my gracious goodness! Whateva did I do ta deserve ta be slapped so viciously! Why, and... so unceremoniously at that?" She whimpered indicating pain, but kept her famous southern drawl in effect as she expelled a slight laugh. The laugh was just enough to intimate to those around her that even though the slap had been entirely unjustified and had surprised her completely she was being mature about it and graciously excusing Abby for her horrendous behavior.

"Why, I haven't the slightest idea what I possibly could have said or done…," she dropped her sentence at the perfect moment to feign total surprise and to confirm to her peers that she had just been attacked without provocation. She made certain that all indications pointed to her innocence at having supplied any reason at all to have caused the unjustified attack.

"My heaven's sake! Why, I am just so… so… shocked!" She exclaimed quietly. Fanning herself earnestly, she continued, "Did any of ya'll hear me say anything ta deserve such ill treatment?" she empathized the words *ill treatment*. Carefully, but quickly she observed her audience. She had to ascertain that no one had heard the terrible shocking accusations that she had just bestowed on Abigail Anderson but she was certain that if they did she wasn't going to give them a chance to reply. Her comments absolutely needed to remain between herself and the girl whom she hated with all her heart.

To her satisfaction, every one appeared to be staring at her in surprise and confusion. Unconsciously nodding her head in satisfaction that her crime remained unknown, she continued, exaggerating her drawn out, famously known, southern drawl, she rubbed softly at her inflamed cheek. "Why I most absolutely neva?" With these empty words so simply spoken, she feigned surprise, disbelief and her innocence all in one.

Still satisfied that she was receiving the results she craved from the crowd she continued, "Really, did any of ya'll see her slap me?" Again she inquired, her intent this time to carefully judge the immediate replies and reactions of her audience. Without waiting for an answer she continued her charade non-stop.

"Why, I just can't possibly imagine what our dear Abby could be so upset over? I swear! I only told her the *absolute truth*!" She moved to defend her obvious statement that had caused the offending slap by emphasizing her final words. "I truly just don't know why she felt she needed ta *slap* me and to degrade me so horrendously and publicly at that?" Again she feigned her confusion but put her emphasis on the word slap. Coyly, she stared in dismay at each person in the murmuring crowd gathering around her seeking sympathy. Noting some doubt among her friends, she wisely decided it was in her best interest to force fake tears to run down her cheek as proof of her unexpected surprise regarding Abby's behavior to her gawking audience.

"Elizabeth Whatley! Whatever did you say to our dearest Abby?" Elaine Wolfe, Abby's best friend, had rushed over the second she saw Abby run from the room. She angrily confronted Elizabeth. "Abby would never have run out of here like that if she didn't have a very good reason!" She hurried to assure the murmuring guests now in attendance of the unexpected disturbance.

"Why my dearest Elaine," Elizabeth mocked Abby's friend, "I am quite certain that I haven't the slightest idea of whateva you think you are referring to?" Elizabeth smartly retorted as she spun to glare directly upon Elaine. Her expression momentarily flashed a vengeful warning to Elaine not to contradict her.

Satisfied that Elaine's sudden silence meant that she had taken heed of her warning, Elizabeth turned her attention back to her audience again and continued to feign her innocence. Nervously, she fingered the yellow satin sash of her newly designed *Parisian* gown. Ordered direct from Paris, Elizabeth's ball gown was created in the latest fashion unseen as yet by the guests in attendance. It was meant to bring immediate attention to her from those attending the ball. She had taken great pains to look absolutely beautiful for this nights festivities. In order to ward off any blame for her intended actions, she knew it was important that she present an aura indicating her supremacy of those around her. Wearing the newest fashions would have the crowds envying her and wanting to be in her good graces in order that they might glean information from her regarding her knowledge of the newest fashions for their own interests.

Her mother had advised her that this night she was going to need all the favorable attention she could get in order to justify her innocence regarding the cruelties they intended to bestow upon Abigail Anderson. Because together they had worked very hard, at carefully but deliberately planning the destruction of Abby Anderson and Jeffrey Browning's recent engagement.

Elizabeth hated Abby with a passion. A year ago, Elizabeth was certain that Jeffrey was just about to ask her for her hand in marriage. But at the very moment he went down on one knee, her hopes had come to an abrupt end as his attention was taken by the vision of Abigail Anderson's grand entrance into the room.

Abby Anderson had just made her first coming out debut by attending the Harrison's spring ball last year. Indeed she was a vision to behold as she pranced easily into the great ball room on her father's arm.

Jeffrey had taken one look at the flashing red head and her dark green eyes and was immediately smitten with her. The vision of this lovely woman with yards of yellow silk swirling all around her as she moved was all he could concentrate on. Unconsciously he had risen from his bended knee totally forgetting about his flirtations with Elizabeth, whom he had never intended to seriously propose to. He'd simply been enjoying his game to play with the daft girl's affections. Elizabeth's obvious desires for him had amused him greatly right up to the moment he had seen the vision of the girl enveloped in yellow. However once he laid eyes upon the golden vision his body had moved immediately in Abby's direction and all thoughts of Elizabeth were completely forgotten. Elizabeth's jealousy began at that moment and she'd had a full year to inflame it to the point of uncontrollable hatred. Upon Abby's and Jeffrey's engagement announcement, she could think of nothing but to find a way to destroy her adversary in the hopes of turning Jeffrey's attentions back to her.

Elaine decided to ignore the dare. Angrily she insisted, "Stop it Elizabeth! I am quite certain that you must surely know exactly what you have said to our dear Abby! So now, dearest sweetie, why don't you please enlighten the rest of us all?" Abby's best friend sent a dare of her own straight back to Elizabeth by mocking the girl's famous southern drawl.

Fire flashed from Elizabeth's violet eyes as she pivoted her attention once again onto Elaine. The crowd was murmuring loudly anticipating the cat fight between the two women. Abby and Elaine were not the only ones who had suffered occasionally from Elizabeth's unkind mouth spouting her inappropriate comments, actions, and yes, lies about themselves on more than one occasion or another. Some in the group were not certain that Elizabeth had not deserved the slap after all.

Elaine could only imagine what had sent Abby into such distress. Everyone present at the ball knew how jealous Elizabeth Whatley was of Abby. It was very apparent to all that her jealousy had blossomed since the public announcement of Abby and Jeffrey's engagement only a week ago.

Glaring her warning a second time at Elaine, Elizabeth snubbed her nose in the girl's direction as she sarcastically retorted.

"Well darling Elaine, since you think you know so much, why don't you just go and ask your dear, dear Abby, for yourself!" Turning her nose into the air she faced away from Elaine dismissing her haughtily.

With her back facing Elaine again, she made it clear that she fully intended to ignore both Elaine's challenge and her presence. She began fanning herself in earnest in order to cover her second smile of victorious delight. Continuing to completely ignore Elaine's continued protests, she turned and addressed the ball patrons around them.

Laughing lightly behind her fan she said softly, "Oh it's nothing, really! Come, everyone, shan't we all just return to our delightful dancing!" she encouraged everyone to leave Elaine's presence before they found out more than she needed them too.

Without interrupting her own conversation she quickly continued, "Why my dearest Mr. Jim Tucker, how very handsome you are looking tonight! And how very lucky I am that I do believe you owe me this next dance." She began flirting outrageously with Jim as she boldly grabbed his hand, and quickly dragged him to the dance floor where she could completely dismiss Elaine and her continued demands for an explanation. She felt no shame at abusing her friend Jim. She always used him to help cover her actions whenever he was available. That she hurt him publicly in front of his friends again mattered not one bit to her.

Angrily, Jim accepted Elizabeth's hand. As he swung her into the first steps of the dance he jerked her roughly to let her know he was irritated with her. Although he hadn't heard the conversation between Abby and Elizabeth, he definitely knew that yet again, Elizabeth had just used him unforgivably. He had looked forward to an opportunity to openly court the raven haired, violet eyed, girl tonight, but now she had deeply embarrassed him in front his colleagues. Although he craved her attention this was not the way he had dreamed of receiving it. Yet again! He admitted to himself.

"I don't suppose you would care to enlighten me on what you have said to Abby Anderson?" he harshly inquired as he expertly glided Elizabeth thru the first steps of the popular new waltz.

"In due time dear, in due time," was Elizabeth's sly answer. She smiled and tapped him on the chin with her fan then quickly spun away from him to her new dance partner for the next step of the waltz.

Reluctantly letting go of her hand, Jim wondered what he had seen in her to begin with. She was definitely beautiful. His heart jumped each time he saw her shining blue-black hair, violet eyes and dainty heart shaped chin and hourglass body. But he knew there was something wrong about her.

He couldn't put his finger on it. Maybe it was her lack of concern for others that bothered him? Jim doubted that any man, including himself, would ever be fully comfortable in Elizabeth's presence. Unfortunately, it was too late for him. He was already madly in love with her and had been for a number of years. He had lost his heart to her when he was the tender age of sixteen and he first met her at a summer barbeque. She had flirted outrageously with him in her intent to make the other young gentlemen around her jealous. She had gone so far as to kiss him behind the big oak tree pretending to be soliciting his favors, while she made certain that other young men caught her in the act. Thus they were assured that they could probably experience the same kiss and who knew what other enticements from her.

As with most young men and their first kiss, Jim had lost his heart to her at that moment. But unlike the fortunate others, he had never been able to put his attentions away from her from then on. Right then and there he made the decision to make her his future wife! However it was now four years later and he had not succeeded in his attempts to entice her to marry him at all. Quite the contrary, she simply used him every opportunity he was near her and then dumped him immediately when she no longer needed to use his affections to her advantage. She had hurt him endlessly with her flirtatious behavior with other men right in front of him, but he could not overpower the hold her attractiveness and that first kiss still held over him. He knew he would continue to suffer in silence until some day he would make her realize that she was meant for him.

He dreamed of the day when she would accept him as her knight in shining armor. Then she would know that it would be he, Jim Tucker, who would protect her from her own self destructive ways. "Ah love, sweet love, what is a man to do when he has no control over his own heart?" He mused silently to himself as he jealously watched her glide from partner to partner expertly flirting with each of the men dancers in turn.

Frustrated and embarrassed at being summarily dismissed, Elaine decided to excuse herself from the group and left the ballroom to look for Abby. She was doubly frustrated with Elizabeth. Not only had Elizabeth summarily dismissed Elaine in front of everyone but, once again, she had gotten away with another one of her many acts of cruelty.

Elizabeth's warning glare had also not been lost on her. She knew that if Elizabeth really wanted to destroy Elaine's blossoming relationship with Robert Grayson, Elaine's fiancé, she would jump to the cause and with her many charms and expertise she probably would succeed at stealing Robert from Elaine. Of course Elaine knew that Elizabeth didn't give a care about her precious Robert and never would, but she wouldn't think twice about using and abusing him just to hurt Elaine and Elaine was not about to allow Elizabeth to do that.

"Have you seen which way Abby Anderson went?" Elaine stopped long enough to ask Harriet Harrison, the patron of the ball. Harriet was avidly conversing with several of her matronly companions in the romantically decorated hallway of the huge Savannah mansion. They had been complimenting her on the gigantic basins of pink and yellow roses strategically placed among the white and blue lilies that were lining the elaborately decorated hallway leading to the ballroom but had been interrupted by the girl rushing hastily through the center of them. Now their gossip had turned to the girl in hasty retreat.

"Oh my goodness!" Harriet excitedly declared to Elaine, "Abby just ran right out here in front of us all! You know we'all just had to scatter so very quickly to avoid being knocked down by her. Do you know whateva has happened to her, Elaine? My gracious sakes, I think the poor girl was crying too! Oh my, I do so hope she is not ill?" Harriet was genuinely concerned for Abby. She fancied herself to be an acting mother to Abby, since Abby's own mother had died so young in Abby's young life.

"I just wish I knew! I most definitely am going to find out as soon as I find her!" Elaine replied ruefully over her shoulder as she hastily continued on her way to search for Abby.

"Oh dear!" Harriet wrung her hands, "I'm so certain this untoward incident is just absolutely going to ruin my ball! Absolutely just ruin all my plans!" She lamented to her woman companions. "My hard planning will all have been for naught! Oh dear! Whatever shall I do now?"

Her lady friends gathered around her quickly, reassuring her that Abby's problem was not her fault. Clustering her among themselves, they continued to gossip about Abby as they maneuvered their hostess into the grand ball room.

"I wouldn't be worrying overmuch," Sarah Bennington winked at Harriett. She tapped her friend lightly on the shoulder with her unopened fan, "In fact, I shouldn't be at all surprised if you won't owe our dear Abby for the delightful success she will have made of the Ball for you," she sneakily whispered in her hostesses ear as she continued speaking louder with, "Come now girl's. Let us all try to find out just what has happened? Who knows, maybe, Abby's going to make this year's ball the most talked about event of the year!" she exclaimed.

"Oh, do you think so?" A shaken Harriet replied. Her genuine concern for young Abby immediately disappeared as she quickly realized her own advantage at Abby's bad behavior. Her demeanor suddenly changed from worry for her self-declared ward, to feeling selfishly excited and hopeful in succeeding at hosting the greatest Savannah social event yet another year in a row.

"Why most absolutely I certainly do! Why Harriet, my dear, you know just how very much we all look forward to your annual spring ball! Why, it's simply the most exciting social gathering of each and every year!" Sarah's southern drawl was comforting to Harriet's ear. She was salivating thinking of the great success this scandal could make of her endeavor to make this year's ball the grandest ball ever!

"Really…? Do ya'll think that I did well with the decorations for my spring ball?" Dismissing Abby's plight, Harriet fished for compliments regarding her hard work and very expensive planning.

"You most certainly did!" Her many friends hurried to assure her. "Why, Harriett dearest, I simply adore the gorgeous flower arrangements you have selected this year. These, yellow and pink roses, just make those absolutely perfect white lilies standout all on their own." Sarah said. She and her friends all chorused together continuing to babble on and on about the daisies intermixed with pale pink rose buds and blue morning glories. Rolling their eyes upward, they clasped their hands together to indicate their approval.

"Why it most certainly just brings all the fragrances of springtime to one's mind! And goodness gracious me, the way those candles are reflecting on your brand new polished ballroom floor, why they are just lighting up the grand letter "H" you have inlaid in the middle of all your gorgeous new hardwood. Why, dearest, what can I say, but it is simply beautiful! Just simply beautiful!" Commented one of the plump busybody ladies determined to compliment her hostess in hopes of becoming one of her actively sought out companions. Any acknowledged friend of Harriet Harrison might as well have earned the key to the city!

The women were all jealously fighting each other for Harriet's attentions. The comments of the women continued their praises on and on culminating with, "We absolutely must enlist your helping us with the planning of Savanah's great Fourth of July picnic for this year." Steadily, her women friends maneuvered Harriett into the crowd where they all began urgent inquiries regarding Abby's hasty untoward retreat.

Meanwhile, Elaine fruitlessly continued her search for Abby. She found Abby's cloak still in the cloakroom and all of her personal items were undisturbed in the room the young ladies had been assigned to use to prepare themselves for the evening's festivities. A search of the kitchen, the servant quarters and the grounds turned up nothing. The drawing room and the library were over filled with male guests who were smoking, gambling at cards and drinking. Elaine chose not to enter the male dominated library as she spied Abby's father engrossed at a table playing a game of cards. She elected not to alarm him as she didn't really know what had happened to Abby. She decided it was unnecessary to disturb him because for all she knew, Abby was probably dancing again in the ballroom by now and was probably in no harm at all. Besides, being the only woman in this room filled with smoking and alcohol consuming males intimidated her.

Heading into the Solarium she quickly perused the occupants. Hastily she fled the solarium feeling uncomfortable in the room filled with young couples enjoying themselves. Some were enjoying themselves way too much for Elizabeth's comfort zone. Many chose to believe that the huge plants in the room were hiding their openly shared affections with each other. Elaine blushed profusely. She hastily exited the room staying only long enough to ascertain that Abby was not one of the Solarium's inhabitants.

Elaine eventually gave up on her search to find Abby. She had searched silently and hadn't asked anyone if they had seen Abby. She didn't want to add further embarrassment to Abby by informing anyone who wasn't already aware of the scene that took place in the ballroom only minutes earlier. Finally she decided that Abby must have calmed down and returned to the ball. Besides she began to worry about leaving her own fiancé alone. There were many young beautiful girls attending the ball. Most of them were hoping to secure their own futures by meeting their new husbands to be, among the many good looking young men in attendance. With this unsettling thought, Elaine overcame her worry for her friend. Instead, she felt the need to hastily return to the grand ballroom to spend some time enjoying her own fiancé Robert Grayson.

A very distraught, confused and angry, Abby Anderson fairly flew as she exited the Harrison mansion. Running through the ornately designed frosted double glass doors of the ballroom she created quite a stir of gossip. She flew down the long entry hallway and straight out the front door of the Harrison's Savannah home. Hot tears continued to stream down her face unchecked. She never saw the shocked faces of the few guests and servants she passed. Her hasty flight caused several of the guests to lose their balance. Some quickly grabbed their cocktail drinks to prevent them from spilling. Others stared at her in open astonishment! Comical and rude remarks regarding the spectacle she was making of herself, began flooding the first floor and the grand entry hallway.

The ornate umbrella stand at the front door flipped over spilling its contents as the ruffle of her skirt caught on the tip of one of the many guest's umbrellas. One of the long pink taffeta ruffles of her ball gown tore loose from her dress and dragged behind her. Never stopping, she allowed the dress to rip further as she tripped over the ruffle and immediately lifted the skirt of the dress above her knees. She was providing the gentlemen she passed a delightful view of her pink stocking legs and lacy pink pantalets. Women gaped at her in disapproval. Various women slapped their male partners who were openly enjoying the sight. Oblivious to the spectacle she created, it never occurred to Abby that she could do herself great injury if she were to trip over the many yards of pink ruffles flying in all directions around her.

"Missy, ye best slow down afore ye hurts yursef!" Warned the Harrison's negro doorman in his half-hearted attempt to stop her. He was exhausted from greeting all of the many arriving guests.

Paying him no heed, Abby continued running down the many steps of the mansion's grand front entry. She quickly weaved in out of the way of the many waiting carriages. Her fast movements excited some of the horses causing the carriage drivers to strain at the reigns to control the agitated teams before they trampled anyone accidently. She ran through the main driveway gate straight through the continuously arriving carriages and onto Exeter Lane. She continued to run non-stop the additional two blocks to her own home. The flying ruffles of her dress caught on several bushes. She dragged them in the dust and mud beneath her. One of her slippers came off. Oblivious to the pain in her foot caused by the rough street gravel beneath her bare foot she continued her running non-stop.

Arriving at her own Victorian home, she threw open the iron gates and ran across the circular driveway fronting the entry. Never stopping, she bolted up the twelve stairs leading to the frosted glass double doors. Tears blinded her as she threw them open without ringing or waiting for the doorman to assist her.

Sobbing loudly she continued running two steps at a time up the grand staircase and into her own room. She slammed the door of her room and threw herself face down on her bed. Kicking her legs wildly in the air she commenced beating the soft feather mattress with both of her fists. Crying loudly she screamed into her pillow "It's a lie, a lie, I know it's a lie! It cannot be true! It just can't be!"

Eventually her huge sobbing turned to whimpering and then became muffled as she fell into a deep sleep. She began having several restless dreams. The vivid dreams caused her to thrash and turn in her sleep. None of them made any sense to her nor could she remember them the following morning.

Back at the Ball, the musicians restarted the music. For the time being, everyone had dismissed Abby's shocking comments and hasty exit. They were having far too much fun to worry about Abby. Besides, they were confident that Abby's delicious escapade would be added to their drawing room gossip sessions during the days immediately following the ball.

Abby's father, Charles Anderson, was engaged in an enthralling game of poker in the library. He was totally unaware of the passing of time and he had no knowledge of Abby's hasty exit. The card game lasted until four in the morning. Finally Charles bested his partner, host, and good friend, George Harrison.

Bidding George a goodnight, he searched for Abby. Except for a few couples unwilling to end their night of enjoyment, the ballroom was deserted. He assumed that Abby had been escorted home by one of their many family friends as was usually the case. Donning his beaver hat and cloak, he picked up his ornately carved silver wolf head cane, nodded a goodnight to the very sleepy doorman and calmly walked home whistling a merry tune, enjoying the unseasonably warm weather.

Jeffrey Browning, Abby's intended, was on a business trip to Washington D.C. where he had high hopes of attaining the future position as Georgia's youngest ever Governor. Therefore he had not attended the ball and he was not to learn of the incident involving his fiancé until after his return to Savannah.

Chapter Two

Abby awoke suddenly from her deep sleep. Unconsciously, she stretched her arms sleepily towards the warm sun shining brightly through her bedroom window. She sleepily acknowledged that it must be morning already. Quickly she withdrew her arms and held them close to her sides, realizing how sore they felt. Blinking her swollen eyes, she sat up groggily and surveyed her mussed up chenille bedspread. Her gaze drifted around the room in a state of confusion. Bewildered, she lowered her head to her lap and alarmed herself as she saw the condition of her pink ball gown that she was still wearing. The beautiful dress was torn and filthy. She picked at the torn, shattered satin of the ripped ruffles. Surprised to see that the bodice of the dress was half separated from the skirt.

The shameful events of the previous evening slowly began coming back to her. She grimaced as she tried to remove the tangled ruffles from around her legs. Noting that her feet and legs were filthy, she was startled to see that there was dried blood on her many cuts, scrapes, scratches. She moved her legs and realized that her entire body was very bruised and sore.

Her initial reaction was confusion. Then she remembered her great flight away from the Spring Ball. Her demeanor immediately changed from one of confusion to heavy despair, completely filled with shame. Against her will, she reviewed the evening's events in her mind. Closing her eyes she tried to pretend it never happened because she did not want to believe what Elizabeth had taunted her with. She tried to tell herself it had all been a dream. Then she opened her eyes and again perused the tattered dress and noted her bruised and cut legs. Finally she had to admit to herself that it was no dream and her arch enemy, Elizabeth Whatley had given her the information that was to destroy all her future dreams and the life she had known prior to last night's events. Tears began to fall down her filthy dried tear stained cheeks a second time as she realized the true impact of Elizabeth's revelations.

Elizabeth Whatley had confronted her with vile accusations regarding her birth. She had accused her of being illegitimate and therefore informed her that she was not the appropriate bride for her beloved Jeffrey Browning. For the first time in her young eighteen years she had been given cause to suspect the details of her birth. Abby remembered that she had verbally abused Elizabeth publicly, then vehemently denied Elizabeth's vile accusations and without warning she had struck the girl soundly. Then she had run away taking her embarrassment and shame with her. Now her life was as shattered as the dress she was wearing.

Thoroughly depressed and hugging her knees, she sat rocking herself backwards and forwards. Abby took time to think about her past. Deep inside herself she had to acknowledge that Elizabeth's story rang true. There were many inconsistencies in her childhood that were unaccounted for. "If Elizabeth is right, whatever am I to do?" She questioned her empty silent room.

Abby slowly sat up and picked up the tattered ruffles of her pink ball gown. Mrs. Gray, Savannah's highly sought after dressmaker, had painstakingly designed the gown especially for her. Abby originally did not plan to attend the ball as her fiancé, Jeffrey Browning, was not in town to escort her. How she wished she had stayed true to her own desires, but she'd relented and agreed to go once her father convinced her that her friends would desire to congratulate her on her engagement and upcoming nuptials. Due to her late decision she had decided to wear the pink dress that was to have been a part of her wedding trousseau. Now it was in tatters. Filthy and torn, it would never be repaired or worn by her or anyone ever again.

The confused girl dropped her head into her hands. Slowly she began to shake her head back and forth. As depression took hold of her she didn't desire to cry. Her tears were spent from the previous evening. She stood and surveyed her surroundings. Her bedroom was the same as it had been yesterday. Everything was exactly as it had been left. Her bureau still held a disarray of her brushes, and powders, rouge and the pink lip gloss she'd hidden from her father. Her four poster bed with her white Chenille ruffled spread was still made except now it was wrinkled and filthy from the dirt Abby's ragged dirty dress had deposited on it during the night. Her half-finished wedding gown hung on the door of her armoire waiting for her to try it on for further seaming of the skirt to the bodice. The sleeves were pinned awaiting the dainty pearl edging on the diamond shaped cuffs.

Abby looked about her in a daze. Catching sight of herself in the full-length heavily waxed mahogany self-standing mirror, she perused her reflection. Her jaw dropped in surprise as she surveyed the damage she had done to her body. Her tangled long red hair hung in dishevelment about her shoulders. The curls of the uplifted coiffure had fallen. Some of the long curls had become undone and hung against her long ivory neck. Now they were severely tangled and had bits and pieces of shrubbery in them. Searching her face, Abby stopped and stared at her normally cheerful green eyes. She cocked her head in surprise. She was looking at someone she did not recognize. Oh, the reflection was of her of course, but the person staring back at her was not the same young woman who only yesterday had pranced in front of this same mirror highly excited, anticipating the dancing she was soon to enjoy.

The vision of the woman looking back at her had a resigned acceptance in her eyes. Gone were the bright laughing green eyes that normally greeted her cheerfully each morning. In their place were overly bright tear stained dark emerald green eyes with tiny hardened black pupils. Although her mother had passed away before she was old enough to understand the loss, now for the first time in her life, she experienced grief. The type of grief that was so severe, that a person immediately aged from the experience. Her neck seemed longer. She held her head stiffer. Her reflection said she was more regal, stronger somehow, as if she had acquired a new resolve for her existence.

Slowly she gazed at the remainder of her body. Standing in her tattered pink dress she gazed upon her breasts. They no longer appeared small and soft. Now they seemed to stand straight up and pertly announced to the world that they were in control. She grimaced ruefully as she thought how silly this seemed. At any other time she would have laughed hysterically at such a ridiculous thought, but today the best she could accomplish was barely a grimace. Her gaze continued downward to the tattered ruffles of her underskirt. The voluminous taffeta skirts were torn away from the waistline of the dress and her silk matching pink pantalets were showing through the gaping hole. Her stockings were filled with runs and holes from her relentless running. She was wearing only one of the daintily embroidered pink dancing slippers. She determined that the other one must have come off during her run. She closed her eyes as she realized the spectacle she must have made of herself to all of Savannah. Her stomach lurched as she felt the shame and embarrassment of it all.

Abby stood silently perusing herself in her disarray for several seconds. Suddenly she began to rip off the pink ball gown. She grabbed the skirt and tore it from the bodice and fairly kicked it away from her body. As for the bodice, she ripped it off of her as if it were a poison that she had to free herself from immediately. She could not get out of it fast enough.

Finally freed from the dress she threw it across the room and stripped herself. She poured cool water from the white milk glass pitcher that had once been a treasured belonging of her beloved mother's, into the matching bowl on her washstand. She began violently sponge bathing her entire body. She felt so much shame that she didn't have the courage to call for her maid to prepare her a hot bath. Only precious seconds away from feeling sheer hysteria, she attempted to wash away the sins she never knew she possessed until last night at the ball.

Finally she quit scrubbing her body, mainly because the bath water was filthy rather than because she was completely rosy clean again. She washed her hair and scrubbed herself until her skin glowed rosy red from the vigorous scrubbing she had given it. Donning clean underclothes from her bureau, Abby turned hastily to her wardrobe to grab a day dress to wear. Her hand stopped in midair as she came face to face with her half-finished wedding gown. Suddenly, she lost her resolve and sank to the floor staring at the half finished dress. Sitting thusly, blankly, she continued to stare at the dress for several minutes. She didn't have the courage to allow herself to accept that this dress would never be worn by her.

Thus it was that heavy set Old Pelly, previously her mother's personal maid, now hers, discovered Abby as she entered the room to do her normal daily ritual of awakening her young ward.

"Good Mornin!" Old Pelly's voice stopped dead in her tracts. In shock she surveyed the condition of the room and was startled to see her ward sitting in her underclothing on the floor in a trancelike state staring up at her wedding gown. Mumbling, she immediately went towards Abby intent on finding out why she was sitting there so quietly. On her way she picked up the skirt of the pink ball gown and stared at the disheveled garment in amazement. She began to mumble to herself. "Goodness gracious chile, whatever has ya done, girlie?" The old woman began picking up the remainder of the pink dress and attempted to smooth it as she discerned the gown's tattered state. "Oh my, Oh my! Abby, is ya a' right?" She urgently asked her ward turning to stare at the motionless girl still sitting on the floor. Dropping the dress she went to Abby. She bent down and placed her hands upon the quiet young woman's tear stained face. Gently she raised Abby's face to a position where she could look into the blank empty eyes of the girl. Calling Abby's name repeatedly she attempted to awaken Abby from the trancelike state. "What's happened to ya chile?" Urgently she coaxed Abby into a standing position and then she put her arms around Abby and tried to hug her.

"Now, u jes tell yur Old Pelly what's wrong wif ya!" She urged her ward to communicate with her.

Still dazed, Abby turned her gaze directly on Old Pelly and then asked, "Why? Why did you not tell me the truth, Old Pelly?" she accused the old woman coldly. Old Pelly cringed from the girl's voice filled with anger.

Surprised and caught off guard, Pelly cocked her white bonneted head to the side as she attempted to discern the content of Abby's shocking accusation. "What ya mean, girlie, Old Pelly ain't never lied to ya," she evasively replied with a narrowed look in her right eye. She rubbed her hands nervously across the front of the white apron she wore over the huge brown bodice of the dress as was her habit when she didn't know exactly what to say or do or whenever she felt the need to tell a white lie.

Old Pelly and her husband, Old Trey, the household butler, were freed slaves. Formerly they were the servants of Deanna Lynn, Abby's mother. Charles had given them their freedom when Abby's mother died. They had elected to stay on with the family as paid employees. Old Pelly was there when Abby was born, and she became the only mother figure that Abby really accepted since the death of her natural mother when she was only five years old. Abby and her father now considered them to be family members rather than employees.

"Well, then why did you not tell me this so called truth that you claim you never lied to me about?" A fully conscious, very angry Abby swung on Old Pelly and demanded her question to be answered. "And don't you lie to me Old Pelly, because now I know the truth! Elizabeth Whatley was so kind as to tell me all about the truth last night at the ball!" she sarcastically stated, "And you had better confirm the truth to me right now!" she demanded of Old Pelly.

Pelly's heart sank. She had known the truth of Abby's parentage before Abby's father knew. She'd kept the secret for years. She knew that one day the truth might come out but she had prayed that this day would never come. Now it was here.

Taking a huge breath she reluctantly turned to look Abby in the face. She recognized that there was no denying the truth any longer.

"Wal then yo just sit down right ere on dis ere bed chile, while Old Pelly tells ya what I knows. I doan xactly know what all that big mouth brat Lisabeth done tole ya, but Old Pelly, well, I'se ain't a gonna lie to ya no more. It's bout time ya knew anyways," she muttered as she proceeded to give Abby the few details that she knew. She finished by suggesting that Abby ask her father for the remaining facts that were still unknown to her.

Abby was stunned! She had so hoped that Old Pelly had nothing to tell her and that would prove that Elizabeth was indeed a horrific liar. But Pelly's comments left her at a loss for words. Now she sat on the bed in silence as she digested the tale Old Pelly related to her. After a moment of silence she stared directly into Old Pelly's eyes and demanded firmly but quietly, "You can leave me now Pelly, I prefer to be alone."

"But chile, ya doesn't need to be by ya'sef right now," Old Pelly countered. "Come oer here and lay yor head on my lap and Ise'll jes brush them tangles from yur hair," she offered to assist Abby as she was reluctant to leave her alone after the strong blow she had delivered.

"I asked you to leave now, Pelly. Don't make me ask again," Abby demanded firmly. She took Pelly by the arm and fairly pushed her out the heavy wooden door to her room as she slammed it shut in her face.

"But chile, you needs yur Old Pelly right now," Pelly countered as she ducked quickly to avoid being hit in the face by the fast closing door. "Oh dear, I knows dis day is gonna be a lot of trouble for dis ere fambly! Yor'e Mama ain't never gonna forgib me! I bet she be a turnin in her grave right bout now," Old Pelly began muttering as she gave up hope of Abby allowing her to comfort her. She turned her huge girth and muttered all the way to the grand staircase and continued her muttering on the way down. At the bottom she turned towards the kitchen. Wringing her hands she mumbled to herself "Yup, God's gonna punish dis ere family today, he shor is, he is a' gonna punish dis ere family today!" She shuddered as she realized the curse that was now upon them.

Abby turned from the shut door ignoring Pelly's pleas. Her view connected with her wedding dress hanging on her armoire door. Shaking her head, she dismissed the dress and selected the lime green day dress with the white lace cuffs and collar. Donning the dress, she proceeded to detangle her hair and put it up into a matronly bun. Glancing in the mirror she dipped her head in a short quick nod acknowledging approval of her appearance. Grimacing as she slipped her sore feet into her black satin day slippers she quietly left her room.

Walking determinedly and with her head held high. She headed towards her father's private office that doubled as his library. Pausing for a moment before the tall imposing double Oak doors, she shook her head to clear her mind and gather her courage. Then with a determined look on her face she raised her hand to knock firmly on the imposing doors.

"Come in!" Charles Anderson absently invited his unknown guest to enter. His nose was buried in the paperwork he was preparing for his office for Monday's upcoming business.

"Good morning father," his daughter greeted him boldly.

His mind was still absorbed in his paperwork and Charles missed the tone of her voice. As usual he gave his nonchalant welcome to her and beckoned her to come in to his private domain. "Good morning daughter? Sleeping in I see. It's about time you came to tell me of all the congratulations you received last night on yours and Jeff's engagement! I expect you received the support of many of your friends?" He absently babbled on as he continued to peruse and direct his attention to the important financial documents before him.

'You could say that", Abby firmly answered him in a strangled voice that was not lost on her father.

Looking up at his daughter in surprise, he discerned the difference in her appearance. Narrowing his right eye he carefully studied her. There was a marked difference in her. One he didn't like. He found himself to be inept at describing it, as if the right words eluded him. He sensed trouble but being unaware of last evening's debauchery, he was totally unprepared for Abby's cold attitude and demeanor.

Coughing lightly to clear his throat he inquired timidly. "Is something wrong Abigail?" pausing briefly he discerned her continued silence and deliberate stare so he tried again. "What's bothering you Abby?" This time his paperwork dropped to the desk in front of him and the content was totally dismissed. Deep dread fell over him as he felt the cold unresponsiveness of his daughter and the once cozy warm room's atmosphere suddenly became quite cold. For some reason the room seemed to grow very large emitting a feeling of being strangely empty to him. His skin began to prickle with fear in regards to his daughter's strange behavior and impromptu visit.

"Why father, whatever could be wrong?" Abby snidely replied. "After all, why shouldn't I be surprised now that I have been informed that I am not your natural daughter?" She blurted out her accusation angrily. Starring deliberately at her father, she dared him to deny her claim. She experienced a perverse pleasure in the shock she saw register in his eyes as his face went pale.

Taken momentarily aback, Charles fought for a way to regain control of the conversation. Gaining an ounce of courage, his color returned and he countered her idly, indicating that he thought she was being ridiculous.

"Why Abigail Anderson, whatever are you talking about?" He picked up his ledger documents again and pretended to peruse them by adjusting his spectacles. Looking at his paperwork he attempted to indicate to her that their importance was greater than her ridiculous statement. Thusly he intended to dismiss her intimated claim.

But his eyes could not concentrate on a single word and his heart was beating faster and faster by the second. He wished the floor would suddenly envelope him and remove him from the room rather than to have to confront his daughter on the long feared and completely avoided conversation he was now being forced to have without any warning. To himself, he was terrified, and all he could think of was "however did she find out?" His answer was forthcoming almost immediately.

"Why Father," Abby condescendingly replied, "Elizabeth Whatley was more than willing to tell me that I am not your natural daughter, but rather that I am the daughter of a whore! That's right! You heard me right, she told me I am the product of a "WHORE!" Abby could barely restrain the anger she felt within her heart, and definitely could not stop it from showing in her over loud and force full voice. "Elizabeth was also kind enough to tell me that my *REAL*

JUDON GRAY

father is unknown." Abby was clear to emphasize the word *real* as if that one word alone contained all the hurt and humiliation she was now to bear. "Then she told me that everyone knew my mother was a tramp! Can you imagine how I felt hearing this in front of all my friends who were supposed to be supportive of my engagement, Father?

Momentarily she stopped to angrily swipe at a tear that had begun to develop in her eye, but quickly she recovered and continued, this time her comment was slightly softer and filled with anguish, "Do you think you can explain all this for me, Papa? Instantly her anger recovered when she realized the man in front of her was not really her Papa. "Oh excuse me! I meant *Mr. Anderson,* of course? She spat out his formal surname angrily as she corrected the error she had made regarding her former claim of parentage.

Suddenly feeling her knees weaken, she lowered herself stiffly into the room's great leather chair. She was torn between breaking down in tears and attempting to keep tight control of the situation and her temperament as she awaited her father's answer. The latter won out as she sat straight up in the chair and tilted her head in command of her father's reply. The sorry truth was she wanted to claw his eyes out! In fact to claw out anybody's eyes right about now would do. She was so angry she visually saw herself as a vicious snake writhing on the ground shaking its rattle's in anticipation of a strike. She felt a heavy need to strike at anything anywhere. Immediately she fought to dismiss the repulsive vision. Her temper cooled slightly in the process.

"Why Abigail Anderson! Whatever are you lamenting about? Of course I'm your father! What is this Mr. Anderson business?" Charles feigned for time as the shock of her accusations settled upon him.

"Come now father, or whoever you really are, don't try to lie to me. It's past time for me to understand what these comments of Elizabeth's are really about. Why is it that Elizabeth Whatley knows this information and I am the fool who had no idea?" She countered her father's question. Before he could answer she continued.

"Of course you can continue to deny Elizabeth's accusations, however she announced to the whole of Savannah the facts of my birth at the ball last night. How kind of her to do your duty for you, don't you think?" She caustically exaggerated and threatened her father. "My dear, dear, father, you may attempt to lie to me, but however do you intend to continue to deny it before all of Savannah?" she taunted him mockingly.

Charles stared at his daughter in shock. Of course she was correct. He could no longer hide the details of her birth now that Elizabeth had made it public knowledge to the whole of Savannah's society. But how could Elizabeth Whatley have known? He stood up from his desk and walked to the library window. There he grabbed hold of the long edge of the emerald green velvet curtain for support. The room was quiet for nearly five full moments before he coughed slightly to clear his throat. He knew he had lost and it was now time for him to tell the truth to his daughter regarding her parentage.

"Abby," he began ruefully, "I truly never intended not to tell you the truthful facts of your birth." Another half minute passed as he stalled for words, "Perhaps I was waiting for the right time, or maybe I just wanted a little more time." Stopping he swiped at his balding head as if to find the words he searched for among the few red hairs that remained.

"Goodness, the truth is…," again he stalled to search for the correct words and decided there just weren't any, so resigned, he continued, "I guess I just plain didn't have the courage to tell you." He finally admitted. His heart constricted when he saw the look of satisfaction and pain cross Abby's face at his admittance of the truth of his failure towards her. She sat quietly daring him with her eyes to continue.

"However, now that you've been told and it is apparently public knowledge all across Savannah," he paused, suddenly realizing the critical social position they both were now facing. He shuddered involuntarily as the public humiliation and shame they were both soon to experience sank into his consciousness. "I suppose it is past time for me to tell you the details involving your birth." He sighed heavily, keeping his back to her. He visually cringed as she threw her next assault at him.

"Yes father, why don't you tell me all the sordid details of my birth! I bet I am just going to be so delighted to hear all the juicy details that no one ever bothered to inform me." She was so angry she was enjoying deliberately insulting him. It never occurred to her that he was painfully suffering at the hands of Elizabeth's accusations as well.

Charles was shocked. Never had he seen his beautiful daughter act so hatefully. He couldn't understand the hateful anger she was directing on him. He had always had a wonderful relationship with his little girl whom he was so proud of. Now, her demeanor scared him. He had never been affronted by any woman in this manner and he didn't quite know how to handle it. That his little girl was very angry and upset at him was obvious, but he had no idea how to calm her.

"Abby, it's not like you think, there are no sordid details. It's just that, well that, your mother, my beautiful Deanna Lynn, who was and still is, the love of my life…" He paused again looking for an explanation his daughter would accept. "Well," he continued, "The first time I looked at her I knew I would love her forever." Her father declared his passion for her mother then he paused momentarily before he continued, "But…, unfortunately…, I was not the love of her life." He quickly blurted out the painful fact, admitting the truth of his farce of a marriage. "Actually, your mother settled for me because she had no other choice." Charles turned from the window and sat back down at his desk. He placed his hands on his head and his eyes began to water. He glanced up at Abby beseeching her to understand.

Abby looked at her father. For the first time in her life he appeared small, kind of pitiful even. She no longer knew him anymore. Sitting there behind his huge mahogany desk, his 5'6" thin gaunt frame seemed to be swallowed up by the huge desk. He appeared almost comical behind the massive piece of furniture. His tearful heavily freckled face appeared pathetic to her. He was vigorously rubbing his hands across the top of his already balding head. Carrot red hairs mixed with coarse gray were appearing in his hands as he pulled them from his scalp without realizing he was doing so. She looked at his tearful eyes and for a split second she almost relented. But then remembering he had been lying to her for years, she sat up straighter in the huge leather chair that nearly swallowed her. She said, "I am waiting, Mr. Anderson, tell me all of it and leave nothing out." She hardened her gaze upon him unforgiving, demanding and daring him to open his soul to her.

Wringing his hands he stared at his daughter. Weighing his thoughts carefully, again he began, "Well, I suppose I should begin at the beginning." He turned to look at her and saw that she was not going to relent but was impatiently waiting for him to continue.

"It all began when I came to Atlanta, nineteen years ago. I was a graduate of Georgia State University and was seeking a position as a banker in Savannah. Well, as you know, George Harrison, our good friend and neighbor was a loan officer at an accounting firm. We met during an interview and he hired me." Here he paused and gathered his thoughts regarding his past, "A week or so later George invited me to his home for dinner. He informed me that he had out of town visitors and their unmarried daughter was with them. He told me that this young lady needed an escort for the evening. He enticed me by telling me that she was a beautiful spirited red headed Irish Lassie, and that I would really enjoy my evening as her dinner escort." Charles stopped for a moment as he savored his memory of the first moments he had looked upon Abby's unusually beautiful redheaded mother whose daughter favored her to a "T."

"Please continue" Abby prompted him coldly.

Blankly Charles looked at Abby and brought himself back to the present. "Well, as he was my employer, I couldn't turn him down so I agreed to attend his dinner invitation. She was beautiful Abby, so beautiful, I couldn't believe my luck," the admiration he felt for her mother glowed in his eyes. "She looked so much like you. I fell in love with her instantly. After dinner the ladies retired to the parlor for tea and Mr. Harrison, your grandfather and I retired to the drawing room for cigars and a game of…, well…, poker," he finally admitted lamely.

"And?" prompted Abby impatiently.

Looking again at Abby, Charles turned his face away so that he couldn't see her reaction and then he blurted out where he had left off. "Well, the sorry truth is that I won that poker game and my prize was…" well…, the prize was your mother!" He finished quickly and then he glanced at Abby to see her reaction to this shameful news. However, her facial expressions remained carefully guarded. Sighing, he continued, "I wasn't informed until later that I had been played for a fool. I had been invited to dinner for the sole purpose of becoming a husband to your mother.

"Really?" she caustically commented. "Well don't stop now!" Abby prompted as she barely held her tone from being overly vicious and sarcastic at the same time. The shock of his story only humiliating her further.

Charles nodded at her as his heart sank into his stomach, after a brief pause he continued, "Apparently, your mother was in love with another man. His name was Scott St. Claire." He fairly spit out the name of the man whom he had hated and been so jealous of throughout the many years since his marriage. "He and my Deana Lynn were very much in love before I ever met her. She told me that she had agreed to marry him. However, prior to the formal announcement of their engagement, her Scott was the victim of a fatal accident. They said his horse threw him in a jump and his neck had snapped. I was told that he died on the spot."

Here he paused again to gather his thoughts and deal with the shame the innocent man's death brought to Charles for his inability to stop his hatred of him. Hating a dead man all these years and nothing he could do about it had helped him to raise Abigail with all the love his heart could offer. The feeling of superiority he received over the dead suiter of his beloved wife, had provided him a form of ugly comfort. He'd felt strangely triumphant in raising the dead man's little girl, which somehow managed to sooth his jealousy throughout the years.

Embarrassed he glanced at Abby and after a moment he continued once again, "You see, Abby, I was informed that your mother and Scott St. Claire had been," he paused and searched for the word to explain the sensitive subject that he was being forced to discuss openly with his female daughter, "well they had been *intimate* with each other prior to their engagement." Again he blurted out the offensive word quickly. "I am afraid that you are the product of their *love affair*." He was shocked by his own reaction to his last two words. Apparently the hated jealousy in his heart even after all these years was immediately awakened all over again.

He feared Abby's reaction and dared to glance quickly at his daughter to see the effect of this embarrassing part of the truth she was demanding from him. He was surprised that he was met with the same stony emotionless glare from her. "How can it be that she has no feelings about all this?" He questioned himself in wonder? She waved her hand to prompt him to continue. In truth, she was horrified and embarrassed, but stonily she refused to let him see.

"I had won the poker game." He picked up on his story again, "but instead of being given the monetary rewards on the table, I was made a proposition by your maternal grandfather. I remember that I thought he was joking. He told me of your mother's plight and explained that she needed a husband right away. He asked me if I would accept his daughter in marriage and raise her child in lieu of my monetary wining's?" Again he looked at her for her reaction to this sordid fact. She simply blinked and waited. He wasn't even certain that she had heard him correctly. However, he decided to continue,

"Of course I couldn't believe my luck. I had fallen in love with her instantly, so of course I consented and your mother and I were married within the week. To your mother's credit she was against this, but she was made to see the sense of our marriage. She knew that it was the only way she would be allowed to keep you and that she needed me to protect you. After the wedding, your maternal grandparents set us up in this home as a wedding gift, and presented me with her dowry. Then they left. They have never contacted your mother, yourself or I ever since. They even refused to acknowledge that they had a granddaughter. I guess they couldn't face what they had forced their daughter to do." He stopped and searched his mind for the details of his past he had lived so long ago.

"Twice I tried to contact them. The first time was when you were born. The second was five years later when your mother died. On both occasions I was informed that they did not know me and had no desire to hear anything I had to tell them. I was turned away and eventually just gave up on them." Again he paused remembering the truths behind his insane marriage.

Abby waited for him to continue. She was afraid to prompt him. Scared of what he was going to say next.

Finally, he looked at her, and swiped vigorously at his eyes attempting to dry the tears of self-pity that were forming unbidden by him. Sniffing he blew his nose with his kerchief and continued, "Later, I was informed that your grandparents had packed their bags, sold out their Atlanta home and moved to Europe. I know nothing more of them to tell you, Abby." He paused but then decided to tempt her to forgive him by reminding her that he had no one else but her in his life to love him.

"I'm so sorry that there is no heritage that I could pass on to you. My own parent's died early in my life. I think I was eight or nine. It was a distant uncle who raised me and he did so reluctantly. When I was of age he immediately put me into private boarding schools and then he sent me off to college by using my small inheritance. Once I had graduated, I was informed that his duty to me was finished. I found myself all on my own from that day forward. That's why it's only been you and me Abby girl. All these years, it's only been you and me since your mother's untimely death." He voiced his last hope praying his daughter would understand and forgive him.

Charles was caught up in the sorrow of the tale of his lonely life. Sniffling he continued wiping at his tears and blowing his nose. Years ago, he had come to terms with his devastating heartache. But now here he was again, his heart break renewed as he related the sad details to his one and only daughter. That she was not his natural born child was of no importance to him, as she had no other living father and since she was put in his arms on the day of her birth, it had been easy for him to accept her as entirely his own child. Sometimes he even succeeded in believing that she was his natural child and never ever gave any thought to the dead man who had actually created her. There was one fact that he had never disclosed to anyone and he also kept it secret from Abby now. His beloved Deanna Lynn had never allowed him to touch her physically and therefore there had never been any chance at all for a child to be born of his own. Again he felt the shame of allowing his wife to reject him.

Gathering his courage and swiping at the tears that were now coursing down his face he looked at Abby and attempted to finish his tale. "Well, That is all there is to it, Abby. That's the facts of your birth." Here he stopped and looked again for a response from her. He received nothing in return. Trying to console her somewhat he continued with, "I would give anything to tell you otherwise, but I can't. I don't know how Miss Whatley knew this information, it was supposed to be kept secret, known only to myself, George and your grandfather." He attempted to apologize for his lack of knowledge that his secret had been disclosed by someone other than himself. His apology fell onto her deaf ears and he knew he had failed yet again.

Silently thinking for a moment, he attempted a plausible explanation, "I supposed that the rumors started when your mother and I were married. After all, whoever would have supposed that your mother would marry the likes of me when she could have had her pick of all the gents in the county, in the whole state of Georgia for that matter? She really was uniquely beautiful!" His voice caught in his throat as he faced his sorrow at losing his beloved Deanna Lynn again. Quietly he relished her memory to himself.

Remembering that Abby was staring at him waiting for any additional facts he could give to her, he continued with, "I suppose that your birth only seven months after the wedding didn't really help." He looked at his daughter sheepishly, ashamed. He beseeched her with his eyes to forgive him and to be understanding. His hands felt so empty. He had nothing to give to her to comfort her. His story had no cushion to it. He knew there was nothing he could do but pray that she would come to understand and accept the details involving her birth.

Abby's emotions were swinging in all directions. The truth had been confirmed. She was not her father's true and natural born daughter. Elizabeth was telling the truth about her birth. She had been correct in saying that Abby had no place in Savannah's elite society. Abby had to accept that her lineage was not true. Thereby she had to accept that she was not the woman Jeffrey Browning needed or could afford to take as his wife. His political future required his wife to be perfect, without blemish. "The people of Savannah are going to have a heyday over this one!" She dared to allow the comment into her thought process.

In that moment she saw her future. She was wearing black. She saw herself as an isolated crabby old spinster lady. She pictured the children of Savannah calling her names like "old witch" and "crazy old spinster" and throwing rotten food at her house as they played in the streets in front of her residence. Hanging his head, her father did not see her body violently shudder as her heart shattered inside her from the cruelties of her vision.

Looking up, Charles waited for a response from Abby. She sat very still. Her expression never changed. Coldly she looked at the man she had tenderly loved and called father over the years. Now he was just a stranger to her.

"So that's it. This is the story of my coming into this world?" She half questioned and half stated the fact to him. Coldly she said, "Thank you for your honesty and truthfulness in telling me." Without any words of comfort for her father, she stood up and smoothed the skirt of her dress. Sedately she walked to the library door. Stopping, she turned to face her father. Speaking in a business tone, she said to him, "You will excuse me I'm sure while I retire to my room to consider the information you have given to me." Not waiting for his reply, she left her father's library closing the door quietly behind her. Walking sedately, her head held high, she headed in a trancelike state down the long hallway to the grand staircase.

In the library, Charles gave way to the pain in his chest and stomach. Placing his head in his hands, he began sobbing in earnest. He cried not only for the pain his story had caused his daughter, but also for all the pain and loneliness his life had held. He cried for the love he had never received from his wife. He cried for the pain he felt from losing her to an early death. He cried because he blamed himself that he was unable to give his wife the love she had so desperately craved but would only accept from her deceased lover, Scott. He cried because he recognized the mockery he had made of his own life in his attempt to do something noble. He had failed to fulfill his own needs to be loved and comforted.

Now suddenly he realized that it had never been his place to protect his beautiful Deanna Lynn. It had never been his right to raise the beautiful girl who was the daughter born of the union between Deana Lynn and Scott St. Claire. It tore him apart to admit to himself that Abby was not his natural daughter. Suddenly he no longer felt pride in the successes he had accomplished with his life.

The horrified, yet blank cold stare in Abby's deep green eyes haunted him telling him how wrong he had been. Although his heartache was debilitating, he knew he would have done it all over again, just to feel the pride he felt each time he'd had the pleasure of introducing the beautiful Deana Lynn as his wife. And for the nobility he had felt in having protected her and her little daughter and in the joy of having had a daughter to raise as his own. His heart was shattered. He was unable to face the next moments of his life. He felt as if his life had ended. Ironically, his life as he knew it up to today had ended only partly when his wife had died. Today the rest of it came to an end. The problem was that Charles had not died with it.

Abby moved in a daze as she reentered the foyer. She failed to see Old Trey, heading for the door on his way to answer the bell. Walking right past him she never heard him mention to her that the day promised to be beautiful.

Old Trey looked at her in bewilderment. "My lands, Pelly don tole me dat dis was to be a strange day, but I doan think she knows just how strange it tis?" He mumbled to himself while he turned to answer the door. His feelings were slightly hurt by Abby's negative response to his greeting. Her bright happy smile was always a high spot in his otherwise boring days. Not knowing about the conversation just held in the library, Old Trey assumed that Abby was just remembering the Ball. "Tis shore a strange look fer a young lassy to have on her face after a night of dancing and merry making. And her goin to be married and all," he continued to mutter to himself in a lowered breath as he turned the glass door knob to admit their waiting caller.

Abby continued her journey up the stairs. She rounded the corner and passed out of sight just in time for old Trey to answer the door to Elaine.

"Good Mornin Missy Lainie," he welcomed her into the Anderson home.

"And a Good Morning to you too Trey," replied Elaine cheerfully as she entered the Anderson's foyer. "Is Abby up yet?" She inquired.

"No'm, I'se afraid she still be a sleeping, but I sure will tells her yo was here to visit wif her." Old Trey calmly lied to Elaine. Old Pelly instructed him earlier that they were not to let anyone in to see Abby, He knew better than to question his wife. He attempted to turn Elaine towards the doors to take her leave.

Determined to speak with Abby, Elaine pressed her point, "Oh may I go up and wake her? I really want to discuss the last evenings Ball with her." She said as she lowered the yellow polka dotted sunning umbrella that matched her pretty yellow polka dotted day dress. She looked fresh as a daisy. Old Trey noted to himself that Elaine must have had a wonderful time at the Spring Fest Ball. However, he knew better than to go against Old Pelly's instructions.

"Wal now Missy Lannie, I'se not so sure that Old Pelly won't hit Ol Trey in dis ol head of his, if n I was to let you go up there and wakes the lil missy up. Old Pelly, she don tole me that Miss Abby needs her rest this yere morning and I surely don't wants to get me ol head hit." He ducked his head sheepishly with the huge brown corneas of his eyes starring wide open at Elaine. Again he steered her back to the door as he insisted again to Elaine that he had to make certain no one was to disturb Abby.

He looked at Elaine with such a comically tragic look, that she burst out laughing. "Why old Trey, you have the eyes of a sad puppy dog!" she laughed, "Oh very well then, I will simply come back in a couple of hours or maybe tomorrow morning to check on her again. But now you be certain to tell her that I am coming so she won't leave. You hear me now, Old Trey?" She playfully instructed him as she replaced her yellow lace gloves and opened her umbrella. Turning she allowed Old Trey to assist her in stepping back outside of the Anderson home and into the bright warm sun shining day.

Turning her back on the house as Old Trey closed the doors behind her, she descended the steps. Slightly frustrated, she frowned. She really did want to find out what had set Abby off so emotionally last night.

After last night's futile search for Abby, Elaine had decided to return to the ballroom. There she spent the remainder of the evening with her fiancé Robert. Quite frankly, all thoughts of Abby had flown from her mind. Her evening had been filled with romance and promises of love as she and her Robert spent their time together planning for their upcoming wedding and future life. It was way past midnight before she remembered about Abby again and that was too late to worry any longer. Although she hadn't seen Abby during the remainder of the evening, and since no more had been said about the incident, she assumed that Old Trey's indifference simply meant that Abby must be just fine. Therefore she now turned her walk in the direction of the Harrison's mansion to thank her hostess for the wonderful evening that her careful planning had provided the ton.

Abby turned down the hallway toward her bedroom. Once there she entered the room and ignored the fact that the housemaid, Ginny, had cleaned the room and removed the soiled and torn ball dress.

Standing before her bureau, she stared at her reflection in the mirror. "So, it's true! It's all true!" She spoke out loud to her own reflection. "Now what shall I do?" She continued to stare at herself in the mirror and never saw her reflection at all. Her thoughts were running rampant in her head. "One thing is for certain, I now know that I can never marry my darling Jeffrey! Why, this scandal will ruin his reputation and his chance to become the future Governor of the state of Georgia. Oh dear, why as a prominent politician, my adorable Jeffrey has so much promise and he can give so much to the people of our State and yes, later, even to the people of our country someday! Oh dear!" she lamented. "How can I ever stand in his way? Under no conditions could I live with myself if I were responsible for destroying his future!" Although she was adamant that she should protect Jeffrey, she failed to see that she really wasn't all that upset over her own lost future.

"I must do something, but what?" She continued voicing her thoughts. "I don't know how I could ever face Jeffrey again after he finds out about me. Anyway I will be so ashamed and embarrassed as he will probably feel he needs to break off our engagement. And as for that snide little Elizabeth Whatley, well, that little witch was finally right about her many accusations she loved to throw at everyone and this time she threw it at me!" Abby felt a thrill at using cruel language to describe Elizabeth. "It kills me to have Elizabeth to be the one who has brought me to this horrendous truth, but there is nothing I can do about that now either!" she reasoned. "Oh dear! Whatever am I to do?"

Continuing to talk to herself she voiced her conclusions as was her habit to do in the privacy of her own room. "So obviously, I am of a notorious birth! I cannot face anyone ever again, much less that horrible Elizabeth. I will simply die if I have to admit to her face that she was right! The horrible truth is that she is correct about my not being a proper bride for Jeffrey. Why, now that I know, I simply can't be the wife he needs. I am certain that I am now the talk of this town. Oh! How horrible it all is!" Abby was so upset she failed to recognize that by releasing Jeffrey from his betrothal to her, she was simply handing him over to Elizabeth on a silver platter!

Wringing her hands she turned and began pacing back and forth in her room. "Dear God! Help me!" She pleaded. Raising her hands and eyes upward she spoke in anguish, "Oh God in heaven and all the angels above, please, please tell me what I am to do! I beg of you!" With her hands still in midair she pivoted and found herself staring at her open Armoire. Her vision landed on the arm of her violet traveling dress that had been especially made for her trip to Europe with Jeffrey for their upcoming honeymoon.

"Why of course, that's it! That's it!" She excitedly repeated it over and over. "Thank you God, I knew you would tell me what to do!" Relieved she went into immediate action.

Grabbing her traveling valise from the corner of her room, Abby quickly dumped the contents on the floor. Rapidly sorting through them she selected a few essential garments from the pile on the floor. Then from her bureau she grabbed her hair brush and ornate silver hand mirror, her lip gloss and rouge, throwing them into the bottom of the bag. Then going to the Armoire she grabbed four of her best day dresses and one evening dress. She squashed these items, a nightgown and some undergarments into the bag. She had to sit on top of the bag to help her close it.

Opening the hidden drawer in her jewelry box that had been her Christmas gift from Jeffrey, she grabbed the stash of money she'd been saving for her wedding present to Jeffrey. Counting it, she placed half of it in her reticule and the other half she carefully placed inside the hem of her suit skirt where she snipped a small hole. Finally, she changed into the violet traveling suit. Quickly she rearranged her hair to accommodate the matching hat with the Black and blue green peacock feathers. She donned it and carefully placed a hat pin through it to hold it in place.

Giving herself a final perusal in the full-length mirror, she nodded her head in satisfaction. Grabbing the valise she walked quickly to the door. As her hand reached for the glass doorknob, she stopped and stood motionless for just a second or so. A tear spilled from her eye as the full realization of her actions became aware to her.

Setting the valise down, slowly she returned to the Armoire. Tenderly, she removed her wedding dress and lifted it high by the hanger and stared at it. Suddenly she threw it across her bed. Returning to her bureau she opened the top drawer. Decisively, she reached in and picked up her sewing shears. Walking to the wedding dress she stared at it for a full moment. Lovingly she touched the white silk bodice that had been painstakingly embroidered with white silk threads and real pearls. Running her fingers across it, she caressed the dress. Hot tears slid down her cheeks. Frowning, she angrily wiped off the tears with her wrist. Stealing herself she firmly grabbed the dress and began to cut it into small pieces. Her tears were streaming in rivulets down her face. She scattered the pieces of the dress across the room. "There!" She nodded in satisfaction. Speaking softly to herself again she smudged at her tears, "Well that's that! There will be no wedding to Jeffrey now!" Wiping one hand against the other to finalize her actions she silently opened her door and peeked outside.

Ascertaining that no one was present, she grabbed the heavy valise and headed for the grand stairway. Silently she descended. Quickly crossing the floor, Abby opened the right side of the double doors and quietly let herself outside. Hastily looking in both directions, she made sure the coast was clear. Bag in hand, she walked sedately to the street corner and hailed a cab giving him instructions to take her immediately to the train station.

Chapter Three

Arriving at the train station Abby paid the cabby. Alighting from her carriage, she hefted her valise in one hand and securing the strap of her reticule over her left shoulder, she headed for the ticket office. She stared in awe at the hustle and bustle of people at the station. Having always led a protected life, she experienced a momentary ounce of fear. "Whatever am I doing?" Said a little voice way deep down inside of her. Quickly she dismissed the voice of indecision and made her way to the ticket window.

Standing before the ticket clerk she was startled back to reality as the clerk inquired, "Destination please, Miss?"

Caught off guard, Abby heard herself say, "Pardon me," she quickly gulped and then before the ticket master could repeat himself she said, "Oh, ah…, please give me a one way ticket for out west, please, kind sir."

Looking at her strangely the clerk replied, "Well, train only goes as far as St. Louis, Missouri, Miss, that's the gateway to the west, and you' will have to make other arrangements once you get there." He informed her.

Starring the clerk straight in the eye, Abby boldly responded with, "Well then, I will take one ticket to St. Louis, please." She had no idea what he meant by other arrangements but she figured she would find out after she arrived in Saint Louis.

"Yes mam. That will be twenty-five and a half dollars then." The clerk informed her and motioned for her to deposit the money into the bin beneath his barred window.

Reaching into her hand bag, Abby carefully counted out the fare. She placed it in the bin and patiently waited as the clerk began to recount it.

"Name please," he asked her.

Startled by his simple name request, Abby panicked. Quickly looking around her she spied an advertisement of a young boy eating a sandwich that his mother had made for him using bread made from *Creosota* brand of flour. Looking the clerk straight in the eye she said to him, "Creosota, that is my name, it is Lydia Creosota." She pulled the Lydia out of thin air.

"Sure thing Miss Creosota," the clerk replied. Again he looked at her strangely. He handed her the issued ticket to Saint Louis. Then he instructed her to wait outside at the gate for her train. He added that she should hurry as the train should be arriving any moment.

Abby absently thanked the clerk, picked up her valise and made her way to the gate. "I sure do run into some strange people on this here job!" The clerk thought to himself as he watched her pick up her ticket and turned her attention away from him. He automatically dismissed her from his mind and began helping the next in line.

Thus it was that Abby found herself waiting for the westbound train to St. Louis. Missouri. She was so busy looking around her that she did not take time to consider what she was really doing.

There were people everywhere. She had never mixed with so many people. She had always been among the elite society of Savannah and the only time she was in a crowd was at a ball or an established gathering of the women folk of Society. She'd never gone to the market with Old Pelly or any of the other household help. As such she was shocked to realize that the world was so full of so many different types of people.

To her left she watched as an obviously harassed mother tried to round up five small children who were running in circles. At the same time the woman was trying to quiet a sixth child, a newborn baby in a basket that was being used as a bassinet for the young baby to travel in. Her oldest child looked to be about eleven years old. He was causing more trouble than help to his mother as he tried to quiet down the smaller five. To her right she saw a young couple. Apparently they were newlyweds bound on their wedding trip. They had eyes only for each other. Once again Jeffrey popped into her thoughts but before she could miss him, she was bumped into by one of the running children.

Grabbing her valise and catching her balance at the same time, she narrowly missed stepping off of the gate decking and falling into the mud below her. Catching her balance, she absentmindedly accepted the mother's apology. The harassed mother grabbed the errant child by the collar of his shirt and yelled at him to behave.

The gatekeeper was walking up and down in front of the gate trying to determine that everyone was at their proper loading locations. "Nice day for travel young lady," he nodded to her as he checked her ticket. In her haste, Abby had not noticed the day. She stole a few moments to take it all in.

The temperature was a comfortable seventy-three degrees. The wind was gently blowing. A bright blue cloudless sky held a brilliant sun shining brightly all around her. April 03, 1849, "yes it is a good day to begin a new life," Abby acknowledged silently to herself as she nodded and agreed with the man on his polite observations. This affirmation seemed to erase some of her nervousness. Announcing its arrival the train whistle suddenly blew loudly in her ear causing her to jump. Her stomach lurched as she realized that this was it! Her life was about to change completely and to what she had no idea! It was now twelve O'clock Noon and the train was exactly on time. She decided that this was a sign that leaving Savannah was the right thing for her to do.

As the train came to a lurching stop the steam emitted from the braking engines engulfed her. Some of the passengers on board began quickly descending. Other people just as quickly began climbing on board. Abby was jostled and shoved by the crowd. When it was her turn to board the train she was pushed again and she missed the step. Unable to catch her balance, her heart stopped momentarily. Horrified, she knew she was about to land face down in the mud.

Startled, her stomach muscles jumped as she suddenly felt strong arms catch her and lift her up as if she weighed nothing at all. Clearly embarrassed, her face beet red, she found herself staring into the laughing blue eyes of a tall blond headed stranger. He was grinning cheerfully and was wearing a very strange looking hat. Instantly she noted his thick honey blond curly hair needed a trim and that he had a mustache that curled slightly upwards at the corners.

Visibly unnerved, she mumbled a quiet "Thank you," to the stranger and turned her back to him making a second attempt to board the train steps as quickly as she could so she could escape from the strange man who helped her. For some reason unknown to her his presence made her very nervous.

"Whoa there, little filly," the stranger quickly said. "Is a thank you all I get for stopping you from ruining that purdy purple dress you're a wearin?" The stranger questioned her speaking in an unfamiliar drawl that Abby had never heard before. She found it strange, slightly melodious and even stranger it was to her liking. Although he mispronounced some of his words, such as purdy, he spoke with a sing song effect. She decided she liked it a lot!

Flustered, she turned to him and replied. "Oh! Of course, how ungrateful of me," she murmured softly. Opening her bag she withdrew a coin to give him. "Watching her and realizing she was about to tip him for helping her, he suddenly burst into loud laughter.

"Now I wasn't referring to a reward," he said. Just a pretty smile along with your thank you ought to do the trick!" He smiled and winked at her.

Embarrassed, Abby nervously attempted to give him the smile he wanted. She replaced the coin in her purse and fumbled for words to make amends, "Oh pardon me, I really am so sorry. I guess I never expected to lose my balance that way." Gathering her courage a little she said "Please accept both my thank you, and also my smile." She managed a rather shy yet bigger smile to bestow upon her benefactor. She had no idea that she was being flirted with or that her smile was encouraging the stranger to continue remaining in her company.

Still blushing, she quickly turned her back on the stranger and boarded the train. Moving down the aisle, she looked for a seat. She almost sat next to the mother with all the little children. Deciding quickly that her nerves would never handle the commotion of the children or the chattering of their mother she selected an empty seat near the middle of the car. Setting her valise on the floor in front of her she sat down next to the open window. The hard wooden seat was uncomfortable. Abby settled in and prepared for her journey to begin. She turned her view to the window. Startled, she was dismayed to see the tall blond stranger had settled his long, lean body into the seat facing her. He kicked his traveling bag under his seat and smiled directly at her.

"Oh no, now what am I going to do?" she thought to herself. She was very uncomfortable with a strange male staring at her. Abby decided to ignore him. Barely nodding at him, she turned her gaze to the window.

"The name is Jordan," he said to her, "Joseph Alan Jordan. I'm on my way to Saint Louie and then I intend to find a wagon train to carry me the rest of the way to Californy. Yep, gold, I hear, I hear they've got gold everywhere in Californy, and I intend to have my share!" he volunteered his business to her without her invitation. He was offended with her for ignoring him. He figured if a woman was brave enough to travel unescorted, she was an open invitation to whoever crossed her path.

Abby ignored the man and did not grace his unsolicited comments with an answer. Indecision and fear gripped her thoughts. "A wagon train?" She thought silently to herself. "I know the ticket clerk said the train only went to Saint Louis, but whatever in the world is a wagon train? Oh no, now I really don't know what I'm going to do when we get to St. Louis." She added the additional worry to her already overloaded mind.

Joseph continued to attempt to converse with her, "So now, little lady, are ya by chance also heading for Californy? Will I have the pleasure of yur comp'ny on the wagon train?

Abby was becoming irritated with him. She had no destination but she did not intend for this strange man to find that out. She angrily graced him with her attention and admonished him sharply! "Sir, you are certainly quite forward!" She vehemently told him. "Why, we have not even been properly introduced and here you are asking me all these personal questions," she found herself rudely blabbering the first words that came to her mind with no consideration of their content.

"Well pardon me lil Missy!" Taken aback, the stranger dipped his funny looking felt hat at her in apology, "But ya will find as we begin heading west that yor high fallutin manners will be of little use to ya out here! In fact I warrant ya should begin to let go of them before they git ya in some real trouble Missy!" he retorted. "And as for us being properly introduced, I did introduced myself to ya. It were you, who didn't introduce yourself back ta me. So I guess it's you Miss, and not me who is being so forward!" He finished and smiled smugly at her. To his self he made a mental note, "Boy, this little lady certainly needs someone to take care of her. Hmmm, this might just become a bit more interesting than I thought." He smiled realizing that he liked this latest idea.

Abby was mortified that anyone should speak so rudely to her. She replied, "Well!" then turned her face away from the stranger and proceeded to look out of the window determined to ignore the rude man. However, she had taken time to silently look him over. He was rather good looking. Although he was tall, and a handsome blonde, he was dressed very strangely. She had never seen anyone wearing a red-checkered shirt, under a brown jacket made of what appeared to be from the same leather fabric as her father's great chair in his office only the stranger's jacket had long thin strings hanging from the yoke and sleeves. He wore a red kerchief with white printed paisleys on it tied around his neck. She didn't understand why he was wearing it backwards. "Why would anyone wear a scarf around their neck with the full end in the front" she wondered? He looked like he was prepared to sit down to dinner with his napkin tied in place around his neck. She smiled slightly as she envisioned him as a five year old boy being instructed on the correct manners at the dining table. "How strange is that?" She pursed her lips tightly to keep from giggling out loud. "And those pants! What kind of pants were those?" Abby had never seen a pair of blue jeans. To top it all off he had stuffed the legs of his jeans into a fancy pair of light brown boots that looked like they were made of animal scales and had funny decorations that resembled lightning in white jagged stripes going up the sides. But none of the above were as amazing to her as his hat was. The ridiculously shaped, light beige colored item was so tall! It was large on top with an indent in the middle. Where it touched his head the sides fanned outwards and were curved upwards! "How ridiculous is that!" she thought to herself. "Whatever can he be thinking wearing a thing like that on his head?" Abby was unable to hide her amusement. Before she laughed out loud she quickly covered her mouth feigning a small cough. The train lurched into action. Staring out the window, her stomach muscles jumped as she watched the city limits of Savannah disappear behind her.

Joseph slouched in his seat. As if he could hear her thoughts he picked up his brand new Stetson, dusted it off and re-curled the curves on the sides. It was his prized possession. He had it specially made before his trip to Savannah to visit with one of his cousins. He had hoped his cousin would go on to California with him but on his arrival he found that his cousin was now married and about to become a new dad. So Joseph had decided to proceed west to California on his own. He placed the Stetson on his head and pulled the brim low over his eyes. Slumping in his seat, he sat peering at her from under the huge hat and pretended to sleep.

Actually, he was checking her out. He certainly liked what he saw. The bright sunshine had made her hair look like hot flames and that had caught his attention immediately while they were waiting to catch the train. The large crowd of passengers made it difficult for him to move next to her. But that glowing red hair had drawn him to her like a magnet. He'd arrived behind her just in time to catch her as she fell. She was tiny in her dark violet traveling suit, but if he was any judge of women, he knew she had a perfectly formed body beneath all that wool. One look at her fear filled green eyes was all it took for him to be completely mesmerized by her. She had a pert little nose with a very slight sprinkling of freckles across the bridge and full red lips that she kept trying to hide with her gloved hand. He vowed to himself that somehow he was going to find a way to kiss those freckles the first chance he got, not to mention her full red lips. He had the feeling that she could match him passion for passion in any kiss. Joseph found it very difficult to take his eyes off of the gorgeous woman before him.

As the train drew further away from Savannah, Abby began again to fear her rash actions. Her thoughts began to haunt her in earnest. Her facial expressions were showing her indecision. The fearful expression on her face was not lost on Joseph. He quirked his right brow and wondered what she was so scared about. He was an excellent well trained tracker. He could smell when things weren't quite right. He concluded that maybe she might be running away. He continued to watch her from under his hat brim.

Abby's thoughts wandered in earnest. She knew she had no idea where she was heading. Maybe she could use her education to secure a teaching position. Then her thoughts switched to Jeffrey. "Good heavens," she said to herself, "whatever have I done?" She came to the realization that she would never lay eyes on her beloved Jeffrey again. Nor on her father for that matter she also admitted to herself. Even though she was angry with him, he had been her lifelong trusted companion. He had been the best father to her for all of her eighteen years. Suddenly missing Jeffrey and her father, she grabbed her valise intending to quickly jump off the slowly chugging train. Just as she reached for the handle of the valise and began to rise from her seat, the train lurched into full throttle and she fell back into her seat with a hard thump. It was too late to back out now. Now not only the train was in full throttle, but also her hastily un-thought out trip was in full throttle as well! For the first time she accepted the realization that she was scared to death!

Abby's throat constricted as she realized what she had done. A tear slowly slid down her cheek before she could stop it. Joseph saw the tear but kept it to himself. He knew for certain that something was definitely wrong with this little gal's world. He decided then and there that he was going to stay by her side whether she liked it or not.

It would take a full week to reach Saint Louis. Periodically the train stopped at various locations. The passengers were allowed to disembark for meals. If the train stopped near a town around dusk the passengers were allowed to find a place to rest for the night. The long train trip provided Abby with ample time to consider the consequences of her actions.

She had refused to accept to face the stares of the elite society of Savannah. There would have been those who would have been kind and attempt to hide their knowledge of the scandal she had now become the central character of. She knew she would fall to pieces in front of those kind souls. Then there would be those hateful self-righteous snobs, including Elizabeth Whatley and her mother. These persons would feel justified to snub her openly and make hateful remarks to her and about her to others. They would spread malicious gossip regarding her birth behind her back. She would be filled with shame and embarrassment. She knew she would want to run and hide. Knowing she couldn't face the Savannah elite society, she had left. She found peace in her decision to find a new life for herself. She hoped to find it quickly before her stash of money dwindled to nothing.

Finally she faced her thoughts regarding Jeffrey. A vision of her upcoming wedding appeared in her mind. She saw herself in her beautiful white wedding gown walking down the aisle of the Presbyterian Church she and her father attended. Pink roses with little white rosebuds were attached to the end of each pew. A wide white satin ribbon was strung from pew to pew attaching the bouquets of white rosebuds and lilies. Her father was leading her down the aisle.

Envisioning herself in the beautiful satin and lace gown she smiled as she sought out the detail of it. The front of the gown ended below her waist in a deep "V" edged with genuine pearls. At the hips it began to flow in wide rows of lace continuing down the exceptionally long train of the gown. The bodice was embroidered with pearls in the shape of tiny rosebuds. The deep heart shape plunge of the neckline covered her breasts with the same lace that graced the skirt. The full train of the dress was edged in pearls and draped a full six feet behind her. The sleeves were puffed from the shoulders to the elbows and then gracefully narrowed to a small point over the wrist. She had drawn the design of the gown herself including the veil, crowned with a pearl coronet in the same small rosebud design. Suddenly she remembered the dress was now in shreds. Tears slid down her cheeks before she could stop them. Grabbing her skirt she bent to wipe the tears from her eyes. For a little while she was able to clear her thoughts. Then she drifted into a deep sleep as the humming of the train lulled her senses.

Her earlier vision of her wedding turned into a dream. In the dream she smiled contentedly as her father placed her hand in Jeffrey's. It was when Jeffrey promised his troth to her and placed the ring on her finger that the dream became a nightmare. The hand accepting Jeffrey's ring was not hers. Those were not her fingernails that she saw. She struggled to see herself in the dream. Finally she saw her face only it wasn't hers, it was Elizabeth Whatley's face and Elizabeth's hand that was accepting Jeffrey's ring! It was Elizabeth, not Abby, who was wearing Abby's beautiful wedding dress! It was Elizabeth who was adoringly looking into Jeffrey's dark brown eyes and sultrily saying "I do." Not Abby! Suddenly Elizabeth turned away from Jeffrey to stare straight at Abby. She glared smugly at Abby and taunted her by saying very loudly for all to hear, "SEE ABBY, JEFFREY BELONGS TO ME! NOT TO YOU ABBY ANDERSON AND YOU NEED NEVER FORGET IT!"

"No! No! Noooo…!" Abby jerked wide awake to hear herself mumbling her insistent denial. Huge tears were streaming down her cheeks.

"Hey? Ya ok, little lady?" Someone, was grabbing at her wrist, attempting to awaken and calm her.

Dazed and in shock, Abby instantly awoke and stared in a semicircle around at her surroundings. It took her a few minutes to realize where she was and that it was the stranger named Joseph, who was inquiring if she was all right. She felt pressure upon her wrist. Looking down she quickly pulled her hand away from the strange man who was lightly holding it. The other passengers near her were all staring at her with concerned looks.

Slightly shaking her head, Abby smiled and wiped her tears. She apologized. "Oh! Excuse me. I'm so sorry," she said, "I didn't mean to alarm any of you. It was just a nightmare, that's all. Just a nightmare," she paused for a second and saw the people nearest to her were all still staring at her. Sheepishly she continued, "Really, it was a rather silly nightmare, you know, the kind we all have now and again, don't we?" She hoped the other passengers would accept her feeble explanation and leave her to her own worries and fears. Some of the passengers smiled back at her in agreement, the others simply dismissed her and returned to minding their own business. Joseph continued to stare at her, worried, his expression was puzzled.

Abby began to shake from shock. Again tears began falling freely in salty rivulets down her cheeks. She couldn't stop them so she quickly ducked her head to hide them and opened her purse grabbing for her handkerchief to wipe at them. Startled, she felt Joseph's weight settle on the seat beside her. Using his red kerchief he gently wiped her tears away.

Compassionately, he put his arm around her and pulled her to him in such a way that she was hidden from the other passengers. He began whispering gently in her ears. "Now don't you worry anymore honey, I don't know who or what has hurt you, but I'm here now and I'm going to take good care of you."

Heartbroken, unable to stop herself from accepting the comfort he offered, she buried her face in his chest and quietly sobbed her heart out until she fell into a fitful sleep once again.

She awoke with a start! Realizing she was still in Joseph's arms she sat up immediately and disengaged her body from his. Embarrassed, Abby pulled herself together thanking him for his kindness. Allowing her to remove her from his embrace, he nodded to her, mumbling something about it was his pleasure and returned to his own seat. She felt his silent message telling her that he was there to care for her if she decided that she wanted him to. Nodding her gratitude, she watched him lower his hat over his eyes and feign sleep.

Instantly she felt lonely again. After her nightmare, she refused to allow her mind to wander. She struggled to clear her mind by concentrating very hard on the view of the countryside passing before her eyes. Slowly she calmed herself and began to enjoy her trip.

Chapter Four

After the train left Savannah it wound its way through several small towns and cities including the larger cities of Huntsville, Alabama, and Vicksburg, Mississippi. The long trip continued winding northwest towards Nashville, Tennessee. After leaving Nashville, it continued northwest into the state of Kentucky heading towards the small city of Louisville. The terrain was beautiful. Thus far the trip was uneventful. Except for small talk now and again Abby was able to limit her concentration to her present position. Gradually she came to terms with her actions and accepted that her decision to leave was the best decision she could have made.

Occasionally she spoke to the other passengers. She met a few people who had hopes of taking the same wagon train that Joseph had mentioned to California. It seemed that everyone was searching for gold. Even the harassed mother with her husband and seven children were heading to California to stake their claim and try their hand at panning for gold. Abby began to feel comfortable among the other passengers. Except for a very sore bottom and stiff legs, she looked forward to the train ride as it continued on its journey towards the still greatly unsettled Midwest.

As long as she kept her mind clear of her past life and Jeffrey, she was able to control her pain. Her father seldom entered her thoughts. She'd already dismissed him along with any thoughts of her past home life from her active mind. She now saw herself as a continuous traveler with neither past nor future, only the present. She knew she needed to formulate a plan for her new life, but for the life of her, she couldn't come up with any ideas that appealed to her. In the end, she decided to put it all in God's hands and prayed that he would lead her directly to her new life.

Joseph had assumed an air of silence. Except for a handful of small polite comments he did not press Abby for any information. Keeping his silent promise to her he shadowed her every move. He was behind her at every stop to help her find her way to meals, sleeping quarters or whatever she needed.

She had accepted him to be her silent guide. She was beginning to worry about what she would do when he went on to California and she would be left on her own.

Several days later they found themselves on the stretch of countryside known as the Dixie trail. It ran between Nashville, Tennessee through the southern lands of Kentucky and headed north into the city of Louisville. Breaking their silence, Joseph decided to ask her for her name again.

"Mmm... my nnname?" Stammered Abby, she was surprised to realize that in all these days of traveling together she had never introduced herself to the only person who had made himself helpful to her. Abby stumbled to reply. "Now what name was it that she had given to the ticket clerk?" silently she searched her brain quickly for the answer. She had almost forgotten that she had used an assumed name.

"Creo.., Creo something? Oh yes, that was it!" She smiled slightly in brief confirmation of her memory.

"Why, my name is Lydia Creosota." She triumphantly told Joseph. He nodded but his instincts told him that she was lying. It made sense to him that she was most likely traveling under assumed name. He could also tell that she seemed to have no idea where she was travelling to. He had decided that morning that he was going to suggest to her that she try her luck in California also. His dilemma now, was how was he to suggest it to her without scaring her away from him. So he remained silent and the question remained unasked.

Suddenly, breaking the silence she spoke to him, "I'm sorry. I really have been rather prudish. Now that we have been traveling companions for a few days and nights, I suppose I really should have introduced myself to you. My name is Ab...," she started to tell him her real name was Abby, but quickly she remembered her assumed name and pretended a cough as she corrected herself, "Lydia Creosota, as I have just told you," she reaffirmed her name and smiled at Joseph. "I recently lost my family and I am traveling west alone. I realize that you have gathered this much about me. There really isn't anything else to say. Suffice it to say that I am looking for a new life and a new beginning. I do wish to thank you for all of your kindness towards me. I want to assure you that you have been very helpful to me and your efforts are not going unappreciated." She smiled prettily at him and hoped that her explanation would satisfy his open curiosity about her. Somehow though, she still felt that he didn't fully believe her.

In return, even though Joseph had nodded his acceptance of her explanation, the fact was indeed that he did not fully believe her. However he did admit to himself that she was finally being partially truthful to him.

As they entered the more mountainous regions of southern Kentucky, Abby became delighted with the scenery around her. Spring time was arriving with a bang. The dogwood and redwood trees were beautiful. They were in full bloom sporting bountiful white and pink blooms. Likewise, the redwoods had thousands of tiny purple beads on them. Some had burst into bloom and others were just beginning to turn to a glorious reddish purple. She was amazed in their beauty. Along the sides of the train tracks, the natural weeds were blooming filled with wildflowers of every color. "What a picture to paint!" she thought. Looking past the train tracts were open pastures where livestock grazed on the wild grass and wildflowers scattered here and there. She was delighted watching the many horses and cows leisurely enjoying their days eating the fresh growing hay. Many of the fields had been plowed for the new crops that were being planted. Looking at them she became homesick for Savannah and the spring seasons she had looked forward to each year. Shaking her head, she refused to let her memory take control. She refused to allow her delight at seeing all the pretty mountains they were winding through and around bring memories of her past back to her active mind. She knew that it was paramount that she simply forget the past as quickly as possible and look forward only to the new adventures that lay before her.

Joseph could not resist telling Abby about a coveted secret of the traveling folk.

"Lydia, look at the mountains out of the corner of your eyes, while you are facing forward." He instructed her. "As the train moves swiftly by them you will begin to see the profiles of people carved into the stones of the mountains."

It took Abby a few moments to discern faces in the rocky cliffs they passed. All of a sudden she began to see profiles appear in the jagged stone edges of the dynamited mountain passes. Excited she avidly called out to him each time she successfully saw another facial profile. Once, she swore she could see the profile of the United States President himself. Alan smiled. He hoped he would have many enjoyable hours with her. He'd seen many beautiful places out west that he would love the chance to share with her.

They arrived at the small Kentucky town called Bowling Green just in time for lunch. The town was known for many caves including the famous one called Mammoth Cave. Joseph and Abby disembarked to eat a quick lunch and exercise their tired legs. Joseph told Abby that he was sorry that they would not have time to actually visit the caves. He explained to her that he had seen them before and that she would have been absolutely amazed by the pure un-believable size of the caverns, Mammoth cave in particular. He suggested that they could take a different train on another day and stay here for a few days to give them time to visit the caves with him.

Abby politely declined his offer. She definitely was not ready under any circumstances to stay in a strange town with a man she barely knew. The very idea was appalling to her! She didn't acknowledge that she basically was already doing this as they stayed overnight in various towns as part of their train trip. In her mind, she had the train and the crewmembers and passengers all to protect her and keep her safe as if they had become her new family for the time being. And although the thought of not seeing the caves was disappointing, she knew she also had limited funds with her. She needed to be very careful with her few remaining dollars or she might not make it to her unknown western destination where she intended to begin her new life.

Engaged in polite conversation about the community around them, neither of them noticed the gang of six rough looking men boarding the train. Without speaking among themselves, the six men suddenly split up. Two men went to the rear of the passenger train car. Two others sat at the front of the car. The other two sat down in the seat across the aisle from Joseph and began openly perusing Abby. The conductor walked back and forth calling "All aboard!"

Joseph's sixth sense was alerted. He looked around him and noticed the two men who seemed to be discussing Abby quietly. He could barely hear them whispering to each other, but he could not discern their mumbled conversation. He decided he was being overly paranoid.

Joseph remained a bit disturbed by their attention to Abby. Without success he continued to strain his ears in an attempt to overhear their conversation. At the same time he was surprised to realize that he was feeling a twinge of jealousy. When had he become so protective and possessive of this woman? A woman whose name he acknowledged that he really didn't know. Assuming the men were simply enamored of her charms, he failed to realize he should have undone the hammer strap of his holster, which presently housed his loaded Colt six-shooter. Unknown to him, the men did intend to do them harm.

The whistle blew, smoke filled the air and the train lurched ahead. Their journey continued. The next scheduled stop was Louisville, Kentucky.

Chapter Five

Silas Johnson sat in the same leather arm chair in Charles Anderson's library that Abby had sat in as her father disclosed to her the truthful facts of her birth. His great girth made him appear stuffed into a tiny kid size chair. The current appearance of the now strained chair was completely the opposite of the vision of the petite young girl whom the chair had seem to swallow on the day that Abby had sat in it to ascertain the horrific unknown details of her birth. He snapped his cigar case shut and shook his head as he listened to the story Charles Anderson was telling him. Instead he lighted the cheroot he had chosen from the box presented to him by his host. Having heard enough of the confusing tale, he interrupted Charles and queried, "I realize you are suffering a great deal of sorrow right now Charles, however, what makes you think your daughter was kidnapped?"

Throwing both of his arms upward, vigorously rubbing his forehead, a frustrated Charles replied, "I don't know that she was kidnapped, Silas. I don't know that she wasn't kidnapped either. In fact as I have told you, I don't know what has happened to her at all!" He was sitting behind his huge desk. Again his small body looked ridiculous behind the huge mahogany desk. "But one thing I definitely know for certain is that she isn't here and no one saw her leave," he concluded adamantly pointing his right index finger directly at his friend.

"Well, I'm hesitant to say so, as I know you do not wish to hear it, but it appears to me that your daughter may very well have left of her own accord," Silas countered. Unknown to Charles, he was using one of the tricks he employed to attempt to confuse his clients in order to ascertain the truthful facts involved. He took a long, slow drag on the Cuban cigar and continued, "Kidnappers usually don't take items of clothing with them. If, as you say she was kidnapped, why would some of Abby's clothing and her valise be missing? I might add that you have received nothing in the form of a letter or telegram from a kidnapper. If I understand you correctly, you have heard absolutely nothing regarding the whereabouts of your daughter." He dumped his ashes in the crystal ash tray that sat on the mahogany Queen Anne table next to the settee. "Are you quite sure that you wish to engage my services to find her? It appears that she just might wish to be left alone. Why don't you just wait a little longer and see if you hear from her. Maybe she'll come to her senses and return on her own accord." Silas dropped his suggestions to Charles in order to determine exactly how worried his friend was. He was aware of the gossip regarding Abby. Charles had enlightened him on the truth behind the raging rumors. He felt that Abby probably had left of her own accord, but would probably come to her senses and return home after she had taken a little time to think things through.

"Do you mean to tell me that you are going to do nothing at all?" Charles slammed his bony fist on the top of his desk as he yelled at Silas. Silas was his very old friend and a very successful, well known, sought after Pinkerton detective. Charles' accounting firm often hired Silas's detective services when they were hunting down a missing client, money, etc. "I can't believe you can't see the immediate danger she must be in? Why, it's my fault…" Charles hung his head in despair, "I haven't a clue what has happened to her. I don't know if she is alright, or hurt, or whatever? Where can she be? How could she just leave? She knows that without me or Old Pelly she has absolutely no protection. She's never been in this outside world by herself. She has no idea of the dangers she will encounter. As my great friend, I am asking you to help me Silas. You simply must help me!" He adamantly pleaded with his friend.

"Alright Charles, calm down now, I can plainly see how upset you are. I will do everything in my power to find your daughter. Only, I must warn you, if she did in fact leave of her own accord, she may not wish to return home right away. You need to understand this and be prepared." Silas carefully searched Charles face for signs that he did understand the warning. Softly, he asked, "Can you handle this possibility of disappointment, Charles?" Waiting for Charles to answer, he took another drag from the flavored tobacco. He attempted to dump the ashes of his cigar but missed the crystal dish and they fell onto the expensive east India rug. Straightening himself to a standing position, he leaned forward to reach into his briefcase for his pen and notepad. His jacket seams were stretched to the maximum to accommodate his huge girth. There was a slight sound of ripping cloth as the back seams of his vest ripped under his jacket. He coughed lightly to cover the sound.

Too upset to have heard, Charles rose and began pacing back and forth in front of the emerald green velvet drapes covering his two library windows. His hands were red from continuously wringing them behind his back. Back and forth, he wore the path he was creating in the expensive India carpet. Finally he answered Silas, "How can I possibly handle such a sharp cruel disappointment?" He whispered. "I suppose that at least I will have the comfort of knowing that she is alive." He paused for a moment. His voice filled with anguish, he began to speak his thoughts, "Oh if only I had realized how distraught the news of her birthright would be to her. I would never have waited so long to tell her. I should have conditioned her a long time ago when she was too small to realize the damage that has been done to her reputation."

Slamming his right fist into his left hand yet again, he continued speaking but this time his tone was loud. Voicing his deep anger and desire for revenge, he continued, "I wish I could flog that Elizabeth Whatley. That little societal snob has always been a thorn in my Abby's side. Everyone knows she wants Abby's Jeffrey. That vixen has no conscience when it comes to what she wants! I wish I could have her blackballed from Society! In fact I wish I could have her hung!" he declared vehemently.

With regret and disgust in his tone he countered his own desire for revenge, "But her father is far too important to our firm for me to do anything but bow down to his beck and call. It sickens me that there is nothing I can do," he spat his contempt on the floor in front of him. But I'll get that spoiled little black haired witch! You just wait and see Silas, I'll get that little snob if anything has happened to my daughter! She will get what's coming to her, I'll guarantee you that! Some way or another I will find a way to repay that little gossiping witch!"

Determinedly, he stamped his foot soundly into the highly polished wood floor. Shaking his head from side to side he began pacing back and forth in front of the windows again. Silas noted, his beleaguered friend was filled with intense grief, anger and worry for his daughter's welfare and her unknown whereabouts.

"Now, Now, Charles, you are understandably upset." Accepting the seriousness of the situation, Silas stood still as he ground out his cigar into the ashes of the crystal ashtray. Striding closer to his friend he continued to attempt to console the highly distressed but comical little man. "Forget about the Whatley brat. You're right, she's a snob, but what we all need to worry about now is finding Abby. Besides, you really shouldn't be so free at voicing threats in front of me, even though she deserves it. You know, I am bound by the law to report all I know. Our friendship is certainly strong, but, I'm asking you not to put me in the position of going against my oaths."

Taking his pen and notebook he prepared to take detailed notes. "Now Charles, once again tell me everything you can about Abby's disappearance. Take your time and be very careful to be totally truthful without exaggeration or condemnation. At this time, I need every factual detail you can remember to help me to find her," he stressed the word *factual*! Silas continued to attempt to calm his friend down. Secretly glad that he was not Charles Anderson. If it had been his daughter he knew that he would do more than have Elizabeth Whatley blackballed from society, he would see to it that she disappeared from the face of the earth, his oath be damned!

Charles once again launched into the story of the discovery of Abby's disappearance. "Ok," his relief apparent at his friends intent to help him, "apparently Abby's friend, Elaine Wolfe, came to visit Abby earlier the morning after the ball but she was told by Old Trey, that Abby was supposedly still sleeping. So Elaine said she elected to run other errands and return to visit with Abby later. She did not come back to see Abby until this morning.

That's when Old Trey knocked on Abby's bedroom door and Abby didn't answer his knock. Then Old Trey looked for Old Pelly and asked her to look in on Abby and tell her that she had company. Pelly says she knocked lightly. Then she opened the door a tiny bit and peeked into the room to see if Abby was still sleeping. Old Pelly told me she was shaken when she discovered the shredded wedding gown, and the contents of Abby's overnight valise all over the floor. After that she checked the armoire and realized that Abby's traveling gown and a few other garments and her valise were all missing. She claims that's when she started screaming. She says that's when she sent Old Trey to go to the accounting firm and bring me home.

Elaine's side of the story is that she ran up the stairs two at a time as soon as she heard Old Pelly screaming. She said Old Pelly kept screaming, she's gone, Oh my lord, my baby's gone? Elaine said she was shocked at the mess in Abby's room."

Charles continued to inform Silas of the tragic story. He told Silas that he had immediately left the office and had arrived home in record time. He tried to listen to Old

Pelly's babbling lamentations. Before he knew what was going on, both Old Pelly and Elaine were sobbing loudly and both of them were explaining their stories to him at the same time. Charles shook his head. Placing his hands over his ears to demonstrate to Silas the horrendous screaming the two women were doing in their attempt to relate their side of the story, one on top of the other. He had not been able to understand a thing that they were trying to tell him.

Elaine was bawling loudly and stating that she should never have trusted that Abby was ok, and that it was all her fault that Abby had had no one to confide in.

At the same time Old Pelly was trying to pick up the room and then she just threw it all back on the floor again along with herself. She just sat there on the floor rocking back and forth holding her head in her hands. She kept moaning, "My poor, poor baby, she done left and I doan know what she be a gettin' herself in for and it all old Pelly's fault cause I'se thought she was a sleepin like a babe, and that the shock would wear off and she would be OK agin by dis mornin! When she didn't come to dinner, I tol em all ta just let her sleep cuz she was tired from all de dancin'. I never did know my baby was gone! I never did know!"

Silas stared in amazement. His eyebrows arched fully upward at the comical picture the small balding red headed Charles presented as he attempted to recite Old Pelly's side of the story in her southern Negro dialect. To prevent himself from laughing loudly at his troubled friend, he lowered his eyes and began painfully pulling on the corners of his gray haired handlebar moustache.

"So Silas, now you know the scene I was confronted with when I entered the room and tried to sort out the problem. Both women tried to tell me their side of the story at the same time. Eventually, I realized that something was terribly wrong and that Abby was not part of the babbling ladies in the room. Finally I was able to deduce that they were trying to tell me that Abby was missing." Stopping to blow his nose and wipe the tears from his red freckled face, Charles sniffed and finished.

"So I tell you Silas, what else besides kidnapping could have happened to her. I simply can't entertain the idea that she would just take off on her own. To endanger her life by leaving without someone to protect her, why it's unthinkable! Abby is far too intelligent to do anything so thoughtless or stupid." He told Silas. Charles Anderson truly believed his daughter had been kidnapped.

Silas thoughtfully listened to Charles. He was writing careful detailed notes in his notebook. In an attempt to console Charles one final time he said, "Try not to worry, Charles. I will do everything in my power to find Abby as quickly as I can."

"You will keep me informed when you hear something, no matter how trivial it may seem?" Charles earnestly implored his friend.

Silas closed his notebook with a resounding snap. "Don't worry Charles, I'll do what I can and you'll be the first to know as soon as I find anything out, even if I have to send you information via Pinkerton's Messenger Service over the wire." He picked up his gray felt hat and placed it on his head. Completely stubbing the cheroot out, he threw it into the crystal dish. Picking up his brief case he walked towards the library door saying, "I'll let myself out. Don't disturb yourself, but do try to get some rest Charles." Quietly, Silas left the library and let himself out the front door of the Anderson home.

Charles never heard his friend leave. He remained sitting at his desk holding his head in his lap oblivious to the tears that were flooding his spectacles.

Silas Johnson's carriage turned the corner and disappeared. In the same moment that a very happy, good looking tall young man holding a huge bouquet of pink rosebuds mixed with yellow daisies strolled down the lane and turned into the Anderson walkway. The excited young man rang the doorbell in quick succession timing the musical notes to the tune he was humming. He removed his new brown derby hat and waited for Old Trey to admit him. Happy to be back in Savannah, the young man had rushed over to visit Abby, his fiancé. Unknown to him, he was about to discover that he, Jeffrey Browning, was in for the shock of his young life.

"What do you mean she is gone?" He yelled loudly at Charles. A flustered Charles was trying to explain to Jeffrey what had happened. Once again they were in Charles library. Charles was feeling engulfed by the darkness of the room and the tragedy that had unfolded in that very same ornately decorated setting.

"Are you trying to tell me that my Abby thinks that I would not want her if I knew she was not your natural daughter?" Jeffrey spoke adamantly as he slammed his checkered tailored jacket down on the leather settee. He began pacing back and forth in front of Charles desk. "Come on Charles, I don't intend to hurt you further, but everyone knows the gossip. Why, just look at her! We all knew that she probably was not your natural offspring. But of course no one would have wanted to hurt you or Abby by telling you of these vicious suspicions. Suffice it to be known that we were all willing to accept Abby without question as part of Savannah Society. You and Abby have certainly earned the respect of our townsfolk. And anyway, nothing would ever have been said once she had become my wife. I would have seen to that." Jeffrey raved on and on.

"You know how much in love with your daughter I am. I'll find her! I promise you that! And when I do, you better be prepared to give her away to me right then and there. I warn you, Charles Anderson, I will not wait another second to make her my wife. Do you hear me Charles Anderson?" Jeffrey instilled his intentions towards Abby firmly on a completely baffled Charles who could think of nothing to say. Charles just sat there gaping at the young man. Relief was slowly sinking in to him as he realized that Abby and his reputations just might not be totally destroyed.

"I just can't believe she would leave me like this!" Jeffrey continued as he wore a new path in the priceless carpet in front of Charles desk. Back and forth with complete bewilderment and surprise on his handsome lean face, he ran his perfectly manicured long fingers, through his short curly dark brown hair, newly cut and styled for his political debut to Washington D.C.

"Whatever could she have been thinking? I'll just have to go find her! That's all! I will just start looking for her right now!" Jeffrey declared grabbing for his hat and coat.

Charles stood up and began pushing the papers towards the back of his desk! "I'll take a leave from the firm and go with you, Jeffrey!" He stated adamantly.

"No Charles, that's not a good idea!" Jeffrey boldly assumed control. "You'll just slow me down. Besides you need to be here in case she returns home. She'll need to know that she is loved and forgiven and that she can expect no shame from anyone. The details of her birth were not her fault. You need to be here for her if she does come home before I can find her. Do you understand me Charles?" He stopped and stood still for a moment as his mind searched for a place to begin his search.

Disappointed, Charles sat back down. "Well, I agree that someone needs to be here in case she returns on her own. However, you will probably find her faster if you join up with Silas Johnson. I have just commissioned him to look for Abby. You know of him. He's the best detective that the Pinkerton firm has to offer. I know that if anyone can find her it will be Silas." Standing, he walked to Jeffrey's side. Grabbing up Jeffrey's jacket, he stuffed it into the anxious young man's hands as he guided Jeffrey out of the library, down the hall to the entry's ornate double doors. "Go now and catch up with Silas. I suspect he will be packing his valise at his apartment and that he plans to leave immediately. Go quickly Jeff! Find Silas and may God go with you both!" He commanded Jeffrey. As an afterthought he threw in a final demand, "Telegraph me the minute you find out anything!" In his hurry, Charles practically pushed Jeffrey out the open double doors forcing him to run down the front steps two at a time to prevent himself from stumbling over his own long legs.

Without replying but with a backward wave of his hat, Jeffrey replaced the brand new derby back on his now excessively mussed up hair with his right hand, while he hailed a cab with his left. He jumped into the cab and instructed the driver to take him to Silas Johnson's posh hotel apartment handing him the address that Charles had hastily given to him.

He formulated his plan as the driver made the short trip into the downtown district of Savannah. He knew that he would have to insist that Silas let him join with him in his search for Abby. "It probably won't be easy to get an old goat like Silas to agree, but I'm not taking no for an answer!" He affirmed to himself. Then he turned his thoughts towards Elizabeth Whatley and her devious attempt to break Abby and himself apart.

That beautiful, raven haired wench had been a lot of fun to flirt with, but no man in his right man could ever trust her to keep her love sacred to him. "I enjoyed playing with that beauty, but I never intended to ask her to wed me! Had I never laid eyes on Abby, I still would not have asked that raven haired witch to be a wife to me," he affirmed and shuddered slightly at the thought of Elizabeth as his wife. His thoughts began to run rampant as he impatiently awaited the cabs arrival at Silas's hotel accommodations.

The train lurched as it left the station in Bowling Green, Kentucky. Five miles later it came to a screeching halt as it suddenly jumped the tracks. The passengers felt a huge jolt at the lurch. Some of them suffered injuries from falling baggage and some actually bounced out of their seats onto the floor of the coach car.

"What the Heck?" Joseph asked to no one in particular as he tried to regain his dignity. He had lurched out of the seat and was sitting in a heap on the floor starring at Abby's knees. He looked so comical and surprised that Abby burst out laughing. At the same time, she was trying to redo her hatpin into her hair as her bag had fallen near her head and knocked her hat off.

Laughing, Joseph attempted to rise. From out of nowhere a gun butt hit him on the head. Stunned, he momentarily stared at Abby, then blackness engulfed him and he fell over on his side at her feet. Abby screamed. A filthy hand covered her mouth and an arm grabbed her tightly around and under her chest. She was lifted out of her seat as if she weighed nothing at all.

Struggling for breath and kicking, Abby tried to free herself. She heard a rough voice demand. "Ya'll sit still and don't move! Keep yur hands in front of ya and close yur eyes. Follow my instructions and no one gets hurt. Unnerstand!" The strange dialect warned her to be very still. She felt a kerchief smelling strongly of male sweat being tied around her nose and eyes. Another kerchief tasting of old dirt was stuffed partly in her mouth and tied at the back of her head. She struggled to free herself and kicked at her assailant. Then she felt intense pain fill her head as the same gun butt used to knock out Joseph, slammed against the top of her own skull. Instantly she passed out and hung limply in the outlaws arms.

Ralph Greening, lead man of the six man crew of outlaws continued bellowing his orders to the passengers. Then he instructed his second in command, "Ok, Jim sling her over yur shoulder, and git er off the train. Tom, ya give im a hand. Larry, check em all for a gun and make sure they ain't loaded. Then throw them guns out them windows. Put the bullets in yur pockets." He added as an afterthought.

"Ricky, git their cash and valuables. Buck, tie this one up and make sure he ain't gettin loose." He kicked Joseph who remained passed out on the floor, his forehead bleeding profusely. Stepping over Joseph's midriff he waved his gun at the passenger's instructing them to handover to Ricky, their valuables, including wedding rings and any money they had.

As the train derailed, each outlaw immediately covered their face with a bandanna to hide further recognition. Quickly they hurried to follow their leader's instructions. The outlaws flashed their guns in every direction, as a warning for all to obey them and not to move. As Ricky took some jewelry and a purse from an elderly matron, she fainted and hit the floor. Her husband went to grab her only to be hit in the head by Ricky's gun butt and left lying on the floor on top of his wife.

Buck tried to take the gun from the husband of the woman with all the children. A struggle ensued as the husband tried to keep the gun and shoot Buck. Buck dropped it in the struggle and it went off. The man jumped up in an attempt to grab and restrain Buck. Ricky, always the one quick to shoot but slow to think, pulled the trigger on his six-shooter and shot it twice. The women and children passengers began to scream. Everyone stared as Buck and the woman's husband fell to the floor.

"Dammit Ralph, Jim asked now what are we going to do?"

"Ya stupid idiot!" a very irritated Ralph glared at Ricky, "How many times have I told ya, yur trigger happy! I told ya absolutely no body was to be shot!" Now look what ya've done. Ya just put us into some serious trouble. Ya'd better pray that I can get us out of this one." Ralph was extremely angry with his trigger happy gang member. His angry facial expressions scared the children on the train. They began crying earnestly. Their Mother was bending over her husband attempting to cradle him in her lap, moaning over and over as she checked her husband for signs of life.

"Larry, check on Buck," Ralph demanded, "Is he dead?"

Before Buck could move, Ricky answered for him, "Naw, but this one is," he said kicking the woman's lifeless husband in the legs. The man's wife screamed again grabbing her husband's lifeless body to her chest. Other's reached to help her only to be stopped by Ricky with his gun pointed directly in their faces. They withdrew and sat quietly filled with fear now that someone had been killed. The severity of the situation became very apparent to everyone. Buck sat up and grabbed at his upper thigh where he had been nicked by the gunshot of the man Ricky killed.

"Dang it! If I had a rope I'd hang ya myself, Rick! Ralph commented angrily. He decided they'd best leave as quickly as they could. "Let's git the heck out a here as fast as we can," he ordered his crew as he brandished his gun in a passenger's face. With Abby dangling from Jim's shoulder, the outlaws backed toward the rear door of the passenger car.

"Remember what I said" he spoke to the passengers. "Ya kin see how trigger happy my buddy is. He warned the passengers maliciously. No one moves, and no one else gets hurt! Do you understand me?" With that final warning the outlaws exited the train and slammed the door shut behind them. They hurried to a clump of nearby trees and mounted the the horses they had waiting for them. Quickly they rode off before anyone else could realize what exactly had happened.

Earlier that morning they had derailed the track and placed a tree trunk in the path of the train and then they had tied fresh horses to the nearby tree ready for their fast get away. They had planned their kidnapping of Abby to a careful successful conclusion. They galloped westward, across the hills towards the cavernous mountains as fast as they could. Abby was bouncing up and down. In their haste, she had been thrown across the saddle face down in front of Jim. He held onto her with his legs and one arm as he expertly guided his steed with his other hand.

Back on the train everyone remained still, scared to move. Silence overcame them all except for the crying children and the lamenting wife. They were still in shock. This was the last thing they had ever expected to happen. The woman whose husband had died continued to sit on the floor rocking the lifeless body of her husband in her arms. She was in shock. Her seven children were crying as they stared at their father in their mother's arms in disbelief. John, the oldest son, did not accept that his father was dead. He stared at the still and motionless form of his father whose blood was spilled on the floor around him beseeching him to stand and walk and be ok. Suddenly he realized that this nightmare was real. Bolting to the door of the train, he tried to open it only to find that the outlaws had jammed it shut with a rifle through the handle on the opposite side of the train car. Frustrated, John began hammering on the door with his fists.

"I'll get you! I'll get you for this!" He cried again and again to the back sides of the departing robbers. Sobbing he gave up and slid to the floor. His other brothers and sisters and the infant all began to cry louder. The mother, in her sorrow, didn't notice or care. She just kept rocking her husband in her lap, moaning as she begged him not to leave them all alone. Tears flooded her face and dripped onto her dead husband's lifeless body.

A passenger poured water from his cantina on the old man and wife to revive them. Other than a few bruises they seemed to be ok.

This was the scene that met Joseph's eyes as he came to. He attempted to sit up. Rubbing his head gingerly on the injured spot he saw his hand was covered in blood. He tried to remember what had happened. One of the passengers came to his aid and offered him some water, "What happened?" Joseph asked.

"I reckon we were just robbed by a gang of outlaws," the other man answered him as he wiped the blood from Joseph's head using Joseph's own bandana. "Strange though, they took the girl with them," the passenger told Joseph as he finished wiping the blood from Joseph's forehead.

"What girl?" Joseph asked. Suddenly he realized that the stranger was referring to his friend, Lydia." Joseph jumped to his feet almost fainting again as blood rushed to his injured head. "Oh my God!" he yelled, "Where's Lydia?"

"I told ya mister, they took her," the passenger said.

Joseph sat on the seat to regain his balance. Holding his bleeding head in his hands he shook it in an attempt to fight the dizzy feeling and make some sense of the situation. He couldn't understand why they had taken Lydia unless it was because the big one had taken a fancy to her. The outlaw had stared at her a great deal. Maybe they took her to hold her as a hostage. He questioned the passenger about this, but the man said he had no idea. Joseph immediately began formulating a plan to rescue her. He figured the outlaws would probably head toward the caves. He was grateful that he had visited the caves previously and had some knowledge of their layout. He figured he knew where they would be hiding her.

Chapter Six

Harriett Harrison's drawing room overflowed with the buzz of gossiping ladies. It was customary to visit the hostess a day or so after the ball to offer her their congratulations in appreciation of her efforts.

The parlor was furnished with two Queen Ann arm chairs, several matching side chairs, a rose damask settee and several three legged mahogany tables. The ladies held fragile patterned gold rimmed china tea cups and saucers filled with the peppermint tea topped with a tiny fragrant mint leaves. The annual spring ball was the main topic of discussion. Abby's slanderous episode certainly added fuel to the flames of Savannah's eager gossipmongers.

"I just can't get over the way Abby Anderson ran out of the ballroom with her dress hiked to her knees! Why her pantalets were showing!" Eagerly, Johanna Johnston opened the subject of Abby as she accepted her cup of tea that Harriet had personally poured for her favorite guest. She covered her mouth with the side of her hand to feign her shock. Johanna was Mrs. Harrison's closest friend and confidant. Between the two of them, Savannah elite knew they had better watch their P's and Q's and toe the line if they wished to remain acceptable prominent members in Savannah's current activities. "Why it was simply scandalous!" Her snicker cracked a bit with her aging voice. The remaining women in the room couldn't wait to nod in acquiescence.

Although the ladies were supposedly speaking to the women nearest them instead of eavesdropping on Johanna's conversation with their Hostess, Johanna made certain that her voice was loud enough to catch all of their ears. Most of the genteel women politely covered their mouths with their opened fans, or lace gloved hands in an attempt to hide their muffled laughter. They were all delighted that Johanna had the courage to open up the subject. All ears turned immediately in her direction waiting for the next bits of gossip. All of them had been trying to think of a way to do the same without looking overly interested in Abby's shocking behavior and hasty exit.

Although, Harriett Harrison was slightly fearful that her precarious position as head lady in town might be damaged by Abby's un-lady like behavior, she could not resist responding to the gossip. Hiding her voice behind her fan she quietly smiled at her friend indicating her appreciation on the opening of the subject of Abby. Immediately she lowered her fan slightly and loud enough for the entire room to hear her, she chimed in with, "Why, I never, I could've just fainted, I was so shocked! My dear, dear ladies," Exaggerating her best southern drawl, she began addressing the crowd of women in the room. "Why, ya'll know, that if I had any idea, why, "any idea at all, that Abby would be so…," pausing to search for words for the right effect she continued, "shall we say *uncouth* in her behavior? You know, what with her foul accusations and terrible physical behavior and all," she loudly whispered her shocking revelations as she paused the pouring of her tea pot, still holding it suspended high in the air for effect. Quickly she gazed around the room to see and hear what her guests had to say in response. She was rewarded by the concurrent gasps and head nodding that swelled encompassing the huge drawing room.

Resuming the pouring of tea to her elaborately dressed guests she continued, "Well, had I known Abby was to act so rudely, I most certainly would never have extended her the invitation to begin with. Surely ya'll do realize that I had no idea she was going to act so inappropriately! Of course ya'll do know that, don't ya'll?" She nodded her head and actively searched for an affirmation from each of the ladies present. She was determined to make certain that her own reputation had not been damaged and that she suffered no blame for Abby's unacceptable behavior. Portraying sympathy for Abby, she continued, "I am most certain that our poor dear Abby must have had a very good reason for her scandalous behavior." Thusly she threw the topic to the ladies at large for all of them to speculate over their own ideas regarding Abby's shocking behavior.

"Of course she most certainly did!" Jewel Whatley replied smugly to Harriet. "It's my understanding that it was the complete truth that set Abby off! Yes, the whole truth, and my very own daughter, Elizabeth, was only trying to protect Abby to prevent her from public embarrassment at a later date." She attempted to justify her wicked daughter's unjust actions against Abby. Her intent was to hide her daughter's attempt to damage Abby's reputation thusly assuring the breakup of Abby and Jeffrey so Elizabeth could steal Jeffrey from Abby without recompense.

If the truth were known, it had been Jewel who had informed Elizabeth of her suspicions regarding Abby's scandalous birth. Jewel was the one who had slyly instructed Elizabeth to make certain that the accusations were made public during the ball so that all of Savannah society could witness Abby's demise. Both Jewell and her daughter intended to do whatever it took to break up the young couple's engagement. While Elizabeth fancied that she was in love with Jeffrey, it was Jewel who definitely wanted the match between Jeffrey Browning and her daughter, Elizabeth. Such an advantageous marriage between Jeffrey and Elizabeth would definitely elevate the social stature of Jewel as well as her daughter and their entire family not only here in Savannah, but in Washington D.C. as well.

Jewel was delighted that Elizabeth had complied and done her part to destroy Abby. However she was immediately dismayed when she heard that Jeffrey was not at the ball. She had been so sure that Jeffrey would publicly disclaim his betrothal to Abby upon hearing the truth behind the scandalous birth of his precious fiancée. Then it would have been Abby's disgrace that would have broken the engagement and Jeffrey would have been free to publicly turn his intentions towards Elizabeth without Elizabeth or her family suffering any social demise for having made Abby's disgrace public. Now, that no one had heard from Jeffrey, Jewel was completely unsure of the results of her timing in the scheming of herself and her daughter's attempt to destroy the union of the young couple. She was dying to know if Jeffrey had found out at all by this time.

"Oh! Mama, we all knew exactly what you are trying to do, please, just give it up!" Interjected an irritated Amelia

Whatley, the younger sister of Elizabeth. Amelia liked Abby and had tried very hard to become a close friend to her but since she was a year younger, Abby had not really accepted nor rejected her friendship. Amelia had jumped for joy when she heard of the betrothal between Abby and Jeffrey. She felt the two of them were perfect for each other. Receiving the calm, caring personality of her father she had been spared the jealous nature that was instilled in her mother, Jewell and her older sister, Elizabeth.

Jewel was taken aback and embarrassed by her younger daughter's comments and chastised her immediately.

"Why Amelia Janet Whatley, whatever do you mean? Surely you are not implying that your sister, Elizabeth, or I, your very own mother, had anything to do with Abby's crude behavior at the ball, are you?" Her warning glance at her daughter was ignored by Amelia as she huffed and prepared to respond.

Quickly, before Amelia could open her mouth to reply, Elizabeth spoke a little too loudly in her mother's and in her own defense. "Of course, Mama and I had nothing to do with this! Whatever are you implying Amelia? I think you should just hush your mouth right now!" Quickly she admonished her sister and followed with a threat to warn her sister to hush immediately. "You know you were only just old enough to attend the ball this year. I'm sure Mama or our very dear Mrs. Harrison," she stopped speaking momentarily to politely incline her head toward her hostess, "would not want to exclude you from Savannah's next social gathering. You wouldn't like that, now would you, my dearest sister, Amelia?"

The veiled threat did not go unnoticed by any of the women in the room. Most of them raised their open fans to cover their shocking facial expressions of embarrassment. It was uncomfortable being forced to witnesses this personal family squabble in the Harrison's elaborately decorated and polished parlor.

Elaine jumped up from the Queen Ann chair she was sitting in nearly knocking it over onto Johanna who grabbed the highly polished wooden back quickly to prevent an injury to herself. Speaking up in Abby and Amelia's defense. Pointing her finger directly at Elizabeth's nose, she angrily countered, "Elizabeth whatever you said to Abby to destroy her is totally unforgivable! I for one shall never forgive you!" She declared her public accusation against Elizabeth vehemently.

"Oh be quiet, you ninny, you don't know what you're talking about" Elizabeth rudely replied!

"OH! I most certainly do know what I am talking about, Miss Elizabeth Whatley busybody! And so do you!" Responded Elaine angrily. "You forget, Elizabeth, I was there. You were the person whom Abby accused of being a liar!"

Elizabeth's face turned a bright shade of red. She immediately screamed her retort back at Elaine! "You did not hear what I said to Abby, so how do you know what I was lying about?" Elizabeth looked smug in her own defense. That she had just convicted herself of the horrendous crime escaped her.

"Stop it! I simply can't sit here and allow you to lie in your defense any longer!" Elaine threw her fan at Elizabeth hitting her on her chest." Angry tears were now streaming down her cheeks. She was very angry at Elizabeth. Her stress level was sky high as she blamed Elizabeth for Abby's absence. Up to this point in time, she was one of the few people in town that knew that Abby was currently missing. Most of the ladies in the room including Elizabeth and her mother were not aware of Abby's absence as Elaine had just discovered it herself only a few hours earlier just this morning.

"We all know you and your mother just want to break up Abby's engagement to Jeffrey!" She sobbed out her accusation pointing her finger at both Elizabeth and then swinging around to point it at Jewel also.

The jaw of every elite lady in the room dropped to her chest in amazement at this blatant public accusation. The huge gasp emitted from each of them all at once reverberated around the room. It was later said that the white Irish lace under-curtains on the many massive windows in the room had suddenly flown straight upward as if a large blast of wind had just entered. However, the windows were shut and locked tightly due to the still slightly chilly weather of the early spring season. The room became totally quiet as all the gapping jaws turned in the direction of Jewell and Elizabeth anxiously awaiting their retort to the harsh accusation.

Elizabeth's face turned beet red in anger. While her mother's face became a complete wash of ash white. "Why I never" Jewel began, she grabbed her dainty lace handkerchief and put it to her nose, "I do believe I'm going to faint!" Her voice faded as she allowed herself to slump backwards into the damask rose covered cushions of the settee in a pretended faint.

Mrs. Harrison immediately rang for the serving maid instructing her to bring in the smelling salts. The ladies sitting beside Jewel jumped to their feet and began fussing over her as they fanned their handkerchiefs in front of Jewel's nose. Anxiously they waited for the smelling salts to arrive.

Jeffrey Browning's mother, Elenora Browning, was sitting paralyzed in her chair completely stunned. Her cup of tea fell from her hands and hit the floor shattering the dainty tea cup. The remainder of its contents bounced onto the imported expensive pink and blue rose Persian rug, staining it under her feet. "Surely you don't mean that?" She whispered hoarsely to Elaine. The thought of her family being part of a scandal terrorized her. It had taken her many long years to attain her high position in Savannah Society. With the men of her family all being political in nature, her family certainly couldn't be involved in any type of scandal. Beside herself, she didn't know how to act in front of her cronies. Standing up shakily, she felt her knees collapse beneath her. Rubbing her forehead, she slid to the floor. Everything blackened around her. The two women nearest to her jumped to pick up her slim body but found that her dead weight made the task impossible. They left her on the floor and began fanning her earnestly while other women hurriedly called to each other.

Sarah Bennington volunteered the obvious, "Oh my! Now our dear Elenora has fainted! Dear! Dear! Where are the smelling salts? Harriet where is your girl? Oh dear! Oh dear?" The gossiping buzz reverberated throughout the room. The room was filled with panicking women all chattering at once.

Jeffrey's sister, Bernadette, suddenly burst into laughter! "Surely you can't think my brother would leave Abby for the likes of you?" She pointed her index finger at Elizabeth. She hadn't even realized that her own mother was now lying on the floor in a dead faint! In her state of hysteria, she began laughing uncontrollably. Soon several of the ladies were all laughing. Some uncontrollably and some rather nervously. Later they admitted they never knew what was so funny.

"Are you implying that I am not good enough for your brother?" Elizabeth's violet eyes bulged from her scarlet face. It was definitely taboo to be a party involved in breaking up a marriage or betrothal in polite society. Anyone who did was guaranteed serious consequences including becoming completely blackballed and expelled from the societal activities of the city.

"Neither Elizabeth nor I would ever be a party to a betrothal split!" Jewell heatedly interjected. Jumping off the settee, she perused the facial expressions of the other ladies in attendance only to ascertain whether or not she had succeeded in fending off their disdain of herself and her daughter.

Jewel's sudden recovery from her faint without the aid of smelling salts was not lost on them. They were looking at Jewel with huge round eyes and raised eyebrows. Jewel stuttered as she realized they knew she had faked her fainting spell. Quietly she attempted to regain her dignity by sitting down on the settee. Fanning herself, she pretended to be feeling weak from her pretended faint.

The room remained electrically charged with emotion from the shocked visitors and their hostess. In the years to come each of these polite ladies of society bragged that they had been right there in Harriet Harrison's drawing room when this historic gathering took place! Over the years their story became exaggerated until the truth could no longer be ascertained correctly.

Elaine's mother, soft spoken Sarah, immediately attempted to allay her daughter's dangerous rash accusations by defending her. "Why Elizabeth, and you also Elaine, Please sit down now and behave yourselves!" She attempted to chastise both of the angry females hoping to calm the room. "Of course Elaine, never implied any such thing!" Sweetly she attempted to comfort Elizabeth by removing Elaine's stinging accusation before all mayhem broke out. "And I believe we all know you nor your mother would ever attempt to break the betrothal between our Abby and her dear, dear Jeffrey. Why everyone knows how deeply in love they are with each other. No one would want to, or could for that matter, break their betrothal up. They are so full of love for each other." She nodded her head to affirm her comments to her audience. As her gaze was directed in warning upon Elizabeth and Jewel not to contradict her defense of their actions, they both retreated, sitting quietly, smoothing their satin dresses around them.

"Why Sarah, my Elizabeth and I absolutely congratulate our Abby and Jeffrey on their impending marriage, do we not, Elizabeth?" Jewel blatantly lied. Her eyes beseeched her daughter to hold her tongue before she managed to have them blackballed completely from the group.

Elizabeth's face was still red, but had cooled to a slightly lighter shade. "Why certainly not, mother dearest, you know that I would most certainly give my blessings to Abby and Jeffrey. She began to comply with her mother's unspoken request but she could not resist adding, "However, where is our dear Abby? Rumor has it she has left the city with no explanation?" She looked pointedly at Elaine. Everyone gasped openly at this juicy tidbit. It was so obvious that Elizabeth felt animosity regarding Abby's betrothal to Jeffrey.

Jewel threw her hands in the air and huffed. "Elizabeth! Why can't you take the hint and shut up?" She unthinkingly ordered her daughter loudly. In her exasperation with Elizabeth, Jewel failed to pick up on the bad vibe in the room that was again being directed upon herself, as well as her daughter.

Caught off guard, Elaine spoke immediately in Abby's defense, "It's all your fault that Abby is not in town, Elizabeth, none of us knows where she has gone!" Surprised by her own outburst she quickly covered her own mouth with her hand as she realized that she had just publicly disclosed Abby's secret disappearance. Moving her hands from her mouth to her head she fell back into her seat and began crying in earnest. The stress of her missing friend was more than she could bear. Too late to recall her mistake she gave in and admitted her intense fears for Abby. "Oh I do so worry for her!" Suddenly glaring at Elizabeth she accused her yet again. "Elizabeth Whatley, You had better not be the cause of any harm to her, or I'll see to it that you pay for your part in all this mess!" She severely and openly threatened Elizabeth! Gasping again, everyone in the room pivoted their heads forgetting about Elenora who was still lying in a dead faint and looked from Elaine to Elizabeth and her mother and back and forth again and again. The room was in total chaos filled with murmuring voices!

At Elaine's open threat, Mrs. Harrison quickly intervened, stopping Elaine from continuing any other threats and possibly incriminating herself. Quickly rising from her seat, she spoke over Elaine. "Oh my dear, Ladies, can you believe it, our hour is up! My goodness it went so quickly today. How fast an hour can slip by when we are all having so much fun!

She began gathering her friend's still filled teacups and saucers from their unsuspecting hands as she continued. "I have so much to do! I simply must prepare myself for this evening's special dinner. We are entertaining the Governor of Georgia, don't you know?" She just stepped over the still body of Elanora laying on the floor in her attempts to grab the tea cups and urge her guests to leave. "I am so very grateful to ya'll for keeping me company today. However, I'm afraid I simply must bring thus ummm…, shall we say delightful visit to a close."

She nearly fainted herself from her fast moving efforts and continued non-stop with, "Oh thank heavens' at last my maid has finally arrived with the smelling salts and our dear Elenora is now awake and feeling better! You are? Aren't you Elenora?" she rudely asked the weakened woman who was now sitting in a chair again. Harriet never stopped in her quest to throw her friends personal belongings to them as she herded them out of her parlor and in the direction of her front door.

Quickly Mrs. Harrison continued before Elenora could answer with any words but only a slight nod in agreement. "My maid shall see all of you out now. I apologize but I simply must ask you to leave quickly please, and if you don't mind we shall all reconvene next week." Expertly she corralled the last of the women towards the door of her parlor stuffing their belongings into their bewildered and shaking hands. The dismissed ladies comments of gratitude to their hostess for her entertainment went unheard as they noisily dispersed.

"Do have a good afternoon, ladies," Harriet called to the retreating women as she quickly shut the door behind the last of them to leave. Turning to her confidant and best friend, Johanna, she grinned from ear to ear. "Johanna dear, wasn't this a delightful session?" She burst into giggles!

Johanna winked at her friend, concurred with her and burst into laughter also, "Just Dandy Harriet! Just Dandy! This visit is one for the record books!" she remarked proudly as she retrieved her own cloak and left Harriet to congratulate herself.

Harriet smiled and laughed with delight clasping her hands together as she practically danced her way up the stairs to her boudoir.

Outside on the landing Elaine deliberately bumped Elizabeth. She whispered, "You better watch your back, Elizabeth, you most certainly have created enemies in corners you might not be prepared for," she warned the angry girl.

"Elizabeth shook her raven hair and whispered back. "I will get what I want Elaine! You mark my words no-one will stand in my way! Not you! Not Abigail Anderson! Nor anyone else!" She sneered. Tossing her curls she donned her bonnet and pushed Elaine out of her way as she haughtily descended the steps of the Harrison mansion.

Elaine gazed after her adversary. Her eyes became cold as steel, as she whispered loudly, "Not if I have anything to do with it" she vowed!

Chapter Seven

Ralph Green and his fellow cohorts made good time as they rode away from the train. Abby's ankles and wrists were bound with rawhide. Barely breathing, her body was slung over the saddle in front of Jim Owens. He was a raunchy dirty looking man. Long black straggly hair hung from under his tattered felt cowboy hat sporting a bullet hole in the front of it. His clothing was filthy. His body stench was filling Abby's nostrils. The horrible smell and the beating she was taking from the bumping of the horse awakened her from her unconscious state.

She remained silent keeping her eyes closed. Confused, she realized that she was tied and being held hostage. Noting her momentary attempt to rise, Jim pushed her back down and placed his huge smelly leg on top of her backside. Realizing she was trapped under the man's filthy smelly leg she panicked. Her memory failed her in her attempt to understand how she had gotten in this predicament. The jolting of the galloping horse and her head hanging in a downward position was extremely painful. She was unable to rationalize her thoughts.

Terrified, she had no idea what to do next. Her breathing was becoming more and more difficult. Panicking again, she began to writhe and wriggle in front of Jim nearly causing them both to slide around on the back of the horse. Attempting to scream, Abby began choking and gagging from the filthy rag still stuffed in her mouth. Jim grabbed her by the hair to pull her into a sitting position. He reined his horse in and stopped, calling out to Ralph. "Hold up will you, she's come to. I need to sit her up before she falls off. She's going to throw up and choke to death if I don't remove this gag from her."

Ralph and others reigned in and stopped. "Better hurry it up!" Ralph ordered him. "We don't need a posse of men catching up to us before we make it to the caves." He threw out the unnecessary warning to Jim.

"Don't ya think I know that a ready," Jim answered smirking as he struggled to still the writhing girl. "Would you mind giving me a hand over here? She's a little filly but all this squirming and kicking me is making it hard for me to git her into a sittin spot? Stop it, you little witch!" He slapped her across the face as she managed to punch him in the groin with her knee.

"Hold still! We will shoot ya right here and now if ya give us any more trouble!" Ralph warned her. He walked his horse over to the girl and grabbed a handful of her thick red hair and jerked her head upright. He ripped the bandana off her eyes. She rewarded him with a hateful stare.

Ralph just smirked and grabbed her other arm and practically threw her upright into a sitting position in front of Jim who grabbed her tightly around the waist to hold her still. Ralph pulled her hair and shook her hard in warning. Touching the tip of his six-shooter on her nose, he warned her not to scream. "Keep quiet! You hear me missy, I'd just as soon shoot ya, as look at ya? If you wanna live, stay still and give us no trouble. Ya hear me?" He questioned her harshly to be certain she took him seriously.

Abby willed herself to calm down. She quit squirming and sat still except for violently shaking her head and making illegible noises.

Ricky realized what she wanted and said "Hey boss, I think she wants you to take that gag off-n-er so she can breathe."

Larry chimed in with, "Go ahead and take it off her boss, she can scream all she wants. Ain't no one gonna hear her way out here."

Ralph realized Larry was right, they had made good time and were in isolated territory now and no one was near them. He ordered Jim to remove the gag. To Abby he said, "Little lady one sound out of you and I'll have Ricky eliminate you right here and now and leave your body for buzzard pickins! Ya un-erstand what I'm tellin ya?" He poked her in the chest with his gun.

She nodded and gulped for fresh air. Catching her breath, she looked straight at Ralph, staring coldly at him she said, "Yes, I understand! I'll be quiet," she rasped, her voice and throat were dry and irritated from the gag, "You needn't worry about that." She quieted down and then asked for a sip of water to ease her aching burning throat but her request was not granted. To herself she vowed, "But I'll see all of you dead and buried if I get out of this alive."

"Let's get ta movin then!" Ralph nodded at the others. The outlaws grabbed their reins and holstered their guns. Looking around for any trouble and seeing nothing in the distance, Ralph suddenly took off at a gallop. The others followed. Abby tried to sit stiff and straight as a bone. It was very difficult with the bouncing horse, but she was determined to make Jim as uncomfortable as she possibly could.

The train wreck site was filled with confusion and chaos. Further examination had shown that the train had hit a log that had been placed strategically in the way of the train wheels and the track had been dislodged from the normal position which caused the train to run off the tracks and crash into the log. The wreck was causing serious delays to their schedule for arriving in Louisville on time. The conductor and engineer were trying to get the engine back onto the tracks. They had sent back to the town of Bowling Green for the Sheriff and some wagon teams to help right the train and repair the tracks. It was important that they get to Louisville as quickly as possible in order to keep their scheduled route from suffering additional delays down line.

The sheriff arrived within three hours and began his investigation immediately. The dead man and his family were loaded onto a wagon and taken back to Bowling Green. The Sheriff assured the woman he had arranged for them to have a place to stay and burial arrangements for her husband. He also assured her that he was doing all in his power to find her husband's killers. The Mother was in a severe state of shock and simply allowed the deputies to lead her. She barely understood the Sheriffs instructions to her and the children didn't really understand what was happening to them. The passengers on the train who had gotten to know the family a little were devastated in their inability to help them.

The passenger who helped Joseph told the sheriff about the woman who had been kidnapped. He explained to the Sheriff that the robbers had ridden off with her as a hostage. He also indicated to the Sheriff that Joseph knew the woman better than anyone else on the train.

Joseph was sitting impatiently as the Sheriff questioned him about Abby. His injury to his head was being stitched by the town's physician at the same time. "I told you Sheriff, for the umpteenth time, I don't know anything about her except that she gave me her name as Lydia Creosota. I was just kind of trying to keep an eye on her cause she seemed to be scared and all alone. Sides she was kinda purdy, if ya know what I mean." He was deliberately trying to show no interest in Abby other than that of a man looking for a good time.

The Sheriff suggested he join with the Posse to find her but he knew he intended on finding her on his own. Keeping his inclinations to himself, he declined the Sheriff's invite and once again he feigned a lack of interest in her other than for her female charms and her shapely young body.

"Well, the other passengers are telling me that the two of you were tight as a wad together!" The Sheriff replied. He was attempting to shake Joseph into admitting he was interested in the girl. He didn't believe Joseph's story of disinterest.

"That's only cuz I was a tryin to git her attention. Like I said, she was kinda purty and all. Figured she'd give in in a little while and we could have, well ya know, have some fun or something." He deliberately lied to the Sheriff in the hopes that he would be left alone so he could go after her. Realizing he was defaming her character he quickly added, "Sides, she looked like she needed someone to, ya know, protect her somewhat. Guess I didn't do a very good job of it though," he mumbled rubbing his sore head and gingerly touching his new bandage. "Are you through with all of these dog-gone questions?" He impatiently asked the Sheriff. "I sure don't want to miss my train to St. Louis," he continued to lie.

"Well, I reckon I had you figured all wrong." The Sheriff gave him a tricky look attempting to size him up hoping for one more attempt to get him to go with the posse he continued with, "I hoped you would want to go along with me and a posse to go after her. We could use your help in identifying her."

"Well, heck no!" Joseph quickly replied. "All I want to do is get back on the train and get on my way to St. Louis, I got a wagon train to catch," he lied again. What he really wanted was to get as far away from the Sheriff as quickly as he could. He planned on buying a horse and high tailing it out of there as fast as possible to find Lydia on his own. He didn't want to be a part of any controlled slow posse. He knew that if Lydia had been harmed in any way he would probably kill the bastard that did it and the last thing he needed was a lawman around to throw him in jail for murder.

"Wow, you are some protector," the Sheriff insulted Joseph. "Guess you ain't made of the right man stuff after all!" He taunted Joseph threatening his male ego. He hoped that would bring Joseph around, but Joseph's half grin and negative shake of the head told him he was just wasting valuable time. "Be on your way then. We don't need jerks like you in this town anyway." The Sheriff summarily dismissed Joseph by doffing his hat in Joseph's direction. Giving him a disgusted look, the Sheriff turned his back and began talking to the others about the wreck and robbery.

Smoldering inside at the insults to his man pride, Joseph picked up his prized Stetson, six gun and holster and climbed back on board the train. Once inside he took a seat. Looking out the window he caught the Sheriff's attention. Giving him a big grin and a wave, Joseph leaned back in the seat, stretched his arms over his head and lowered his Stetson over his eyes, indicating that it was his desire to take a nap while he waited for the train to resume its journey.

The sheriff glared at him and shook his head. Then he turned his back on Joseph. He walked away to prepare his posse.

Immediately Joseph jumped up from his seat and grabbed Abby's reticule and traveling bag as well as his own personal effects. Jamming his Stetson hat on his head he covered his blond hair and his bandage. Then once he ascertained that he was not noticed he slipped out the back door of the passenger car. By walking on the opposite side of the train and mixing into a small crowd of passengers that were walking back to the town of Bowling Green he was able to make it to the livery stable without the sheriff or anyone else taking notice of him.

Arriving at the livery stable, he bought two horses. His was a beautiful black stallion. For Lydia, he purchased a chestnut mare with a white mane and tail. The mare appeared gentle enough, but still young enough to gallop at a fast pace if it became necessary in his attempt to free Lydia. He also purchased two saddles. He paid the livery man and handed him an extra twenty dollar gold piece.

"What's this for?" The livery hand asked.

Joseph winked and replied "For keeping quiet about this purchase" You never saw me and I was never here, right?" Joseph questioned the man.

"Yep, ya got it! Heck, you ain't even here right now Mister!" the livery hand winked at him as he pocketed the extra money.

Joseph nodded at him and reached for the gear to saddle the horses he'd just purchased. "Make certain you remember that, because I would certainly hate to return here some night and have to make you pay for having had a loose mouth," he quietly threatened the livery hand.

"Yes sir, I hear ya! Don't worry, you're not the first nor the last, I figure, who paid me to keep my tongue quiet. Your secret is safe with me." The livery man hastily assured him. It was none of his business anyway he reasoned.

Joseph nodded his head satisfied that he could trust the man to keep quiet. He saddled up and headed to the general store where he bought some food and a few camping supplies. Pulling his Stetson low to cover his face he rode, slowly to the edge of town away from the train wreck.

Surreptitiously, he looked in all directions to be certain no one paid him any attention. Once he cleared the view of the townsfolk, he kicked his horse in the side and holding on to the reins of the mare he took off at a gallop in the direction of the caves. He had a lot of lost time to make up for. About six hours he reasoned.

Chapter Eight

Abby awoke to complete darkness. Straining her eyes to see, only complete blackness returned. Her tongue was stuck to the roof of her mouth. She was parched and hungry and couldn't remember the last time she had eaten. Straining to hear, she attempted to discern her surroundings. But all she could hear was a deafening silence. She tried to remember where she was and how she got here.

She remembered waking up in a face down position on a foul smelling man's horse. There were six men and she didn't remember how she had become among them. She recalled that they had allowed her to sit up and took a gag out of her mouth then they had galloped away as fast as they could. Since she had been gagged, she wasn't sure if she was one with them or who she was. She couldn't remember anything except for the foul smell of the man whose saddle she was lying across in front of his lap. She figured she had passed out again at some point during the ride. She recalled that they had ridden well into the night. She could not remember when they had arrived. She had no idea where she was or how she had gotten here.

She tried to focus in the darkness. There was a tiny line of light way above her. From the cold hard rocky ground beneath her she decided she might be in some sort of cave. It was too dark to be near any outdoor night light from the moon. Finally her eyes began to focus somewhat. She began to discern the dark shadows of rocks and other items around her. Running her hands beneath her, she felt the rough wool of a horse blanket. She discerned that she was lying on it and that it seemed to have some softness and give to it. Feeling under the blanket she felt straw. Someone had made her a pallet to sleep on.

It was damp and chilly. She was extremely cold and began to shiver. Reaching behind her, her hand came in contact with a damp rock wall. The ground was filled with loose sand and gravel. Feeling in front of her she couldn't tell what else was there. Once again a huge empty blackness met her eyes. Again, she strained her eyes in the darkness to see. It didn't help any. The light from above was not enough to illuminate more than a few feet around her. She tried to get up only to find that her ankles were still tied together and she was tethered to something preventing her from moving very far. Her head was pounding. Listening intently, she could hear the drum of low voices but their words were not legible. To her dismay, she accepted that she was still in the possession of the six men whom she could not recall having ever seen before she awoke face down in one of their laps as she rode double with him on his horse.

Straining, she was able to smell the odor of strong coffee and roasting meat. Her stomach began to cramp as the smells reminded her body of its need for food. She sat up holding her stomach to ease the cramps. Slowly she rocked backed and forth looking for relief. Her bladder was full. But at this moment that was the least of her worries.

She finally accepted that her first surmise was correct. She was definitely in a cave an abandoned mine, or something similar. "No one will ever find me in here," she surmised. She almost began to cry but then decided to take her chances and call for someone to come to her aid instead.

"HELP! She tried to yell but was surprised to hear her voice cracked and she barely could emit a dry hoarse whisper. Her throat was so dry. Trying desperately to summon enough saliva to wet her mouth, Abby tried again. "Hey! Hello! Anyone out there?" This time her voice was a little stronger and a little louder. She hoped someone had heard her because all of the low voices suddenly ceased.

A few seconds later, she heard footsteps. The shadow of a man carrying a barely lit candle formed in front of her. She was momentarily blinded by the sudden appearance of the dim light after the complete darkness.

"Well, wha'd ya want?" Ricky coldly asked her.

"I'm hungry and thirsty and I'm so cold." Her voice trembled as she boldly told him her needs.

"So, do ya think I care?" Ricky smarted back at her.

"Get her some grub, Rick, and try to remember we have a lady in our presence." Ralph's voice rang out from the darkness to her right. His unknown presence startled her. She recognized the voice as the man who threatened her life if she made any noise. He must be their leader she figured. What she did know of him was that he was one mean man. She jumped and tried to locate him in the darkness.

"Aw alright. Don't know why ya want to keep her alive. Nobody is gonna answer yur telegraph anyway. As for her being a lady, well, ladies are only good for one thing in my book and I just might try her out a little later." Rick replied to Ralph.

"Touch one hair on her head before I let ya and yur dead meat! Got it!" Ralph cuffed Rick on the head and kicked him in the shins. Rubbing his legs below the knee, Rick glared at him.

"Ow! Stop it!" he yelled, "Well, what else is a female good for?" He threw back at Ralph.

Ralph started in his direction with his fists in a ball and his arms ready to swing at Rick. Rick ducked. "Aw, I ain't about to touch that filly, she's too damned skinny for me anyway. I was only funning with ya, Boss." Rick protected both his cocky reputation and himself so Ralph withdrew.

"Like I tole ya, git her some feed. But keep yur damned hands to yurself if n ye ever want to shoot that gun of yur'n again!" Ralph warned him. Rick glared after Ralph's back but he knew better than to disobey his leader. He went to dish out some food for Abby.

She looked at Ralph who had struck a match and lit a small oil lantern. Finally she was able to see a little of her surroundings. She couldn't discern much. There just seemed to be a whole lot of rock everywhere.

"What did he mean by telegraph?" She asked.

"I know who ya are." Ralph replied. "Saw yur picture on the wanted poster. Said ya was missing. Someone put up a big reward for ya." He answered her.

"You're crazy. She said, "I don't know what you are talking about. I'm not missing and I'm not worth any reward. You're just wasting your time."

"Yea, ya know who ya are. Yur that Anderson woman, missing from Savannah, Georgia. The paper said ya've been missing for a couple of weeks now. The description matches your looks to a "T," so don't try to fool me. Me n the boy's is gonna collect on that reward and then some maybe," he hinted that they were interested more in a huge ransom amount instead of the generous but smaller reward that he had read on the missing poster.

Abby appeared to be confused. She did not reply. Finally she said the smartest thing she could think of. "Well, if you want a reward, you better see to it that I am not harmed any further." She rubbed her head where they had hit her with the gun butt. She had a huge bump on her head. Her body was bruised and sore. Her face hurt too. She had a huge bruise on her left cheek and her lips had dried blood on them. They were scabbed and were peeling from the dust and the dryness.

"Is that so? Well ya just see to it that ya do as yur told, and maybe, just maybe, yu'll not get hurt," he caustically replied.

Rick brought her a plateful of half cooked beans and some roasted rabbit meat along with a hot cup of coffee and a hard cold biscuit.

"Leave her hands untied so she can eat, Rick. She won't go anywhere. The only way out is to pass by us. You can retie her when she's finished filling her belly." Ralph instructed his cohort. To Abby he said, "Call when ya finish. We'll see to it that ya can relieve yurself and then we will tie ya back up for the night. If you're half as smart as I think ya are, ya will eat every bit of that, cuz ya aint gettin no more till tomorrow night."

Ralph and Ricky turned and walked away taking the lantern with them. Left in the dark she managed to move into a sitting position. For a few moments she just sat and tried to figure out what to do. She didn't even know if she was in a cave and old mine, a tunnel or what. Even though it was dark, she was glad she was alone. She didn't feel as threatened as she did when she was in the company of the outlaws. She rubbed her untied wrists together to get the blood moving in them again. They felt like pincushions. Her wrists were sore. She rubbed dried blood from them caused by the ropes that had burned her skin and cut through it.

Feeling in front of her she reached for the hot coffee and plate of food. She was ravenous so she ate hurriedly. The beans were hot, causing her to cry out when she put them in her sore mouth. But she didn't spit them out. She remembered what Ralph had said about getting nothing else to eat until tomorrow night. She also wanted to be certain she ate everything she had been given because if she grew lucky enough to find a way out of here, then who knew when she might have a decent bite to eat again.

"I wonder what he meant when he said I was that woman named, Ander... Andres.., what was it he said? I've never heard that name before." She considered what the outlaw had said. "I don't even know who that is," she mused to herself, I'm, I'm…. she dropped her fork in surprise. Suddenly she realized she didn't know who she was. She couldn't remember her name, her age or where she had come from. Abby sat there in bewildered shock. Staring at her half empty plate. She couldn't think. Unable to eat any more or even to move, she stared blankly into the darkness. She began to wish she had paid more attention to the name that outlaw had mentioned.

She strained her brain trying to remember who she was. Rubbing her head didn't help. The top of her head was so sore from where the gun had struck her. She recalled the splitting pain she had felt in her head as they were riding. The pain had been so intense that she had panicked and started kicking. "I don't know how I got here," she mused unable to ascertain how she came to be in the outlaws company. That's when she realized that she could be suffering from amnesia. Her heart sank to the pit of her stomach. She realized that even if she was lucky enough to get out of this mess, she didn't know where she belonged or to whom.

Maybe she was this Ands, Andres, woman or whatever he had called her. If so she might have a chance of returning to her life, but what if she wasn't the person on the reward poster? What if the person who printed the poster and offered the reward decided not to pay for her or couldn't afford to pay the ransom they demanded for her? What if whomever it was simply laughed in the outlaws face and told the outlaws to take her away with them. How could she live with these men? It would be horrifying. Even worse, what if the outlaws didn't want her with them? Where would she go? What would she do? Dear God, what if they decided to just shoot her? Suddenly she collapsed in tears and began sobbing uncontrollably. "My God, help me!" She secretly cried unto the heavens. About an hour later, the outlaw named Larry Sheldon came to take her plate from her, she was just sitting there staring into the dark, her mind a blank.

"Is ye finished eaten yet, Miss?" Larry politely asked her as he raised his lantern to see her. He was an outlaw, but he was older than the others. She was surprised to see that he had asked her respectfully if she was finished eating and he had addressed her as Miss. He seemed quieter and less demanding than the others she had dealt with. I've come to take yer plate and walk ye outside for a few minutes so ye can take care of yur business he continued to speak. I've brought a lantern so's ye can see where ye is going."

He placed the lantern down out of her reach and took the plate from her hands. She just stared at him with a puzzled look in her eye. He untied her ankles and she tried to stand. Larry grabbed her as her weak legs buckled beneath her. "Easy there, Miss," Larry said. "Yev'e got to get some blood back in them there legs of yurn. Ye'll be a right in a minute or so and then we'll go.

She hung on to him tightly. Unknown to Larry, her amnesia made her weak in the knees more than her bindings had done. She decided not to tell the outlaws about her amnesia. She figured the only thing that might save her was if they thought they knew who she was. Slowly she straightened and said, "Thank you, I think I'm alright now. You can let go if you'd like. I'm not going to go anywhere. I don't know where I'm at or how to get back to where I was. Apparently I am at your mercy." She told him. He seemed hesitant to let go of her, so she said, "Just help me to the outdoors. I do need to take care of my business." Despite the darkness and her situation she felt her cheeks blush at the personalization of the statement regarding her own physical needs. Holding her hand with his left hand, he put his right arm around her back to support her. They began moving down the path to the cave entrance. She looked him over and was surprised to note that he seemed to be clean-shaven. He had bathed, and was wearing clean clothes. "Maybe, I can trust this one," she made a mental note.

Abby took stock of her surroundings as they walked. With the light from the lantern she was able to discern that she was in a very massive cave. They stayed to the right side of the path and followed the wall of rock. There was a four foot wide walkway along the rock wall and beyond the four feet there was a huge cavernous drop off. Abby realized that she would have fallen to her death if she had tried to make an escape on her own. They walked along the walkway for about fifty feet. There she saw the campsite of the men. They had blanket rolls lying around the center of a fire pit. There was a coffee pot, a pan and some scattered dirty tin plates. The fire was lit, but had died down to just a few flames with red coals but the half empty pot of beans still hung on the tripod over the dying embers. None of the outlaws were there. She wandered where they had gone, but lacking trust in all of them she kept quiet and didn't ask Larry fearing he might lie to her.

On they went for another forty or so feet. She began to feel a breeze of slightly warmer but fresher air from outside the cave. Bending down, they went through a tunnel about three feet long. Then suddenly they were in the great outdoors. The night was beautiful but cool. There was a gentle wind blowing. Clouds moved steadily across the path of a full moon that provided light for her to see. Even though it was in April, with all the dramatic things that were happening to her it seemed as scary as all hallows night pending a brewing storm.

Larry led her to some bushes on the darker side of the cave. There he tied one end of a long strand of raw-hide to both of her wrists and the other end loosely to the trunk of a cedar tree. Then, he spoke, "Miss, ye jest go behind these ere trees and do yer business. When yer through ye jest call out to me and I'll come for ye.

Abby tried to tell him that she needed at least one hand loose so she could maneuver her needs, but he declined her request as he felt that she would be able to untie herself if he gave her a free hand. Upset, she nodded her head in dismayed acceptance. Wondering how she was to manage, she stepped gingerly into the woods behind the tree.

"One more thing, Miss," Larry called out to her, "doa'n ya be a thinking of untying that there rope, cause this woods is full of rattle snakes and mountain lions not to mention there's these here holes in the ground around here that ye could step into only to find them to be bottomless pits to the caves not to mention the pits of quicksand. If you want to live, I suggest ye follow my instructions to ye," he warned her.

His warning comments gave him comfort that he had nothing to worry about in so far as she might try to escape therefore, he took his time and lounged on a leaning tree and enjoyed a few minutes to himself. He was really exhausted from the day's events. The stress of planning and succeeding with the kidnapping was now quickly taking a toll on him. He began to feel jetlag and his attention to details began to lessen greatly.

He listened for Abby's answer, "Don't worry" she assured him as he heard the snapping of twigs from her footsteps as she gingerly searched for a small clear area in the brush to take care of her physical needs. "I told you I have no intention of leaving." She took his warning seriously. Nervously, she looked around her for the hidden dangers he mentioned.

Once she found a spot that looked safe and private to her she began to take care of business. She called out from the bushes. Curiosity and the fear of the danger in the woods got the better of her in the dark night, she called out to Larry to make certain that he was still there. "Where are the others at?"

Larry replied to her, "They be a takin care of the horses and the chores. Don't worry none bout them. They're just round the corner. I'd appreciate it if ye would hurry on up there, I want to get ye back inside afore they finish up. I got to tell ye, Miss, some of them ain't like me. They be rough characters. Not meaning to scare ye or nuttin, but some of them would like to do harm to ye, if ye know what I mean Miss. It would really be best if ye just hurried your business up and let me get ye back inside as quickly as I can. That's why Ralph put ye in the back behind the rest of us. He said it was safer for ye there all by yeself."

Hoping to comfort her after putting a scare into her, he kept on rambling. "It sure is a purdy night out here. Kind of cold though. Them there stars in the sky are so bright! And them clouds are blowing past the moon really fast and all. Kinda has the feel of rain coming. Yes, Miss, it sure does feel like it might rain. I hope Ralph gets this business over with before it does. Sometimes Miss, when it rains, these caves can take to flooding real bad." He continued his nonsense chatter for a while and he failed to realize just how much time had passed.

Finally he ran out of things to say. So he just sat on a big rock and began to be engrossed in his own thoughts until he dozed off. Suddenly he awoke and realized he had no idea how long he had been sitting there. Worried, he shook his head to wake himself up fully. She should have been done by now.

"Ye finished yet, Miss? He called in the direction of the woods but not too loudly as he didn't want his boss to hear him. Ralph was a mean man and very difficult to work with. He didn't want any problems from him. The last thing he needed was something to go wrong. Listening carefully, he failed to hear any answer from her. He walked closer to the path she had taken and tried again a wee bit louder, "Miss, I asked ye if'n ye were finished yet?" Again he strained his ears but he did not receive an answer from his charge. The hairs on the back of his neck rose involuntarily. Panic overtook him, "Now Miss, I need ye ta answer me. Can you hear me?" He commanded her to answer him a third time.

Walking to the tree where he had tied the rawhide rope he bent over to pick it up. Calling to Abby again he pulled on the rope. Relief momentarily flooded him when he felt the tension on the other end of the rope. "Miss, I don't want to come back there and catch ye in a compromising position, but if'n ye doan answer me…? Holy Moley!" He exclaimed as he stood there in disbelief looking at the cut end of the rawhide that he had jerked a second time a little harder. The harder pull had dislodged it and it had come flying back at him swinging at his face. His heart sank and he knew he was in deep trouble. "Where are ye, Miss? Where did ye go? Ye alright, Miss?" He asked while he went into the woods hoping against hope that he would find her.

Larry spent a good half-hour searching for her. He knew he wasn't just in trouble he was in serious trouble now! "Good God," he said, "she's escaped. God I know I haven't been a good Christian man but if I ever needed ya this would be it cuz Ralph is going to shoot me now!" How well he knew that it would take prayers and help from heaven to get him out of this mess.

Scared to tell Ralph, he sat for an additional thirty minutes, stalling for time. Finally he decided, "Well, tain't nothing I can do but go and tell him I reckon." With that Larry picked up the remainder of the rawhide rope and went in search of Ralph and the other outlaws.

Chapter Nine

Abby proceeded to raise the now filthy purple skirt of her traveling suit to begin doing her private business. Feeling intimidated by the vast shadows of the trees against the bright patches of moonlight that came and went according to the fast flow of the coming storm clouds, and the sudden hoot of an owl, she decided maybe some conversation would help to calm her nerves. "Where are the other men at?" she barely got the question out before the Owl hooted again and she heard crackles of twigs in the woods near her. She flushed in fear all over again, but she listened intently for Larry's answer as well as to her surroundings. Awaiting his answer, a hand suddenly covered her mouth. Simultaneously, an arm grabbed her tightly around the chest for the second time in less than twenty-four hours. She wanted to scream both in fear and pain, but couldn't because her mouth was so tightly covered. Without warning, she found herself staring into a tall blond stranger's deep blue eyes that were imploring her to be silent and still. He had quickly pivoted her around to face him and removed his hand from her lips. She didn't know who he was but she hadn't seen him among the men who still held her captive. She almost screamed again. But Joseph began to whisper softly to her.

It's Okay", Lydia, it's just me, Joseph. I've come to rescue you. Be quiet now. Don't make any noise while I cut this rope you're tied to.

Abby stopped her struggling. She was stunned. She didn't recognize this man but apparently he knew her. He had called her Lydia and said he had come to rescue her. She decided if he knew her as Lydia, then she couldn't be this Abigail person that Ralph was expecting to receive a handsome reward for when he returned her to her supposed loved ones. That left her with the option of remaining with her kidnappers or worse. What if the people who posted the reward said she wasn't the girl they were searching for? One thing was for certain. She did not want to remain with the outlaws! Having no idea what to do or where to go if she was left on her own she quickly decided to see what this man had in mind. After all, he seemed to know who she really was. He had called her by the name of Lydia and didn't seem to suspect her to be anyone else. And she hadn't seen him among the group of men who were holding her hostage so hopefully he wasn't meaning to do her any harm.

Joseph released his hold on her as soon as he felt her quiet down. "Be real quiet," he whispered. They could hear Larry Sheldon talking to her in the near distance. Joseph continued whispering, "I'm going to cut this rawhide, and then we need to get out of here superfast and quiet. We have only got a five minute or so margin to work with. So when I cut the rope follow me quickly!"

Abby nodded. She didn't let one sound escape from her. She just stared at the handsome stranger before her. Surely her life couldn't have been that bad, if this handsome guy who seemed clean, and treated her respectfully, had come to her rescue. She decided to do whatever he instructed of her. Even though she didn't remember him, she decided that he seemed the best choice of her two options at present. Just in case though, she determined it to be wisest not to tell him that she feared she suffered with amnesia. "Nope, that was best left a secret at this time!" she privately resolved.

Joseph made one swipe of his knife and cut the rawhide quickly freeing her from bondage. He looped the long end around a bush, He was hurrying and didn't take time to secure it tightly. He figured it would only buy them a few moments anyway if Lydia wasn't there to reply to the man who was calling to her from the edge of the bushes. Grabbing Lydia by the hand, he led her quietly through some more unruly brush and shrubbery to the top of a low hill. At the bottom of the hill's other side she saw two horses waiting for them.

They started running down the hill, but it still took a couple of minutes to reach the horses. The urgency for them to get away quickly kept Joseph nervously pushing Abby to limits she struggled to succeed at. He had no idea of the soreness in her body, or the current state of her mind. He signaled for Abby to mount the gray while he proceeded to untie them. She stood in front of the gray but simply stared at the mare. She looked confused.

Joseph quickly mounted his stallion and turned to signal her to follow him quickly. He was stunned to see Lydia just standing there staring at the saddle of her horse. "Oh my heavens!" he thought to himself, "She can't ride a horse!" He never for a second considered that she might not know how to ride a horse. "Well, this changes things!" he noted to himself as he quickly dismounted and fairly ran to her side. Scaring her again as there was not a second for him to explain, he simply grabbed her around the waist and hoisted her off the ground and placed her in the saddle. The pain in her back and side almost made her faint. She struggled to breathe when he released her and barely heard him instruct her to place her feet into the stirrups and hold tightly to the saddle horn. "Don't let go and don't fall off!" he whispered as loudly as he dared to her. Quickly he grabbed hold of the reins of her mare and then jumped into the saddle of his own stallion. As fast as he dared he began to walk the horses quietly away.

"Now what am I going to do?" he was worrying as he quickly tried to make changes to his get a way plan. He reasoned, "If she can't ride, then I'd better find a good place to hide with her, because we can't make enough good time to beat the kidnappers back to the safety of town. He searched in his mind and with his eyes for a good hideout that wouldn't be too obvious for the kidnappers or the posse to locate. He didn't want the posse to mistake him for one of the kidnappers and shoot him before he could prove who he was and that he wasn't kidnapping but rather that he was rescuing her from the kidnappers.

Searching his mind avidly for a solution, he decided the best thing to do was first to head in the direction of town and then to circle back and hide behind the cave entrance on the opposite side of the trail back to town. He hoped the kidnappers would think that Lydia had escaped and would naturally attempt to make it back to the safety of the nearest town. With a little luck they wouldn't realize that she had been rescued and therefore maybe the horse's tracks would be ignored. But he decided not to take any chances.

He continued to ride in the direction of town for approximately two additional miles. As he intended to mislead the outlaws, Abby was startled when he suddenly stopped the horses without giving her any warning. Immediately she panicked and felt fear that the outlaws would catch up to them.

"Why are we stopping?" she whispered, but Joseph simply put his finger over his lips indicating for her to be quiet. Then he dismounted and opened his knap sack. He selected two shirts and two bandanas. Tearing them into eight pieces, he raised the hooves on both horses and tied the rag around and under the bottom of each hoof on each horse. Then he took the reins of both horses and walked them off the trail until he reached a rocky area. Turning the horses, he headed back in the direction they had just come. He continued to walk the horses down the rocky ground away from the trail but back toward the caves.

Abby's heart pounded in fear! "Surely he wasn't taking her back to the outlaws?" she feared, but decided to stay quiet and look for any outlet she could in case she had to try to escape all of them including the handsome stranger whom she thought was trying to help her. Praying silently that God would not let her down, she kept silent and held on tightly. First immense fear filled her as she recognized the area they had just left and realized they were almost next to the cave she'd been a prisoner in. Then relief flooded her as they continued on past the caves and kept riding throughout the night. Circling as wide as he dared, Joseph led them past the area where he had rescued Abby.

Abby still said nothing. She was traumatized from the terror she had experienced. She stared ahead with her eyes wide open seeing nothing in particular. Concern overloaded her sense of security when Joseph had stopped, bound the hooves of the horses and then turned around again. She began to feel overly fearful. "After all," she reasoned to herself, "she really didn't know who this man was and maybe his intent was not to rescue her at all but rather to claim the same ransom that the kidnappers were after." Considering this she came to the conclusion that since she had no clue where she was or who she was, she just kept quiet and decided to trust him to get her to safety. She did, however make a mental note of the placement of his rifle stuck in his saddle just in case she might find herself in need of it. She had never shot a gun. She prayed she would do it right and shoot straight if she had to use it.

"Please GOD," *HELP ME*!" She fervently prayed over and over again silently within herself. "Help me to make the right decisions to get out of this mess alive and by all means, please let me know who I am."

Meanwhile Larry located Ralph and the others watering and feeding the horses down by the stream about a half mile south of the hideout cave. He dreaded telling Ralph about the woman's escape. "If they didn't ave me horse, I prolly would a just mounted up and rode away meself!" Nervously he resorted to his broken Irish accent in his thoughts as he convinced himself his best option was to be truthful. He realized that he had to tell Ralph cause without his horse, he would die out here all alone not knowing the terrain at all. He'd even considered hitting himself on the head and knocking himself out, and waiting for them to find him. Then he could claim the woman had done it to him. But he acknowledged that his male pride would never allow for that much less would he be able to face his fellow outlaws and live through their making fun of him for being bested by a weakened female. He knew they would tease and torment him forever never ceasing their tirade.

Ralph glanced up as Larry approached, "Well, did ya git er fixed up fer the nite?

Larry hesitated before answering. "Okay, here goes...," he thought to himself. "Better be ready to duck!" Speaking carefully he answered Ralph.

"Well, boss, I reckon I've got a bit of bad news," he began, "just don't quite know how to tell ye?" he finished lamely. He was on guard waiting for Ralph's reaction.

"If'n you know what's good for ya, ya better not tell me anything my ears don't want ta hear." Ralph turned from filling his canteen and warned him sternly. Larry knew his boss meant business too!

Larry's stomach began to flip flop as he said, "Well, it ain't no good news, Ralph," he stalled for time.

Ralph's cheekbones began to tighten and the veins in the side of his neck and head began to pulsate. "Oh, surely ya ain't gonna tell me…,"

Larry decided to just get it over with and prepared to duck.

"She got away boss!" he blurted out then ducked as quickly as he could but Ralph managed to cuff his left ear with his fist spinning him to the ground. Holding his bleeding ear, Larry got up quickly and tried to back away from Ralph at the same time he continued with the details in hopes of defending himself, "I did it just like ye tole me to! I tied her up jes like ya said and everthin!" He began to fear for his life as he quickly turned to look at Ralph and saw that Ralph was headed right for him both arms held high, cocked at the elbow and his massive hands balled into fists. Ralph's face was a deep red purple filled with his rage.

Larry turned and began to run. He kept moving forward but tried turning his head backward to see if Ralph was gaining on him. He was determined to keep trying to put distance between him and the very angry man he called Boss. He kept attempting to haltingly babble out his story as he retreated and he became more and more breathless. "I waited…, for her to finish…" (*Come on breathe, man breathe! He subconsciously urged himself!*) "her business and then I pul't on the rope and when she din't come out and then I pul't it agin…..," his voice was breaking as his heart was pounding in need of air, "and then I figured she was still on the other end cause it felt tight…," now he was really gasping hard for air, but he continued, "but when I called to her 'n' she din't answer again so then I tugged it right hard, and the darn thing came a flying through the air and hit me square in the face!" Larry fell over a log as he finished his story but it didn't make any difference. Ralph's overly big fists suddenly made contact with Larry's face and he punched Larry until he lay limp and broken and he blacked out from the pain.

The other kidnappers had stopped what they were doing and stood still watching the drama unfold before their eyes. They were ready to duck from Ralph's rage if it became necessary. Trigger happy Ricky, had his hand on his gun ready to draw and shoot if he had to protect himself against his angry boss's rage. They all knew that Ralph had an uncontrollable temper. They had seen how far Ralph would go when he was angry. Outright murder was not out of the question.

"Ricky, get me a bucket of water!" he commanded. Ricky rushed to do as he was bid. He grabbed the bucket and ran to the creek bottom to fill it and then ran back to Ralph splashing the water everywhere as he handed it over to Ralph. "Well don't hand it ta me, ya idiot," Ralph commanded! "throw it on that sorry loser!"

Larry spluttered and sat up as the freezing water hit him in the face! He was barely coherent and trying to remember what had happened. He heard his Boss's angry voice again and he cringed at the words.

"Well, did ya search for her?" Ralph asked the nearly comatose Larry through clenched teeth.

"Course I did, Boss." Larry could barely answer. "There weren't no sign of her no wheres! I couldn't find any tracks cause it was in the dark side of the cave. An there weren't no moonlight a shown'n." Larry hastened to explain, while examining his injured face with his hands looking for the source of blood dripping into his right eye.

"Ya freak'n idiot!" Ralph screamed at him. "What the sam heck did ya take her to the dark side for?" he was taken aback by Larry's stupidity. "Don't ya know ya couldn't keep an eye on her from there?"

"I'm sorry Boss," Larry tried to apologize, "I was jes trying to give her some privacy, Ralph. She promised me she weren't goin anywhere, she said she war to scared of the snakes and mountain lions and the quicksand spots I tole her to be on the lookout for." Larry tried to cover for his error in judgment.

"Snakes and mountain lions, and quicksand!" Ralph roared. "What kind of crew am I dealing with?" he questioned himself and then he hauled off and and slammed his right fist into Larry's face and left fist immediately followed into Larry's stomach. Larry doubled over spitting blood and teeth. He fell to the ground unconscious again.

The other outlaw members stood and stared at the scene before them spell bound. All of them had their hands posed ready to reach for their guns and draw. But they were paralyzed into inaction.

Ralph turned to his horse and grabbed for his rifle. He mounted and began yelling instructions to them. "Well what are ya'll standing around for?" he deliriously questioned them. "The rest of you stupid jerks get your gear and go find her!" he commanded them into immediate action. They saddled up and were mounted and moving within five minutes. Larry remained unconscious lying in a heap on the ground with blood flowing from his broken nose and sliced open jaw.

Ralph looked at his badly bruised hand, kicked at Larry in the leg and when Larry didn't respond, he turned and went to his horse to finish saddling him. He mounted the steed and then left the injured man lying in the dirt. He carefully picked his horse's way to the darker area Larry had indicated that he had taken Abby to relieve herself. He dismounted and began looking for tracks. Without consistent moonlight to help him it was too dark for him to find a single clue. After attempting to find her for an hour, he decided to give up before he disturbed any clues that he might find when daylight came.

"Stupid idiot!" he cursed referring to Larry. "We will have to wait till morning to search for her. That dad blamed fool very well may have just cost us a fifty thousand dollar reward." He was so furious he stamped his foot into the ground startling his horse. The horse reared. His forelegs came down directly on top of Ralph. At the last second, Ralph threw himself out of the way. He stood up and grabbing his horses reins he jerked on them so hard the horse neighed in pain and stomped his front foot again. Ralph turned to his gathering crew and said "Let's get back to the cave and get some rest. If she's on foot she won't get far tonight. He remounted and swung his horse back in the direction of the cave and their campground. The remainder of his outlaw group warily followed him in.

"Hey Boss, where's Larry?" Jim dared to ask.

"Who the heck is Larry?" was his boss's sneering reply.

Jim shut up and they all knew that Larry was no longer considered one of them and they had better be careful what they did next.

Chapter Ten

Silas Johnson had his valise almost packed and was about ready to leave. Just a couple of quick items and he would be on his way to the train station. He had published a telegraph with Abby's description and a reward notice for fifty thousand dollars that Charles Anderson had offered for the safe return of his daughter. Silas warned him not to post a reward for Abby, but Charles Anderson had insisted.

Silas shook his head as he remembered arguing with Charles about posting a reward that huge. Charles had only insisted by demanding, "Do it Silas! Do it right away!" So Silas had stopped by the telegraph office on his way to his hotel suite and posted the notice. Through the miracles of telegraph, the notice had immediately been sent by wire to several different telegraph offices in cities across the nation. They were also posted on the walls of the Sheriff's offices, telegraph poles, etc., for the general public to see.

Silas was afraid that someone might take advantage of Abby and seriously harm her in an attempt to collect the reward. He still maintained that Abby had left of her own accord. All the evidence pointed to the probability that she had not been kidnapped. Who would have taken the time to shred a wedding dress when hurrying to kidnap someone, he reasoned. Then there was the fact that there had been no ransom letter. If she had left of her own accord, she would be visible to the public on a daily basis. The offered reward would be easy money to many. Not just men with immoral conduct but even hungry every day American citizens would want to collect the reward posted for Abby. If her disappearance was her own decision, she would not realize the danger she was in. She would refuse to return home and anyone would be inclined to kidnap her just for the reward and some might demand even more as ransom. Silas was very worried for Abby. He knew the reward had just made his job all the more difficult. He had very little time to find her if he was to keep her safe from harm. Mumbling to himself he said, "I hope Charles and all of Abby's friends are praying that someone somewhere is protecting that girl." With that he snapped his valise shut and headed for the door of his room.

Silas jerked his hotel suite door open and barged through the entryway. Moving too quickly and not taking time to watch his step his right eyeball made contact with Jeffrey Browning's balled up fist. "What the he…?" He exclaimed, dropping his valise and covering his right eye with his now free right hand. Almost simultaneously, he let out another howl. "OW!" He yelled again as his heavy valise landed directly on top of his right foot squashing his toes.

Jeffrey appeared stunned for a second and then he burst into laughter.

"Just what do you think you are laughing at?" Silas blurted angrily. "Aint you ever seen a man in pain before?" He had commenced hopping up and down on his left foot attempting to cover his eye with one hand and at the same time attempting to grab his injured foot with the other.

Jeffrey was laughing uncontrollably. In between gasps for air he attempted to apologize.

"Sorry sir, I didn't mean to laugh, for that matter I didn't mean to poke my fist in your eye," again he broke into uncontrollable laughter. I was just attempting to knock on your door when you opened it and barged right into my fist before I could knock! Ha… Ha… Ha! He continued to guffaw as the image of Silas's surprised expression kept reappearing in his mind.

A seriously irritated Silas hopped back into the room towards his bed. He dropped his huge form on the lower left corner. Immediately the bed collapsed taking Silas to the floor with it. Silas bounced off of the mattress and landed with a loud thud on the hard wood floor in a sitting position with his legs spread eagle in front of him. He had thrown his huge arms into the air in an attempt to stop himself from further injury.

Jeffrey immediately envisioned an over large bird, trying to fly but couldn't lift himself into the air. His laughter increased until he began to choke. He couldn't help himself. Trying to curtail his out of control laughter, he entered the room and attempted to help the comical man by reaching out his hand to help Silas rise from the floor.

Silas slapped his hand away and said, "Who are you anyway? What is it that you want?" he angrily demanded. "Ooooh that smarts!" He whimpered, rocking his huge frame back and forth to cover the intense pain in his buttocks and lower backside. He kicked off his shoe, then tore off the sock and examined his toes for broken bones.

Thanks to Jeffrey's fist, his vision was blurry. Tears of pain were running down the right side of his puffy red face. With his free hand he was trying to rub his bottom side.

"Well?" He choked out, "Answer me boy! Who are you and what is it you want? Owww, Oooh! That smarts!" He moaned again and again.

Jeffrey tried very hard to control his laughter. First laughing and then frowning, he nursed his injured pride at having his hand slapped out of the way. Again, he attempted to apologize to Silas.

"I said I'm sorry sir, truly I am. I did not mean to cause you injuries, you, it's just that…, well, you looked so funny! Ha! Ha! Ha!" Again he fell into heavy laughter at the memory. Looking down at Silas sitting on the floor, his face bulging red with anger, Jeffrey immediately controlled his laughter and held out his hand to assist Silas to a standing position a second time.

Jeffrey realized he was being rude by laughing and that his rudeness might stop Silas from allowing him to accompany him on his search for Abby. The memory of his missing Abby immediately calmed him down. He became serious.

"I'm Jeffrey Browning, Sir, Miss Abigail Anderson's fiancée. Charles Anderson sent me to find you." He explained. "He said I should accompany you in your search for Abby," he quickly threw in as an attempt to force Silas into allowing him to go with him. Noticing that Silas had thrown his hands in the air shaking them and his head negatively he realized that Silas was about to deny him, so he firmly insisted, "Now mind you I refuse to take no for an answer!"

Silas again slapped Jeffrey's extended hand out of the way. He refused both Jeffrey's offer to help him rise a second time, and his request to accompany him to find Abby.

"You've got to be an idiot if you think I'm going to take a clumsy oaf like you with me!" Silas was gruff with his retort. "In fact, you're an absolute screwball if you think you are going anywhere with me!" He nodded his head harshly to affirm his rejection of Jeffrey. Again he attempted to rise but failed to pull his huge girth up off of the floor.

"Begging your pardon sir, but I feel I must bring to your attention, that you are the one who opened the door and barged right into my uplifted hand without looking where you were going!" Jeffrey foolishly defended his innocence regarding Silas's painful incident. He didn't take the time to consider that his putting Silas on the spot of being responsible was not going to endear him to Silas any and therefore would most likely make it that much more impossible to gain Silas's agreement to allow him to travel with him to search for Abby.

"And I might add that it was you and not I who dropped your valise on your foot and then sat too hard on your bed causing it to collapse and make you hurt your own butt, sir!" As he spoke, Jeffrey retrieved Silas's heavy over packed valise. He replaced the items that had fallen out when the bag had burst open as it landed on Silas foot. Closing the door behind him, he reaffirmed his intention of joining with Silas to find Abby.

Silas gave up trying to lift his huge girth off the floor. He realized that nothing he could say was going to deter Jeffrey from going with him so he decided to trick him. Lifting his arm in Jeffrey's direction he said, "Well then, I see that I haven't any choice but to allow you to accompany me. Grab my hand boy, can't you see I need help getting off this floor!" He demanded, totally dismissing Jeffrey's previous attempts to help him up. Finally he stood. Shaking the dust from the hardwood floor off of his trousers and attempting to straighten his brown pin striped suit, he replied to Jeffrey's admonitions earlier.

"Young man, I do not feel like letting you off the hook for my grievous injuries. So if you want to go with me you've got one hour to get your things and meet me at the livery stable. Mind you, I won't wait for you. Not one red second!" he warned! "So you had best be there within the hour or you will miss your train and your chance to accompany me!" He harrumphed loudly as he stated his offer. "Now get going so I can get on my way!" he ordered.

"Yes sir!" Jeffrey quickly nodded his head in relief at being allowed to go. Slamming his derby onto his head he was already out the door calling back to Silas, "I'll be there sir, mark my words! Right on time too!" Bounding out of sight, he lurched down the carpeted stairs of the Hotel, three at a time, dodging a couple of hotel guests expertly in his young haste.

Back in his room, Silas began to put his sock and shoe back on. He knew, he and not Jeffrey, was responsible for his injuries. The truth was, Silas was a bit clumsier than most. He attributed it to having his thoughts on his cases and not on his feet and their whereabouts. He had deliberately miss-lead Jeffrey into thinking that they would meet at the livery station. He intended to take the train, and he intended to take it alone. All by himself! Yes! He did not need anyone

else around to help him trip and fall. After all, he knew he
could do a perfectly fine job of that all by himself.

Upon reaching the bottom of the curved polished
staircase, Jeffrey ran past the hotel desk clerk and out the
door. He dodged to the right of the bell boy. In the process
he managed to knock over several pieces of luggage the bell
boy was attempting to cart into the hotel. He did not stop
to help or take time to apologize to the bell boy.

Three minutes later he reached his own home. His valise
was still packed with the clothes he had taken with him on
his trip to Washington DC. Grabbing it and writing a hasty
note to his parents saying only that something had come up
and he had to leave again and that he would write them later,
he slammed his bedroom door shut and descended the two
sets of stairways in his parents three story newly constructed
Victorian town home two steps at a time. Running through
the front entry hall, he quickly handed the note to Baxter,
his family's butler and called over his shoulder as he jerked
opened the door and made a quick exit, "Baxter, make
certain my father gets this note!" He instructed the butler.

He was out of hearing range before Baxter could reply
in his quiet monotone voice. "Yas sir, Masa Jeffrey, I'se
surely will." Baxter was standing in the doorway Jeffrey
had left open. He had his overly thin head and long neck
extended through the doorway looking around the corner
towards the end of the street but Jeffrey was nowhere to
be seen. The whites of his surprised eyes were completely
visible surrounding his black corneas. Shaking his head, he
withdrew from the entrance and closed the door mumbling
to himself, "Now wha's up wit dat boy?" He asked out
loud in his monotone voice. He was accustomed to making

comments when no one was around to hear him. Talking to himself was how he kept himself company during his long, lonely, mostly uneventful days.

Jeffrey hailed a cab and arrived at the livery with fifteen minutes to spare. Finding the stable hand he inquired if a large man named Silas Johnson had been by. The stable hand replied, "No sir, ain't been no one here in more n a hour or so."

Jeffrey checked his watch. "Well, saddle me up a horse and throw a bed roll on the back if you have an extra one." He instructed the hand.

"How much am I going to owe you?" He casually inquired at the same time checking his watch again. He still had five more minutes. He stood leaning against the gray weathered wood of the stall, awaiting Silas. Suddenly he quit counting out his money and stared straight ahead into the bright sunlight of the street outside.

"Aw heck no! Don't tell me!" He muttered out loud as he heard the train whistle blow announcing the impending departure from town. "That fat old man duped me! Well, I'll be a monkey's uncle!" Stuffing his money back into his wallet, Jeffrey called to the stable hand. "Never mind, I won't be needing that horse or bedroll after all." Immediately, turning towards the street, he began running in the direction of the train station.

The stable hand sarcastically muttered under his breath as he began to unsaddle the horse he had just saddled. "Saddle me up, unsaddle me, don't these crazy folks know I've got better things to do like rubbing down the horses and mucking all these ere stalls?" He complained to no one in particular.

Jeffrey had remembered Silas's last words to him. Silas had mocked him and warned him "*not to miss his train.*" Well, we'll see about that, Mr. Silas Johnson, you're going to be one surprised old man when I show up at the station in time to not *miss my train.*" he chuckled as he emphasized the last words to himself. He relished imagining how angry Silas was going to be.

He arrived at the station with minutes to spare. He rushed to inquire from the ticket master in his iron cage, which train had a Mr. Silas Johnson boarded and was it still at the station? The ticket master didn't think twice about telling him that Silas had booked an all-inclusive ticket covering several cities and stopping at the end of the line in Saint Louis, Missouri. He was treated as a peon by Silas, and he was still smarting from being dismissed as totally unimportant to the self-important detective.

"Well has it left yet?" Impatiently, Jeffrey asked the man.

"No sir, got two more minutes afore she leaves the station."

"Wonderful!" a relieved Jeffery exclaimed! "Well, then sell me the exact same ticket would you?" Jeffrey ordered him. "Do it in a hurry if you would be so kind." The Ticket master was more than willing to comply as Jeffery had paid proper respectfulness to him in his employment position.

Paying the required fair as quickly as he could manage, Jeffrey grabbed the ticket and his valise. Immediately he turned and ran straight past the wanted posters that had been taped to the walls of the train station.

In his haste, he failed to see the one with a drawing of Abby. Her description was written all over it. Pulling his valise behind him he managed to knock the poster advertising Creosota flour to the floor. It was a shame that he didn't realize he had just passed up a very important clue. So important that it would have saved both himself and Silas a great deal of grief and extensive travel if only they had known.

Jeffrey boarded the passenger car of the train and headed straight for the seat beside Silas. Throwing his valise onto the shelf above the windows, he plopped his tall body down next to a very surprised and frowning Silas Johnson. Smiling facetiously, Jeffrey turned to Silas and said, "Well, you told me not to miss my train. Didn't you?"

"Dad gummit Boy, I thought I had thrown you off the tract on this one."

"Not when it comes to my Abby!" Jeffrey declared! "I'll do whatever it takes to find her and that even includes putting up with a crotchety old man like you Silas Johnson!" Jeffrey settled himself in his seat and reached for the paper that Silas had been reading.

"Well, you might just be of some use after all," Silas admitted, "since you were smart enough to figure out what I was up to." Silas replied a little unsure of his decision to accept Jeffrey on this trip with him. "But I warn you boy, this one's going to be a tough one. We've got our work cut out for us." Reaching over and jerking his newspaper out of Jeffrey's hands, he bellowed in his booming voice, "Rule #1, don't ever grab my paper or anything else out of my hands, you understand?"

Jeffrey, released his hold on the newspaper, but not before he kept one page of it for himself. "My you are an old grouch, aren't you he commented back at Silas.

"Yes, and you better watch your P's and Q's if you want to stay with me until we find Abby," Silas ordered him.

"So, what clues have you deduced so far? Jeffrey changed the subject.

"None." Silas calmly replied.

"None?" A startled Jeffrey asked him.

"Yea none, Jeffrey." Silas acted as if Jeffrey was deaf and hadn't heard him. Then he continued, "However, I asked that bigoted ticket master if he saw anyone who resembled Abby? But he said he had just come on duty. Said he'd been off for the whole week. Something about becoming a new dad, or something." Silas answered absent-mindedly as he continued to read his paper.

"Well, you got any ideas, or any plan of action?" Jeffrey inquired?

"Yea, we are going to take this train to Saint Louis which is as far as it goes. And we are going to ask everyone we see at each stop if they have seen a girl that matches Abby's description. Hopefully, we will get some leads to go on." As an afterthought he sarcastically asked Jeffrey, "Hey, since you re such a genius, what ideas do you have?"

"Well, I just happen to have a tintype of Abby with me!" Jeffrey proudly announced! He pulled his pocket watch from the breast pocket on the inside of his vest. Opening it he showed Silas the miniature photograph that had been taken of himself and Abby when they were walking in the city park 2 weeks ago. A man had sat up a temporary camera apparatus and had charged him a pretty penny to have a tintype made of his beloved Abby. He would have paid any price to have her picture available to him as he traveled extensively initiating his new political career.

Now the tiny picture of Abby's beautiful face nearly caused him to breakdown as he remembered the reason he was on this trip to begin with. He was taught that "men don't cry!" But right now he would have liked to break down and do just that. It made no sense to him that she was gone. He became silent as he remembered the night the picture was taken. They were having such an enjoyable walk and unknown to Abby he had the ulterior motive of asking her to be his wife. Suddenly in front of all the people walking in the park around them he'd dropped to one knee, and asked her to be his wife. She had blushed demurely and gasped in pleasant surprise. Then she accepted the diamond ring he had selected to give her and said "Oh yes! Of course I will Jeffrey!" Then she had allowed him to chastely kiss her on the forehead.

Now, his chest experienced a sharp pain as he remembered that he was here because he had no idea where she was or if she was all right. He never questioned the fact she may have chosen to leave him. To Silas he said, "I figure this picture will help us a lot more than any questions will."

Silas glanced at the tiny portrait of Abby. He was slightly embarrassed that Jeffrey had more in his hand to accomplish this case with than he had in a formulated plan to find her. "You better give me the portrait boy." He ordered, his hand extended.

"You're crazy, you old goat, I'm not ever parting with this picture. It's all I've got to hold onto until I have the love of my life back with me!" Jeffrey replied adamantly as he snapped the watch closed and returned it to his vest pocket.

"Oh, all right!" Silas unwillingly gave in but not without establishing his own authority over the tintype. "But whatever you do, don't lose that picture! It might just be the most valuable tool we have to find her with," he warned Jeffrey at the same time he made it clear that he didn't trust Jeffery to be intelligent enough to hold onto the tintype.

The train whistle blew and the conductor yelled, "All aboard!" With a sudden jolt, the train started on its way. Both men settled down for the first stage of their trip.

Silas continued reading his paper. He was anxious to find the girl for Charles Anderson, his close friend and also to close this case for his Pinkerton office in quick order to sustain his excellent reputation with the firm.

Jeffrey, anxious and nervous, praying that soon he would have his beloved Abby back in his arms again, settled back and lowered his hat over his eyes. Immediately he fell into a light sleep and he began dreaming of Abby. In the dream Abby was beckoning to him, but the more he reached out to her, the farther she floated away from him. He kept running towards her, but she continued floating away from him. As the train picked up speed, in his dream he ran harder and faster towards her, but no matter how hard or fast he ran she became even smaller and farther away from him.

The train whistle blew again to announce they were arriving at the next stop. With a start Jeffery awakened from the dream to find that he was sweating profusely. After the dream he felt shaken and much more worried than before.

Chapter Eleven

Morning came way too soon. Ralph woke up at exactly six am which was his habit. He rolled over and sat up. Immediately his mood darkened when he remembered that all of his hard work and planning had failed. The girl was on the loose again and he had to start all over to find her as fast as he could. It wasn't going to be a pleasant day for him or his men. He vowed to see to it that no one rested until she was back in their possession.

Jim, always the dependable one, had already risen and had hot coffee brewing on the fire he refreshed from last night. He also had a fresh batch of biscuits made and some slab bacon was frying in the small iron skillet he carried with him at all times. Ralph grabbed a biscuit without waiting for the bacon and filled his tin cup with the coffee. Walking to the other side of the blazing fire, he kicked Ricky, Tom and Buck in the legs.

"Get your sorry selves up and eat yurself a biscuit and git some coffee. We're out of here in five minutes." He ordered nastily.

Groaning and mumbling, Buck and Ricky sat up. Rubbing their sleep filled eyes and pushing at their unkempt hair, they took their time to stand. Tom reached for a biscuit and poured himself a cup of coffee.

"Hey? Did Larry show up last night?" He dared to ask.

"Who gives a hoot about that stupid idiot?" Ralph answered angrily. "That sorry son-of-a-whatever just cost us fifty grand! I don't give a crap where he is or even if his sorry butt is still alive. And if any of ya'll have any ideas of taking precious time to check on that worthless piece of crap, then ya might as well get yur gear and get out of here as well!" He informed them angrily. "Now git a move on it! I mean it! I'm not waiting longer than two more minutes for ya'll to be packed and on the road looking for that gal. She can't have gotten far," he finished by reaffirming his hopes to himself. "Put out that fire and eat that bacon as quick as ya can swallow it!" It was obvious to the men they had best comply quickly so they grabbed a biscuit and ate the half cooked bacon at the same time as they rolled their blankets and packed their few belongings onto their pack horses. They seldom bothered to shave or wash up anyway so they didn't waste any extra time on these menial daily tasks. In less than ten minutes the group was ready to begin searching again.

Larry stumbled into the camp covering his broken nose with his bloody kerchief. His stomach was in severe pain. He was walking slowly, bent over slightly. He held his arm across his stomach. With his other hand he was leading his horse. He was very grateful that Ralph had left the horse with him. A man could die way out here all alone. "I didn't mean to let her get away, boss. Didn't do it on purpose, ye know." He said to Ralph.

Ralph pivoted and glared hatefully at Larry, "Ya'd best shut yur mouth before I break all yur teeth too! Git some food and coffee in yur belly and get a move on it if yur gonna help us to find the gal. Ya better be the one that finds her if you know what is good for ya. Ralph continued to chastise him harshly. Mount up with the others and let's get on with finding her! Larry quickly gulped down his hot coffee, painfully pulled himself onto his horse and tried to catch up with the others who had already headed for the escape site to begin their search for Abby.

At the far side of the caves from town, Abby awakened and stirred. She discovered that she was being held in a tight arm lock under her breast by the sleeping stranger who had rescued her. She lay very still, as she was very scared and didn't want to awaken him until she took time to think about her predicament. Lying on the hard cold ground, she was very cold except for the side of her body that was touching Joseph. That side she noticed was quite warm. She wished she dared to turn over and warm her front side against him as well, but she was scared to death of what might happen if she should. She had never slept in a man's embrace before. She found it nerve-wrecking yet, sort of enticing. For some reason she craved more of the man. Immediately, she chastised herself for thinking such insane thoughts.

She perused the strange denim jacket lined in a red plaid flannel that was partially covering her keeping her upper body slightly warm. Very slowly, she turned her head slightly to look around her. The memories of her previous evenings escapades came flooding back to her. Recounting the events, she remembered awaking in a cave, being fed and then taken to relieve her bladder still tied up as a hostage. From out of nowhere this man in whose arms she was lying had rescued her. Who was he anyway? Did she know him? Was he a friend, relative or good heavens, could he be her husband? Why else did she seem so comfortable in the arms of this strange man? She tried again to remember who she was and what else had happened. All she succeeded in doing was making her head pound severely.

Carefully she tried to disengage herself from the stranger. She studied his face slowly searching for some sign of resemblance about him that she could remember. Nothing came to her. She moved, trying to get up. Joseph awoke when she attempted to disengage his arm from around her breasts. Their eyes met. For a brief second they stared at one another. His blue eyes caused her heart to jump. Surprised, she did not understand why her chest had constricted and why did that strange tickling feeling suddenly happen in her lower abdomen. She gasped slightly from the shock of the strange feeling.

Her green eyes stared at the handsome stranger. They were filled with questions and fear. He sensed her unease. Letting her go he rolled over and stood up. Picking up the bedroll he began rolling it up. "We are on the other side of the caves. But, we still need to be very quiet," he warned her. We have no idea where the men might be that took you from the train."

"Train?" She silently considered the word. She remembered the outlaws but nothing about any train? Confused she stared at him but did not ask him any questions. She was afraid she would let the cat out of the bag regarding her state of amnesia. She feared that if the stranger meant to harm her, knowing she suffered from amnesia, might just give him the excuse he needed. She nodded to indicate her understanding that she must remain silent. Attempting to whisper, her voice was hoarse and raspy due to her ordeal and the cold moist weather. "What, do we do next?" She asked him coughing quietly to clear her throat.

Joseph, placed his hand on her forehead. He was concerned about her health. "Are you running fever?" he asked.

"No, I don't think so. Just a little sore and I'm very tired." She both reassured and informed him.

"Okay, Well, I'll try to take it easy for you." He comforted her but remained concerned.

"So? What's next? She asked again. She was hoping he would tell her something that would tell her more about whom she was and why she was here.

He rubbed his long thin fingers through his blond hair. "I guess we will lay low for a couple of days and watch for any signs of our discovery. Then I guess we will head on to Saint Louis from here on horseback." He said to her. If we are lucky, we still might be able to catch that wagon train heading to California."

"California?" She thought to herself, "wagon train?" She tried to concentrate on these words to see if they meant anything to her. Nothing came to mind. "Who am I?" She questioned herself. "Who is this man, is he my brother, or cousin or husband maybe? Oh God! Whatever am I going to do?" As was now becoming her habit she once again beseeched the higher powers. Out loud she asked, "Will you teach me to ride the horse?" She fervently hoped that he had known that she couldn't ride before all of this had happened. But if that was so, why did he bring her a horse? What if he didn't know her after all? Then that would mean he was trying to steal her from the outlaws for the same ransom they mentioned. She became afraid of him again.

"Yea, you didn't do that bad," he barely whispered to assure her. "Actually, you managed to hold on pretty well. That's the hardest part. You know, just keeping your balance. After that it pretty much seems to come naturally to you. You do realize that a horse is the only way in or out of this countryside?" He asked her.

"Of course!" She assured him, even though she didn't have a clue if what he said was actually true. "I just don't want to cause us any problems, getting out of here," she covered. If a horse was the only way out of here, well maybe then he did know her, she reasoned.

"Don't worry," replied Joseph. "I promise to protect you and take care of you to the best of my ability." He was finished tying their bedrolls behind their saddles. He handed her a piece of the store bought jerky he'd purchased in Bowling Green yesterday. Sorry, "we can't make a fire because it might be seen or smelled. So that means we can't have any coffee or a hot meal, OK? But there is some water in this canteen, so drink up. It's going to be a while before we can stop to refresh ourselves," he took time to caution her.

She nodded and followed his advice.

"Just chew on this and it should relieve some of the hunger in your stomach until we can find something better and some fresher water to drink. Ok?"

She nodded again. He walked up and put his arms around her to lift her onto the saddle.

His touch caused her to jump nervously.

"I'm sorry," he said, "didn't mean to alarm you. I'm just going to lift you up into the saddle. Grab hold of the pummel and pull yourself the rest of the way up into a sitting position." He whispered softly to her while holding her tightly against his chest. His heart beat wildly.

Never had the touch of any other woman stirred his blood so hot on such a simple touch. "What's the matter with you, idiot? You haven't got time for this kind of thing." He silently chastised and reminded himself. He withdrew his arms as quickly as he could.

She smiled timidly, nodded and whispered back. "Sorry, didn't mean to jump. Everything that's happened and all…" she stumbled to explain her reaction. She didn't want him to think she didn't know who he was in case she was supposed to know him. The truth, she admitted to herself, was that she didn't know why she practically jumped out of her skin every time this stranger either looked at her or touched her. "Surely, I must belong to him, or at the very least I must know him?" She questioned herself, "Oh God, I just wish I knew who I am."

Joseph turned his back to her and quickly mounted his stallion. His hands and arms were burning where he had touched Abby. He tried to ignore the sensations he felt every time he was near her. He couldn't explain why touching her created this strong physical response in him. Oh sure he had had his share of women in cat houses and such, but no woman had ever drawn this need to fulfill himself as this one did. Usually the women had to work hard just to entice his interest.

He refused to glance in her direction. He was afraid that she could feel his discomfort. He didn't want her to think that all he wanted from her was to take advantage of her and then leave her. He wanted her to know that it was his intention to protect her and keep her safe. "Good gosh, this is going to be one long hard trip for me to get through." He dared to admit to himself as he turned his horse away and started picking his way north and westward deeper into the forest around them. Without looking at her, he began instructing her quietly on how to maneuver her horse to follow his.

Always heading north and west and away from Bowling Green, Kentucky, they continued walking their horses. Slowly and quietly they picked their way through the underbrush and rocky paths. Joseph kept inside the forest as he was trying to keep away from any actual roads, or worn paths, where the outlaws or the Sheriff's posse would likely be looking for them. He decided it would be wisest to keep the hooves of the horses covered for as long as the fabric remained in tack.

Abby hung onto the reins of her horse. At the slow pace they were traveling she began to feel more confident with her ability to learn to ride her mount. She patted the horse lightly on the shoulder and whispered to it that everything was going to be just fine.

She began to watch the honey colored mane of her horse bounce up and down in tune to the rhythm of their cadence. Eventually, she let her fears subside and she began to enjoy the ride. She felt secure with this stranger. Although she knew that at any moment she might be spotted and taken hostage again, for some reason she just didn't feel any danger would come to her as long as she remained with this stranger.

Just eight miles away on the east side of the caves, heading in the direction of town, a very angry Ralph sat on his horse. They had searched for hours. They had found a trail of footsteps that had led them to horse tracks. It appeared to have been two horses. They had carefully followed the tracks for two miles towards town. Then it began to rain lightly. Their hopes of following the tracks any further died as the rain washed the hoof prints away.

Angry, Ralph decided to take his anger out on Larry. Balling up his fist he rushed his horse in Larry's direction. Larry turned his horse around and kicked him into a gallop. Lying low in his saddle to stop wind resistance, he galloped away as fast as his horse could go. He knew his days with this group had come to a close. In fact he knew that his very life was in danger. He figured he had better head southward to the southern states and attempt to lie low for a while. He certainly didn't need to run into any one in this gang ever again. To do so might end up fatal for him.

Ralph cursed when he was unable to release his anger by injuring Larry some more. Ten minutes into the chase he stopped and did not try to chase him any further. He knew his horse was spent. He admitted that he had no idea what to do next. Couldn't tell where the girl and her rescuer had gone, north, east, south, or west? No one knew. He turned to the other four remaining men. Let's get out of here. Head back into town. Maybe we will pick up a clue there. Together they rode the remaining 20 miles back to the town of Bowling Green.

Chapter Twelve

Six days and five nights later found Abby and Joseph approximately forty miles south-east of Saint Louis. Joseph figured two more days in the saddle and they should arrive in time to secure a wagon to continue their journey west with the wagon train. He was hoping that they had not missed the last wagon train out for the season. He knew they were pushing a strict time deadline.

He was still trying to find a way to suggest to Abby that she should go to California with him. He knew very little about her. What he did know is that the past few days convinced him he wanted to keep her in his life forever. Perplexed, he repeatedly asked himself, "What do I want this filly around me for? I'm not the kind of man that wants to settle down and have a passel of young'uns. Not to mention a home with roots and all the work it will take to keep it maintained" he mused silently as they trotted at a steady pace towards Saint Louis. "Sides, I m a loner, got to claim my stake and find gold. Maybe I just better dump her in Saint Louis and consider myself done with her?" He nodded to himself in satisfaction.

Looking over at her as if to let her know of his decision, his chest suddenly constricted with a longing he had never felt before. "Dad gummit why does she have to be so beautiful?" The unbidden thought flitted through his thought process. He knew he was kidding himself. There was no way he could leave her behind in Saint Louis. He wanted, no, he needed her with him.

Staring at her with a sideways glance he watched her unbound long red hair blowing freely with the wind. The lengthy tendrils curled around her head and blew wildly out of control. The evening sunset glistened through the long strands making it shine like real burnished gold.

Joseph had presented a valise to Abby filled with female apparel and indicated to her that it was hers. She thanked him and pretended she knew it was hers. However her hurried search of the contents did not help her to remember who she was. But it did reveal that she had not packed any clothing suitable for riding horseback. So, earlier that morning, Joseph had handed her one of his blue denim shirts and a pair of his jeans and instructed her to put them on. She had tied the jeans around her tiny waist with a rawhide rope and folded the legs up into cuffs to shorten their length. The top two buttons of her shirt were unbuttoned to help ward off the heat of the day.

He watched her fascinated by the rise and dips of her breasts moving up and down in rhythm with the cantor of her horse. Coughing slightly, he nearly choked as he watched the near erotic sight. "Better look away while you still can," he instructed himself.

At that moment, she turned her face to him and asked, "How much farther do we have till we get to Saint Louis?"

Her green eyes were shining brightly as she squinted into the sun. She appeared angelic with the evening glow of the sun surrounding her. Glancing in her direction, he nearly fell off of his horse. Pulling himself up with his reins he righted himself back in his saddle. "Get a grip, old boy!" He warned himself silently. To Abby he replied, "About forty or so more miles, I think," he answered her.

"Oh!" She acknowledged his answer and turned to face forward. Her thoughts began to taunt her again. For nearly a week now she had been trying to remember who she was. She still had no memory of her past life. She didn't have a single clue who this handsome stranger riding beside her was either. What she did know was that so far this stranger had not attempted to harm her. They had been together for several days and he had been protective at all times. Not once had he tried to touch her inappropriately.

Which brought up another question? Could he be her husband? If so, surely he would have tried to make love to her by now. She suddenly blushed. "Make love to her? Where did that come from?" Then she realized that she had no knowledge if she was still a virgin or what making love really meant? "WOW! This is so ridiculous! When will I have answers to these many questions?" she wondered. As for the stranger, maybe he was her brother. No, that didn't make any sense as they didn't have any family resemblance and he had not referred to her as Sis or sister, cousin, or any other words that would have indicated that they were related.

He had called her Lydia, but that's all he had mentioned. She was hoping that he hadn't realized that she had not called him by name either. She remembered he had told her his name when he rescued her but she was so shocked she wasn't certain if he said it was Joseph, or Joe or Josh, or whatever? If he figured that out, he might guess about her amnesia and that could be very dangerous for her. So why would a complete stranger act as if he knew her and that she should know him? "Will I ever regain my memory?" She wondered.

Hoping to relieve the constant pain in her head she attempted to turn her thoughts away from her dilemma. Deciding to attempt some small talk, she turned to look at Joseph. Instantly she jerked on the reins of her horse. She had caught him staring directly at her with a look of pure longing on his face.

Caught unawares, her horse suddenly stopped. She fell to the ground from the unexpected jolt. A sharp pain in her buttocks indicated she had landed half on and half off a smooth rounded rock. She looked so surprised that Joseph had to cover his mouth to keep from laughing. Rolling onto her knees, she began rubbing her bottom end to relieve the pain.

Suddenly Joseph's hand was helping her to stand. Without warning, he grabbed her to his chest and hugged her tightly. "Are you alright?" He huskily whispered his worry in her ear. She nodded but was unable to reply. His embrace was squeezing the breath out of her.

"Good Lord, don't ever pull on the reins like that," he admonished her. Gently he rubbed her hair at the same time unmindful that he was still squeezing her to his chest. "I should have told you the horse would balk when his bit is tightened without warning. Are you sure you are all right?" he asked her again. Her muffled answer made him immediately release his hold on her.

"Yes, I'm fine!" She managed to squeak out as she gasped for air. "I just got the wind knocked out of me for a moment there!"

"Hey, I'm sorry, didn't mean to squeeze the remainder of your air out," he immediately released her and apologized to her with a sheepish grin on his handsome face. "It was just that…, well, I," he stammered trying to search for the right words, "I reckon I was just scared ya might of been hurt." He lamely attempted to explain.

Looking up at him she saw the genuine concern for her that he felt. "It's ok!" she muttered under her breath. "Oh and Thanks for caring!" she playfully said blushing as she smiled prettily at him.

Simultaneously they burst into laughter realizing the silliness of the whole situation. Abby caught her breath as she watched his glistening blue eyes staring at her. The sunset was behind him. With his blond hair blowing gently in the wind, the sun created a golden halo around his entire body. She turned away from him immediately and without thinking she bent over in front of him to pick up the hat he had lent to her to provide shade for her face from the sun.

Joseph did a double take. Immediately he turned and stomped to his horse. Taking the reins in his hand he began to walk the horse off the current path they were now following and deeper into the thick forest at a super-fast pace. This woman made his knees go weak every time he looked at her. One moment he wanted to throw her on the ground and make passionate love. The next moment he knew he would kill himself if he did. She certainly didn't need to be treated like the common women he had been used to bedding. "But, Oh! The intense longing she made him feel was becoming unbearable for him!" he admitted ruefully.

Abby picked up the hat and turned to see that Joseph had walked away from her. For the most part she was still innocent of the physical power between men and women, she had no idea that she had openly invited him to peruse her bottom side by bending over in front of him in such a seductive manner. She was not aware of her female effect on him. She wondered what she had done to upset him.

"Is everything ok?" She called to his swiftly retreating back.

His nerves were grating beyond control. Barely able to contain his movements, he answered a little harshly, "Just fine!" He lied to her tensely. He walked his horse deeper into the woods picking up his pace.

"We'll make camp here!" He called to her, "Tie up your horse and then if you don't mind see if you can come up with something for us to munch on. I'm starving and I bet you are too. Supplies are in the pack. I can hear a stream close by. You can get some fresh water there." He rambled on and on as if trying to get control of himself. Grabbing his rifle from its storage location, next to his saddle, he added. "We're out of meat. I'm going to find us some. I'll be back in a bit!" Quickly he disappeared into the forest. He had to get away from her fast and he knew it!

A bewildered Abby stared after him. "Now what's his problem?" She wandered. But a slow smile spread across her face as she watched his long legs and lean body disappearing from her line of site. Nodding, she admitted she liked what she saw. In fact, she really liked what she saw. Beginning to hum a lively tune Abby prepared a camp for them for the night. She gathered loose timber and started a fire. Then she went to the nearby creek and refilled their water canteens with fresh cold water. Upon her return to camp the fire was blazing so she put on a pot of coffee for them.

She also made up their bedrolls for the night. She placed them next to each other just as they had for the past few nights. She felt safer close to him. The woods were scary enough to her. Wild animal calls throughout the night along with occasional rustlings. Once they heard a wolf howl. All of this was frightening to her citified ears. But even more, there was still the threat that the outlaws could find her at any moment.

Joseph returned thirty minutes later holding up two freshly shot squirrels. Abby was checking on the biscuit bread she managed to whip up from the few remaining ingredients left in their stash of supplies. She had never cooked anything before in her life. But she'd been very observant of Joseph as he had prepared the biscuits for them earlier. Also, she had carefully watched him strike a fire using just a flint and some kindling.

She was feeling very proud of her accomplishments. Hearing Joseph's arrival, she stood up and faced him. He held out the two bloody squirrels to her. Clasping her hand over her mouth she barely stopped herself from vomiting at the sight of the bloody animals. Quickly she spat the fluid out of her mouth and bravely pretended that nothing was out of the ordinary.

Joseph was surprised by her behavior. "So, our little Lydia has never seen anyone with a fresh kill before," he surmised silently and decided not to mention anything. He did make a mental note though as he felt this clue might tell him some more about Lydia. He was still unaware that Abby suffered from amnesia. He just knew very little about her to begin with.

Turning his back to her he unsheathed his knife from his belt and began to skin and gut the squirrels. "How'd you get the fire going?" He asked nonchalantly.

"How do you think?" She sarcastically replied. Do you really think that I don t know how to build a fire or make a biscuit? Nerves on edge she waited for his reply. She hoped he didn't realize that she didn't know if she ever had known how to build a fire or make biscuits.

Sorry. I didn't mean to sound demeaning. I just didn't know you knew how." He told her lamely. "Those biscuits smell really good," he complimented her as he washed the meat and speared them on a freshly stripped from its bark, green tree limb to be roasted over the flames. He had brought only the one pan to cook in and it was full of biscuit bread. Talking idly they sat together and consumed their meager, but hot and delicious meal.

After satisfying their hunger, Joseph stomped out the fire. He hadn't seen anyone following them since his rescue of Lydia. But he was still on guard. However he felt it was enough to finally make them a fire the previous evening to warm them up from the chill. Then this morning he had made the biscuits for their breakfast before they started on the trail again. He was pretty certain that they were in safe territory for now. However, he knew he would seriously be on guard upon their arrival in the populated city of Saint Louis. At the speed they were going he determined two more days in the saddle should put them at their destination.

The weather was taking a turn for the worse. Except for the first night he had rescued her, he and Abby had been able to sleep on the separate bedrolls he had purchased for each of them. They had slept within sound, sight and in reach of each other for safety's sake. Usually he attempted to stay awake as long as possible until he was certain they were alone and she was not in danger. Then he tried to get a few quick hours of sleep during the wee morning hours before they left camp. She was not aware of the sacrifice he was making for her safety. She usually fell asleep instantly as the trip and her ordeal had completely zapped all of her energy reserves. Tonight the wind began to pick up and the temperature dropped quickly.

Fully satiated and feeling a little proud of her self, Abby admitted she was tired and went to her bedroll to attempt some much needed sleep. About an hour later, Joseph broke the silence. "Sleeping yet?" He softly asked her.

Out of the darkness came her soft shaky voice. "No…, and I can't seem to sleep." She yawned, but admitted that sleep was eluding her.

"Is something wrong?"

I'm, just a little bit cold!" she admitted to him. In fact she was shivering so bad that she wasn't able to disguise the shaking in her voice.

Joseph felt his heart jump. "Well, now what do I do? Can't just let her freeze to death." He mused. To her he said. "Come over here, we can sleep side by side and keep each other warm. Sorry, but it's not wise to light a fire and let it burn tonight. We are in an open forest and there is nothing to conceal the flames and the wind is too strong anyway." He explained his concerns to her.

He waited quietly. She did not respond. "It's ok, Lydia, I promise, I won't harm you. Come on honey, you know I've never harmed you. You're going to freeze to death if you don't." He coaxed her to comply.

Nervously, Abby considered her options. Once again, she asked herself, "Who is he? Am I married to him? Is he a relative or friend or what?" She didn't feel that they were married as he had made no demands on her, but he also did not appear to be brotherly or to act like a cousin either. "What should I do?" she prayed. As usual, she received no verbal answer. "But if I don't lie beside him, I am going to freeze to death!" Her cold body would not stop shivering. Deciding on the most reasonable alternative, she rolled up her bedroll and went to lie next to him. "I know you won't hurt me," she whispered to him, more to convince herself than him. Also, she didn't want him to be alarmed by her hesitation just in case he did know her. She lived in fear that he would put two and two together and guess her amnesia predicament.

Quickly enveloping her within his arms Joseph grabbed her bedroll and spread it on top of both of them. "G-nite, sweet dreams!" he whispered in her ear.

"You too, sleep tight!" she drowsily answered as her cold body began to warm and relax against him. His warmth was erasing the pain of her bruised, sore, tired body. She felt comforted in his arms. For the first time in days she felt safe again. A deep sleep came almost immediately to her.

Joseph was not so lucky. Stiffly, he lay beside her afraid to move a muscle. He didn't wish to wake her. Mostly, he feared he couldn't trust his own body not to become aroused by her. It was excruciating to feel her softness in his arms and not be able to satisfy himself. He tried to turn his thoughts away from her curvaceous body.

He began to concentrate on the dilemma they were in. Because he didn't feel they were in any immediate danger, his thoughts kept returning to the woman in his arms. He wanted desperately to take her here and now and make her into his own woman. He didn't know for certain but he didn't think she had any idea how a man's body could make her feel. Right now, he was having a terrible time holding back from teaching her himself. Forcing himself he had to accept that it would be the very worst mistake he could make at this time. Her breathing was gentle and rhythmic. His last conscious thoughts were, I'm going to push two days mileage into one tomorrow. We've got to get to Saint Louis tomorrow night. There is absolutely no way I can take another night of torture like this one. Then concentrating on her rhythmic breathing he managed to fall into a deep sleep beside her.

A few hours of sleep revived him. Awaking before daybreak, he looked at her in his arms. He tried to sleep some more but his thoughts began to wander. He began thinking about the beautiful woman lying in his arms. "Who was she really?" he asked himself. "Why was she so sad on the train, but since the kidnapping, she hadn't mentioned the train or anything that had happened regarding the robbery of the train or her own kidnapping for that matter. In fact instead of being sad she seemed to be empty and bothered by something. But what?" he continued to examine the facts.

For one she hadn't asked about the welfare of the other passengers. That negligence seemed completely out of character with the little bit he knew about her. She had always shown concern for the other passenger's levels of comfort. Strange that she hadn't asked about the family who lost their father. As it were, she was just beginning to trust in him and had become a little talkative before the kidnapping. Now, he got the feeling that she sometimes acted like she didn't know if she trusted him or if she should fear him.

"*OH MY GOD*!" Suddenly his body jerked in surprise! She stirred slightly, mumbled something and fell back to sleep. Settling down, he resumed his thoughts, What if that hit on her head had injured her seriously. "That's it! That explained everything including why she had not called him by his name since he had rescued her. This little gal has lost her memory!" Triumphantly he congratulated himself on discovering her secret.

Staring at her peacefully sleeping face, his eyes were filled with concern and sadness for her. He tightened his arms around her protectively and almost soundlessly he whispered directly in her ear. "Oh honey, don't you worry. I'll protect you, you will never have to worry! I will always be here for you through thick and thin! I give you my promise!" he assured the soundly sleeping exhausted girl. "But why didn't you tell me, you little minx?" He asked her telepathically. Don't you know I would never hurt you? No sirree! Not for the world, and if I've got anything to do with it neither will anyone else!" It was at that moment the he realized he was in love with her. Vowing to never leave her side, he knew he no longer had any choice. He had to make her go with him to California on the wagon train. He just had to figure a way to convince her to go with him without alarming her.

Realizing that for some unknown reason, she did not want him to know of her amnesia. Giving it some thought he decided he wouldn't tell her that he had guessed her secret. In the meantime, he intended to look harder for clues to find out who she really was and why she had been on that train in the first place. "Ironic," he mused, "never thought I would want to settle down on a farm with a wife and a passel of kiddos." He smiled at the mental picture their future could be and suddenly he couldn't wait to do just that.

Frowning, he intently shifted his gaze to her face. "But what if you are already someone else's wife?" The question came out of nowhere. He gazed upon her. Mentally he asked her the question expecting no answer. "Man o' man, I can't take that! Maybe we'll never know. Then again, maybe I don t want to know!" Holding her thusly he knew he didn't have a clue where this relationship was heading. Eventually he fell asleep again.

The next morning bloomed bright, chilly and very windy. Abby awoke in Joseph's tightly held embrace. She started for a moment and then remembered their agreement to sleep keeping each other warm during the cold night. Admitting she was warm, she felt refreshed and ready to take on the day before her. A slow smile of content blossomed across her face.

Without disturbing him she turned her face to look at him. He had been true to his word. He had not attempted to violate her or touch her in any way other than to keep her warm and safe beside him. She felt relief that was immediately followed with disappointment as she wondered what she had missed. "Gracious sakes, what can I be I thinking?" Turning slowly she attempted to ease away from Joseph trying not to awaken him.

He stirred and opened his eyes. Their eyes locked. Her eyes were incredibly green and his, a clear bright blue. Staring into her green eyes he momentarily lost his senses. She looked at his eyes and saw deep into his soul. A silent understanding passed between them. They felt safe and secure in each other's arms. Suddenly embarrassed, Abby pulled away. Her cheeks immediately turned a bright shade of pink. Standing a little awkwardly, she dusted the nights sandy dirt from her clothes and then walked towards their supplies.

Joseph watched her go. His empty arms left him feeling lonely. Sighing, he also stood, stretched his arms wide and inhaled the fresh air of the morning. Abby looked up at him as she was folding the blanket they used. Watching him stretching, her knees went weak. The last thing she needed was to have this stranger see her fall in front of him! She turned her back to him and chastised herself smiling slightly.

"Morning," she whispered shyly.

"And may it be a good-morning to you too!" Joseph responded good- naturedly. "Hope you slept well," he fished for her feelings regarding their previous night spent in each other's arms.

"Yes thank you, just fine," blushing, she answered him shyly and turned her back to him again as she began to pack their supplies in preparation to leave.

Joseph placed his hand on her shoulder. She jumped! "Sorry, didn't mean to startle you none, just wanted to get some of that good biscuit bread you made yesterday before you pack it up," he said.

"Oh," she said, "sure thing, hoped you enjoy it." She smiled timidly at him as she passed him the remainder of the biscuit bread.

"Want some?" He broke the bread in half and handed her a piece.

"Yes, thank you." She took the biscuit bread and sat down to munch on it. Suddenly she was feeling very self-conscious and totally nervous.

He was as jumpy as she. They both felt the unspoken tension in the air around them beginning to build. "We'd best be on our way then," he said. I'll get the horses saddled while you finish gathering these things up." He picked up his gun belt, buckled it in place and walked towards the horses.

"Sure thing! She was grateful he had ended their uncomfortable morning. She reached for the second bedroll.

She screamed!

Joseph dropped the saddle he was lifting and ran to her. Standing, paralyzed with fear, she was staring into the eyes of a huge rattlesnake that was rattling his tail at her in warning. The snake was poised and ready to strike.

"Don't move!" Joseph cautioned her quietly. He didn't have to warn her to stand still. She didn't hear him anyway. Her heart hammered her fear. She just stood there, paralyzed unable even to blink as she stared in a trance like state into the eyes of the six foot snake.

Slowly but determinedly, Joseph carefully dislodged his six-shooter from his holster. Taking quick but careful aim, he shot the snake in the head. The snake's body wriggled and jumped all over the ground, his head shot clean off.

Abby fainted on the spot.

Dropping his smoking gun, Joseph barely caught her in his arms before her body hit the ground. Visibly shaken, he gently laid her down. Using the pointed end of his rifle he picked up the huge lifeless head and the remainder of the snake's body and tossed it into a deep ravine in the woods on his way to the flowing stream a few yards from their camp site. Filling his hat with water, he hurried back to Abby. Kneeling, he lifted her limp body onto his lap. With his dampened kerchief he carefully dabbed at her face. He was very worried that she might not resume consciousness after all the trauma she'd experienced.

The sudden cold water on her face caused her to stir. Joseph breathed a sigh of relief. Sitting up she burst into tears and threw herself into Joseph's arms. The snake had been the final straw. All the shock and pain of the past weeks had taken its toll. She began crying hysterically. Joseph did the only thing he could think of. Rocking her back and forth in his arms he patted her head and consoled her assuring her everything would be alright.

Eventually her tears began to slow. She lay limply in his arms, her body shaking occasionally as she released another huge sob. Joseph placed his finger under her chin and gently raised her face to look into her eyes. Her tear stained face made his heart lurch. Grabbing her to him he kissed her swollen lips, gently at first and then harder. Surprised, Abby responded to him immediately. The pit of her stomach felt funny. A yearning began inside her leaving her wanting something she couldn't describe. With his tongue, Joseph enticed her to open her swollen lips. His tongue entered her mouth and tasted her. She couldn't think. She could only allow him to do as he wanted. She answered his kiss with a passion to match his own. She never knew the sensations she was feeling existed. She couldn't remember if she had ever been kissed before. But she didn't think she could have forgotten the sensation this kiss provided her with.

Suddenly, Joseph grabbed her arms and pushed her away from him. He stood up and turned away from her. He bounded into the woods never looking behind him.

Abby was confused. She didn't know what had just happened. It felt so good and he had thrown her away. Now she felt ashamed, exposed and embarrassed. She stood there looking after him and wondering what she had done wrong to upset him.

Twenty minutes later he still had not returned. She'd finished gathering their personal items. Not knowing what else to do she was sitting on a rock waiting for him to return. Half of her was afraid that he had left her there all alone. The other half of her reassured her to wait patiently for him and he would be back soon.

Without warning, Joseph appeared behind her leading the two horses properly saddled. Never speaking to each other they loaded their gear and mounted.

Breaking the silence, Joseph suddenly spoke firmly, "We have to make it to Saint Louis today. We have to ride hard and fast and won't be stopping!" Turning, he kicked his horse into a gallop. Bewildered by his sudden abrupt behavior and demand to make one day out of two days travel, Abby quickly followed suit.

Joseph was angry and ashamed of his actions. The very last thing he wanted to do was to take advantage of her. Too much had happened to her already. He didn't want to add to her confused state of mind. Doggedly he pushed their horses forward. He stayed in front of her and didn't look behind him to see if she was following. He refused to allow himself to think of her. He concentrated on the path in front of him and on keeping an eye in every direction to search for any danger they might be in.

Abby, watched his back. She had no idea what he was feeling. She only knew she had done something wrong. What it was she had no idea. She kept silent and allowed him to lead them to Saint Louis as fast as he could. She actually had trouble trying to keep up with his black stallion. The steed's shiny long black tail flew in the wind in front of her. Abby gave up thinking. She rode in complete silence concentrating hard on keeping up with Joseph.

Chapter Thirteen

Silas and Jeffrey arrived in Bowling Green, Kentucky. Descending the train they took a minute to absorb their surroundings. Small town, small train station, seems quiet, Silas observed as he made mental notes. Speaking to Jeffrey, "This place is probably a waste of our time. You go ahead and check with the station master. I'm just going to walk around a bit and stretch my legs. They get a lot of pain in em just sitting on those wooden seats all day." He motioned for Jeffrey to leave. Reaching into his vest pocket he withdrew a cheroot, lit it and took a long drag.

Jeffrey saluted him both with the intent of acquisition of his orders and mocking of Silas at the same time. He pivoted on his heels and headed straight for the station master's office as ordered. "Boy what does that guy do to earn a living?" he mumbled under his breath but loud enough for those near him to hear. "It's always, Jeffrey, do this! Or Jeffrey, do that! I didn't come along to be his errand boy! I'm a future politician for the state of Georgia and soon enough I intend to be his Boss as his state Governor!" He declared loudly to the townspeople he passed. He had been so embarrassed by Silas' constant put downs and orders to him in front of everyone aboard the train. Many of the passenger's actually had raised eyebrows as they listened to the older man berate the younger one constantly. To publicly declare his independence wasn't really intelligent but it certainly made him feel better for the moment. Silas had wandered into the nearest Hotel looking for a soft chair to sit in while he enjoyed his cigar and privy to Jeffrey's tirade.

Jeffrey was becoming extremely irritated with the whole situation. Silas always passed the menial tasks to him. So far they had received blank stares when they showed Abby's picture. No one had any news of her. Jeffrey was beyond ready to find Abby. He wanted her found yesterday, not tomorrow. Each day he became more fearful for her life. His chest ached nightly when he was alone with his thoughts. The only reason he stayed in Silas' company was his need to find Abby. He detested the old man, considered him to be a lazy bigot and he couldn't wait to get away from him.

His intelligence cautioned him against striking out on his own. Silas's Pinkerton experience could prove to be their best bet to find Abby. Therefore he stuck out his relationship with Silas, but that did not stop him from wanting to punch the odious man in the mouth and tell him a thing or two.

Walking into the station, memories of the day he knew he was in love with Abigail assailed him. After half-heartedly courting Elizabeth Whatley for nearly a year. Suddenly he met Abby and she became the focus of his life. Of course he knew her as Charles Anderson's little girl because they had walked the same streets to school for years. But since he was four years her senior, he'd never given her a second thought. After leaving town for four years to attend Yale University,

Abigail Anderson had grown up into the vivacious woman he was unable to ignore at last year's spring ball.

While flirting idly with Elizabeth Whatley he was having another enjoyable evening similar to all the other social events he usually enjoyed. Flirtatious Elizabeth was always good for his ego not to mention some extra unacceptable hugging and kissing, etc. Although he knew she expected him to offer her marriage, he had no intentions of doing so.

Elizabeth was beautiful, but he sensed cruelty in her. Maybe it was her beauty that kept him from feeling she could truly love only him. Or maybe it was that she appeared more interested in what he had to offer her financially rather than what she saw in just him. His family's wealth and political stature had made him the most desirable single male in Savannah.

Then Abby, escorted by her father, entered the ballroom. Jeffrey glanced in her direction, saw her flaming red locks, and bright green eyes. The room suddenly had been filled with a glow all around her and he knew at that moment he was now smitten for life!

Completely forgetting Elizabeth and her charms, he rudely left her standing staring at his retreating back as he hastened to confront Abby's father. Greeting Charles Anderson without taking his eyes off of Abby, he said, "Charles Anderson! My good man, how good it is to see you this evening," he began shaking Charles hand vigorously and without a pause, he continued, "may I have the pleasure of formally being introduced to your daughter, sir?"

Little Charles Anderson puffed his chest to twice its normal size. It was his daughter who had caught the eye of

Savannah's most eligible bachelor. Charles was pleased to see the dismayed looks on the mothers who had daughters of marriageable age.

But Jeffrey never heard Charles introduce his daughter. He'd already grabbed her hand and dragged her to the dance floor before her father could finish his formal introductions. Thereafter, he claimed all her dances and refused to allow anyone else to spend a single moment much less to allow any of the other male guests a chance to dance with her. Jeffrey smiled to himself remembering his beautiful Abby. Eleven months later he proposed and was elated with her acceptance. Charles demanded they wait until Abby was nineteen to marry thus their scheduled wedding was to have been this coming September.

But now, the wedding was on hold. The residents of Savannah held their breath waiting to hear if there was to be any wedding uniting the two lovers at all. Gossip spread freely regarding the delayed wedding. Most prayed Abby would be found safely and the wedding would come to pass as planned. But one family in particular was profusely against the wedding. Elizabeth Whatley and her mother were frantic with fear that Jeffrey would find Abby and all they had worked for would have been for naught.

"Excuse me sir, I wonder if you could help me?" Jeffrey tapped the station manager on the shoulder. "This woman is missing. I was hoping you may have seen her?" He feared another disappointment.

The station manager was busy with problems of his own. Glancing quickly at the watch, he automatically began to turn Jeffrey down and walk away. Suddenly he doubled back. Taking the watch from Jeffrey's hand, he looked at it closely. "Now, jes hold on dere jus a wee minute," he said. "Ya know, I do believe's I has seen this yere little gal. Gib me a minute to finish with dese passengers 'n' I'll be right with ya!"

Jeffrey's hopes soared sky high! The man's strange accent was music to his ears. Finally they had a lead! He was so impatient to learn what the station master knew that he followed him everywhere he went. He nearly tripped the poor man twice in his anxiety to hear news of Abby.

Jeffrey was still waiting when Silas came huffing and puffing into the train station ticket office. Finding Jeffrey he bellowed across the room to him. "Find out anything?" He called loudly across the waiting room. Fully expecting a negative reply, he was anxious to find some supper and a room for the night before re-boarding the train again early tomorrow morning.

He was surprised to see Jeffrey quickly wave to him to come quickly as he replied, "Yes sir, I think we've got something here!" Silas stopped his advancing walk in midair. "What'd you say boy?" Had he heard correctly, finally a lead? Well it was about time! He went to stand next to Jeffrey, who informed him that they were waiting for the station master to tell them what he knew. Impatiently they both waited hoping their search would soon come to a successful end.

"Yep thaa'd be heer!" The station manager declared finally free of his other responsibilities, he had turned to the two men and taken the picture and studied it carefully.

"You're, sure? You've seen this girl?" Questioned Silas assuming immediate control stepping quickly in front of Jeffrey blocking him from speaking directly to the station manager. He wasn't about to let Jeffrey take credit for finding Abby before he was able to settle the case himself.

"Oh yeaa, thaa'd be heer for sure I aam!" the station manager replied affirmatively.

"Well man, let's have it!" demanded Silas. "Tell us what you know."

"Where is she?" Jeffrey fairly yelled at the poor man. He pushed his way back in front of Silas. There was no way he was going to allow Silas to take credit for finding this important piece of news. He felt his knees nearly buckle beneath him as his heart leaped sky high!

"Wa…ll now ya'll jest hold yeer horses," the Station Manager slowly drawled. Tapping his index finger to the side of his head he paused deep in thought. "Now all I know is dis yeer is de gal dat waas taken from de train durin de robbery a few days ago, yep, twas near bout not quite at a week agoo." He calmly announced to the startled two men. Dismissing them he returned the picture to Jeffrey and advised them, "Yee'd best go to de Sheriff for de details of it all." Then he completely ignored them and returned his attention to his job.

Silas immediately turned and headed for the Sheriff's office.

Jeffrey, however, grabbed the station manager by the neck of his shirt and demanded, "What's that you say? Robbery? What robbery, Where's my Abby? Is she ok? You'd best tell me what you know, mister. Tell me right now or I'll…!"

"Put that man down you imbecile!" Silas yelled at him. If you want the details, you'd best high tail it to the sheriff's office with me. That's the only place we'll get the truthful facts anyway.

Stunned, Jeffrey looked at the red faced man he had hanging by the shirt collar high into the air. The station manager's bulging eyes were filled with fear as he attempted to breathe air into his constricted throat. His feet were barely touching the floor. Jeffrey realized he was practically choking him to death. Immediately Jeffrey dropped his hold on the man and began apologizing profusely. Then he ran to catch up with Silas.

The shaken station manager straightened his clothing. Regaining his composure, he mumbled, "Humph! These yeere passengers, 'r' a goin ta be ta end of me one of dese here days!" Shaking his head and fixing his tie, he resumed his work.

Jeffrey and Silas entered the Sheriff's office. No one was present. Jeffrey's heart sank. Silas began to look for clues. On top of the Sheriff's desk he found the missing poster of Abby. Silas began skim reading the handwritten notes the Sheriff had written all over it.

"Mister, you'd best be a puttin' them thar papers right back where you got em!" The unexpected voice came from the back room. The Sheriff's older deputy hastily entered the room. He grabbed the poster from Silas's hands. "This here is *official* business!" he boldly declared. "It tain't here fer no strangers to walk in off'n the street ta just up and read it!" Proudly he expressed his disdain for the unwelcome guests intruding on his domain.

"Excuse me sir, I do apologize," Silas quickly attempted to soothe the man and then went into an explanation of his actions. "It's just that this is the girl that I have been commissioned to find. Allow me to introduce myself. Silas Johnson, Investigator for Pinkerton Services at your service." He said bowing slightly and removing his hat respectfully. His voice intimated his authority. He handed the deputy his Pinkerton card as identification. If there was one thing he had learned in his profession, it never did any good to antagonize anyone in the Sheriff's department or any official investigative lawful authority if he both desired and needed their help in solving a case.

The Sheriff's deputy allowed his vision to slide quickly over Silas's card. Sniffing in indifference and showing his disdain for the Pinkerton agent, he indicated, "Wal then, ya can both jes set outside and wait fer the Sheriff! He oughta return here in a bit!" Directing them to the door, he quickly dismissed them both. They heard the door slam behind them and the bolting of the lock made it clear that they were not welcomed in this office. His deputy's unfriendly response was to prevent them from learning that he had never learned to read. He also was upset that someone was here to interfere with the Sheriff in the settling of his case.

Jeffrey and Silas looked at each other in dismay. The hope in Jeffrey's heart was plummeting fast. Silas pulled his eyebrows downward indicating his frustration at the added delay. They were both anxious for news of Abby and they wanted it right now.

Accepting that they had no choice but to wait, Silas decided to sit on the only chair in front of the Sheriff's office. The wicker chair creaked and the seat bulged under his weight. Settling himself comfortably, he lit another cheroot, took a drag and closed his eyes, resigned with the knowledge that they had no choice but to wait.

Jeffrey paced the boardwalk. Angry at having to wait he slammed his right fist into his left. "God, why are you stopping me from finding my Abby? Don't you realize the longer we take the more danger she's in?" he silently implored his creator His anger and attitude grew more and more out of control as time passed and the Sheriff failed to show.

Unknown to either of the two impatient men their efforts to find Abby were in competition. At the far end of Main Street of the very town they were in, across from the Hotel, Ralph and his four remaining crewmen sat drinking whiskey at one of the local saloons.

"Fifty grand!" Ralph lamented again, "right in our hands! And even more if'n I had my way! If I ever lay eyes on Larry Sheldon again, I swear he'll be a dead man!" His anger had not cooled any in losing his hostage due to the carelessness of his comrade in crime.

Tom downed his whiskey, "Come on Boss, it weren't Larry's fault. He didn't know someone was gonna help the gal ta git away." He attempted to point out the obvious, but Ralph wasn't having any of it.

"Why the hell are ya a side'n with that worthless jerk for?" He angrily replied. "Ya do know that the idiot just cost us more n fifty grand don't ya?"

"Well, sure I do boss, but, I figure it weren't none of hiz fault cuz he only did xactly what ya told im ta do."

"Well, maybe ya'd best go find him and join up with him then!" came Ralph's ugly reply. "One things for sure, I certainly don't need any more screw balls on my team!" he smarted. Turning to the bartender his booming voice ordered, "Bartender, git some more whiskey oer here! Doan nobody do their job right anymore?" again using his ugly attitude he sneered deliberately at the bartended fully intending to insult the innocent man.

Trigger happy Rick pulled his gun from his holster and spoke up. Waving the gun in the air he took the opportunity to gain favor with his boss, "Doan ya worry yur self none, boss, ya still got me on yur team!" he bragged.

"Put that stupid gun away, ya ignorant trigger happy foolish idiot!" ordered Ralph. Dismissing his loyal comrade in crime by turning his back on him, he continued muttering under his breath, "That's just what I'm afraid of! A bunch of stupid jerks and idiots! Yep! That's my crew all right! What ever happened to the days when ya could get a crew ya could count on?"

He grabbed the bottle of whiskey from the bartender who was refilling his glass causing the whiskey to spill all over the bar. "Just leave the whole damned bottle, would ya?" he nastily commanded the bartender as he threw his coins across the top of the polished mahogany bar.

He turned his back to walk away from the bartender who expressed a wave of relief as he was about ready to grab for his shotgun under the counter in case he needed to defend himself. The bartender had trained himself to keep out of his patron's business. He knew the importance of keeping a blind eye and a deaf ear to the rough outlaws that frequented his establishment. But this man's disgusting attitude was seriously trying his last nerve!

"Yes Sir! Your wish is my command!" Retorted the bartender under his breath as he grabbed a towel and began cleaning up the spilled whiskey. He picked up the coins that Ralph had thrown on the bar and the few coins that had missed the bar and hit the floor. "This is a group of bad men. This one in particular is the troublemaker type," he mentally noted. "All of em look ready to pull a gun and start shooting." Glancing downward he made sure his own shot gun was cocked and loaded. It lay in easy reach under the bar where he could quickly grab it if he needed. He learned a long time ago that a loaded gun ready to shoot was a good thing to have in this kind of work. "Too bad the sheriff's out with his posse searching for that girl or I'd send for him through the backway!" he kept his thoughts private from the gang's ears never realizing the men were speaking of the very girl the Sheriff was searching for.

The rest of the crew kept their mouths shut. They knew better than to rile Ralph up when he was this angry. Sides, they didn't have a clue what to do next. As always, they were waiting for instructions from their omniscient leader.

Ralph sat at the bar for another hour. Other than small talk, the rest of the crew sat quietly playing poker at a table in the back of the room. The bartender relaxed and began to ignore their presence. Finally, totally inebriated, Ralph said. "One of ya get yar backside over to the sheriff's office an snoop fer some clues. See if ya can find out anything. See if they found the girl or what?" he slurred his words as he slammed the empty whiskey bottle down on the table in front of himself.

His four crew members stared at Ralph in amazement. No one volunteered. They all had wanted posters on them. It was obviously suicidal for any of them to go to the sheriff's office. They didn't have the brains to run an operation but they certainly had enough brains to avoid the sheriff or his crew.

"Well, are ya all a bunch of chickens or something?" Ralph slurred, sneering at them.

Tom spoke up, "Boss that ain't really all that good of an idear. We could git thrown into jail ya know."

"So, do ya think I'd leave ya in jail?" sneered their drunken leader in return. "If'n I did that how would I find out what ya learned, ya idiot?"

The crew looked at each other questioningly. Ralph's statement did make some sense, however, none of them trusted Ralph to get them out of jail. Particularly because the declaration was made under his inebriated condition.

"Boss, why don't we just split up for a bit, and walk the streets. Ya know, talk to the manager at the train station, the general storekeeper, the barber? Maybe we can get some info from the local gossipers?" Jim suggested a more intelligent scenario, shuffling his deck of worn out marked cards.

Ralph didn't appreciate being outsmarted. To stay head man in the gang he knew he had to be firm and demanding with his answer. "Well, since ya'll 'r' such chickens...," he paused to shake his head disgustingly at them sneering at each one in turn, "guess we'll just take the chicken way out and do as Jim sez! Tis jes gonna be a whole lot slower is all!" he sneered again after delivering the drunken slurs to his men intended to ascertain that they all knew he was still the leader of their gang. "Meet back ere in a couple a hours!" he commanded them and then he threw the empty whiskey bottle at the bartender and sauntered drunkenly out the door.

He knew Jim's idea was more intelligent than his had been. He just couldn't stand his foreman being more intelligent than he. His damaged pride accelerated his anger.

Drunkenly striding down the street he came upon Mabel's Pleasure Palace. "Well now! Ain't this jes a fine place find my lonely lil self in front of!" he entered and coarsely yelled "Where the heck's Mabel? Can't ya'll see this here man's in need of some female compny?" he hiccupped and waited for Mabel to arrive and satisfy his needs.

The remaining outlooks looked to Jim for instructions. Jim downed his whiskey, stood up, hitched his pants, and said, "Ricky, check out the train station. Tom, don't ya need a haircut? Buck, head on over to the doctor's office, have him look at the wound to yur leg, find out if he's treated a gal with red hair."

"Yea, and what are ya doing?" Ricky asked snidely, resentful of taking orders from someone other than Ralph. Ralph's confidence in Jim irritated Ricky to the point of jealousy.

Jim turned and looked him in the eye. "I'm gonna shoot ya if ya don't get a move on it!" He pulled his gun and aimed it at Ricky's midsection.

Quickly, the crew grabbed their hats, downed their beer and whiskey, and scattered to do their assigned instructions.

Jim nodded his head and sat back down. "Bartender?" he called, "git me another one of them thar bottles of whiskey!" he commanded. Never could stand that Ricky guy, shiftless, mean spirited lazy jerk if n ya ask me!" he mumbled as he drank his drink.

Meanwhile, Ralph was enjoying himself immensely. Mabel had sent him on to Loretta. She was a buxom brunette, and was lathering her attentions all over him. Of course he had to pay a high price for her. He lazily relaxed and decided she was well worth the money. His temper eased and his injured pride healed as he listened to her words praising his male ego. An expert in her trade, she knew to keep quiet about his inebriated state that was disabling him from performing.

Finally she tired of playing with him. She told him his time was up unless he wanted to pay for a longer session with her. He laid back. Patting her bountiful behind. Lighting one of the cigars she kept in her room for just such an occasion Ralph asked her what the local gossip was. She told him several small things that were happening in town but nothing about the train robbery and Abby. Stretching, he stood and prepared to leave her. Throwing money on the bed beside her he said he had to go.

Pocketing her money she said, Sure thing sweetie, any time you want a woman, you just come see sweet little Loretta. I'll make ya feel better, I promise." she flirted, winking at him. Ralph slapped her hard on her rear and left heading back to the bar where he had left his crewmen to discern their findings.

Ricky didn't do any better at the train station. The robbery gossip had been laid to rest. Most folks in town lead busy lives, and the excitement faded quickly so most had already forgotten about it so he headed back to the bar empty handed of any news.

Buck winced as the Doctor treated his now festering wound. "Can't believe you been walking around with this one." Commented the Doctor as he stitched. "You leave it like this and you'd be a dead man in a week or so from the spreading of this infection."

Buck cringed as the Doc continued to dig in the wound to clean out the ugly yellow greenish site. "Doan suppose ya been treatin any other patients recently," he painfully croaked as he gripped the sides of the table he was lying on.

The Doc looked up at him questioningly, "Anyone in particular?" he asked as he pulled a piece of the bullet from deep inside Buck's left leg.

"Yea! A redheaded woman!" Buck nearly fainted from the pain as he answered the doctor. "She got kidnapped a week or so ago from the train." He blurted out without consideration of secrecy. He immediately grabbed the edge of the table and gripped it even tighter when the pain increased as the doc stuck a needle filled with penicillin into the area of his wounded leg. EEOOWWWW! Doc! Watch it that hurt's!" Buck exclaimed.

"Nope, haven't treated any red headed women lately," the doctor calmly replied. Mentally he decided to inform the sheriff about Buck. Something sounded a little fishy to him. "Well now," he finished bandaging Buck and instructed him on caring for his wound. "That'll be five dollars," the Doc patted Buck on his shoulder and led him to the door with his hand extended.

"Five dollars!" Buck was amazed! "Boy, you docs make a killin' off n a man in pain, don t cha? You docs don't need any banks to rob, ya just rob sick people." He insulted the Doctor. Mumbling to himself he continued, "Now I ain't got no more drinking money." But he paid the Doctor and left heading back towards the Saloon.

Tom got a real nice haircut at the barbers, but he also struck out in the information department. He paid the barber and headed to the Saloon also.

At the Saloon, the five men gathered around their whiskey, relating to each other what they had accomplished.

Jim blatantly lied to Ralph and claimed he'd been to the general store and the livery, but there was no news there either. Ralph would have shot Jim on the spot if he had known that the storekeeper and the livery hand were the only ones in town who could have described Joseph's description to them.

Deciding they had hit a dead end, the decision was made for them to continue traveling towards Saint Louis. They hoped to find Abby along the way since she was heading there on the train they sabotaged. It was decided that they would hit the trail again in the morning after they had some more whiskey and card playing. Besides, Ralph wanted to visit with Loretta again.

Finally the Sheriff returned to his office. Before he could tie up his horse to the hitching post he was instantly confronted by a very angry Jeffrey and an irritated Silas. Jeffrey bombarded the Sheriff with questions about Abby. Silas calmly walked up to Jeffrey and put his hand on him to silence him saying, "Good lord man, give the Sheriff here a minute or two to get himself organized." He hoped his attempt to calm Jeffrey would win them the support of the local law office. He had seen immediately that the Sheriff intended to ignore Jeffrey. "Forgive us my good man, but this young man is as impatient as a pig trying to get to the food scraps." Silas tried to win the sheriff's cooperation. To himself he wondered, "Why did I ever let him accompany me anyway? Oh yea, he fetches and carries pretty good, that's why!"

Calming down, Jeffrey bit the inside of his mouth as he gritted his teeth. He wanted to knock Silas down and would gladly have eaten the sheriff in order to get news about Abby. He glared at Silas, but obediently shut his mouth.

A half hour later they had the information they needed regarding the train robbery. They knew that Abby had been kidnapped and a posse had been formed to find her but had no luck in doing so. They were told about the man she'd been sitting next to on the train. However, the sheriff assured them the man had shown no interest in her and had declined to be a part of the posse. The Sheriff gave them a description of Joseph at Silas's insistence. They were dismayed to learn that the posse had tracked the kidnappers for only twelve or so miles before they lost the trail due to rain. The Sheriff also told them that he was telegraphing other towns for any information they might have. Other than that," he'd said, "my investigation is pretty much at a dead end. Hope you men have better luck than I did." He slapped them on the back and led them to the door.

Leaving the sheriff's office, Silas said, "Well, that didn't tell us much but at least we know she did head in this direction and that she has been kidnapped. Guess, I was right about her leaving home on her own accord. Darn' kept telling Charles that I didn't think she'd been kidnapped from Savannah. He ignored my warning him not to put out that reward poster. I just knew it was going to put Abby into additional danger and sure nuff that's just what it did!"

Jeffrey said nothing. Completely devastated beyond words, he couldn't think. His beautiful Abby was in the hands of six outlaws. Suddenly he felt he was going to be sick. "What kind of man would have just let any woman, much less one as beautiful as Abby, ride off in the company of outlaws and not attempt to protect her like that guy on the train anyway, who the heck was he? Did the sheriff call him Joseph somebody or other?" He asked Silas and to himself he questioned, "did she know him, or even worse was she traveling willingly with him and if so wherever did she meet him and when? Suspicious jealousy crowded his heart preventing him from thinking clearly. "My head hurts, so, what do we do next?" he rambled his jumbled thoughts to Silas.

"Don't rightly know just yet. Let's go book a room at the hotel, shake the traveling dust off of us, and then eat some dinner. That'll give me a chance to go over everything. Hopefully I can develop a plan of action for us to take from here." Silas suggested.

As there was nothing else he could do, Jeffrey nodded in agreement. Together they walked across the street and down a block to the hotel. Spending around thirty minutes freshening up they met up in the dining room of the establishment. Extremely hungry by now Silas ordered a steak dinner and devoured it quickly. However, visibly upset, Jeffrey said he couldn't eat anything but eventually he picked lightly at a salad.

After dinner, Jeffrey pressed Silas, "Well, what have you come up with?"

"Nothing at the moment," Silas admitted calmly, "the only thing I do know is that I have to put a stop to that reward poster. If we don't she could be in even greater danger than she is right now. I'll send a telegraph to Charles tomorrow and inform him of what we've learned today, and I'm going to insist that we pull the poster. He isn't going to like it, but surely after hearing what's happened he'll accept it's for the best."

"I have to agree with you." Jeffrey answered. "Gosh, I'm drawing blanks too. I haven't got a clue what to do next. Maybe we should take the same trail the posse did. Maybe we can find something they missed?" he suggested.

"Could be, but then it could be a waste of time too," Silas didn't relish the idea of putting his great girth on a horse and suffering through the up and downs of a horse's choppy gait. "It's late, we ought to get some rest and then maybe hit some of the local gossiping stations in town. Maybe we will hear some more regarding her intentions or whereabouts."

"I supposed I could use a soaking bath and a shave anyway," admitted Jeffrey ruefully rubbing his growing beard.

"Good idea, but remember to listen more than you talk," Silas warned him. You can actually harm her more if someone who knows something finds out that you are looking for her. Be totally discreet. Don't disclose any information about yourself or that you are searching for Abby. Don't show anyone her picture! You will only endanger her further. Remember, I can't stress it enough. Your job is to listen! Don't talk and don't ask questions! From now on we will confine our questions to the law." He instructed Jeffrey firmly.

Jeffrey agreed to do his best to learn what he could.

Silas said he was going to check back at the sheriff's office and then maybe at the general store along with a few other places. "Let's get some sleep for now. We can meet here in the morning over some breakfast and see what we can come up with before noon tomorrow. Then we will meet back here for lunch to discuss our findings. Hopefully we will know what direction to take by noon tomorrow."

Jeffrey agreed. In silence they finished their dinner. Jeffrey went in search of a barber and a worn out Silas turned in for the night.

Morning dawned bright but overly cool. It had rained during the night and a front had come through. Jeffrey and Silas wondered if Abby was sheltered from the weather or in danger from it. Jeffrey couldn't help feeling jealous. He wondered but didn't voice his concerns, if she was keeping warm in another man's arms. He knew the sheriff had told them the man on the train had left her to her own devices, but somehow, he couldn't believe it. His jealous nature was accelerated when he thought of Abby with anyone other than himself. In an angry mood, he and Silas attempted to eat breakfast. Jeffrey once again didn't have an appetite, but Silas encouraged him to eat hardy as they might not be able to enjoy a hot meal for a while. Jeffrey reluctantly tried to do as Silas suggested but his meal tasted like dried paper to him. He was anxious to hit the road in search of Abby and was irritated with Silas for taking his time. Eventually, Silas put down his fork onto his empty plate but then he asked for some more coffee.

Jeffrey's impatience hit the roof. Angrily he said he would wait for Silas outside. He got up and left the table and headed outdoors. "If I knew where to go or what to do, I'd leave that old man right here right now!" he mumbled under his breath. Taking the initiative, he went back inside and told Silas he was going to ask at the general store if anyone had any use full information for them.

Silas nodded his agreement but as soon as Jeffrey was out of sight, he decided to order himself some pie to eat with his coffee. "Kinda nice to let that youngster do all the work! He commented to himself. I'm getting too old for all this physical activity. I'll just let him do the leg work and I'll be the brains of this outfit!" he concluded to himself as he bit into the juicy cherry pie before him.

Ralph and his gang had saddled up and left town in the early dawn hours heading towards Saint Louis. They intended to take their time, in order to check some of the back roads as well as the main route to Saint Louis. "It might cost them a little time, but it also might turn the girl up again," Ralph had assured them.

It was fast becoming a contest as to who would find her first. Only neither team of men knew they were in competition with the other.

At noon, Jeffrey and Silas met for lunch to compare notes. A very excited Jeffery had found out that two different shady looking characters had been asking around town about the train wreck and in particular about the pretty girl that had been kidnapped. One of them had been foolish enough to let it out that he'd heard that the kidnappers no longer had her in their custody but that they were trying to find her again.

Jeffrey said the he had been at the barber's for his morning shave, when he had overheard the barber telling one of his customers about a stranger coming in for a haircut yesterday. The barber was saying, "Funny part about it is that the stranger told me that he had heard that the girl had been rescued by someone who had just two horses with him.

Silas didn't the sheriff say there were ten men in that Posse? If I remember right, the Sheriff didn't mention anyone else was searching for Abby? Did he?"

Silas was surprised by this information. "I went back to the sheriff's office and the local doctor was there. He mentioned that he had a patient yesterday who had a wound about a week old. Said the wound was really festered. The thing was the fellow had also asked him if he had treated a young red haired gal recently."

"It sounds like we may have something here. If you put what you heard and what I was told together it appears that someone did rescue Abby from the kidnappers. Then if the general store owner is correct about the story he told me of a young blond haired fellow with blue eyes buying supplies and food for what he had termed a little camping in the wilderness just a few hours after the train was wrecked and the kidnapping..., Well then?" he left the unfinished statement hanging in the air.

"Hey, that description of the man from the store is the same as this Joseph guy that the sheriff described to us." Jeffrey slammed his fist down on the table interrupting Silas and exclaimed, "I'll bet you that it is the same man who was on the train with Abby! They are both probably on their way to Saint Louis as we speak!"

"Suddenly, Jeffrey visibly paled. Did Abby willingly leave him for someone else? That couldn't be the case, besides, when could she have met anyone else? No other man was gone from Savannah who was in their social group. His serious jealousy began to set in again. Pulling his mental state together he said, "I don't know about you, but I'm taking the next train to Saint Louis." He announced.

Sounds like we need to get back on the train today and head to Saint Louis as fast as possible!"

Silas nodded in relief. He would much rather be riding on an uncomfortable train seat than on a bouncing horse. "Right! The train leaves at two this afternoon. We'd better hurry to pack our gear and be on it." Silas confirmed their plan of action. There was no way he was going to allow Jeffrey find Abby before he did. His job reputation depended on it!

Chapter Fourteen

Saint Louis was a bustling city. People were everywhere. Abby felt the city definitely seemed lacking in something, but she couldn't put her finger on it. Everyone was hurrying past each other without greetings between them other than an occasional slight nod. It seemed as though everyone was the "only" one in the city. They seemed to ignore the presence of anybody around them. The stores were extremely busy. People entered and exited the stores faster than Abby could count them. Wagons were being loaded with large volumes of supplies.

Wagons and horses filled the streets. Carriages were few. It seemed most people were either riding horses or guiding wagons pulled by huge teams of several horses down the deeply rutted muddy streets. Most of the wagons had funny round looking canopies made of white canvas stretched across the top over a rounded wood frame. One was being pulled by a team of two huge looking animals that she had never seen.

Seeing her puzzlement, Joseph explained to her that they were called Oxen. "That's a good sign, hopefully the wagon train is still in town," he added.

"Oh so this is what constitutes a wagon train." She silently surmised as she nodded her head acknowledging his explanations. Something was going on everywhere she looked. The noise was deafening. She felt a sense of abnormality and unease. Feeling nervous, she suddenly wanted to leave Saint Louis as quickly as possible. She missed the quiet she had enjoyed the last few days with Joseph traveling alone with him in the woods.

Searching her memory, Abby tried to ascertain what it was about this strange city that gave her such unease. A vision of a tree lined street with large ornately decorated homes flashed into her mind. She saw a street with people walking leisurely. The gentlemen were doffing their hats in greetings to others and beautifully dressed ladies were smiling beneath the shade of their parasols. Just as quickly the vision faded and try as she might, she couldn't recall it again. "Where did that come from?" She shook her head as the momentary vision blurred and in response to the sharp sudden pains she felt in her head, from concentrating so hard to recall it. Her head always hurt when she tried to remember things. To clear her head and ease the pain, she concentrated on the commotion around her. Here, everyone seemed coarser in their manner and in the clothing they wore than those people in her momentary vision. Some of these folks made her want to hug her reticule and personal items closer.

Filled with amazement and a little frightened, unconsciously she inched her horse closer to Joseph. He reached over to pat her hand. "It's ok. We shouldn't be in the city but a day or two," he reassured her.

They continued navigating through the heavy horse drawn carriages, covered wagons and horse traffic on the main road into the city. Joseph was steadily heading west to the far end of town away from the ferry they had just ridden to cross the great Mississippi River.

Abby had never seen so wide a river. The current was so fast she was certain that they were going to be washed downstream. The river traffic was extremely busy. She feared their ferry would collide with another boat. She saw a huge white boat that had wheels made of paddles that were three stories tall. The tremendously large wheels were churning through the muddy water making the boat go. It was fascinating to her. The name on the side said *The Mississippi Queen*. Abby loved the looks of it and wondered what it would be like to be a passenger on it.

Joseph called it a showboat. She didn't know what that meant. He said it was filled with heavy gambling, card playing, and the like. She looked confused with his explanation. It was as if she should have known what he was referring to but the simple truth was she had no idea what he meant. But the words gambling and card playing upset her for a reason she was unable to determine.

Joseph knew that if there were any wagon trains left in town they would be set up on the western edge of the city. He hoped they had not missed the wagon trains. He knew they took to the trail early in the spring season because it was a very long, difficult three month long trek to California. He had heard of the many difficulties the wagon train folk encountered. Originally, he'd planned to follow one of the trains but not to join up with it. He liked being free to come and go as he pleased. But now that Abby was with him, he knew he was going to need to join up and outfit a wagon for her. He was praying they wouldn't be too late to join up with one because then, he reasoned, they may need to travel hard all alone and hoped they caught up with one. He was determined to make it to California before he missed success in the great gold rush.

"Oh well, no matter what, we'll need a lot of supplies anyway." He unconsciously nodded his head to confirm his thoughts as sound planning. He had taken it for granted that Abby was going with him. There was no way he was staying in Saint Louis when there was gold to be found in California, and there was no way he was leaving Abby behind. He'd decided that he would simply hogtie her and put her in the wagon and take her with him anyway if she declined to accompany him. Considering his irrational thoughts, he decided it was past time to ask Abby what her plans were. Gathering his courage, he cleared his throat and broached the sensitive subject.

"Lydia, now that we are in St. Louis, what are your plans?" slyly he looked at her to see her reaction. He hadn't confided to her that he knew she was suffering from amnesia.

Abby was stunned. His question took her completely off guard. She had not thought about her predicament any further than their arrival in Saint Louis. Not knowing her identity had kept her from any final decisions.

"Uh….What do you mean?" She stalled for time hoping her question would prompt him into telling her something about herself.

"Well, you never really said what your plans are," Joseph prompted. He was hoping she would remember on her own. He did not want her to guess he knew of her amnesia. When they were still on the train, she'd mentioned her plan was to go west seeking a teaching position.

"Well..., truthfully, I..." she hem-hawed as they slowly made their way down Main Street on their horses, I, umm..., where was it you told me that you were going?"

Quickly she tried to avert the conversation back to him, and therefore to buy herself some more time to determine what she was going to do. At the moment she knew only that she was petrified. This bustling yet primitive city scared her to death. So did the thought of finding herself on her own here all alone.

She really didn't know what she would do if the handsome stranger was no longer with her. In a matter of speaking, he had become her only family. It seemed to her that they had been and would be together forever. Now for the first time, she realized he may no longer wish for her to accompany him. Maybe he was ready to get rid of her! That thought magnified her fears. She couldn't think clearly to search for an answer to give to him.

At least he hadn't dragged her to the sheriff's office to collect on his reward for finding her. That is if there really was a reward. She was not only confused at not knowing who she was but also she did not feel that she was anyone who would be important enough to have a reward posted for her. Now she was really concerned as to who this man was and why he had taken such excellent care of her? It was all too much! What would she do if she found herself suddenly all alone? That thought made her heart lurch upside down with fear. She was glad they hadn't had time to eat yet. She felt that she may lose the contents of her stomach at any moment.

Of course she didn't know a single soul in Saint Louis. That is as far as she knew she didn't. What if she was from here? "No, that couldn't be, this place feels too alien to me!" She acknowledged silently and prayed that she was correct.

Joseph watched her carefully, he could sense the fear in her so he casually replied, "Yea, I'm going west to Californy to try my luck at a gold stake. I hear gold's aplenty way out there. Told you I want to find my share," he offered hoping to jumpstart her memory.

She was trying to deal with the realization that this wonderful man who had taken such good care of her was obviously not her husband. "Well then who is he?" She wondered. He obviously had no idea what her plans were any more than she did. Therefore, he couldn't be a relative or anyone else she knew either. Where had she met him and why would he have risked his own life to rescue her? "What ever shall I do? It is far past the time to make this decision."

Speaking without thinking she blurted, "Well, reckon I'm heading west also. Maybe I can try to find a teaching position." To herself she asked, "Now where did that come from, sounds like a good idea though. Maybe he'll be around to protect me if we end up on the same wagon train," she hoped. The one thing she did know with certainty is that she wanted as far away from this strange city as fast as she could arrange it and she definitely was reluctant to let the handsome stranger out of her life. She felt that she would surely die on her own if he wasn't there to help her get through all this unexpected drama.

"Surely with all the folks heading west they are in need of a good teacher. What do you think?" She looked to him for reassurance.

Joseph's heart flip flopped. He had been so worried and now she made it all easy for him! He dropped his question.

"Would you mind if I escort you while we are on the wagon train?" For a split second he feared she would deny him.

She immediately turned to stare at him openly. Quickly he continued. "Uh, that is," he stumbled, "I don't mean to be suggesting anything harmful or disgraceful to you, you understand, it's just that I would like to make sure you are safe while you travel west. It can be very dangerous on these wagon trains what with all the wildlife, Indians, and other dangers…," he trailed off hoping to advise her to be concerned for her own safety but not to scare her too badly at the same time.

"Oh! Would you mind? I mean, that is…," she stammered unable to say her thoughts thinking she was being overly provocative, "well, I'm trying to say that I would appreciate that very much!" She rushed to reply and felt total relief that she had found the courage to accept his protective care. "I have to admit I haven't any idea what to do or where to go. You will be so helpful to me if you will continue to accompany me. I feel that I can trust you. I mean…, I…, well, you haven't hurt me or anything, is all I meant?" She stumbled, embarrassed and blushing profusely at her quick acceptance of his offer to accompany her. More strongly she continued, "After all, if you had intended to do me harm I feel you would have already done so. You've certainly had the opportunity over the past few days. That is…," She turned her overly red face away as the vision of sleeping in his arms and his passionate kiss engulfed her recent memory.

"Now Miss Lydia? Surely you know that I never had and never would have any intent to harm you?" Joseph adamantly reassured her. He decided to help her memory a little. "You know on the train when we met, that I promised you that I would watch over you and that's just what I have been doing. This may not be the time or the place, what with us riding horses down a busy thoroughfare, an all, but I want you to know, that there is something about you that just makes me…, well…, that is…," it was his turn to stammer for words, "I have come to care for you very much." He declared, "You have my word. I will protect you to the best of my ability." He let go of his reigns with one of his hands and reached over to hold her hand as he sincerely assured her from his heart.

She had the grace to blush. "Thank you Joseph, I truly am relieved to know that I can count on your help." She answered him. She was careful not to speak from her heart. She didn't know if she belonged to someone else. Silently, she prayed, I hope I am free, because I'm very much falling in love with this kind man who's done so much for me." Internally she was petrified. What would happen to her if Joseph did find out that she was married or obligated to someone else. Would he fight for her? Or would he leave her to whomever it was she couldn't remember? Worse, would he turn her over to the law and walk out of her life? She didn't think she could go on if he did that.

Looking at her from the corner of his eye, he could see the distraction on her face and the fear in her eyes. "Why won't she confide in me and tell me about her amnesia?" He wondered. "No matter, she must have a reason. As soon as I get a chance to get away, I'm going to do some snooping around and find out what I can. Reckon the sheriff's office would be a good place to start." He confirmed his private thoughts with a slight nod of his head. "Trouble with that is what will I do if I find out she belongs to someone else?" His heart caught in his chest. *My life would be so empty without her. I think I'd go stir crazy if she belonged to another man! Oh well, all the more reason I need to find out about her, I guess. Before it's too late and I kidnap her for myself."* He ascertained.

They reined their horses in at the end of the street. Dismounting, they tied them to a hitching post in front of Dan's Western Supply Depot. "Lydia, why don't you go inside and cool off a bit. You can look for the supplies we will need on the trip. I'm going to search out a used covered wagon and secure us a team. After that, I'll be back to load up and pay for the supplies you gather. Got it? Don't worry everything's going to be fine!" He reassured her and smiled to himself thinking *"Oh Yea! Everything's going to be more than fine now!"*

She nodded her head at him. Removing the hat he had lent to her she walked inside the store.

"Morning Miss! Warming up out there a ready?" The store clerk attempted to small talk with her as he noticed her flushed appearance from traveling.

She was extremely exhausted. They had ridden until late afternoon yesterday. Around six, Joseph stopped them only long enough to rest the horses briefly and for them to eat a bite and take care of personal needs. He'd told her not to make camp as he felt they should continue on to St. Louis, riding through the night.

Again, she was surprised at his suggestion to travel straight through without rest. "Why did he want to travel at night," she wondered? "Had he seen someone following them?" The look of panic had shown on her face as she had nodded her acknowledgement. Then she voiced her questioned to him and asked him if he had seen someone following them?

Rather than tell her the truth, he mumbled as he returned his rifle to his saddle strap, "Something like that." His comment put enough fear into her that she didn't question him again. Instead she hurriedly packed their food and gear and mounted to leave looking around her in fear.

Joseph saw her look of fear. He hated to give her false worry, but he knew it was for the best. He wouldn't be able to control himself if they spent another night in each other's arms like the previous night and he knew it! Turning his back to her he mounted quickly, and took off at a gallop. It never occurred to her that he was uneasy with the thought of spending an additional night alone with her in woods.

They'd ridden all night. The trip was much slower going during the long night hours. The moon was full and provided plenty of light for them to navigate with. The remainder of the trip was tiring but uneventful. Eventually she let go of her fears as Joseph did not seem to be overly worried.

Early this morning they'd arrived in the city known as the Gateway to the West! Also known as the up and coming great city of Saint Louis, in the territory known as Missouri.

"Yes, it's warming up quickly," she attempted to give the store clerk a quick, but evasive answer. She began looking around her at all the different goods the store offered.

"Could I help you find something?" The clerk asked her.

"Looking around her in confusion she had no idea what to select for their trip. She looked at the clerk in relief and said, "Yes, thank you, we are joining a wagon train to California, could you please advise me on the appropriate stock that we will need to take with us on the wagon train?" Timidly, she allowed him to help her.

"Sure thing Miss? Be right happy to oblige ya," he said leading her over to the far side of the store. Barrels of flour, lard, canned goods, cooking utensils, quilts, and even a feather mattress to fit in the bottom of the wagon, were among the items he suggested to her. She said, "Gather it up and my husband...," she stumbled and blushed pink knowing she openly lied to the clerk, "will be here to pay for it shortly."

Meanwhile Joseph had found his way to the Sheriff's office. He asked the sheriff if he had any news of a red-haired girl that had been listed as missing.

Hmm? Let me see, the Sheriff answered him thinking. There was a poster came through the other day regarding a girl that was missing. Said she had red hair I believe. Listed her name as Abigail Anderson. If I recall correctly. Sound like the girl you are looking for? He asked Joseph.

"No, the girl I need information on is named Lydia Creosota." He totally forgot that she was most likely travelling under an assumed name.

The sheriff shook his head. "Nope, can't say as that name has surfaced anywhere."

Thanking him for his time, Joseph shook his hand and then asked, "Should anything come up regarding the name of Lydia Creosota, could you be kind enough to get word to me? I should be in town until tomorrow morning. I'll be with the wagon train area heading out of town to California." He made certain that the Sheriff would know where to find him.

"Sure thing," said the sheriff absentmindedly. He had plenty of things on his mind right now. He certainly didn't have time to worry about someone he had no knowledge of.

"I'll send my deputy down to the wagon train, if I should happen to hear anything." He replied absentmindedly.

"Thanks!" Joseph called over his shoulder as he rushed from the office. Secretly he was relieved. Maybe she was just a girl who had no family left as she had told him on the train. Short of time, he hurried out of the Sheriff's office and walked past the wanted posters without looking.

If he had looked he would have seen the two men ripping Abby's poster off of the wall. The big one was angrily saying. "Dad gummit! I asked for these posters to be pulled. Can't get anyone to do anything right. The huge man mumbled as he crumpled the paper and threw it in the trash. He and the second man turned to the Sheriff to ask if he knew anything about the girl whose portrait they showed him from inside the younger man's pocket watch?"

"What you got here?" Joseph asked Abby as he entered the store.

Both the clerk and Abby spoke in unison to tell him what they had selected. Laughing at each other, Abby backed away and let Joseph and the clerk go over the supplies they had gathered. She walked around the store looking at the wares, etc., for sale. Walking to a mannequin in the window she fingered the pretty cream colored calico dress on the mannequin. "Too fancy for a day of work on the farm, but just right for a woman to wear to a party or a church social in the west," she thought to herself. Times must be a lot harder in the west she supposed. She had fancier gowns in her traveling bag. But this one was obviously more practical for her new life than those she had brought with her. Again she wondered why she had such fancy clothing in the valise the handsome stranger had given to her. She wished she had the courage to ask him his name, but that would give her amnesia away and she was still too scared to do that.

She looked at the dress longingly but decided it would not be wise to spend her dwindling stash of cash on it. She did not remember that she had additional cash hidden in the hem of her skirt. She fully intended to split the bill with Joseph for the wagon, horses and supplies he purchased when they were together privately again.

Joseph watched her pick the skirt of the dress up and run her hand across the pretty smooth cream colored sun flowered print. It was trimmed with a green ribbon sash. He longed to see her in the dress. The green was the same bright color as her eyes. Turning his attention back to the store clerk, he added some further instructions on items they would need. Then he paid for the supplies and called Abby to return to him.

"Lydia, I think we have everything we need in here. Let's go to the livery across the street and bring the wagon I found back here to be loaded." He took her arm and guided her from the store into the street. There is something we need to discuss before we will be allowed to join the train."

He was reluctant to tell her the news he had been told regarding their traveling together.

Alarmed, Abby followed him to the livery. As they crossed the street, he explained to her that he had found a wagon train heading west in the morning. They were to leave at seven. "But, my dear, we have one problem," he told her hesitantly.

"Ok, so what's the problem, do we have time to fix it?" she asked him pointedly.

"Well, I certainly hope so," he stalled. "He didn't quite know how to tell her the difficult news. "The train master has a rule," he began and then just dove in, "He refuses to allow a single man and woman to travel together as friends or even as relatives. As a couple, we have to be married to travel together!" He looked down at her to gage her reaction.

She stopped in the middle of the street staring at him her mouth gaping open. "But… bu… b,…?" she sputtered.

Quickly, before she could be seriously hurt by the transgressing traffic, he pulled her to safety on the other side of the street. He interrupted her, "I know, we aren't married," he said.

"Well, what do we do?" She asked him incredulously. One thing at least has been clarified, the handsome man in front of her was certainly not her husband. Abby's face blushed at the embarrassing predicament they were in.

"Before you say anything, hear me out," he said, "I've given it some research," taking her arm he urged her to continue to the Livery stable. "I have a couple of options for you to consider. Of course the first one is that we can get married. She whirled on him. But before she could speak he continued. Or we can do option two."

"And just what would option two be?" She was sarcastic. His last statement assured her that marrying her was something he didn't want.

Reminding herself that she didn't really know if she was married, she calmed down somewhat and let him speak to explain his option two to her.

"Now don't be getting upset or anything," he warned her, "I just felt that maybe you or maybe both of us might not be ready to get married, so I asked around for some other solutions."

"I see." She let him know that he had her full but insulted attention.

"I was talking to this fellow who told me he had a similar situation when he was traveling out west with a female cousin, said he had the same problem. He told me that he knew of a, well…, a not so honest preacher. He said the preacher agreed to do a ceremony for them in front of the Wagon Master and to give him a fictitious license. He said it worked for them. He and his female cousin had a fake ceremony, signed the license in front of the train master and went out west together." He didn't tell her that it cost the man a fat $50.00 bill for him to retrieve the license later and have it destroyed before it was ever filed in the courts.

Mortified and embarrassed, Abby felt like a loose woman. At the same time, she didn't know if she was already married. So this seemed like a plausible solution to their problem. "But will we sleep in the same wagon?" She asked him timidly, her face beet red she turned away hoping he wouldn't see her embarrassment.

It was Joseph's turn to be embarrassed. "Well, I figure we can make it look like we do, only I can slip out of the wagon when no one's looking. And I can volunteer extra often for the watch." He offered a solution to their predicament.

She nodded her head slowly in agreement. A lot calmer, she realized it was best for her to choose to remain unmarried to the handsome stranger as she might already be married anyway. So, dismissing her shame, she said quietly, yet with conviction, "I think option two sounds good then. Where can we find this preacher?"

Joseph relaxed. He knew he wanted to marry her, but knowing of her amnesia he had feared that she would balk. He was also aware that she didn't know that he had figured out her dilemma. So he had done his detective work and was pleased to hear that his solution satisfied her.

"Good!" he replied "I need you to go back to the store and ask the clerk for the extra package I purchased. It's something I thought you might need. Ask the clerk if there is somewhere you can freshen yourself up a bit and use what's in the package. I'll be back to get you in an hour or so. You okay?" He asked her wiping a tear from her face. He was completely upset to have to humiliate her with a false marriage but he didn't know what else to do.

He would have married her on the spot in order to avoid humiliating her any further. Her green eyes were filling with tears that she was unable to hold back. He knew she was suffering from amnesia and that she didn't know if she was married or if she was free to marry him. He could only imagine the thoughts going through her mind. How he wished he could just fix all her problems for her but he knew that she had to handle some of them in her own timing.

Saying nothing she nodded and returned to the store. Joseph watched her go. Then he left to find the dishonest preacher.

Seven PM that same evening, Abby stood beside Joseph in front of the dishonest preacher with Randolph Bushing, the Wagon Train Master, and Mr. and Mrs Cleotus Broling, passengers on the wagon train who agreed to witness the wedding.

"Do you Joseph Alan Jordan," take this woman, Lydia Creosota, to be your lawfully wedded wife?" Lydia began visibly shaking at the preacher's request to Joseph.

"I do." Joseph looked at Abby. Her small hands were trembling in his.

"Do you little lady, I mean, Miss Lydia Creosota, take this man, Joseph Alan Jordan to be your lawfully wedded husband?" He waited patiently for Abby to comply.

Abby looked like she would like to faint. "Joseph Alan Jordan!" So that was his name, unconsciously she tried but failed to remember having heard his name before. The failure in her memory caused her to assume a momentary trance. Joseph waited anxiously for her answer. Looking down at her he was overcome by how beautiful she looked wearing the same pretty dress she had admired in the store window earlier that morning. Never in her wildest dreams did she think she would be wearing the same dress to her own illegal wedding that very evening!

"What am I doing?" The question flitted through her worried mind.

"You're securing your very life!" Her subconscious screamed back at her. "Now get a grip, find some courage and do what you have to do!" Her conscious took charge of her emotions.

"Well, do you?" The preacher asked her again. Everyone waited on baited breath for her answer.

Joseph gently placed his finger beneath her chin and raised her head upwards to look into her eyes. He nodded his head slightly to assure her there was nothing to fear.

Seeing the honesty and sincerity in his eyes. The trance holding her motionless broke. She listened to a shy voice say the words "I do." Then she realized it had been her voice who spoke.

Joseph visibly relaxed exhaling a sigh of relief and the witnesses all nodded their heads accepting her answer to be in the affirmative and of her own choice.

"Well then, I pronounce you man and wife. You may kiss your bride sir." The dishonest clergyman finalized their ill-legal wedding. He was noticeably relieved as well. For a moment or so he feared that Abby was going to publicize his deceptive practice.

Joseph maintained his intense stare into Abby's eyes. Ever so slowly he bent over and claimed her trembling lips in a chaste kiss.

Mr. Broling guffawed, he chided Joseph, "Come on now boy! You kin do better 'n' that can't cha?" Daring Joseph to claim his new bride in a passionate manner, he patted his wife's behind indicating that their marriage was healthy and surviving well.

Margaret admonished him, "Cleotus, mind yourself! "This young couple knows what's best for them." She hugged Abby and took hold of her hands. "Congratulations, dear. If my Cleotus, or I, can be of any help to you, just let us know. Our wagon is right in front of yours."

Cleotus shook hands with Joseph who winked at him intimating his intention to do better later when he had his new wife alone. Cleotus let the subject matter die and congratulated the young couple properly.

The wagon master placed a hand on Joseph's shoulder and nodded to Abby. He congratulated them as he led them and their witnesses to the preacher to sign and witness the license. Then he cautioned them, "Don't be honeymooning all night, we will be leaving at daylight. We're already two days behind." Then he took his leave to handle other business.

The Broling's walked off hand in hand to their wagon. They were a much older couple completely comfortable in each other's company. "They are so in love." Margaret commented to her husband. "You can see the love they share for each other in their eyes when they said their "*I do's*.""

"Oh, Maggie darling, you are still my sentimental little love bird. Her husband affectionately hugged her close as they took their leave and returned to their wagon to finish preparations for the beginning of tomorrow's long journey.

Timidly Abby dared to look at Joseph. "What now," her green eyes questioned him timidly?

Joseph guided her towards their wagon suggesting his plans, "Let's have some supper and then you can get ready for bed. As soon as I can I'll slip off, I have an errand I have to do, but then I'll be sleeping close by you in the woods. Don't worry, I'll be back in the wagon by five am so no one is the wiser. Just don't let me scare you if I manage to awaken you."

An hour later he made his escape. Being in her presence was torturing his soul. It was next to impossible for him to keep his hands off of her. All he wanted to do was to pick her up in his arms, carry her into the wagon and make passionate love to her and completely make her his wife in every sense.

"Well, what did I expect?" she chastised herself. Of course, she knew he couldn't stay with her. Extreme loneliness hit Abby as she watched him make his escape. "Oh, you knew exactly what you were thinking," her subconscious responded. "You wanted to lie in his arms and feel his body against yours again!" Quickly she retorted to her own lustful thoughts. Yes! That's exactly what I want but I cannot have," she ruefully admitted. Resigned to her farce of a marriage, she entered the wagon and prepared for sleep.

Morning dawned bright with a light chill in the air. Abby awoke with a start. Gazing around the wagon, she remembered her fake wedding the night before. And today she was to begin a journey to California. Quietly she called to Joseph.

"Morning!" He stuck his cheerful head between the canvases on the back of the wagon. "Sleep well beautiful?" He asked her.

Instantly he regretted his actions. She was sitting, stretching her arms upward as she yawned in an attempt to wake herself up. Unawares that she presented him a provocative picture just sitting there on the feather mattress on the floor of the wagon with the quilt they purchased from the dry goods draped across her lap, her bare feet extending outside of the quilt, her dainty toes pointed upward. She was not aware that her long red unbound hair draped her shoulders and pointed to the now drooping front of her half opened night dress. His body jolted at the sight of her rosy cleavage.

Clearing his throat, he immediately retreated. "That was a sight I do not need to see!" He chastised himself. To her he said. "Ooops…, umm…, so Sorry! Uh…, the Coffee's on the fire, we need to eat!" he stammered badly, "We've only got thirty minutes before we're off to Californy!" His shock cleared as he allowed the excitement of their journey that hopefully held riches for the both of them to overtake his feelings of embarrassment and need.

Abby jumped up grabbing the neckline of her nightdress buttoning it quickly. Exiting the wagon she blushed and tried to apologize to Joseph. "I'm sorry, I didn't realize the buttons…," she trailed off as he immediately turned his back to her and busied himself with the camp fire.

"No problem." He rushed to interrupt her with his strangled reply.

"Really Joseph, please believe me, I didn't mean to upset you?" Her vanity was overshadowed by her fear of having embarrassed him especially after all he was doing for her.

"Here, have some coffee," he offered her a cup of the fresh smelling inviting brew. Then he reached for his gun and headed toward the woods.

"I'll be back in a minute," he called over his shoulder to her as he took long fast strides to leave her presence.

"Oh dear, now I've upset him. He must think that I am a harlot! I'll have to do better than this with this illegal marriage." She instructed herself. "From now on I shall sleep in my daytime clothes," She decided as she began packing their things but her heart felt so empty she wanted to sit down and cry.

Joseph returned in time to grab a biscuit and down some coffee before she packed up the coffee pot. He tied their two horses to the back of the huge worn out wagon and helped her to climb onto the buckboard cautioning her to be careful of splinters. He had taken her multi colored quilt and made a makeshift pad to provide a minor cushion for them to sit on. Climbing up to sit beside her, he intended to show her how to drive the wagon. Once he felt she could comfortably handle the team, he would ride alongside on his stallion. For now the stallion along with her mare were tied to the back of the wagon and would follow them along the trail. Her close proximity to him was becoming more and more torturous for his body. It took all his will power to keep from grabbing her into his arms to make her fully and completely his.

"Damned this illegal marriage anyway!" He mumbled to himself as they began their journey together.

He handed her the reins of the team. She looked at him in alarm. He said, "Sorry honey, but you have to drive this team ninety percent of the way. So begin learning right now."

The wagon master gave his call to start the journey. Following Joseph's instructions, Abby flicked the reins and the team began to move. She listened intently as he instructed her on how to release the brakes and gently he helped her with the reins until she got the feel of them. Suddenly the excitement of the journey overcame him.

"Finally! Califony here we come!" He half sung the comment and smiled widely at her. His happiness was contagious and she could feel her own heart flip flopping in and out with joy and anticipation of their new lives to come!

"That's right! Californy here we come!" she smiled and relief flooded her because at least she now had a destination to her very confusing life.

Neither of them were aware that two groups of desperate men were on their trail. The nearest group was Ralph with his four remaining outlaws. To make up for lost time, they'd headed straight to Saint Louis on horseback. Ralph intended to surprise Joseph and Abby at the Ferry landing where they would have to cross the wide Mississippi river to enter St. Louis. He was counting on the girl's lack of experience trekking through the woods, to slow them down.

Ralph wasted five additional days in Saint Louis. He and his crew stood shifts, watching for Abby and Joseph to arrive at the ferry landing.

Unbeknownst to Ralph, Abby and Joseph had arrived a full day earlier than he and his crew. Thanks to Joseph becoming nervous at the idea of sleeping in the woods with her in his arms he had unwittingly saved Abby again. Finally five days later, Ralph decided he had incorrectly judged their victims date of arrival to the bustling gateway to the west. Ordering his crew to mount up, they headed west hot on the trail of the last wagon train out.

The other group was Silas and Jeffrey. They never knew that Joseph was the man they were searching for when they were in the Sheriff's office in St. Louis. They wasted another full week searching for clues of Abby in Saint Louis. That's when they found the store clerk who had helped Abby and Joseph to gather their supplies for the trip. The clerk informed them that he had seen the girl in the picture. She'd been there about a week earlier. He remembered that he thought she and her husband were heading out of town on the wagon train destined to California he informed them.

To Silas's dismay, they bought horses, gathered supplies and headed after the wagon train. They were slower finding their way.

It didn't help that Jeffrey had become completely agitated. His temper was now barely controlled. Hearing Joseph being called Abby's husband had sent his jealousy level to extreme limits. In his active mind he vividly imagined how he intended to tear this guy traveling with his Abby apart limb by limb as soon as he found them. He refused to believe that they could actually be married! The very idea that his beautiful Abigail Anderson, was now riding along with the many "backwards" people of the wagon train was impossible for him to accept.

"Why ever would Abby want to go to an uncivilized place such as this California must be?" according to the sparse information he had gathered about the land in question. Now, he found himself directing some of his anger in her direction. It was her fault that he was forced to make this overly long and very arduous journey just to find her. He considered giving her up to her so called husband and returning home alone. But then he realized the embarrassment he would be privy to when Savannah society gossiped that he was a man who couldn't keep his woman so what could he possibly do for them as the Governor elect of their state. No! He decided he would bring her home any way he could and he would do whatever he needed to accomplish his task.

It all boiled down to which group was going to get to California first? It would take three months to journey over the Midwestern plains and crossing of the Rocky Mountains before the wagon train or any of them would arrive in California. The only good news was that Abigail Anderson was certain to be at the end of the line unless they became lucky enough to find her somewhere along the way!

A month and a half later the wagon train had made exceptionally good time. They had reached the foothills of the Rockies. The trip remained clear of accidents, Indian attacks, etc. Although the uncomfortable daily heat was mounting quickly, the favorable weather helped them to expedite their journey.

To Abby, each day was filled with tons of drudgery work. It became the same routine for them every day. Her tender white hands were now calloused and blistered. Daily, she drove the team, when she was too tired to drive, she rode her mare or walked and let Joseph drive for a while. Each evening they stopped to camp and she cooked their meal and cleaned their mess.

Whenever they came upon a creek or river bed, they stopped to refill their water containers. Some managed a bath and washed their clothing draping it on makeshift clothesline, or over trees, brush, etc. Each morning she cooked again, cleaned again, packed everything up into the wagon again and drove the team even further away from civilization into the unknown wilderness before them.

Occasionally someone became ill. One lady gave birth to a newborn son. This delayed their travel by nearly a day. However everyone was grateful for the rest. They took the time to recheck on supplies, clean their wagons or some just took time to catch up on much needed sleep.

A few of the passenger's pulled out musical instruments at night and Abby enjoyed the folk lore and western songs they sang. The sounds were alien but enjoyable to her. She found herself quickly responding to the fun foot stomping's and hand clapping of the country toons and to the sadness of the ballads she had never heard before.

On a couple of nights they played music for dancing and merry making. Abby loved the music, but for some reason, Joseph always made his escape from her just when they had the opportunity to spend a little time enjoying each other's company. Abby still didn't understand his disappearance was to protect her. She yearned deeply for him to spend time with her. But her hopes were always dashed when he would quickly dismiss her and head into the nearby woods. She began to feel that she was worthless and maybe she had made a mistake to fall in love with him. The good thing from his disappearances was that he was able to provide a stock load of game meat for them to eat. Abby even shared some of it with the Brolin's who were becoming fast friends to her.

Occasionally someone's wagon would become stuck in a muddy rut or a wheel needed repair or a horse needed to be shod. Until now, the terrain had been mostly level. They'd circled west through a growing settlement called Kansas City being built along the Missouri River in an attempt to avoid the Ozark Mountain ranges of Western Missouri and Oklahoma. Steadily, they plodded along, fording rivers in shallow spots and crossing fields of tall windblown grass.

They'd been lucky to have begun their travel in the early spring. It would be late summer before they would arrive in California. This was good. It allowed them to avoid snow and icy weather that would have made it impossible for them to ford the Rocky Mountains. The wagon master had made this trip many times. He knew the exact route to take them mostly over flat and level plains making it easier on the teams of horses to pull the heavily laden wagons. Most importantly he knew where bodies of water were to be found.

Thank heavens the Indian civilizations around them remained peaceful during their journey. It was dangerous business crossing the great territories of North Central America. Even though the news was that the Indian threat was not serious, the wagon master kept a sharp eye out as they travelled and double the watches at night. He wanted to be prepared for any emergency as he knew the importance in expecting the unexpected.

The weary travelers walked most of the way on foot to ease the weight of the wagons carrying their few belongings. Only one person rode at a time in most of the wagons and that of course was the driver of the teams. Slowly they lumbered across the great divide.

Their hopes and dreams for a better life gave the passengers courage to withstand the drudgery of the journey. Many of them daydreamed of finding gold in California. The hope of never having to suffer financial stress ever again was a great motivator to keep them going. The Gold fever of 1849 made the passengers endure what they would have otherwise not survived, without the goal of gold waiting for them at the end of their long arduous journeys.

Some of the passengers gave up on their dreams. Due to sickness or just plain unable to continue under the extreme exhaustion the fast trip was putting on them, they pulled out of the train along the way. They stayed where they were and created new settlements across the Midwest for generations to come. The Wagon Master was not deterred. He was determined to push them hard in order to make good time while the weather remained cooperative.

With the train now approximately half its original size, they arrived in southern Colorado territory near the foot hills of the majestic snow covered peaks called the great Rocky Mountains. They had just left the small but growing settlement of Denver. There they had replenished their supplies, saw the local physician if needed and just took a day to unwind before they began the arduous mountain climb that would, unbeknownst to them, tax every little bit of strength they had left.

Chapter Fifteen

Charles Anderson lay awake for another fitful night. It was August 8, 1949. It was also Abby's nineteenth birthday. He did not wish to leave the sanctuary of his bed and face her birthday without her. Yesterday he had heard again from Silas and Geoffrey. The telegraph said they were still looking for Abby but the trail appeared to have gone cold. They knew that she was on a wagon train heading west. There were so many trains that headed west from Saint Louis that they were having to catch up to each one and search for her. None of the trains had an Abigail Anderson on the passenger lists.

Silas intimated to Charles that Abby was most likely traveling on an assumed name. He refrained from telling Charles that there was a possibility that she had married someone other than Jeffrey. This was making their job more difficult. They had already checked with three wagon trains they had managed to catch up with, but to no avail. The best tool they had to find her was the picture of Abby in Jeff's pocket watch. At every train they ran into they showed her picture and left disappointed in their response.

They searched for other trains taking different routes. But it was time consuming. Each time they had to backtrack and find a new trail that had turned off to a different route. They were becoming very discouraged. No one had any knowledge or had seen a girl who matched the portrait that Jeffrey carried in his watchcase.

That both of them had little experience traveling on horseback across the wilderness did not help at all. They were both fatigued and short tempered with one another. Together they learned to survive in the wild. Silas had traveled west before but never farther than to Saint Louis. Jeffrey was a novice with only the training he received as a kid on camping trips from his father's occasional hunting excursions.

Charles wired them back and begged them not to give up on the search. He promised Silas a huge bonus if he would only bring his daughter back to him. Silas wired back that a bonus would not be necessary. The wires were sent in hopes of reaching their intended destination. As much as possible Silas left telegraph messages at the different settlements or army posts they encountered.

Receiving answers from Charles was difficult, sometimes they caught up with them but most of the time they arrived after the two men were back on the trail and they never received them. Silas wired that he fully intended to keep looking for her. They knew she was alive. They just had to find her. He reminded Charles that he had never failed on a Pinkerton assignment yet and he didn't intend to fail this time either. But he was beginning to doubt himself as this case was turning into the longest and hardest case he had ever been assigned to.

For Charles, life had become pure agony. Each day he went to bed later and later and failed to find sleep. In the beginning he had begun each morning with hope that today he might hear something. By midafternoon his stomach would clench and he'd acknowledge another day filled with total disappointment. He plodded along and kept to his normal routine. From home to the office, to home, to bed, and yet again to the office, to home, to bed, and so on and so on. The joy of life had left him.

He dreaded the daily encounters he had with his friends and business relationships wherein he politely and patiently had to repeatedly inform them that there was still no news of Abby. He had become a shell of a man. His already thin body was looking emaciated. If it wasn't for old Trey's insistence, he wouldn't have risen from his bed each morning. But Old Trey tried to convince him daily that he needed to be in good health for the day Miss Abby came home. Charles tried to comply, but was failing miserably.

He was so consumed with the guilt he felt from hiding the actual circumstances surrounding Abby's birth from her. He continually chastised himself for not realizing how upset she must have been. He'd been so encumbered with his own grief that he totally failed to notice her strange behavior on the morning she'd taken her overly quiet leave of him from his home office. He took full responsibility for her decision to leave. His guilt was slowly but surely sucking the life from his body and soul.

Today, he forced himself to rise from his bed. He dressed and headed down stairs to the dining room. The house felt so strange without Abby. Old Trey and his wife,

Pelly moped around barely doing their assigned duties. The house felt overwhelmed, filled with an aboding depression.

Charles entered the dining room this morning the same as any other and listened to Pelly's normal daily greeting to him. Only now it was delivered in a monotone instead of the bright cherry greeting he was accustomed to receiving from her.

"Morning Masta Charles. Does ya thinks we's gonna hear sumpin today bout our Abby Chile?" She asked, however this morning she added, "Dis be her birfday an I surely wud like to tell cook to bake her a birfday cake." Sadly she was making a poor effort to converse with her employer and friend. She felt it was really a waste of effort, but she didn't know what else to do.

He gave her the same quiet reply. The comment meant to be encouraging but delivered only despondence every day in response to her inquiries,

"God only knows, Pelly. God only knows." He let the words die in the air. Usually the conversation would stop here, but today his heart felt that it had broken all over again as he added, "It would be nice to have cook make her a cake, if she were here to enjoy it…," his voice trailed off, but since she is not…," a deafening silence permeated the room around him.

The clinking of the silver spoon in the sugar bowl sounded deafening in the still silence. Charles, replaced his fork by his plate and sat still and quiet waiting for the clock to tell him it was time to make his daily trek to work again.

Eventually, Old Pelly quit fussing with the china and made an attempt to converse again. "Yas sur I'se unerstands, I'll jes go tell de cook not to bother wif making de cake."

Pelly rambled on glad to make her excuse to quickly exit the gloomy room carrying his uneaten breakfast dishes with her again as she had every morning since Abby's impromptu departure.

The depression in the house had sunk to unhealthy measures. In Abby's room, Pelly had put the remnants of the wedding dress in a box in the closet. She couldn't bear to throw them out. She felt to discard the torn dress would declare that Abby would never return. The sight of the torn strips of lace and satin set her off to moaning and crying each time she picked up another piece. Pelly blamed herself for Abby's departure.

"I shoulda been dere for dat baby!" She was heard to condemn herself time and again. Pelly had gone to the butcher's the morning that Abby had left. However, she blamed herself because she had instructed everyone to "let the chile sleep," upon her return home again with the days dinner in her shopping basket.

Old Trey also blamed himself for Abby's disappearance. He said, I'se shouldn't ta left the front entry darrs un-atented?" He would lament right alongside of Pelly. At night they tried to comfort each other. But neither was able to find relief or comfort while Abby remained missing. Their guilt was too strong. Eventually their own relationship began to feel strained. As the empty days wore on they adopted an air of silence between them.

Today on Abby's nineteenth birthday, Mrs. Harrison sat with her best friend, Johanna in the Harrison's parlor yet again with her weekly guests. Also in attendance for tea was Jeffrey's mother, Elenora Browning, with her daughter

Bernadette, and Jewel Whatley with her daughter Elizabeth. They were conversing about the various upcoming social events for Savannah.

"Oh my dear, it doesn't appear that there is going to be a wedding after all, does it?" Johanna turned the subject to the expected joyful union of Abby and Jeffrey. Currently referred to as the "wedding disaster of the century."

"Well, let's not jump to any conclusions," Mrs. Harrison intoned nodding her head in sympathy in the direction of Elenora intimating that her friend should ask for any news the sad mother might have of the missing young adults.

Johanna acknowledged she understood her hostess's message, and continued with, "Well, how can there be a wedding without the bride to be?" She asked deliberately directing her question in the direction of Elenora's bowed head.

Everyone in the room was hoping against hope that the latter woman would volunteer some news regarding her son and his future bride's whereabouts. Most of the occupants in the room prayed for positive news. Two of them, however, waited on baited breath for the confirmation of any disastrous news that might dash their hopes of stopping the still tentatively scheduled wedding ceremony.

Of course the two women did their very best to pretend that they also wished to hear something positive regarding the two missing adults. In the interest of being politically correct, the remainder of the women tolerated their falsifications. Everyone knew by now the role the two women had played in destroying the wedding. There just wasn't proof enough yet to totally dismiss them from the social gatherings and blackball them completely from Savannah society. Until the proof was presented without any question, the two women's financial status kept their social status intact.

Elenora Browning tensed. This was indeed a sore subject that she did not wish to discuss yet again. "We pray each and every day for the safe return of Abby and Jeffrey, Johanna," she quietly replied with the same answer she had provided each weekly session among her friends.

Jewel Watson immediately jumped at her chance to find out what the current wedding plans were now that the bride and the groom were both missing. At this stage no one knew what was going to happen. Jewel was determined that the wedding should fall through. She still held high hopes for her daughter Elizabeth, to become Jeffrey's wife. She was very upset and thoroughly dismayed that plans were still in progress for the wedding between Jeffrey and Abby even after all she and Elizabeth had done to destroy any future marriage between them.

"Surely, you are not still planning the wedding, are you?" she rudely fished for information regarding Abby and Jeffrey's future plans. Immediately realizing how cruelly her inquiry had been delivered, she continued in an attempt to soften her tone, by adding "My dear, dear Elanora, I feel your pain."

Some of the women immediately covered their mouth with their opened fans, and hid their laughter at the woman's disgusting attempt to cover her bad behavior.

Without thinking, Elizabeth blurted, "My goodness, I just don't see how our poor dear, dear Jeffrey can possibly still want to marry a girl who cared so little for him as to just up and run out on him!" She stated vehemently in her overly famous southern drawl. "Why I would neva, absolutely neva have left our darling Jeffrey in such a shameful mannar! She declared, "Why, unlike Abby," the tone of her voice changed dramatically at the mention of the despised girl's name indicating her deep dislike for Abby, however she instantly returned to her condescending overly sweet southern voice continuing her sentence with, "I would never have disgraced him. I would have stood right by his side for life!" Fanning herself a little too vigorously, she nodded her affirmation of faithfulness directly to Elenora whom she had high hopes of one day calling her "mother." Her innocent expression was comical. All of the women in the room new of her flirtatious nature. Some of the women attempted to hide their humor behind their own fans once again.

The Browning women were not swayed. They both knew the stories that were circulating regarding Elizabeth's many trysts with eligible bachelors in the various rose gardens of their friends each time a social gathering was held. Everyone knew that Jim Tucker was Elizabeth's current conquest.

"Poor Jim Tucker!" The other women in the room were thinking to themselves. But only Bernadette had the courage to voice the thought out loud.

"Yes! Yes! Why our dearest Elizabeth," she mocked the girl by copying the tone of Elizabeth's overly sweet voice, "we are all aware of how deeply your loyalty to my dear, dear brother is?" She sarcastically sneered in reply. The very thought of Elizabeth in her brother's arms sickened her. She held her own affections for Jim Tucker and so far, Elizabeth's very existence was making a match between herself and Jim an impossibility.

"Why, I'm just certain that I don't quite know what you mean? Elizabeth countered. That she knew she had been insulted was obvious to all.

"Why Elizabeth, my dear friend, of course I meant absolutely nothing a'tall, my dear. Why absolutely nothing a'tall!" Bernadette mockingly reiterated, and continuing in the same sickeningly sweet dialect emphasizing her "at tall!" fully intending to embarrass Elizabeth. `

Bernadette's jealousy over Jim Tucker needed assuaging. "It's just that we have all been privy to your loyalty to our dear Jim Tucker!" She looked directly into Elizabeth's astonished eyes declaring her challenge. It was clear that she was more than happy to take on any challenge involving Elizabeth Whatley, whom she now considered as an arch enemy.

Gasps of astonishment were heard throughout the room. Mrs. Harrison harrumphed! "Girls, let us pray right here and now for the safe return of Abby and Jeffrey shall we?" She extended her hands to Johanna on her right and Elizabeth on her left. But Elizabeth wasn't having anything to do with praying for Abby. She pulled out of Mrs. Harrisons grasp. She jumped up from her seat and faced Andrea directly rudely touching her finger on the tip of Andrea's nose.

"How dare you insult me little Miss Bernadette Browning! Because if you think you are any match to I, then allow me to remind you of just how much you have been fawning all over *my very own*, dear Jim Tucker yourself!" She countered being certain that she claimed Jim's affections belonged entirely to her in order to ascertain to Bernadette that she didn't have a chance with him. She continued declaring her innocence to the other women with, "and the mere fact that *Jim has attained my very own affections is* proof that I have no reason to wish our dear, dear Abigail Anderson and her dear Jeffrey any ill will!" she exclaimed vehemently at her adversary. The latter statement was directed to the remainder of the room as a poor attempt to remove any blame placed on her for the current dilemma involving the two young lovers.

Bernadette flushed. She had managed thus far to prevent anyone, especially her mother from noticing her current infatuation with Jim Tucker. She looked at her mother only to see Elenora's jaw drop to her chest, her huge eyes stared questioningly directly at Bernadette. Her hand remained in midair, holding her no longer moving fan.

"You don't know what you are talking about Elizabeth! You and your mother are both just upset that you can't have Jeffrey and all his money and social prestige that a marriage to my brother could give you!" Bernadette retorted angrily using her own voice. Her face was red as a turnip.

"Oh my!" Both Harriet Harrison and Johanna Johnson said in unison.

"You little witch!" escaped from Jewel Whatley's mouth before she could stop herself. All eyes in the room pivoted from Bernadette to Jewel. The ladies jaws dropped to their chest in their surprise at Jewels blatant accusation directed at Andrea delivered publicly before them all.

Bernadette and her mother both rose at the same time dropping their tea cups onto the highly polished floor, shattering the expensive and irreplaceable patterned china. "We all know that what Bernadette has spoken is the truth. But Bernadette, I..." Elenora began but was rudely interrupted by Jewell.

"Why that is a flagrant outright lie!" Jewel screamed in Elenora's face.

"Mama, are you going to let her call me a witch?" Bernadette innocently asked turning her attention and anger onto her mother's shoulders. Her own tears were now running fast down her rosy red cheeks. Then she continued, "Mama, are you just going to stand there and allow that horrible woman to disgracefully insult us like we are nobody at all?"

Bernadette was horrified at being called such a name but she had immediately forgotten that she had asked for it all by herself in her jealousy regarding her infatuation for Jim Tucker.

The exact same request was made by Elizabeth to her own mother at the very same moment! Elizabeth was being held back by her mother before she struck Bernadette physically in her anger at having her sins being pointed out publicly before all the ton.

"Ladies, please Ladies, calm down now. I'm sure no one meant to be harmful to the other," Harriet attempted to soothe everyone's flaring tempers even though she knew it would be fruitless for her to try.

"Come Elizabeth," Jewell ignored her hostess attempts to calm them, "we are leaving! We certainly do not need to be or intend to remain in company of such cruel vicious women!" Here she accused the entire room of having insulted them. Now they all stood up and an argument began that no one was ever able to tell anyone else who said what to whom! The room was in chaos once again! Jewel had risen from her chair and ignoring all the women now yelling at her as well as each other she summoned Harriet's maid herself without bidding for assistance from her hostess for her hat and gloves.

Elizabeth indignantly arose upon seeing her mother call for her personal items, and immediately called across the room to the maid to bring her personal items as well. "You are absolutely right! Mama!" she declared and turned her nose up to all the other guests letting them know that she thought she was way above them, and continued, "Why I just absolutely cannot get out of this room and away from these horrible unkind women quick enough." Turning her back to everyone, she took her time pulling on her gloves and fixing here hat to be certain that everyone had time to respond to her outrageous insult upon them all.

Bernadette refused to give up. In her extreme anger, she was determined to tell the truth about Elizabeth's indiscretions. "We all know you are just using poor Jim! Where are your intentions to be loyal to him?" she declared vehemently. The room silenced and on baited breath all eyes pivoted to Elizabeth as they awaited her answer to this horrific accusation of infidelity. They all had wondered the same thing at one time or another.

"Bernadette! That is absolutely enough!" her horrified mother declared. "In fact, I do believe we should also be leaving. My dear Harriet, would you be so kind as to ring for your butler and see that our carriage is brought around front, please?" She also rose and began collecting her personal items about her as she prepared to leave.

"But Mamma?" Bernadette ignored her mother. "Everyone knows it's true! We all know how she is just using my poor, poor Jim Tucker." She burst into tears again and sat down holding her head in her hands. "And as for Jim, why he can't see two feet in front of him!" If he could he would see just how stupid Elizabeth is making him look!"

She was now crying her heart out over her lost opportunity of finding love from Jim Tucker.

"Bernadette, I said that would be enough!" Elenora demanded her daughter to cease. "Stand up! Dry your tears and get a hold of yourself right now!" She commanded, "Get your things!" turning to her hostess, she continued apologetically, "Harriet dear I am so sorry!" she flung her attention onto her hostess, and then left the room as fast as possible heading for the main doors of the mansion. The women who remained turned their unfavorable attention upon Jewell and her daughter.

"Please collect your belongings, we must go!" Jewell ordered her daughter Elizabeth. "We no longer feel welcomed here! She announced to the room full of women. Heading for the door, she was stopped short by Elizabeth's next comment,

"So Mama, I see that you are going to allow her to continue to deface me!" turning on her only ally, she accused her mother angrily.

"Oh shut up Elizabeth Whatley! You've done enough damage with your outrageous and flirtatious behaviors!" her mother threw back at her. She pushed Johanna out of her way and hurried to be able to push Elenora and Bernadette out of her way as well. She intended to be the first to leave the Harrison's Mansion. In some twisted manner she felt that maybe being the first to leave the premises would allow her to retain an ounce of her pride!

The other three women in attendance other than Harriet and her friend Johanna, haughtily exited the room swishing their skirts around each other but refusing to speak to one another. "Well! I never!" was muttered by most of them to no one in particular as they also gathered their personal effects. Their anger had become contagious and everyone was mad at everyone only no one really knew exactly why.

Suddenly the Parlor was empty and ominously quiet again. Stunned, Harriet looked at Johanna with her eyes wide! Johanna's mouth hung open? Simultaneously they began laughing their heads off.

"It just makes my day to see them tear into each other" Johanna choked through her laughter and swiped at the tears rolling down her chubby heavily rouged cheeks. "They are like a pack of wild wolves! Ha Ha Ha!" her laughing becoming uncontrollable.

"Absolutely my dear friend!" Harriet guffawed as she joined in with Johanna's raucous laughter. "I know what you mean!" She spluttered the words, while holding her stomach to relieve the painful abdominal cramps created by her boisterous laughter. But she couldn't escape the vision previously presented and her laughter simply continued even heavier than before. Both of the woman were enjoying this daily meeting far too much!

"Oh Johanna, I just love having them all over here every Wednesday! They entertain us so well!" Harriet continued her loud laughter patting her friend on the back.

Johanna winked at her friend in the midst of her laughter. "They are like putty in our hands! Harriet dear! Just putty in our hands!" she repeated. Their laughter continued but slowed as they retired to the private parlor to do their afternoon's needlepoint.

"Hmmm…, I wonder what delights we will have in store for us next week," Harriet again burst into laughter and Johanna nearly choked on her own laughter in return. They spent quite an enjoyable afternoon discussing the many possibilities next week might present to them!

Chapter Sixteen

Raising her soiled apron, faded from the intense sun, Abby wiped her sweaty dripping face. She attempted to push away the escaping dripping wet tendrils of red hair that escaped the confines of her bonnet. It was terribly hot and humid. There was no wind. The air was suffocating. Dust was billowing from under the horse's hooves, choking her. The train was enveloped in dust with no wind to blow it away. The trail was mostly rocky with almost no greenery and only a few scrubby bushes protruded here and there among the high rock walls rising all around her. The wagon continuously bounced over larger pieces of rock or suddenly the wheels would drop into a rut. Her buttocks hurt! She'd never been this sore in her life. She thought it was bad when she'd been kidnapped, but this was pure torture. She implored the heavens for rain or at least a breeze, but there were no clouds in the blue expanse of sky above her.

She was using her quilt as a cushion beneath her. Unfortunately the damage was already done. Each bounce of the wagon brought her out of the seat and back down again with a thump upon the buckboard. "Oh my where in the world is this Californy?" She grumbled.

Joseph had ridden ahead to speak with the wagon Master and his scout. She was alone on the buckboard trying to control the tired team. The terrain they were trying to cross was dusty with sand and gravel and broken larger pieces of rock that had rolled down the mountain sides. And even worse, it was becoming even more rocky and very dangerous as they advanced further upwards on the mountainous trail.

All around her the great Rocky Mountains loomed. They were absolutely beautiful! Some were still snowcapped. But she was in too much pain to care about their beauty. All she wanted was to be in Californy already and she prayed it would be cooler there or at least there would be cleaner air for her to breathe. She had wrapped the ties of her bonnet across her nose and mouth to help with some of the dust, but her eyes were stinging from the constant specks of dirt flying in all directions around her.

"Whoa boy!" She called to her horse as the wagon hit another huge rock. She bounced again then released an overloud "Ouch! That one really hurt!" Inspecting her bottom, while still holding the reign's in control, she ruefully pulled a six inch splinter from her buttocks area that had penetrated her skirt and pierced her tender sore skin. "Oh, please Lord, give me a break!" Her eyes rolled heavenward in exasperation!

Joseph kept a close eye out during the whole trip for the kidnappers as well as the normal dangers of the trail. The wagon master had no knowledge of the kidnappers. He was not looking for them. He was unaware that Abby and Joseph might bring additional danger to the wagon train and his other passengers. Joseph happened to ride up in time to hear the wagon master conversing with five male strangers. He stopped his horse short and listened to the men indicate they were also heading to California. Joseph had never seen the kidnappers up close. They had knocked him unconscious before he had any idea that trouble was brewing. "He didn't remember their voices either. The men were asking the wagon master for permission to ride along with the wagon train.

Alarmed, Joseph experienced a feeling of extreme unease. He slowly backed his horse away and watched the men converse from a distance. He knew that six men had robbed the train and kidnapped Abby. This group was only five men. But that didn't rest his unease.

Ralph was saying. "We are just tired of riding alone. Thought ya'll wouldn't mind if we kept company with ya for a spell."

Randolph Bushing, the wagon master, was reluctant to have the men join with the train. He didn't like the looks of them and he took his responsibility for his passenger's safety very serious.

"Well, I like to keep careful attention to the welfare of my passengers on this train. I have a lot of responsibility to them. I'm committed to keep my word to each and every one of them, that I will provide safe travel and unfortunately, that means that I'm not comfortable with adding strangers around them. So I would really rather you fellas just keep pushing on by yourselves. "Sides, we are short on supplies and we aren't looking for any trouble, either." He denied Ralph's request and sent them a verbal warning. At the same time he moved his hand near his hip in preparation to draw his six shooter if necessary.

Ralph noticed the movement of Randolph's hands. "No problem," he was quick to assure the train master.

"We'll just head on down the trail ahead of ya then. Maybe we can scout it out for ya." He offered and nodded his head intimating his understanding and intent not to protest the wagon master's decision. Then he motioned for his men to turn and leave. As they moved on he called back in a gesture of friendship, he offered to hang back and warn the train if they saw anything that they thought might endanger the wagon train as they proceeded up the trail.

Ralph was fuming mad! He'd seen a red haired woman driving one of the wagons on this train who resembled Abby from a distance as they'd ridden up. He figured they would just invite themselves in for dinner and nab her after dark from her wagon. Now he would need to twerk his plan a bit!

Ralph hadn't counted on the wagon master taking his job so seriously. The outlaws rode hard and fast for a few miles further on the wagon train's rocky trail. Rounding a bend they were out of sight, hidden well by the mountains between them on the overly curving rocky path. Quickly Ralph reigned to a stop and ordered his men to move off the trail and hide in the boulders alongside of it.

"We'll wait right ere! When the train comes around this bend we'll ambush em." He laid out his newly formulated plan. "Jim, Tom, ya two rush the lead wagons and Ricky and Buck, ya'll rush the last wagons. Take hostages for leverage. It's best to grab women and children. The more hostages we have the better the wagon master will trade em for one red headed woman." He laughed disgustingly in anticipation and pride at how easy his new plan was going to succeed!

"Oh! And Ricky, try not to kill anyone unless I give the command!" He ordered sneeringly! "Remember, we want the ransom money and that might be hard to collect if we have a bounty on our heads as well. You've already killed one man and hopefully way out here no one will know about it." He reprimanded his trigger happy man as if he were a two year old. They were also suffering from the excessive heat and he was in a very foul mood!

The crew nodded in agreement. He instructed Jim and Tom to ride further down the road to be in position to attack the train's front wagons with him, simultaneously and informed Ricky and Buck that they were to close off the rear so no one, especially the red headed woman could escape.

Ralph looked around him. "Yep this is the best place to make our stand. No need to wait till dark. These here boulders will hide us until we are ready to rush them. And these rocks will provide barriers for us from any stray bullets." Nodding his head at assessments to his crew he motioned for them to take their places. They all began raising their kerchiefs over their faces to hide their identity. Once they were in position, they waited impatiently for the slower moving wagon train to come around the bend.

Abby's wagon was the eighth wagon from the end of the train. There were about twenty seven remaining wagons from the original fifty that left Saint Louis. Totally oblivious to the danger awaiting her, she kept plodding along.

"My arms are so tired! She complained to herself. Joseph had come by on his horse and warned her to keep a sharp eye out. He didn't tell her of the men because he feared she would panic. He just said that the countryside they were about to enter was full of snakes and wildlife and who knows what else, he had added evasively. He did say that if anything happened she should immediately hide under the mattress in the wagon and wait for him to come help her. She nodded and plodded on wondering how hiding under a mattress would keep a rattler from biting her?

After he left she began to think about him. She no longer understood Joseph. Since their farce of a wedding he had avoided her company as much as he could. He didn't speak to her any more than necessary during meal times. She didn't understand his change in behavior. She decided he was mad at her for agreeing to enter into this pretended marriage with him. Maybe he was feeling trapped or something. She couldn't put her finger on it.

As for her, she constantly thought about him. Where was he? What was he doing? Was he thinking about her? What could she make him for dinner? How could she entice him to spend more time with her? With these thoughts she amused herself during the long tired lonely days. She knew she was head over heels in love with him. His deliberate avoidance of her bewildered her and hurt her feelings deeply. She wanted to feel his kiss again. She didn't know if she had ever been kissed before, but it didn't matter because she felt certain that no one ever could have kissed her like he had. She certainly couldn't forget Joseph's kiss. It haunted her day and night.

There were times that she caught him watching her as she did her menial tasks. She would smile invitingly at him in an attempt to engage his company. He always nodded at her and then he would quickly walk away.

Each night after they shared a quick dinner, he'd leave and talk with the other men until she retired. Then he would return to their wagon and pretend he was about to retire with her for the night. When he knew no one was paying attention to them, he'd slip away into the surrounding woods and she wouldn't see him again until day break.

The only times he stayed with her was when he knew it was his time to stand guard. On those nights he would sit uncomfortably at the rear of the wagon after he thought she was sleeping. He would doze a little while he waited for the knock on the wagon informing him it was his turn at watch.

The first time he did this she tried to engage him in conversation. He got up and left the wagon barely acknowledging her. Since then she pretended to be asleep on those nights. She preferred him close to her even if he refused to be company to her.

Entirely frustrated, she told herself that she should have stayed in Saint Louis. "What am I going to Californy for if I am to be alone by myself after we arrive," she'd grumble.

Most of the nights she was alone. On these nights she would think about him and wish he was lying beside her. She wanted to be in his arms. Her body ached to touch Joseph and to be touched by him. Then she would chastise herself for thinking such thoughts. When sleep would come, it was fitful and she would awaken several times during the night listening for him. Occasionally her exhaustion from the long arduous trip allowed her to fall into a deep night's sleep. But upon awakening her first thoughts returned to Joseph immediately.

"Yes, I'm in love with him!" she acknowledged to herself. "What am I to do?" Her sub conscious always replied the same. "There is nothing you can do, you don't know who you are or even if you're already married." Then her conscious mind would begin again to repeat the same prayer she prayed nightly. "Please Lord, help me remember!" Her prayer always felt that it was being left unanswered. Her faith was being questioned. She decided that God was punishing her for something really bad that she must have done, but whatever it was she couldn't remember. She lived in daily misery. She knew she'd blocked her past life from her conscious mind. But she didn't know why? How could she remember why she had chosen to block it if she couldn't remember anything about it? "What a horrible predicament I am in," she would become angry at herself and turn over willing sleep and oblivion to come take control of her and give her mind relief from the many chastising thoughts that were beginning to drive her insane!

Suddenly Abby reigned in her team! The horses balked but came to an abrupt stop kicking up dust and pawing at the trail they whinnied loudly in surprise. The wagon in front of her had stopped without warning. She waited but they didn't move forward. Finally she climbed down and went to see what the problem was. Two riders on horse flew past her without looking at her. They looked familiar to her.

Suddenly she knew exactly who they were! Pivoting on her heels she quickly ran to hide herself in the rocks surrounding the wagon trail.

Joseph and the train master were being held at gunpoint by Ralph at the front of the train. The remaining male passengers of the train were standing in a group quietly waiting. They had been warned not to make a move or Joseph or the train master or both of them would be harmed. Not knowing what to do as long as Joseph and Ronald had a gun pointed on them they stood still and listened to the orders of the ringleader.

"Drop yur guns and move away from these two and they might not get hurt!" Ralph sneered his orders to the passengers. "We're looking for one passenger in particular. When we find her we'll be on our way and no one will be hurt." He demanded their immediate cooperation as he informed them of his purpose for holding up the train.

The men conversed among themselves quietly. Deciding one passenger was better than their families or themselves being hurt they dropped their guns and moved to the side.

Ralph called out, "Jim, Tom, You get em?"

"Yea boss, got two good uns! Right here!" Jim came around the corner of the first wagon with the Carters seven year old twin daughters hanging under his arms. Kicking and flailing their arms, they were screaming in fear! "Put us down mister! Please put us down!" they begged him.

Tom followed dragging two fighting teenage girls who were trying to bite his hands in order to break his hold on them.

The passengers became alarmed! Some of them reached for their guns.

"Drop em and git back where ya war and these ere kids won't get hurt none!" Ordered Ralph pointing his gun in their direction.

"But then, On the other hand, I got no problem wif shootin em all in the head right now if'n any of you give me any trouble!" he warned them nastily. The uneasy men fell back. Ricky and Buck had corralled the remaining passengers to the front of the train.

As their train master, Randolph Bushing felt it was his duty to speak up. "Well here's everyone. Which one do you want?"

Ralph aimed his gun directly on him, "Jes hold on to yere horses. We'll let ya know when we're ready to. Just do as I say and keep your two cents to yarself!" He poked his gun hard into Randolph's ribs. The train master doubled over and his knees buckled. Ralph smacked him in the face using his six shooter. Randolph lost his balance and fell to his knees.

Ralph ordered him to get back up. Randolph struggled to regain his stance and comply.

Joseph kept quiet and prayed that Abby had found a safer place to hide than under the mattress. He searched the crowd and didn't see her among them. His hopes were high that she escaped in time.

Disturbed Randolph remained silent. He was trying hard to figure a way to get to his derringer hidden in the waistband of his jeans. He always carried the small gun just for this kind of emergency. With his hand in the air and a gun pointed on him he decided he'd better wait for a better opportunity to reach for it. "Besides it's a one shot only instrument." He reasoned.

Abby sneaked behind some rocks. She was trembling in fear. Although she was hiding, she was able to see the tense scene unfolding before her. Holding her breath, she waited, hoping they would not find her in the crowd and move on to look for her elsewhere.

Ricky and Buck each grabbed a woman from the group of Passengers. One was holding tight to the newborn infant that had been born on the train.

The infant was now only one month old and he began wailing continuously from the pain he felt from his mother squeezing him while holding onto him so tightly. The other woman and the children hostages were crying, scared to death.

Except for the unnerving wailing of the infant, Ralph decided he had everything under control. He searched the crowd of passengers. "Where the sam heck is she?" he commanded. Where's the red head?" He was angry and felt that they were all guilty of hiding her. He knew she was with them. He'd seen her from a distance. And he wasn't going to give up without taking her with them.

Realizing Abby was whom they wanted the crowd looked amongst themselves for her. Margaret Boling spoke firmly, "There aint no red head here!" She had ascertained Abby's absence and put two and two together. Now she attempted to protect her new friend whom she'd become very fond of. She thought of her as the daughter she never had.

"Yur a lyin, old woman!" Ricky hit her with his gun butt. She fell to the ground unconscious. Abby cringed for her friend as she watched from the rocks she had hidden in.

"We knows she's here. We been a follerin ya for days and we done seen her! Now git her up here! Right now!" Ricky commanded as he shoved at Maggie with his boot, and pushed her husband back into the crowd of men brandishing his gun at all of them.

"Someone, please check on her," Cleotus Broling begged, "At least wipe that blood off of her!" her husband implored the women and children around his wife. No one moved to help Mrs. Brolin. They were scared to death of the outlaws. Trigger happy Rick took over command a second time. "Leave her alone and you shut up!" he yelled at the poor worried husband. Keep yur mouths shut or I'll see to it she never get's up agin!" he warned them all.

Ralph had enough of Ricky's taking control. His jealous nature made him order Rick to lay off. He reminded Ricky and his crew that "No one get's hurt unless he gave the order."

Rick smarted! He had been proud of his control of the group! He enjoyed being in charge. To himself he counseled, that one day, soon if he had his way, he would be boss of this outfit. He just had to get rid of Ralph first. He reasoned privately and began making plans for Ralph's demise as soon as Ralph collected the ransom on the girl they were after!

Worried, Cleotus volunteered "My wife don't know where the girl is. Leave her alone, please. Don't hurt her he begged."

Joseph cringed. Cleotus unknowingly had just given Lydia's only chance away. Now the outlaws knew for certain that she was a passenger on the train.

Ralph turned the gun on Joseph. "You, you got to be the one who rescued her." He reasoned, "Where is she?" He cocked his gun placing it into his chest he cocked the trigger. "I been a watchin ya mister. Seen ya with her. If ya want ta live, call and get her out here right now!" he threatened Joseph!

Joseph shook his head. "No! I'll never give her to you! Over my dead body, I'll not turn her over to the likes of you!" he declared even with the gun cocked and touching his chest. "Go ahead and shoot me!" he dared Ralph.

A gasp went through the crowd. They didn't want harm to come to their new friend Lydia, but neither did they want harm to come to themselves or their families either. Some prayed fervently for Joseph to give her up. The husband of the woman with the infant called out. "I seen her run for the rocks! She ain't even here with us!" he called out from the crowd to Ralph.

Joseph cringed again, he knew they didn't have a chance but he was still unwilling to provide Lydia to these hooligans.

"*Girl!* I'm give'n ya only two minutes to turn up here in front of me afore I kill this one!" Ralph hollered towards the mountainous rocks and warned Abby to show herself by pushing the gun further into Joseph's chest. "Ya got less than a minute or this one's first to go!" Ralph yelled loudly for her to hear him as he stuck the edge of his gun directly on the tip of Joseph's nose.

Joseph flinched but tried not to move. He was praying that Abby was not in hearing distance and wouldn't fall prey to Ralph's threat.

"Put your gun down and let him go! I am right here!" Abby emerged from her hiding place in the rocks. She was holding Joseph's loaded rifle and had it pointed straight at Ralph. Let them all go or you'll be the first to die!" she threatened him.

"Ralph just laughed at her. "Missy thar's five of us and only one of ya! Put that gun down and get yur backside over here!" he commanded her.

"Not on your life!" she answered, "there may be five men in your group but there's only one of you, and you're the one I'm gonna fill with buckshot first! Then I won't care what the rest of them do. You're their leader and you are the one I want!" she replied bravely as she moved closer to him to be better in range. Abby was petrified, she had no idea how to shoot the gun. She was bluffing. She was unaware that she needed to cock the rifle before it would shoot. Trigger happy Ricky, started to move toward her, she swung the rifle's aim, pointing it at him. "Get back, or I'll shoot you both!" she ordered.

He stopped but he didn't retreat. She aimed the gun somewhere between Ralph and Ricky in case she had to swing in either direction. "Release these people," she called to Ralph. "They aren't the ones you want. I am. I **don't** know why you want me, but I know I am the one you **are** after."

"I'll release em when ya lower's that gun to the ground and give yarself up!" Ralph called back to her.

"Don't do it! Lydia, Don't put the gun down!" Joseph beseeched her.

All eyes were pivoted on her. She didn't know what to do. She feared she would probably miss if she shot at them and in turn she just might hit Joseph or one of the passengers instead.

"Alright girl! Put the gun down, Redhead," urged Ralph once more. "Or this one is going to be shot before you can shoot either of us." Again he shoved the gun deeper into Joseph's midsection. Joseph bent over from the force of the blow and gasped. "Don't listen to him, Lydia, don't don...," he tried to tell her but the pain in his chest had taken the air from his lungs.

Abby stared at Ralph for a second. Obviously they didn't want her dead. Maybe she would find out what they wanted without them hurting her. She remembered Ralph had mentioned a reward for her return. To save the lives of the others, she decided to give in. Slowly she lowered the gun to the ground.

"Take me and release them!" she relented and offered herself in Joseph's stead as she laid the gun gently on the ground before her.

Ricky quickly moved over and grabbed her arms tying them behind her with the bandanna he whipped off his face revealing his identity. Ralph mounted his horse still pointing his gun on Joseph and Randolph.

The remaining outlaws mounted without taking their guns off the crowd and the hostages. Ricky mounted pulling Abby up to lie face down in front of him. She struggled, but with her hands bound she couldn't stop him from taking her with them. He slapped her on the butt to pleasure himself more than to make her stop wriggling. She quieted down immediately and allowed herself to hang limply over his saddle. She hated him and his touch on her was more than enough to stop moving praying he wouldn't touch her again. Ricky pulled hard on his horse showing off as he rode up next to the other outlaws.

She dared a look at Joseph. He tried to recover from the pain in his gut. He was looking directly at her. His dismay was evident. He questioned her disbelievingly.

"Why'd you put the gun down, Lydia, Why?" he moaned in pain. He was beside himself. There was nothing he could do but watch her go. He had to respect her decision to save him and the others. All he could do now was watch which way they went as they left and then he would have to track them and rescue her all over again.

Reading Joseph's thoughts, Ralph hit Joseph on the head with the butt of his gun again. Joseph slumped to the ground. The rest of the passengers made to move.

"Don't move! Stay right whar ya are!" Ralph commanded them. "Move and I'll shoot as long as I'm still in range!" he warned.

Motioning to his crew, they all began backing away. Continuing on the trail before them. As they cleared the canyon walls, they turned facing forward and kicking their horses they raced out of sight of the wagon train and the fear filled passengers.

Once again Abby was clinging on dearly for her life. Her bruised bottom was screaming in pain and Ricky's body smelled horrifically. She wanted to retch, but the jostling up and down prevented her from doing so. This time she was conscious but to confused to fear for her life. "Well, here I am again God!" she conversed privately between the bouncing! "When do you intend to let this torture come to an end?" she silently implored with difficulty as her head bounced uncontrollably. All the jostling revived the pain in her head that had been slowly lessening as she came to terms with her amnesia and she'd quit trying so hard to remember her past.

"What could they possibly want with me anyway?" she dared to wonder. This time she felt truly defeated and felt she was near her end. She just didn't have the strength to continue onward much longer.

She had watched Joseph collapse and feared that he had been killed by the men who kidnapped her. Her heart was shattered not knowing for certain if he lived or died. But the one thing she did know was that without Joseph in her life she really didn't care what happened to her anymore.

Joseph became conscious within seconds of the cold water that Maggie poured on his head. At least this time he wasn't bleeding. The wagon train passengers were a hum bug of comments. Noise was everywhere as they all tried to discuss the event and what to do now.

Randolph Bushing looked angrily at Joseph. He was fighting mad. "Who the heck is she, why did they want her?" He demanded. "Why didn't you tell me you two would be an added danger to this train?" He wanted to punch Joseph out all over again, but withheld his temper as over the time they had spent with the train, Joseph had proven invaluable to him and he now considered him more of a true friend than a passenger. "I trusted you and allowed myself to accept you as a trusted friend! Now I'm not so certain," he continued his angry tirade over the injured man.

Joseph rubbed his head and confessed. "I'm sorry Randolph. The truth is that I Don't rightly know who she is. I met her on the train to Saint Louis. She seemed scared and to be hiding something. A few days later the train was robbed by these same bandits that just took her when we were leaving Bowling Green, KY. They hit me on the head that time too. After that they kidnapped her and rode off. Later, I found her and rescued her from them. That's why I was trying to get to California with her." He was trying to quickly relate his story to the Train Master as he was anxious to rescue her again. "I admit, I fell in love with her and I was only trying to keep her safe," he moaned rubbing his head.

"As for who she is, I don't know and she doesn't know either. She hasn't told me but I gathered that she's suffering from amnesia. She told me her name was Lydia Creosota before the train was robbed. I'm not sure that she told me the truth though," he finished lamely.

Randolph was shaking his head in amazement as he listened to Joseph's wildly unbelievable tale. Shaking his head in disbelief, he said, "Well, I'd like to try to find her as I am responsible for her safe travel as well as the other passenger's on this train, but if I leave, the whole train will be at risk." He half asked and half stated to Joseph his predicament.

Quickly Joseph interceded, "That won't be necessary and sides, you got a train to get to Californy. I brought this problem into your train and now I know I have to relieve you of any responsibility you may feel you owe to either of us. I also do not want these people in danger any more than you do. I'm going after her right now! Just stake my wagon to that tree over yonder and be on your way. I'll get her back and then we'll join up with you later if we can find you. Don't concern yourself, I fully realize your responsibility is to the passengers on this train." He reassured Ron, helping him to handle the guilt he was feeling at not being able to go after Abby.

"Well, I could round up some of the men and go with you," Randolph offered reluctantly thinking of the delay searching for the girl would do to his tight schedule.

"Honestly, you've got a schedule to keep and sides, I'm much better when I work alone. That's how I rescued her the first time, Joseph reassured Randolph that he didn't need or want his or the men of the wagon train's help. But he did take the time to apologize a second time for the trouble they had caused and to thank the man for his offer of help. He decided Randolph Bushing was a good man to know and he was honored to have met him and to be called a friend by him.

The worried train master reluctantly agreed to let him go alone. He told Joseph not to worry about their wagon, he would have someone keep driving it with them. "God go with you and when you join up with us again, we'll have your stuff," he added. Sides to leave it here was an open invitation to any straggling Indian's who might be looking for trouble which could in turn put the entire train in major trouble all over again.

Joseph thanked him a second time. And said he'd best get started right away.

"God go with you!" was Ralph's retreating reply. He turned to reorganize his train and get them back on the journey as fast as possible.

Joseph nodded, and began a repeat of his actions on the day of the train robbery. He went to his wagon, grabbed a few supplies, saddled both of their horses and grabbed his rifle. He shook his head as he noticed that Abby hadn't even cocked it. "What guts that girl has!" he announced to no one. "Guess I'm gonna have to teach her to shoot a gun. And I'm doing that as soon as I find her!"

Half grinning and completely worried he began to track the bandits to find his beloved Lydia. He hoped to find them by nightfall and this time they would pay for their continued harassment of his beloved! He vowed! He wasn't going to give them a chance to keep on chasing her anywhere.

Joseph tracked the bandits trail late into the evening. Unwisely, they hadn't taken the time to cover their tracks.

He came upon them just as they were setting up camp for the night. "These guys have got to be some stupid outlaws!" he commented to himself. "Only idiots would actually stop and set up a camp with a lighted fire knowing there was a good possibility they were being followed. Hmmm…, he mused to himself, and I'm going to put their stupidity to good use."

Joseph decided to remain hidden in the bushes till way after dark when the men would be sleeping. He watched as they ate some beans and jerky for their supper. One of them tried to feed Abby. Her hands were still tied behind her back and they had lashed her feet together. In addition they tethered her to a tree. She was in the middle of Ralph and Jim. They weren't taking any chances that anyone could sneak up on them and take her again.

Ralph was certain that the hit to Joseph's head had killed him and he was fairly certain that the wagon train would not come after her. However he decided to be cautious and placed her near him and his most trusted crewmember. He also didn't trust his other crewmembers not to try to take advantage of her. In his haste he'd failed to be cautious about his tracks and the fire. He was congratulating himself on his smart recapture of her and the fifty thousand plus dollars he intended to ransom her for.

Ricky pulled a bottle of whiskey from his saddle bag. Keeping it hidden from Ralph, he, Buck and Tom managed to empty the full bottle in short order. Soon they fell into a drunken stupor. Jim was on sentry duty. Ralph kicked out the fire and laid down lowering his hat over his eyes to sleep. Joseph made a mental note that Ralph had removed his gun belt laying it within reach of him. However, he had foolishly left his loaded guns in the belt. Joseph shook his head in amazement as he took note of Ralph's flagrant ignorance. He wondered how Ralph had ever became the head of this gang.

Sitting patiently from his hiding place, Joseph waited until he was certain that Ralph was sleeping soundly. Around two in the morning, Ralph's loud snores confirmed to him that it was time to make his move.

Once again using the techniques he learned from the Indians he'd lived with he began slowly sneaking up behind Jim. "It's my turn now!" He silently affirmed as he brought his gun butt down on Jim's head as hard as he could.

Jim never made a sound. He instantly slumped over. His scalp began bleeding profusely. Quickly Joseph grabbed the rawhide rope he had with him and tied Jim up. Then grabbing Jim's own kerchief, he tied it across Jim's mouth preventing him from making any sound if he came too. Joseph dragged Jim's heavy body to a huge tree. He slung the rawhide rope over the nearest thick branch and pulled Jim up by the ankles. He left him hanging upside down in the tree, his blood steadily dripped onto the ground.

Silently, Joseph crept into the center of their camp. He thanked God silently for allowing him to have spent that year of his life living among the Indians. There he had learned some very valuable tricks about moving silently, tracking your opponent and other important feats of war fare and survival in the wild. Never making a single sound he gathered each man's gun and hid them in the bushes. Then he walked towards the snoring Ralph. He raised his gun intending to slam the butt of the rifle into Ralph's head but stopped in midair as Abby stirred. She opened her eyes wide and stared in alarm at Joseph.

Putting his fingers on his lips to silence her, he brought the gun down on top of Ralph's temples. Abby winced and looked away. Ralph groaned and rolled over. Blood gushed from the newly opened wound above his temple.

The noise had awakened the deep drunken sleep Ricky was in. He stirred sleepily. Groggy from the alcohol he finally realized something was wrong. He grabbed for his rifle. His look of surprise was priceless as he realized it was gone. He was helpless against the giant man standing above him.

Automatically he reached for his knife, but Joseph sent a bullet straight into his heart without hesitation. Staring at Joseph in surprised, his eyes glazed over and his lifeless body fell face forward upon hard cold ground.

Tom and Buck sat up staring at Joseph still groggy from the effects of the whiskey? They stumbled drunkenly as they tried to stand. Joseph shook his head in disgust as he watched them fumble around for their guns. They were both so inebriated, they looked like a couple of pigs in a pigsty snooting around for some grub. Joseph smiled and aimed his rifle at them. They began backing away with their hands in the air.

Ralph stirred and reached for the small Derringer he kept hidden in his vest pocket. Abby managed a loud grunt from her gagged mouth as she tried to scream to warn Joseph.

Joseph's gun discharged again. Ralph stared at Joseph in amazement fingering the blood that reddened his chest. "Ya…, shot m…e! He tried to say as his eyes glazed over and his life left his body. He laid there, his eyes blankly staring at Joseph in disbelief.

Joseph believed in God. His parents had been certain that he attended church and Sunday school every Sunday. He had learned that God instructed him to care and protect his loved ones. Killing the three dangerous men had to be done and he did it without blinking an eye.

This was the only way he would be able to ascertain Abby's future freedom and give her the peace she needed to live her own life out. It was apparent by their second attempt at kidnapping her that they would never cease to harass and endanger his beloved. Joseph had no idea what it was the outlaws wanted her so badly for. But he didn't care about that. He only knew that he wanted to spend the remainder of his life with her and she had to be free from the evils that threatened her for them to do that.

But for right now, Joseph was sickened by the killings. He had had enough. "You two want the same?" he asked Tom and Buck as he waved the gun in their faces once again.

"No Sir!" They both replied in unison, slowly attempting to back away. Joseph cocked his rifle again and ordered them to stop. They both complied instantly raising their hands into the air in surrender.

Never removing his gun off of Buck Joseph ordered them, "You," he indicated to Buck, "untie her and help her to her feet. You turn around," he told Tom. Tom turned his back to Joseph and Joseph quickly bound his hands tightly. Joseph gave Tom a quick kick behind his knees, knocking him off his feet. Then removing his boots, Joseph tied Tom's feet together with more of the rawhide rope. Buck received the same treatment after he finished untying Abby.

Joseph took Abby's hand. He never took his guns off of the two men.

"If you want to live, you will leave this lady alone for the rest of your lives!" he threatened them. "If I ever lay eyes on either of you again, I'll shoot first and ask question later! Mark my words!" he nodded in the direction of Ricky, Jim and Ralph, now dead to the world.

Tom and Buck knew he meant business. They nodded in agreement. Joseph took his knife and sliced through their clothing until they were left in their red long underwear. With the rest of his rope, he tied their feet together and then he threw the rope looping it over a strong tree branch. Grabbing the now dangling end of the rope he used his amazing strength to hoist both men high into the air. He left them hanging there suspended upside down just like Jim.

"Remember I am a man of my word!" He cautiously warned them a second time. Tom and Buck hung there feeling dumbfounded from the effects of the whiskey and their sudden captivity. They acknowledged his threat with mumbled sounds and by trying to nod their heads. Alarmed, they watched Joseph pick up their boots and the remains of their clothing. He left them not caring if they died or managed to escape. He walked back to the camp where Abby was watching everything happen in shock, disbelief and total relief all at the same time. He walked to the fire and threw the two men's boots and the remains of their clothing into the still smoldering coals. Flames immediately flared and the items were soon burned to ashes.

Non-stopping he walked straight to Abby and took her in his arms and hugged her as if he would never let her go. She began crying from the shock. Several minutes passed but he refused to quit holding her tightly in his arms. Eventually her sobbing stopped and she pushed away from him enough to look up into his face. Her eyes questioned him and thanked him both at the same time. Tenderly Joseph disengaged them from each other and took hold of her hand. Then he led her away from the bloody camp and the dead men, to the hobbled horses of the outlaws. Without a word, Joseph untied their bindings and put their bits on them. Then he took Abby's hand and lead her and the outlaw's horses to his own horse that was patiently waiting for them just a few feet away from the camp.

Finally his own shock at his horrific actions recovered enough from his adrenaline rush that he suddenly stopped and grabbed Abby into his tight embrace again.

"Lydia Jordan, you scared the daylights out of me!" He told her as he held her tightly in his arms.

She clung to him. Bursting into tears a second time. She tried to explain to him, "I couldn't let them kill you! Joseph, I love you!" she confessed her heart. "I can't live without you another second longer! She was still thrilled to have heard him call her by his last name as if she really were his true wife. "And this hiding in the woods away from me every day is slowly killing me! What have I done to make you not want to be with me?" She was shaking from all the killing done in front of her eyes. All she could think was he had to love her very much, because he had killed three men for her. So before she realized what she was doing she'd confessed her feelings of love for him.

He heard her words and they burned joyfully deep into his soul. "Oh Lydia," he said holding her tightly and stroking her hair, "I love you too my little minx! I love you so very much!" He confessed his feelings to her softly in her ears. She moved her head until her tear stained frightened eyes stared into his worried blue eyes.

There was no way he could prevent himself. Immediately he dipped his head and his lips softly captured hers. His kiss was pure oblivion to her. Then her innocent world turned upside down as he kissed her forehead, moved to softly kiss her face and finally he moved to capture her mouth again. This time his lips pressed hers harder and firmer, forcing her to open her lips to him. Her insides melted and her knees went weak as his kiss filled her with all the pent up desire he had been fighting to hold from her for what seemed an eternity to him!

She slumped in his arms and returned his passion to him with her own lips and tongue. They couldn't get enough of each other.

Against his will and with great reluctance Joseph gently pushed her away from him. Her puzzled look questioned him, but he only motioned for her to mount her horse. She looked at him with longing and regret that the kiss had ended.

"I know, woman, I know, I don't want to stop kissing you either, but we will have to ride all night and all day tomorrow if we hope to catch up with the train," he told her. She nodded. Her bottom was so sore, but the events of the day had completely made her forget the pain. She was so relieved that she and Joseph were both alive and the kidnappers would no longer be any threat to her. More than that she was on cloud nine. Joseph had not only rescued her again but he had shown her as well as told her of his love for her. Her world was nearly complete. But not quite! If only she had her memory back. She was disappointed that all she had just witnessed did not return her memory to her.

"So who am I anyway?" riding along the trail in the dark she'd allowed herself to contemplate her memory dilemma. It angered her that she still couldn't remember who she was. Eventually she decided, "It's probably best that way. If I remember who I am, I might have to leave Joseph and never be with him again, and I cannot bear the thought of that," she decided to herself. That was one scenario that she most certainly didn't want to happen. Her love for Joseph had no boundaries. She wanted to spend the rest of her life with him. He made her feel protected but so much more than that. She had felt his love for her and the passion he had in his desire for her. She smiled thinking about the two kisses she had received from him. She wanted more of them. She knew she wanted more than just kisses from him. Unlike other women, Abby had been raised by a quiet celibate father. She was never made privy to the facts of life between a man and a woman and thusly she was still innocent of any knowledge of the physical relationship between a woman and a man. Although she wasn't exactly sure what it was she was craving from Joseph, she was definitely sure she wanted it, whatever it was.

Hanging upside down with his blood rushing to his already inebriated head Tom twisted to look at Buck who was squirming in a likewise position. He croaked out, "Buck, I don't know about ya, but I sure as heck don't want nuttin' more to do with that little gal! Fifty grand or not!" His eyes were huge big and glazed due to the rush of blood from hanging upside down and from the effects of the whiskey.

"Ya got that right! She ain't nuttin but bad luck!" a drunken Buck agreed. Now all they had to do was hope someone came along and rescued them eventually. "In fact, Tom, if we ever get down from here, I think I'm heading south, maybe run into Larry or something." He formulated his future plans.

Buck agreed and said "I'll think I'll join you in that! Hey you think if we swing back and forth, we can catch each other's ropes and try to untie ourselves?" They busied themselves swinging to and fro like monkeys in a tree trying to make their escape.

Unknown to either Abby or Joseph their problems were not yet over. Still hot on Abby's trail was a very determined Silas Johnson, her father's longtime friend and a well know Pinkerton Detective, and her betrothed, Jeffrey Browning. They were getting closer by the minute in their diligent search for her.

Silas was still convinced that they would find her. He'd been a Pinkerton man for over twenty-three years. He was well aware that there would be times that were time consuming and even discouraging in order to accomplish the many projects that the Pinkerton men were famous for. He was among their best because he possessed determination and plenty of patience. Both qualities were adamant in the successes of his endeavors.

Jeffrey, on the other hand, was a very discouraged and extremely angry man. Now, deep into depression, he was living on tunnel vision. His focus was to see Abby at the end of the tunnel. He no longer could see with peripheral vision. Silas feared that Jeffrey was going to collapse on him. His determination to find Abby was so strong that he was unable to sleep, sit or stand still for any length of time. He'd become a driven man. Silas suggested to him that he return home and prepare for his wedding only to quickly regret his suggestion.

Jeffrey came unglued, screaming in his ears, "I will not now on ever return home without her. I would rather die than let that man take her away from me! If you ever suggest that I quit searching for her again, I will punch your lights out! You hear me old man?" Only inches from his nose, Silas felt the spray of Jeffrey's spittle hit his face. The smell of the whiskey Jeffrey had taken to drinking regularly was so overpowering that Silas had to turn his face away from the smell of it.

Silas backed down immediately. But he did try to warn Jeffrey, "Okay! Okay! You can stay with me and keep searching. But boy, I've got to tell you if you don't calm down and put that bottle away you just might be hurting our chances more than you are helping us to find your Abby.

Jeffrey's face turned beet red, he clenched his fists at his side. Raising his hand he threw the nearly empty bottle at Silas. It shattered as it landed at Silas's feet. "You damned fool! You don't know what the sam hill you're talking about!" Unaccustomed to hearing himself converse so angrily, Jeffrey realized he had to get a grip on things. He swung around and threw open the swinging doors of the Saloon and stomped into the street oblivious to the horse and carriage traffic surrounding him.

He knew Silas was right. He just couldn't stop the tremendous need he felt to find Abby. He wanted to be certain that she was securely his again. Completely torn by his emotions he could barely concentrate on the task at hand. Each day they continued to be separated he felt more anger caused by the fear that she was most likely in another man's arms and that he had already lost her. His pride was taking a beating. "Abby, where in this forsaken world are you? I'm afraid of what I will do if I find you in the arms of another man. Heaven help him is all I can say. I'll probably kill the jerk!"

There was one thought his subconscious refused to listen too. Even though the subject tried to enter his conscious many times, he closed his mind to the possibility. "What if it was her choice to be with a man other than him?" He refused to hear the thought much less to believe how real the possibility was that this was a probable scenario. He had been raised in a political environment where a man had to keep his word at all costs. After all he had been through to find Abby, he didn't have the courage to return home and face his faithful supporters, much less than to allow them to see his failure and his massive embarrassment at being dumped by his Bride to be of whom he had bragged so highly about. They would never trust him again. He would become a laughing stock. This whole ordeal could prevent him from securing a political position if his reputation for keeping his word was ruined.

His heart was broken and filled with jealousy. Lately that jealousy had turned from green to black in his heart. He wasn't sure if he could forgive Abby if she had been unfaithful to him. He just knew the longer he took to find her the greater was the chance of her being unfaithful to him. If that should be turn out to be the case, he planned on handling that when and if he came face to face with it. For now it was safer for him to ignore the possibility.

Under this extreme duress, Silas and Jeffrey continued their diligent but exhausting search for Abby.

Chapter Seventeen

The little mining town of Shabby Shacks, located in the foothills of the Sierra Nevada Mountains of California, was well named. Abby, driving their covered wagon and Joseph, beside her on his horse, were traveling down the only street of the small town. The street was only a wide worn out path of mud and ruts wide enough to handle the size of a wagon team passing each other. On either side were a series of small shack like dwellings nicknamed Shanty's. Most were erected overnight and were in danger of collapsing or fire. Made of a quickly erected wooden frame and covered mostly from the scraps of canvass remaining from the wagon trains they were part building, and part tent. Some small businesses had created more than one room. A couple of the new businesses were thriving and the sound of hammers could be heard as they erected buildings for their new town.

The crudeness of the town amazed Abby. However she didn't feel the same alienated feeling she had felt in Saint Louis. Most likely due to all of the Wagon Train's adventures and small settlements they had visited along the way. Instead, she felt a bit more welcomed but mostly just fascination by the prematurity of the expanding town bustling around them.

The closer to the center of the town they came to, the more the hustle and bustle increased. Crude, filthily dressed men were everywhere. Exhausted men sat on the wooden porches of buildings with their backs against the wall. Most of them looked as if they needed to bathe and definitely they needed to shave and get a haircut. Relieved, she saw that there were a few women dressed in calico dresses casually strolling the boardwalks of the buildings. Some were carrying baskets filled with their purchases while other women were being escorted by men who were apparently their husbands, family members or simply their protector's.

To her left, Abby watched in amazement as they passed a shack with a crudely painted sign stating it was *Annie's Dressmaker's* shack. Next to it was a small but completely built whitewashed building boasting a cross at the apex of the roof. She was pleased to see that a church was available to them. Next, she was surprised to note that a small brick building carried both names of the *Shanty Shacks Bank* and the *Assessor's Office* included in one. They continued down the street and saw that there was also a telegraph shack and various other minor enterprises. To her right she saw, the Sheriff's partially completed office and Jail.

Across the street they passed the Assayers shack, a lawyer's partially built office and of course the completely finished Saloon next door to a huge two story gingerbread designed house boasting finished construction of two stories, named *Rubies House of Pleasures*. She wandered what that meant and suddenly she bit her tongue and blushed as she saw two women in their undergarments waving silk shawls at the men below them.

They passed in front of Dan Bigger's General Store. It appeared to be the only general store in the town. Surprised, Abby saw that it had a steady flow of customers. Next door to the store, a two story hotel ended the business interests the town appeared to offer. She had also noted that there were a few occasional side streets offering shacks and crudely constructed dwellings for the living accommodations of some of the town's folk. There also appeared to be several fully built homes located at either end of the main street and behind some of the buildings as well.

Several children played idly in the street. Some were running, others were playing catch. Five little girls were jumping rope in the alley. Between the general store and jail, Abby smiled at them and then she saw a group of mid aged boys shooting marbles. There was an empty red schoolhouse next to the church. Today was Monday and the children were obviously not in school. Her hopes soared. "Maybe they do need a teacher here!" Excited, she turned to Joseph to tell him of her hopes to teach the children for the town.

"Could be," he absentmindedly replied. He was absorbed in his own thoughts. Now that they'd finally arrived in California he planned on staking a claim at the land office. He wanted to start panning for gold immediately. He'd heard stories of huge nuggets that had been found. Some men went from poor to wealthy in less than a second of panning. Now it was his turn. He was determined to strike it rich! Especially now that he intended to make Abby his true wife and begin a family with her.

Joseph's mind wandered to his past. He became an orphan at the age of ten. His parents had homesteaded in the Texas territory of Nacogdoches. The summer of his tenth year, Joseph had remained in the town of Abilene at his father's request to help his mother's injured younger brother who was suffering with a broken leg to bring in his crops and care for their livestock. In Joseph's absence, his mother, father and two younger sisters all died from the yellow fever epidemic in Nacogdoches, leaving him orphaned.

His uncle later succumbed to alcoholism over the years. Due to his addiction he was unable to support his wife and six children. This only made him resent Joseph as he was another mouth to feed. He became cruel towards Joseph. The more he drank, the more he found reasons to use his whip on Joseph. Finally, Joseph had taken his final beating from his uncle.

At the age of fifteen he left in the middle of the night and never returned. He learned to survive on his own the hard way. Drifting from place to place he worked for food when he could, begged when he couldn't and stole when all else failed.

After ten months of wandering he met a Sioux Indian named White Horse who took a fancy to him. He took Joseph with him to his Sioux Indian camp and there Joseph remained for a year learning the many things that White Horses heritage had to teach him. White Horse died a year later in a hunting accident. So that was when Joseph felt compelled to leave the Indian village and strike out on his own. He drifted from town to town again, learned to be a crack shot and how to enjoy life and women. But until he met Abby he refused to allow himself to care for anyone ever again.

Here in Shanty Shacks he was determined to find his final destiny. First he was determined to legally marry Abby regardless of her unknown past. His second most pressing goal was to find gold and finally live in peace for ever more.

He and Abby had discussed their future after their return to the wagon train. Abby finally trusted him enough that she disclosed her amnesia to him. She was surprised and a little angry with him when he confessed to her that he already knew she was suffering from memory loss. She forgave him once he explained that he understood that he felt that she needed to trust in him first before he felt free to tell her that he knew as he was afraid she would come to fear him and his reasons for staying with her.

They decided that once they reached their destination they were definitely going to get married immediately. Neither of them cared about Abby's past any longer. They decided to simply ignore the possibility that she might be married already. They agreed to keep her amnesia as their secret and no one in California would ever know. Besides, they reasoned, no one would ever locate her way out here in the boondocks of California. Their love for each other was so strong they wanted nothing to interfere with their future happiness together.

When they had caught up with the wagon train, the wagon master and the passengers now knew of their fictitious marriage Randolph kept them separated from each other nightly. Now that they were no longer part of the wagon train, they decided to stay together until their wedding could be arranged.

They had spent this much time together without the sanctity of marriage. They figured a few more days to a week was nothing to worry about. But it was important to them both that they held their relationship from further activity until they were legally bound as man and wife. So Joseph told her he would sleep in the same vicinity as she, but he promised to not share the same bed with her until they were actually married.

Now they had finally reached California and they were headed to the land office. On the first day of their arrival they had secured a temporary room at the hotel. The second day Joseph left Abby sleeping soundly in the hotel room to catch up on some much needed rest.

He went on a thorough search of the area. Talking with some of the local men in town, he quickly located an abandoned claim a small distance from Shabby Shacks. There was a small cabin already built on it.

"Looked like a great place to start our life together." he excitedly told Abby. Now she was waiting for him outside of the land office as he staked his claim for the abandoned property.

Waiting on the buckboard of the wagon she smiled. For once she was completely happy. She had her Joseph and they were no longer traveling on that long arduous trail. The kidnappers would never threaten her again. She no longer cared that she had no memory of her true identity. It simply didn't matter anymore. Instead, she was ecstatic that very soon she would become the wife of the current love of her life!

Joseph came out of the land office grinning from ear to ear. "We got it! Abby my dearest love! We got it! Our own little piece of paradise! Oh Happy day!" he momentarily sang the one line tune. "We're going to move in right now and you can start fixing me some hot grub!" He jumped up on the buckboard grabbing the reins, kissed her lightly on the lips, smartly flicking the reigns they were off!

Abby hugged him and held on tightly to his arm. She was chattering none stop about their new home. Then she realized that he was heading further into town and away from the direction of their new homestead.

"Where are you going? I thought you said we were going to our new home?" She asked him puzzled.

He grinned and said, "You'll see. Just be patient." He patted her on the knee and drew the team to a stop in front of the church rectory. Jumping off the wagon, he waved at her, blew her a kiss and went inside. Five minutes later he returned. Jumping back on board, he announced,

"Well, tomorrow morning at ten o'clock you are going to become the legally known Mrs. Joseph Alan Jordan!" he proudly exclaimed.

She nearly fell off the wagon as she jumped up and hugged him. "Oh my darling Joseph, hurry home, I have so much to do before the wedding!" she happily replied and blushed pink in her excitement.

It was all happening so fast. She thought to herself, but Abby didn't care. She was tired of not knowing who she was. Tired of traveling. Tired of worry and fear. She was ready to sit back and enjoy life. She knew they would have a hard time ahead of them as they settled their new place and Joseph began panning for gold.

"Stop at the Sheriff's office, I want to find out who I have to see to become the teacher for this town." She requested.

He looked at her in surprise. He thought that now that they were to be married she would not want to work.

She read his thoughts and said, "Now Joseph, you know that I am going to have to bring in the income for us until you strike that gold of yours!"

He laughed loudly. "Figures," he said, "that I would find not only the most beautiful but the most giving woman in the world to be my wife." He hugged her and continued, Honey you don't have to work. I'll find a way to support us and still pan for gold. Don't worry. Okay?"

"Oh Joseph, you don't understand. It's not so much that I do or don't want to work, look around you. The children in this town need me. They're all running wild and not learning any schooling. By the time our children are ready for school, I want this town to be a good place to raise them. What better way can I help, except by teaching their peers?" She looked at him for understanding.

"Good point!" He conceded, "Wow! Our children? I think I like the sound of that he said as he pulled the team to a stop in front of the sheriff's office.

Abby smiled and said they should have four children. Two boys and two girls!

He laughed happily and said, "Maybe we'd best just take what comes, sweetheart!" Together they laughed!

Abby quickly pecked his cheek with a small kiss and jumped from the wagon. She went in and inquired about a teaching position possibility. It just happened that the mayor of the town was visiting with the sheriff. He offered Abby the job on the spot. She was to start in one week. They wanted to give her time to get her affairs in order. Abby couldn't contain her excitement! She thanked the mayor, promising him to be the best teacher Shanty Shacks would ever have.

As evening settled, they drove onto their claim site. Abby lovingly perused the bedraggled little cabin. It was obvious that it once housed bachelors. A ripped apart old burlap flour bag was crudely hung for a door cover. The windows had a wooden shutter but no glass in them. The porch looked solid though.

"Well...," Joseph trailed off as he surveyed their new home, "welcome home my love!" Joseph jumped from the wagon, picked her up and carried her over the threshold.

Hugging him tightly in her excitement, Abby stepped gingerly inside. She found a one room cabin. There was a rope bed frame in the back of the room. One roughly made table sat in the center of the room with two stools made from tree stumps. A huge stone fireplace covered the far right wall. Various empty jars and barrels littered the room. A shelf had fallen loose from the wall. Everything was covered in dust and to top it off, she jumped when a porcupine ran past her leg, out of the cabin and into the woods scaring her momentarily. They both fell into hilarious laughter.

"Oh Joseph, it really is home, isn't it!" she smiled softly at Joseph and let him hug her tightly. He turned her to face him and captured her lips in his. Their long slow kiss initiated their new home.

Finally he released her lips but still holding her tightly in his arms, he said, "We've waited this long. I'm going to be a gentleman and wait one more night. But woman you better be prepared for me tomorrow night, because I'm going to make you my wife in every sense of the word!" he promised her as he patted her backside.

She blushed profusely. She was happy to know that he loved her enough to give her time to feel securely married before he made her his wife in every sense. She wasn't quite certain what those words meant, but she felt a good woman waited for marriage to find out. She wandered where that thought came from but soon dismissed it. Looking at Joseph she smiled at him and said softly, "I truly love you Joseph Alan Jordan!" then more excitedly she continued with, "Now get busy and unpack that wagon. Let's turn this place into our home and I'll get you some supper on."

He laughed as he said "I love you too. You little minx!" Slapping her irresistible bottom side once again he turned and began unloading the wagon and settling them into their new paradise.

Chapter Eighteen

Tuesday morning awakened Abby to the sun shining brightly in the uncovered window of the cabin. Abby rolled over and listened to a rooster crowing. She'd slept later than she intended. Stretching her arms over her head and her legs as far as she could in front of her, she sat up. "I haven't slept this well in months," she acknowledged. She jumped off the bed and landed on the floor in her bare feet. She wriggled her toes and smiled as she felt her tired aching body slowly become alive. It feels so good to be wearing nightclothes to sleep in, instead of that dirty dress I've been wearing daily for the past three months. She began to dance lightly in her excitement. Looking around her she felt she was finally home and she was loving everything about it!

Last evening they had completely unpacked the wagon. She'd put what few items they had in various places around the small cabin. Then she'd placed her feather mattress on top of the rope framed bed and made it up with the quilt they had purchased in Saint Louis. After the meager dinner she fixed for them, she went outside to enjoy the evening air. Looking at the land around her she'd picked some wildflowers and placed them in an empty can she found inside the cabin. These she placed in the center of the table. This morning everything looked neat and clean and welcoming. She stretched again. Just then Joseph entered the cabin. She grabbed the quilt and wrapped it around her.

He laughed. "Today you become my wife, Lydia! It's not necessary to hide behind a quilt."

Smiling she replied. "I am an unmarried woman for a few more hours Joseph. I want to act like one." She danced past him circling around and around as she poked him on the nose. More seriously she said, "I can't wait to become your wife today Joseph.

"Nor me, your husband," he rejoined her softly.

"Well, step out of here so I can get dressed and we can go to town in time for our wedding." She was laughing as she pushed him towards the door. He grabbed her and held her tightly to him. Brushing her nose with a light kiss he released her and just as suddenly he left her alone to see to the morning's chores.

She watched him go thinking to herself, "This is going to be the most wonderful day of my life!" She hugged herself tightly for a moment and then began tidying up the cabin and dressing for her wedding. Without hesitation she grabbed the calico dress Joseph bought her in Saint Louis. She had prettier dresses in her valise but she felt that they were a part of a life she didn't know. She wanted to become his wife in every sense of the word. Wearing it again allowed her to feel that their first farce of a wedding would somehow become justified and all the embarrassment and lies she had lived would be instantly erased and forgiven by God.

Later, walking hand in hand Abby and Joseph entered the small church in town. Joseph looked down at her. His heart lurched. This beautiful woman belonged to him. He was happy to see her wearing the dress that he had bought her. It seemed fitting that she wore it again to legally marry him this time. Seeing her in the dress gave him the same sense of forgiveness toward his wrong doings in their earlier farce of a marriage as she had felt. He was proud to see that she had placed a garland of yellow and white daisies that she picked from the field by their cabin onto her head. But her face was the prettiest part of her. She was radiant! He was so pleased to finally see her so happy at last. He wandered what he'd done to deserve this beautiful woman and to have earned her love for him.

Reverend Elihu Thadeus Martin, the local preacher, approached them. He looked a bit intimidating to Abby standing tall and thin in his two piece black suit with a round white collar covering his neck. His nose was thin but long and looked a bit pinched, and his hair was balding in the middle but short and slicked down the sides. Abby didn't know whether to be scared of him or if she wanted to laugh.

He welcomed Joseph whom he met the previous day and then he introduced himself to her. Then he beckoned to his wife, Marion and introduced her to both Abby and Joseph. He explained that she was to be their witness to their wedding.

Again Abby almost laughed. Marion was a full figured very short woman wearing a dark gray dress and her gray hair was pulled tightly into a bun. She also wore a pair of gold rimmed spectacles. Her cheeks were rosy and she had a merry attitude about her. Abby noted that the couple was completely different and looked like they couldn't possibly be man and wife. However, she quickly shook Marion's extended hand and accepted her happy congratulations on her marriage.

Marion asked her if they would like her to sing a song for them. Abby smiled and nodded her head. While she and Joseph stood before Reverend Martin, smiling at one another, Marion began her song. Her voice was a beautiful as a songbird. The song she chose was a love ballad named *I Love you truly*!

Abby felt that the song was absolutely perfect. "I am going to remember this day forever!" She thought to herself as she looked into Joseph's eyes.

As Marion finished her tune, her husband began to speak. He mono-toned his wedding sermon first. It was long and he very seriously explained the importance of becoming man and wife and the duties they would be agree to be bound to for each other. He warned them not to take marriage lightly as it was sanctified by God, and needed to be treated with kindness, reverence and true faithfulness to each other. He reminded Joseph that it would be his duty to love and care for his young bride, just as Jesus loved and cared for his church. To Abby, he indicated her responsibility to stand beside Joseph, and for her to be an obedient and submissive wife unto her husband.

Both Joseph and Abby began to feel slightly overwhelmed at their new pastor's description of marriage. They stole a look at each other and both of them automatically knew that everything would be alright for them.

Finally, Reverend Martin got to the meat of the ceremony. He asked Joseph. "Do you, Joseph Alan Jordan take this young woman to be your bride till death do you part?" He was careful to voice the question seriously to Joseph.

"Yes Siree! You bet I do!" Joseph lapsed into his Texas accent in his exuberance!

"Ah hem…!" the preacher coughed and replied, "A simple 'I Do' will suffice Mr. Jordan."

"Well, then, I most certainly do!" Joseph jubilantly replied again never taking his gaze off of his beautiful bride!

"That's better!" the preacher nodded his head and turned his attention to Abby, "And do you Lydia Creosota, take this man to be your lawfully wedded husband?" he prepared his expression to wait patiently for her to confirm her vows.

Abby smiled into Joseph's eyes, and began saying her vows to him, "I d…,"

"NO! She most certainly doesn't!" Came an unbidden booming voice of authority from the doorway of the church.

All eyes pivoted in the direction of the door. "Oh hello Jeffrey!" Abby smiled at him and returned her gaze to Joseph. Suddenly her eyes opened wide. Her expression went blank. Her mouth formed the shape of an 'O,' she looked into Joseph's eyes and immediately fainted, crumbling to the floor before Joseph could catch her.

"Lydia!" Joseph cried as he quickly dropped to the floor to pick Abby up in his arms. He cradled her and at the same time he was trying to push the stranger away from grabbing onto his bride. For a second a tug of war ensued between them.

Joseph was stunned! He swung his fist up and hit the stranger in the chin knocking him backwards and releasing his hold off of Abby. Grabbing Abby tightly to him, Joseph tried to fan her and bring her to. "Who in heaven's name are you? Why are you interrupting my wedding to my bride?" He demanded the strange man to identify himself.

The stranger was sitting on the floor in front of the first pew where he had landed. Joseph had nearly knocked the breath out of him. He was gasping for air and was momentarily unable to speak. Shaking his head and rubbing his chin ruefully he attempted to rise from the floor. He was dressed decently but had the dusty look of having traveled long and hard about him. His three piece expensive brown suit needed cleaning and the stranger himself smelled of having partaken of whiskey. Trying to stand and regain his balance he grabbed for his brown derby hat that had fallen off of him when he fell. Dusting it off he attempted to speak to the reverend, totally intending to ignore Joseph, but he was interrupted before he got a single word out.

"This young man is the young woman's legally betrothed!" Declared a huge heavyset man who was also gasping for breath as he hurried into the church behind Jeffrey. "And no she is not legally at liberty to marry you or anyone else except this young man!" he panted his explanation huffing to get his breath. He was pointing to the young man sitting awkwardly on the pew. "May I introduce you to her betrothed," he took charge of the conversation, "This young man is Mr. Jeffrey Browning, the youngest Senator for the esteemed State of Georgia, soon to become the youngest Governor of said state and he just happens to be this young woman's legally betrothed!" He adamantly declared to everyone in the room.

Joseph was shocked. His absolute worst nightmare had come true. The love of his life actually did belong to someone else and that someone was here to claim her. His heart shattered. What's more she had called the stranger Jeffrey. She knew the man. She had remembered his name. Joseph felt that he was going to be sick to his stomach. He searched the room for someone to help him with Abby.

"Marion, some water please, quickly!" He requested her to respond to him immediately. Dismissing the stranger he attended to his love. He needed time to think. He needed her to revive herself and explain this horrible nightmare to him.

A shaken Marion grabbed the flowers out of the vase on the altar and gave the container filled with water to Joseph. She was confused, her husband was standing still staring at all the people in the church. It was clear that he had no idea what was going on.

Joseph took the vase and dumped the water on Abby's face. She came too instantly, pushing at the water that now had drowned her face and wilted her flowered head band.

She looked up at Joseph and said, "What happened Joseph? Where's Jeffrey?" As she said the name, Jeffrey, her memory completely flooded back to her. "Oh my, Oh no? Joseph…," her voice faded to a stop. The shock on her face was evident. She stared into Joseph's eyes, beseeching him with her eyes to stay with her and help her to understand what was happening.

Joseph released her from his hold and hurried outside. He felt sick of his stomach and was afraid that he was going to heave the contents. He was completely ill from the shock of his shattered dreams.

Jeffrey recovered his breathing and walked to Abby. He sat beside her on the pew Joseph had deposited her on so quickly. She ignored him and her eyes were riveted on Joseph as he rushed out the door. She didn't understand why he had left. She thought he left because he wasn't able to forgive her. She looked from Jeffrey to Silas Johnson in bewilderment. "Silas, what are you doing here?" She asked completely and intentionally ignoring Jeffrey.

Jeffrey began speaking softly to her telling her that he was here now and that everything was going to be okay. "What is he babbling about?" She thought, "Everything is okay already, or it was until he and Silas Johnson arrived!" She shook her head trying to alleviate the intense pain in her head. All sound seemed to be receding from her ears. She fainted again and this time it was Jeffrey who caught her in his arms.

Chapter Nineteen

Reverend Martin and his wife Marion, took control. "Leave her with us they demanded. This young woman has obviously experienced a great shock today. Let us take care of her until she comes too and can think for herself." They demanded more than suggested to Silas and Jeffrey. "You two look like you need to get some rest. There's a hotel down the street. We will contact you when she is ready to see you." Reverend Martin spoke firmly to the obviously exhausted men. He had Marion lead Jeffrey to their bedroom where he was instructed to lay her carefully on the bed.

"That's fine, I will contact you when she wakes up and we determine what needs to be done." Flustered, Marion took immediate control and began covering Abby lightly with a quilt and then she headed for the water pitcher, dipped a rag in it and prepared to wipe Abby's brow. "You can return to the sanctuary now and my husband will see you out!" Marion politely but firmly dismissed him.

She didn't care for the looks of the young man. He appeared frantically out of control and smelled of whiskey. On the other hand she had already learned that Abby was to become the new school teacher and automatically she was concerned that the beautiful young woman may be taken from the town far too quickly for her liking. Besides, there was definite love between this girl and young man they almost married her too. She had witnessed enough marriages to take notice of that fact. On the other hand Marion failed to notice any interest in the girl for the young man smelling of whiskey who had stopped the wedding with his claims of betrothal rights.

The Reverend took the two men by the arm and urged them to leave the church. He walked outdoors with them and pointed to the direction of the Hotel. He did not see Joseph anywhere so he went back inside to help Marion with Abby.

Jeffrey and Silas stood in front of the church arguing with one another. Jeffrey was insisting he stay with Abby. Silas attempted to coerce him to see that Abby needed a little time alone to get her head on straight. Jeffrey refused to listen. He insisted on remaining by the Church. Again Silas tried to warn him that he needed to leave and clean up a bit before Abby saw him again. However still Jeffrey insisted on remaining. He was afraid that Joseph would come and take her away from him although he refrained from telling this fear to Silas. Frustrated, Silas gave up and said he would be at the Hotel if he was needed. He left and started down the street.

Joseph regained his composure. His face was pale and it was obvious that he had been retching. Leaving the rear of the church where he had run for privacy, he returned to the church's main entrance. Seeing Jeffrey he stopped. Measuring him up, he did not like what he saw and knew he was about to confront a very angry and out of control adversary.

Jeffrey looked up and saw Joseph measuring him up. His eyes immediately filled with hate! "Abby belongs to me! Not to you!" he declared vehemently to Joseph.

"That may have been true once, but she's not yours anymore, she made that clear this morning when she was about to become my wife!" Joseph retorted angrily.

Jeffrey rose from the church steps. Now both men were standing sizing up each other.

Jeffrey stepped into the street. The young men began to circle each other their fists balled ready to fight. Jeffrey swung first. He missed, but caught his balance as Joseph hit him squarely on the jaw cutting his lower lip. He lunged at Joseph. The two men fought back and forth hitting and swinging at each other. People gathered on the street to watch them fight. For a full thirty minutes each man attempted to destroy the other. Eventually, they were both spent. Their energy zapped. They stumbled again to a standing position and attempted to swing at each other once more. They missed each other and both of them fell to the ground completely spent. They lay there on the ground saying nothing to each other attempting to catch their breath.

Eventually, Jeffrey rolled to his side and attempted to stand. Without looking at Joseph he placed his arms across his stomach to ease the pain. Bent over and stumbling he ignored the crowd that had gathered. Still protecting his injured stomach and without a single word to anyone, he made his way down the street to the Hotel. He was in too much pain to take the risk of being hit yet again by Joseph and he finally accepted that the worst thing he could do was to let Abby see him in his battered filthy drunken state. He now realized that she had not rushed into his arms but had actually ignored him, no actually she had looked right through him as if he wasn't even there, when she spoke to Silas and not to him.

Joseph watched him leave. He still lay panting for breath on the hard street in front of the church. He took this as a sign that he had won the battle. Sitting up he gathered his remaining strength and asked the preacher where Lydia was? Reverend Martin reached down and gave him a hand to assist him to rise. "Ok, the fight's over, everyone can go on your way now!" ignoring Joseph's request he first addressed the crowd. Then he asked Joseph, "Are you alright?"

"Yes, thank you." Joseph panted his reply as he attempted to straighten his clothing and shake off the street dust. "Where's my bride?" he asked the reverend impatiently for a second time.

"She has fainted again, I'm afraid," the reverend informed him, "I have sent for the doctor but I am afraid she is still unconscious.

"Will you take me to her?" Joseph was trying to be polite, but his anxiety was mounting quickly. He headed immediately for the rectory not waiting for the reverend.

Reverend Martin grabbed his sleeve to detain him. "Son," he said, "I'm sorry but I can't let you see her just yet. There is a question of legality to deal with here and I need to speak with the Sheriff and Judge before we can determine what the law has to say about all this. I suggest you go on home, clean up a bit and let the girl decide what her intent is. I promise to send for you as soon as she awakens and asks me too." Joseph vehemently objected, but the Reverend was adamant that he should leave.

Joseph realized that he was not going to be allowed to see Abby. Disappointed and worried, he picked up his hat and complied with the Reverend's request. He made certain that Reverend Martin knew where to contact him and then he said, "I know you are probably right? But promise me that you will send for me before you let those other men in to see her. I need to know for myself what's going on here." He explained to the Reverend that Abby had been suffering with amnesia for several months now and to the best of his ability he informed the Reverend of his side of the story as much as he knew. "Apparently, seeing Jeffrey is the cause of her fainting, but also I believe she is experiencing an end to her amnesia. I saw the bewilderment in her eyes as she looked at me before she fainted. So, yea, you are probably right. She does need time to get her thoughts together."

"That sounds like a plausible reason for her fainting," the Reverend replied. "But it doesn't explain why you were marrying her if you knew she might belong to someone else." He chastised Joseph for the sin he had almost participated in helping them do.

Joseph nodded, "I realize you are right, and we were most likely about to make a huge mistake, but we are in love and she has no one here or anywhere she could turn too except me." He told the Reverend that both he and Lydia had made the decision to marry anyway as they thought no one would ever look for her way out here in this new fairly unknown land. He explained that they hoped by marrying they would prevent themselves from living together wrongly.

"I understand son, and commend you for attempting to prevent a sinful life, but as your new preacher, I have to inform you that were really doing a great wrong in the eyes of our Lord." He admonished him again. "It's fortunate for both of you that her young man, arrived and stopped you just in time. Now maybe you will have the opportunity to right all of these wrongs!" He assured Joseph that he would get word to him when the girl awoke and made her decision. He then led Joseph over to the wagon and sent him home.

Joseph didn't want to leave, he tried again, but the Reverend was adamant and told him to go home," He then went into the rectory shutting the door in Joseph's face.

Joseph was beside himself. His chest hurt much worse at the thought of losing Abby than it did at the beating he had just taken from Jeffrey.

"What's happened? What do I do now?" He asked himself standing in front of the closed sanctuary door. He reached up to push his tumbled blond hair away from his eyes. When he did he noticed that his hand had blood on it. "Oh wow!" he mumbled. "I need to see Lydia and know that she is ok, but if she sees me like this she will be very upset all over again." He decided he had best do as the preacher told him and at least get cleaned up a bit. Then when the preacher sent for him he would return to see Abby. "Anyways, he is a preacher so I can trust him to keep his promise to me and let me see her before that other yokel does! At least I have that one advantage," he consoled himself as he climbed into the buckboard and turned the team in the direction of their cabin. He tried to calm himself, but the pain of the fight began assailing him as he drove off. Apparently he had taken quite a beating himself, he acknowledged.

Much later that same evening, Abby moaned lightly and attempted to sit up. Dazed, she looked around the room wondering where she was and how was it that she ended up here. Then she saw Marion sitting in a rocking chair watching her. "Where's Joseph, Where am I?" She asked the preacher's wife.

"He's gone home dearie." The Reverend and I sent him home until you're ready to see him. We felt you needed to get your head together and decide what you wanted to do."

Abby rubbed lightly at the bruise now turning shades of purple and black on her forehead. Her head had collided with the edge of the pew when she fainted the first time.

"Oh my…," she mumbled as the memory of her wedding fiasco returned to her subconscious thoughts. She realized now that her memory was completely returned as well. "Oh no! "I'm not Lydia Creosota!" she suddenly blurted out more to herself than to Marion. "I'm Abigail Anderson and that young man who stopped the wedding is my betrothed, Jeffrey Browning, but I don't love him anymore! I love Joseph!" she announced to the astounded Marion.

"Oh my heaven's! What am I supposed to do now? I love Joseph with all of my heart but I am betrothed to Jeffrey. Only I am not good enough for Jeffrey so I left my home and now…, and now…," she paused to think, "now here I am and I don't know what to do. At least I finally know who I really am." She looked at Marion relieved to have her memory back. At Marion's look of confusion, Abby related her story to her from the very beginning.

Marion looked completely stunned as Abby completed her absurd story. "My, my, why that's quite a story dearie," she finally offered in reply. "Frankly, I don't quite know what to say to you. Here, in California, we are not governed by the same social rules and regulations as the southern states of America. We simply follow our heart and pray to our heavenly father to guide us as we do his will," she advised Abby.

Abby looked at her. "I suppose I need to see them both. But only one at a time. Would you please have Reverend Martin send for Silas Johnson for me? Hopefully he can help me to understand the mess I have made of everything." she asked Marion.

Marion volunteered that her husband was visiting with another parishioner, but she herself would go after Mr. Johnson for her. She patted the girl on the head and told her to lie back down and try to rest. She was unaware that her husband had promised Joseph to let him see the girl before the other men did. "Try not to let your thoughts overload you, dearie!" she cautioned her and then left to go after Silas.

Abby paced the room anxiously trying to sort out the mess as she awaited Marion's return with Silas. Their wedding had been interrupted badly by Jeffrey's untimely arrival, but this evening was much worse. After relating her story to the Reverend's wife, she fully understood that her rash decisions and actions caused her to be in this predicament and that she and she alone was responsible for the outcome and any harm that might come to either Joseph or Jeffrey. She accepted that both men were totally innocent of any crime against her and that she was totally to blame for actions that involved them all. She had requested to speak with Silas before either Joseph or Jeffrey as she wanted to know what her legal obligations were and to determine if she was free to marry Joseph or at least to inquire what actions would she need to take to free herself of her obligation to become Jeffrey's wife. She knew in her heart that she could never be a wife to Jeffrey, no matter what happened to her and Joseph. She prayed that Joseph would understand and forgive her for involving him in this horrific mess.

Instead of Silas, Jeffrey suddenly burst into the room. He went straight to her and tried to grab her in his arms, she stepped behind the side of the bed to evade his embrace. She was caught off guard and was not prepared to speak with him yet, but at his insistence, she tried to explain to him that she'd left him because she could not be the wife to him that he needed.

Jeffrey assured her that he knew the story of her birth but her illegitimate birth didn't matter. "Anyway your parents were married at the time of your birth, so in the eyes of state law, your birth isn't considered to be illegitimate. And in fact your birth circumstances are actually not any issue in preventing our marriage at all!" He excitedly attempted to assure her that he didn't care about her birth circumstances. "I still want you to be my wife!" he declared.

Abby's attention was taken away from Jeffrey momentarily as she saw Silas arrive into the room from the corner of her eyes. Most of Jeffrey's statement had fallen on deaf ears. She really wasn't interested in anything he had to say to her right now. Her questioning gaze turned on Silas, demanding him to explain her responsibilities to Jeffrey to her.

However, Silas counseled her that she did have a somewhat legal obligation as the betrothal had been announced publicly and that she needed to keep her legal obligation and return home and marry Jeffrey. He also added that her life was, and always would be, in Savannah. He also informed her that the circumstances of her birth did not take away her rights to inherit Charles estate as he was listed as her legal father on her birth records.

Abby attempted to argue with Silas," But, I'm not legitimately his child. This discredits me and will only bring shame to Jeffrey and this will hinder your career!" she turned her attention back to Jeffrey, imploring him to let her go.

"Not so Abby, Not so, you are wrong about that Abigail," Silas interrupted and turned her attention back to him. "You are still his legitimate heir legally. Yes, there has been gossip and slander regarding the actual facts of your conception, but you have to be strong enough to ignore them. My dear young woman, society is fickle! Once the people of Savannah discern that you cannot be disturbed by their gossip, your story will fade into oblivion." He tried his absolute best to convince her.

"Oh, I'm so confused…," Abby put her hands over her face to cover her dismay. She searched for a way to convince Jeffrey that she no longer wished to become his wife.

Jeffrey had had enough. He grabbed Abby and embraced her tightly. He went to great pains to assure her that he wanted her to return home to become his wife. He also told her that he was glad that he had arrived in time to stop her from making a terrible mistake.

"What do you mean a terrible mistake?" She asked him angrily while she wriggled desperately to free herself from his embrace. "I Lov…,

Again, Jeffrey cut her short. "Don't say that! You and I both know it's not true! He ordered her overly loud. "You suffered with amnesia Abby," he reminded her a little more tenderly. "We both know we belong together. You just didn't remember me for a little while, that's all."

Holding her shoulders firmly, he continued to stare into her eyes willing her to remember the love she'd recently felt for him. His pride totally refused to allow Joseph, or any man, to cuckold him. "Besides, we've publicly announced our engagement." He continued his persuading tactics, "I've made a commitment publicly to marry you and did so as the youngest Senator of Georgia! Now! *I need you to marry me*!" He emphasized his need. "I can't allow any scandal to interfere in my public life!" Again he reminded her of his social obligations in order to accomplish his career goals.

Abby looked at him strangely, something didn't seem right about his last statement. She had tried to let him off easy. She knew her heart belonged to Joseph. What's more she didn't want to leave California. She had only been here a couple of days but she loved it here. Suddenly the thought of returning to Savannah's *high fallutin society*, as Joseph would have called it, seemed lame at best. She had never felt as excited in her whole life as she was just this morning at the possibility of her new life here with Joseph in California, not to mention her opportunity to teach the children of this town who needed her so much. She'd tried to explain her desires to Jeffrey, but he refused to hear her.

Instead he'd gently taken her hand and kneeled beside her at the edge of the bed, shaking his head sadly he said, "Abby my dearest, I am so sorry sweetheart, I truly didn't want to have to tell you," he paused for effect and then continued, "but, your Joseph told me he doesn't want you anymore."

Smoothly he lied to her without feeling any remorse. At her look of disbelief, he quickly explained, "You see darling, your Joseph and I had a fight in the street right here in front of the church earlier. You can ask anyone. There was a huge crowd," he told her in an attempt to convince her. "Your Joseph quit before I could seriously hurt him. He said he'd had enough and that you just weren't all that important to him. He went so far as to tell me that I was welcome to you!" Jeffrey pretended that he was outraged incredulously at Joseph's quickness to accept his defeat and let her go so easily without fighting for her. "Then after that he dusted himself off and he just walked away!" he finished.

Silas's eyes were bulging! He wished he hadn't walked to the hotel and left Jeffrey alone at the church earlier. He knew that there had been a fight as Jeffrey had returned to the hotel badly beaten, but Jeffrey had not mentioned any of this to him.

"Wh..aaa..tt..?" Abby drew the one word question out in heartbreak and disbelief. "I don't believe you!" Violently Abby pushed him away from her. Running to the door away from Jeffrey she called loudly for the Reverend and his wife. "Please, could you find Joseph for me?" She asked, vigorously wiping at the tears that were streaming down her face.

Jeffrey rose from the floor and followed her to the door. There he tried again to embrace her apologizing for the cruelty that fate was dealing upon her.

This time she violently pushed him off of her and demanded for him to leave. She'd told him she would talk to him later after she spoke with Joseph. She'd pushed him out of the room and motioned for Silas to accompany him and then she slammed the door in their faces.

Jeffrey turned and smiled broadly at Silas. "See, I told you not to worry. I've got things under control." He turned Silas in the direction of the door and ordered him, "Why don't you go book a ship for all three of us now." He commanded Silas. "We need to get out of here and back to Savannah as soon as possible. I don't know about you, but I'm saddle weary." He reminded Silas, "Sides, Abby needs to see sights that won't bring back memories of another man to her," he spat out the words referring to Joseph angrily! "Not to mention there are no other wagon trains out of here till next spring. So go on! Book us a ship old man!"

Silas replied in surprise, "But Jeffrey, the girl doesn't…,"

Jeffrey interrupted quickly, "You need to solve this case don't you! Now let it alone and leave it to me. We are all three going home to Savannah immediately!" he reiterated. "Now go get that ship passage booked!" he ordered Silas again only forcefully this time.

Relieved to be on a ship instead of horseback Silas agreed quickly and left to find out how to book a ship from this small town. He did so via telegraph. Even this small town had a telegraph already in use in her fast growth. He also sent a telegraph to Charles and informed him that they had finally found his missing daughter. He informed him that all was well and that they would be home as soon as it could be arranged via a sea voyage.

Totally distraught, Abby paced the floor waiting for Joseph to arrive. It was much later that night that a light knock came on her door. She'd thrown the door open ready to jump into Joseph's arms. But it was the Reverend and his wife who were standing there. Marion's eyes were red. She had been weeping.

The Reverend took Abby's hands and sat her down gently on the bed as he delivered the news she did not want to hear. Joseph was not to be found. The Reverend explained that he had sent a messenger to the cabin to get Joseph. The man had returned to town and told him that Joseph was not at the cabin. He said the cabin was in chaos and her personal items were strewn all over the place. So then he looked for Joseph's possessions and none could be found. He also noted that the horse and wagon were gone as well.

The reverend and the messenger then searched in town for him. They checked the saloon, and the hotel, and even the bank, but no one had seen the man they were looking for. "I'm sorry Miss Abby, but it looks like your young Jeffrey has told you the truth. As far as we can tell it appears that your young Joseph has left you."

Abby stared at the Reverend in both shock and disbelief. Tears slid slowly down her cheeks. Marion hurried to console her. When Abby's tears subsided somewhat, Marion suggested that Abby should probably return home to Savannah with her young betrothed and pick up her life where she had left it. "I think this is absolutely appalling! Too think that your young Joseph could leave so easily. I was certain he was in love with you." She momentarily mused, "Well, no matter now! He is simply not good enough for you! She declared victoriously. Patting the heartbroken girl's back lightly as she spoke her words of wisdom.

Knowing she really didn't have any other choice, Abby reluctantly dried her tears agreed to return home to Savannah with Jeffrey and Silas. She did considered staying in town hoping Joseph would come back. "After all, she could still support herself by becoming the town's teacher." She suggested to Marion.

In the end, however she allowed the Reverend and his wife to convince her that she shouldn't stay in a place that would only bring her more sorrow. They told her that everywhere she went she would be confronted with her unhappy memories and hopes of a wonderful life with Joseph. They felt she would not be able to handle her sorrow.

"Besides, we have seen so many young men like your young Joseph. They come to this town and then they just leave all of a sudden. None of them have ever returned and we fear your Joseph won't either. You really should go home to the life you've lived and are familiar with. And you should do so while you can be escorted by your two family friends. At least your Joseph knows you are from Savannah and if he ever decides to look for you he will probably start his search there." And with those words, Abby let them convince her. It gave her one thread of hope to hang onto.

Chapter Twenty

Three months later, Abby awoke in the bedroom of her childhood Savannah home. She'd experienced a few tense moments when her ship rounded Cape Horn. There was no denying the sailing trip was overly long and terribly lonely without Joseph being beside her. Except for the horrific constant sea sickness, the trip had not been nearly as arduous as the wagon train journey across the mainland had been.

Now here she was sitting up in her very own bed just as if she had never left. The thought flitted through her mind that the last six months might as well have been a huge nightmare.

"This room has not changed. Everything is still in the same place. I might as well be eighteen again. It was all just a bad dream! Just a very bad dream!" she stated aloud to no one. Her voice echoed back at her in the deafening silence of the overly large quiet room.

She swung her feet over the edge of the bed but remained in a sitting position in a fog of thoughts. She recalled her arrival home last evening. Old Pelly had nearly smothered her with her overly large breasts as she hugged her crying tears of joy as she'd repeated again and again, "See, my babie's a'back agin! She shore is! I done tole ya she come back to her old Pelly!"

Pelly and Old Trey were the only persons whom Abby truly was happy to see again. As for her father, she'd hugged him obediently, but her feelings remained strained. Her anger towards him was newly returned after her bout with amnesia and they still remained unresolved. "One day I may forgive him, but not now!" She spoke to the sunshine filtering into her room through her open window.

Abby's thoughts took a new direction. "Why am I back here anyway?" She asked herself. "Oh yea! Cause Joseph lied and ran out on me!" Abby reminded herself angrily. She was extremely depressed. "I don't know what I did for him to leave me without as much as a single word? I reckon Jeffrey was right all along!" She lapsed into some of Joseph's Texan dialect.

"Someday, I'll accept that Joseph didn't really love me," she wiped at the single tear sliding slowly down her cheek.

"Well! Here I am again. Silas said I should count my blessings that Jeffrey still loves me and that he is willing to overlook my illegal birthright and still wants to marry me! Frustrated, she spoke loudly to her empty room. "Stop it! Stop it Abby Anderson! You wouldn't be here planning your wedding to Jeffrey Browning if your Joseph's love for you had been true! So stop thinking about Joseph! He no longer matters! You need to focus on Jeffrey instead!" her confused mind argued within herself.

She had been having this same conversation nearly every morning now for the past three month's journey during her sea voyage home. Always she ended up chastising herself reminding herself that Joseph had chosen to leave her. But as always her thoughts returned to the day she'd nearly married the man whom her heart was still lost to. "That's right! Mr. Joseph Alan Jordan, you still hold my heart!" she ruefully stated to the empty room.

Abby looked into the same mirror that she had perused herself in so many months ago. Again the woman looking back at her was unknown to her. The girl she used to see in the mirror with the smooth peachy cheeks was gone. This woman was definitely matured. Her hair was the same vibrant red, but was bound in a long tight braid that ran down the back of her head. Gone were the flirtatious loose curls of her childhood. This woman had a slightly tanned weathered face with many freckles across the bridge of her nose. Gone was the overly protected perfectly white, almost freckle free, skin that she had been taught so carefully to protect from the sun by the use of ornate parasols to protect her precious complexion. This woman's lips were thinner, stronger! No longer plump or pursed in a joyful smile. They would frown now at the least little provocation. Her once shiny green eyes were blank, empty, emotionless, just green irises rimmed in a thin black line. She stood there staring at herself wondering what had happened to her and who was she now?

Eventually, she shrugged her shoulders and turned away from the mirror. She busied herself with a quick sponge bath. She looked in her Armoire for a dress to wear. The beautiful day dresses all begged to be worn again. For some reason she felt disgust in them. She selected the plainest of them all, a gray and white simple dress with a high neck. She put on the dress and secured her long red braid into a bun. Taking a last look in the mirror she frowned and thought to herself, "At least I can look like a school marm!" But she couldn't even giggle at her own attempt at humor.

Leaving her room she went downstairs for breakfast. She paid no attention to the house as she walked down the staircase and the immaculately polished long hallway into the dining room. Seeing it again meant nothing to her.

Later, that same day, she entertained Jeffrey, his parents and his sister. Plans were made between them and her father for the finalization of her long awaited wedding to Jeffrey. It was decided that they would be married in one month, on Christmas Eve. Abby sat silently allowing them to make the decisions regarding her life. She no longer cared about her future, her depression was deep. Those around her assumed her disinterest was due to the tiredness of her sea journey home. She let them have their assumptions without argument.

Jeffrey was excitedly confirming plans for their wedding. He completely dismissed the fact that Abby had remained in her stateroom for most of the journey home, refusing to speak to him unless it was absolutely necessary. Her few conversations had been polite and limited, cold in nature. Silas indicated his concerns but Jeffrey convinced him that she was suffering from seasickness. Jeffrey was determined to avoid further scandal to his career. He'd adamantly commanded Silas to say nothing to anyone regarding Abby's involvement with Joseph. Besides, he'd assured Silas, she'll come around after we are married and our new life begins.

Abby looked emotionless at her father. "What a peacock!" She sarcastically thought to herself. She refused to see that her attitude towards him was completely unjust and totally unfair to him. She needed a scapegoat to blame and the very existence of her father perfectly provided her that outlet. She watched him standing tall and proud for his short height, his thin face bright and happy as he conversed with his guests. "He's so proud that his daughter has returned home unscathed and unblemished!" She angrily deceived herself, finding pleasure in her not entirely truthful accusations directed at the poor man. She gave no thought to how much he had suffered thinking harm had come to her.

In truth, Charles was relieved that his daughter was home unscathed and unblemished. But not for the reasons, Abby chose to believe. His heart was thrilled for her safe return and for her future to still be intact. His feelings were the same as any loving parent's feelings would be at the safe return of their missing child. In his happiness over his daughter's safe return he completely overlooked her state of melancholy. He also attributed her long journey to be the cause of her apparent disinterest in planning her upcoming nuptials to Jeffrey.

Abby felt disgust for him whit his constant expressions of gratitude to Jeffrey for saving his daughter from further harm and preventing her from being shamed even worse by the ton. Hiding her face in her fan, she sniffed in disgust, watching him.

Elaine arrived just as Jeffrey and his parents were leaving. Abby forced herself to smile and allowed her friend to quickly hug her. She felt nothing but the need to run away from everyone.

"Oh how is it that Joseph could leave me so easily!" She pouted internally. All she could think of was how much she missed him and she was very jealous at the thought that he might be spending precious moments with someone else. She was in no mood for additional company even if the company was her best friend.

As Abby followed Elaine into her bedchamber for their visit, as was their usual custom, Elaine immediately noticed Abby's distant attitude. Forthright as always, she closed the bedroom door tightly and turning to Abby she demanded Abby to explain her attitude to her.

"Come now Abby darling, I know you better than this. Something's dead wrong! Don't you even try to lie to me, Miss Abigail Anderson, you know I can see right through you! So you'd best open up and tell me what's wrong right now!

Startled, Abby looked at Elaine's forthright face. Suddenly she burst into tears, ran into her friends arms and cried like a baby.

"Oh Elaine, it's all so awful, I don't know where to begin," she cried brokenly and told her long horrible tale to Elaine. She finished by begging her friend to keep her story confidential between them.

"I'm so mortified, Elaine, I loved Joseph so deeply and he just left me without a single word! She sniffed. I don't want anyone to know! I'm so ashamed! I traveled alone with him and was about to give myself to him in marriage and oh, I would simply die if anyone ever knew he just up and walked out on me!" She paused wiping her tear streaked face with her kerchief. "But the worst part is, I still love him with all of my heart Elaine. Oh what am I going to do?" She lamented and burst into tears again.

Between sobs she rambled on blowing her nose as she continued, "Jeffrey is willing to marry me, but I don't feel the same for him. I know I don't love him and most likely I never will. I must have simply been infatuated about being in love, but now I know what love really means. Oh! Whatever am I to do, Elaine?" Again she blew her very red nose loudly as she implored her friend for advice.

Elaine gazed blankly at Abby, completely shocked by her story. Traveling with a single man, outlaws, an unlawful marriage, and finally, wagon trains? She reran some of the facts confided to her about Abby's absence. "Abby, I don't know what to say?" She honestly told her friend. "Give me some time to digest this before we decide what you should do?" she pleaded reasonably. "Are you completely certain, that Joseph has left you?" She voiced the one thought that was haunting her friend daily. "If he loved you as much as you thought he did, well..., then I just can't see him giving you up so easily?" she confessed.

"Oh Elaine! I've asked myself that same question time and again. The fact is he was gone, no one could find him. He didn't even leave me a note. Absolutely nothing! Nothing!" she repeated. "Jeffrey said he didn't even want to fight for me. He just left? What else can I think?" she lamented to her friend.

"Hmmm...? Well I don't rightly know?" Elaine noted that Abby was so distressed that maybe she was unwilling to believe that Jeffrey hadn't been entirely truthful to her. So Elaine decided to do some detective work on her own. She attempted to calm Abby by changing the subject.

"Abby, let's try to put this aside for now. I'm going to think long and hard about this for you, but for now, I'm just so happy you are home! My best friend is home, safe and sound and I was so scared I would never see you again!" She hugged Abby tightly. She was trying everything she could to take Abby's mind off of the subject of Joseph.

"You know Abby, she continued happily, while you were gone, Robert Gaars and I were married, and I so missed you at my wedding. It was so empty without you there as my maid of honor. But Robert's and my plans were already made and our parents insisted that we go on with the wedding because of all the expense and all. I'm so sorry you weren't there Abby," she sincerely apologized to her best friend. "Of course I do love Robert dearly, and I'm so happy to be his wife now, and I have a secret, Abby, I'm going to have a baby!" She smiled broadly at Abby.

Abby squealed in delight for her friend! At least this was a subject that she could feel honest true happiness about. It felt good, so good to actually be happy for a while after such a long period of continuous depression. The two friends continued to discuss their lives, catching up on everything that Abby had missed. Elaine related some of the hysterical goings on at the Harriet Harrisons, weekly gossip sessions. Abby smiled ruefully at her part in all the scandalous events, but suddenly Elaine had her laughing her head off at all the ridiculous behavior of the various women. It was several hours later before Elaine took her leave. Abby felt suddenly alone after her true friend left, and just like that her deep depression returned.

Chapter Twenty-One

The following day, Harriet Harrison's parlor was over filled with chattering ladies. "Did you hear? Abigail Anderson is back in town and the wedding is back on!" Their hostess was delighted to be the first to spread the juicy gossip.

"It's wonderful news, dear!" Johanna confirmed. "I was so relieved to hear that our Abby was found safe and well. Don't you think it's just the most romantic tale that Savannah has ever heard? How her Jeffrey went searching for her and found her all the way in California?" She was dying to disclose the additional juicy facts. "Whatever do you think she was doing in California?" She dropped her bomb anticipating the rush of her friends to join in with their own comments.

Elizabeth jumped at the bit. "Well from what I heard," she paused for effect and fanned her nose lightly, "she was up to no good!" She was now desperate to defame Abby since her first attempt had obviously failed.

"Oh, you're just angry that she and Jeffrey are together again!" Her sister, Amelia, couldn't resist some sibling rivalry.

"My goodness gracious! Both you girls just hush now!" Jewell Whatley admonished her daughters quickly before a family fight could ensue. But she couldn't help herself in her own curiosity about Abby's return. Turning her attention to the rest of the room's occupants, she implied her own hearts desires, "Why of course, I'm sure we all would like to know exactly what Abigail was doing in California?" She repeated her daughter's question. She experienced difficulty controlling her own anger at Abby's return to Savannah.

"Then, why don't you just ask her yourself?" Elenora's musical voice came from the entry doorway of the massive parlor. She, with her daughter in tow and her new daughter soon to be, Abigail Anderson, arrived a few moments late for the gathering but just in time to hear Jewell's comment. "I have our own dear Abby, right here with me!" She delightfully announced to the room.

The women stared momentarily in surprise as Abby entered. Angered by Jewel's comment, Abby spoke in her own defense, "Well, Mrs. Whatley and Elizabeth, why don't you both tell me what you think you heard that I was doing in California?"

Not waiting for an answer, she immediately dismissed Jewell and her hateful daughter. Turning she made her polite greeting to Mrs. Harrison. The other women gathered around her, hugging her and exclaiming how happy they were to see her home again. The conversation turned to Abby's wedding plans.

I just believe that I will let my mother-in-law to be, tell you all the exciting plans," Abby turned the conversation over to Elenora. It had taken every nerve in her body to walk into this room and face her peers. She resorted to acting mode to cover her fears. But when the conversation began discussing her wedding plans to Jeffrey, she fell silent. In her heart she really didn't want to marry him. Harriet beckoned Abby to sit beside her as her guest of honor. Accepting her offered cup of tea Abby took a small sip and attempted to block her ears from hearing Elenora's excitement as she related the details of the upcoming wedding.

Looking up Abby found herself starring directly into Elizabeth Whatley's dagger throwing angry violet eyes. The glare was consumed with hatred. Abby shivered involuntarily and looked away. Elizabeth congratulated herself in having successfully intimidated Abby.

Abby's knees went weak. She withdrew within the shell she had fought so hard to come out of. She barely answered the questions the ladies bombarded her with.

Finally, Elizabeth could stand it no more. She was angered by all the attention that Abby was receiving. "Mother, I wish to leave now!" she suddenly demanded loudly for all to hear.

The room fell silent as all the women turned their attention on Elizabeth. Jewell looked at her daughter in surprise. "Leave? Why Elizabeth, we've only just arrived."

"I'm sorry mama, ladies," she addressed them all "it's just that I no longer feel well!" Elizabeth pointedly looked at Abby. "This room is just so stuffy all of a sudden. Why, I just can't catch my breath in here."

"Well, if you are ill, dear?" Mrs. Harrison authorized them to leave.

Abby was red with embarrassment. It was apparent to all of them that Elizabeth was referring to Abby's presence as her reason for her suffocation.

Elaine spoke up on her behalf. "It is stuffy in here." She agreed. "However, I'm certain the air will clear when Elizabeth leaves."

The ladies pivoted their gazes upon Elaine, their eyes bugged at the open hostility Elaine directed upon Elizabeth.

"Oh face it Elizabeth!" Elaine continued. "You're just upset that Abby is back and once again you have lost your chance at Jeffrey." She happily taunted the girl.

Abby instantly dropped her head to hide her shame. Her face blazed red. Elaine's attempt to defend her friend had only succeeding in humiliating her further.

"You witch!" Elizabeth and her mother cried simultaneously at Elaine. "How dare you?" Jewel screamed into the room at the top of her voice.

"You see what I mean Mother, about the air being so stuffy in here!" Huffed Elizabeth, barely controlling herself, she rose and began pulling on her lace gloves confirming her desire to leave immediately.

"Now ladies, that's enough, please sit back down and enjoy this day with us," Mrs. Harrison urged her guests.

"I think it would be wise if I left also," Abby attempted to stand in an effort to make a hasty retreat.

"No you won't dear!" Mrs. Harrison forced her to remain sitting. "However, If Elizabeth is not feeling well, she is most certainly welcome to leave." Harriet defended her guest of honor causing Abby to blush scarlet at being once again the center of attention.

Elenora, her daughter, Elaine and the remaining women in the room began crowding Abby. They wanted to reassure her that she was welcome among them. Their 'well meant' intentions only furthered Abby's discomfort level. It was all she could do to attempt to accept them graciously.

"Well, I have never been so insulted! Come along, Elizabeth, Amelia, we are taking our leave now!" she urged her girls to grab their personal items and she herded them quickly to the door. "We know when we are not welcomed!" Jewel threw her comments to all in the room as she hurried herself after her daughters towards the parlor doors. Finding themselves to be ignored by the other women guests, they left angry and humiliated.

Abby felt oppression settle on her again. Now more than ever she realized that she was committed to marrying Jeffrey. There was no way out of it now. Her heart sank as she politely attempted to accept the ladies many acts and statements of kindness.

Chapter Twenty-Two

"Who hit me?" Wondered Joseph groggily as he regained consciousness. "Where in heaven's name am I? What happened?" Trying to focus he searched his memory. The pain in his head was severe. He attempted to reach his head to inspect his wound and realized that not only was he gagged, but both his hands and feet were tied as well. "What the heck?" Slowly he became oriented with his surroundings. As his faculties returned he tried to remember what happened to him. "The last thing I can remember…?" He squinted from the sharp sudden pain in his head, "is that it was my wedding day. One minute I was the happiest man in town and the next here I am all trussed up like a turkey!" he was frustrated and angry with himself for not knowing how he'd gotten here.

He'd awakened from a terrible nightmare in which he'd seen his bride being led away from him. He'd called out to her begging her not to leave him. He'd declared his undying love to her and his arms were extended begging her not to leave him. The next thing he knew he awoke and found himself gagged and bound lying in this foul smelling dark place that he didn't recognize.

Again, he tried to move his legs. His heart sank as he heard and felt the weight of the chain attached to his ankles. Kicking his legs as far as was possible, he ascertained that his ankles were chained to a huge round post and beam. He could barely breathe through the filthy tasting gag in his mouth, but the stench around him was much worse. It stunk like rotten fish!

"Oh my god! I'm in the hold of a ship!" This realization came more from the sudden rocking of the ship on the water more than from what little knowledge he'd managed to gain from his surroundings. Stopping all movement, he strained his ears, listening carefully for any sounds he could discern. Frantically he prayed that the ship might still be at anchor in port. Feeling the rocking motion was extremely gentle, he decided it was unlikely that the ship had sailed out to the rougher waters of the sea.

"But I still don't have a clue how I got here! Don't worry about that right now, if you want to get out of here you better use some quick thinking and follow it with action before she does set sail! He admonished himself. Immediately he put his creative mind to solving his dilemma.

Working with his tongue and teeth, he finally managed to free his mouth from the gag. Taking a huge breath and nearly vomiting from the fowl air, he silently continued to assess his situation.

"At least now I can breathe!" He congratulated his efforts thus far, but kept looking for a solution to his getaway. "I've got to get out of here before I lay in my own retching mess! Again he struggled to free his hands from the hemp rope that bound him. "I wonder how long I've been here?" Questioning himself verbally helped him to keep conscious.

His head was throbbing in pain, and the rest of his body was so sore, he couldn't tell if it was from the fight he had with Jeffery or some new injuries as well. Continuing with his thoughts he ignored the pain and continuously worked his hands attempting to free himself from the hemp bindings. Suddenly his hand slid out from one of the circles of hemp that bound him.

"Fantastic!" he muttered. He began working the hemp twice as hard. Finally one of his hands was free. He sat up quickly and threw the hemp off of his other hand.

All the while he worked he consciously strained his eyes to see into the darkness. "Those look like barrels over there and I can hear voices coming from above me. Sounds like a lot of moving around up there.

"Now to figure out how to hurry and get this chain off of me!" He continued to keep his mind as busy as possible both to expedite his escape and to take him mind off of the horrific stench. Now that he freed his hands he sat up and inspected the chain attached to his ankles. He nearly laughed out loud!

"What idiot tied me up like this? Sometimes I question the intelligence of men in this world but God Almighty, this is one time that I thank you from the bottom of my heart that you made idiots and put them in this world!" He declared his praises as he attempted to untie the hemp rope attached to one end of the chain with the other end attached to his ankles. Frantically he pulled at the knots binding the rope but they wouldn't budge.

"Well that figures at least someone was smart enough to tie a knot!" he grimaced as his continuous efforts failed to undo the well tied nautical knots. Looking around him for a tool to aide him, he spotted an oil lantern on top of the barrel next to him. He grabbed the lantern and broke it. In the quiet darkness the shattered glass sounded like a bomb going off. Immediately he stopped all movement and patiently waited to see if anyone was coming in response to the noise. When no one came he quickly picked up a shard of glass and began sawing at the hemp rope. "Lucky for me, they didn't stop to think I might wake up and try to get out here cause…," he paused as he managed to cut the rope and unwind it freeing his ankles. "…Cause getting out of here right now is exactly what I'm going to do!" he declared upon freeing himself from bondage. Quietly he moved around searching for a way out of the hold.

Sore and bruised, Joseph examined his head injury. He found dried blood on his forehead. "Thank you lord for letting them hit my head in a place that missed my temples, because I might be lying here dead if that had happened." He continuing conversing with himself. It not only gave him strength to ignore his wounds, but it helped him to think his way out of this mess. Spotting a ladder leading to the upper decks he cautiously climbed and made his way to the main deck.

Peering through the opening in the wide open hold he noticed many sailors busy loading barrels and cargo onto the ship. Slipping among them he grabbed a barrel and hefted it high on his shoulder against the moonlight and the lit lanterns on board the deck. He walked to the loading plank and descended it quickly. By pretending he was one of the sailors loading and unloading stock he managed to escape without being noticed by anyone. Upon reaching the dock, he walked to some barrels, laid down his load and silently disappeared into the darkness of the nearest alley.

He hid there for a few minutes hoping the docks would clear. Shortly after, he heard the captains call to raise the boarding plank. He watched for a while longer as the ship slowly left the dock and set her sails for the wide open sea. "Wow, now that was a close one!" He declared with a whistle under his breath. No one heard or paid any attention to him.

He dusted his filthy clothing and picked some of the dried blood off of his forehead. Then he began making his way off the docks and found himself in the midst of one of San Francisco's roughest neighborhoods known as the Barberry Coast.

No one including the captain realized that he had managed to escape. By the time they looked for him, the ship would be way out to sea. He breathed in a huge sigh of relief.

"Now to find Lydia, I mean Abby!" he corrected himself. "Wow that name sounds strange on my tongue, but no matter, Lydia, Abby, it's not important to me, what is important is that I love that woman and no one, especially that pampas southern social jerk I beat up, is going to take her from me!" He vowed!

Joseph walked down the boardwalk of an unsavory side of San Francisco adjacent to the docks filled with ware houses, saloons and houses of pleasures. A horrible area filled with sailors, passengers, indigents and outlaws. The place ran rampant with daily and nightly crimes. It was unbelievable that many traveling passengers of all social status also frequented the area to board the ships they planned to travel on.

Joseph dismissed it all as of no importance. What was important was that his wedding had gone sour. He'd not been allowed to see the woman he loved with all his heart. He remembered that he'd been sent home to wait until she was ready to see him. The next conscious thing he knew was when he awoke and found himself bound on board the ship.

"When I find out who did this to me, I'll kill them!" He confirmed his thoughts angrily. "And I have a good idea who I'm after," silently he acknowledged that Jeffrey was his most likely assailant.

Taking time to casually speak with a young sailor, he learned that the ship, now sailing on the far horizon, that he just freed himself from was bound for China. Putting two and two together he gleaned that he had been sold into slavery to the ship's captain. Further small talk with the sailor allowed Joseph to ascertain that he was in the city of San Francisco. Not recognizing the name, he mentioned he was in California to mine for gold.

The Sailor volunteered information that he had heard that there was a gold mining town, named Shanty Shacks, about a full days ride north of the city. Joseph thanked the young man for his information and left him.

He avidly began searching for a horse. He rounded a corner in time to hear a drunken sailor bragging to his companions.

"Yes sirree! My buddy and I sure managed to make a small fortune off of that fancy fellow! He smelled of money, so I figures he oughta spend some of it on me!" The bragging sailor continued. "Why I just walked right up to im and asked em what can I do for ya, govnah?" He laughed at his own courageous act.

"That's when he took me an me buddy ere," a second sailor chimed in and nodded over at the first bragging sailor, "over to a huge bag lying in the back of this yere wagon, ye see! Can ya believe it, that tall dandy gave us this here thousand dollars in gold an told us to git rid of the poor bastard he had all tied up in the bag. He even told us to be sure we drowned the bastard, and a course we agreed, but after he left," he snickered here and then continued, "I tole my buddy ere, Why for do we want to drown the poor guy when we could just double our money here by selling the poor chap to the captain. Everyone knows, old captain Kincaid, is a sucker for buying strong men and selling them as slaves once he get's to China?" he was really enjoying telling his story but he became aggravated when his buddy interjected and took the credit away from him.

"So I says! Heck yea! That's what we should do, we'll just sell em ta that captain on that ship headed to China. So we carted him up ta the captain, an tole him what we had in the bag. And then, well this old Captain Kincaid, well, he got this ere gleam in his eye…,"

"Yea, an that's when he tole us ta take the poor chap down into the hold and ta tie him up in the cargo where he warn't likely ta be seen! The second sailor chimed in and stole the story away again.

"Man o' man! Did it ever stink in there! Ya see there was all this stuff, ya know for the voyage I guess, they was even live pigs and cows, and chickens and the poop stink!" he stopped and waved a hand over his nose, "Well, I was sure glad to tie that poor chap up and then get out of there as fast as we could. We found the captain and showed him the proof that the poor fella was all tied up nice and secure like and then he gave us another five hundred dollars each! Yep, me n me buddy ere, we's fixin to do some heavy drinkin and find us a fancy lady or ladies, if'n ya know's whats I mean!" He guffawed at his unexpected good luck!

The Sailors listenting to their outrageous story congratulated them on their good luck. A couple of their friends even slapped them on the back and shook their hands in congratulations.

Joseph continued to watch and listen in amazement just around the corner from all the bragging. He never doubted for a minute that the conversation was about him. He wanted to walk over there and slug them out, but he reasoned that it was more important that he used his time to find Abby. And anyway there was way too many of them and his body was near beaten to pieces as it was.

So he just sat there listening and eventually he heard them say they were going to be on their way to do their drinking etc. Together the bragging seamen walked away sharing the bottle of whiskey between them.

The crowd began to disperse. But a few of their dock friends were envious of their luck. They let them go but Joseph heard the remaining seaman begin making plans for catching them later on during the night and robbing them of the reward monies they had made.

Joseph grinned and nodded his head in satisfaction! "Good, I'm glad to know they'll get what's coming to them." He smiled because he was going to get his satisfaction and he didn't have to lift a finger to accomplish it! Promptly, he dismissed them from his mind and continued his search for a horse.

JUDON GRAY

"At least now I know what happened to me for certain!" he acknowledged and "the dandy" could only be Jeffrey! He was now certain who had done this to him. There was no doubt in his mind about that! Absolutely no doubt at all!

Horse thievery was punishable by death, but right now he didn't really care. He knew that he had only a limited time to catch up with Abby and his pockets were empty of cash. He walked right up to the hitching post in front of a local saloon, untied a horse, mounted him and rode off at a slow pace until he cleared the city limits. Then he kicked the horse into a gallop and rode all night until he reached Shanty Shacks.

If only he had known that at that very moment, Silas, Jeffrey and his beloved almost wife were alighting from a hired cab just a block away from him. They were rushing to be in time to board their own ship headed for Savannah at first dawn.

It was high noon when he arrived back at the cabin. Dismounting his horse he went to the stable and was relieved to note that Abby's horse was still there. He slapped the horse he'd stolen on the rump and shooed it away. He had no desire to be caught with a stolen horse on his property or in his possession and at this point no one had seen him take it or even knew it was gone until it was way too late to track him.

"Give my thanks to your owner for loan of his horse!" he verbally stated to the horse as he slapped it on the rear sending it into a fast gallop. The horse whinnied and then took off at a gallop heading back the way they had come, He doubted it but he shook his head and hoped the horse would find the way back to his original owner.

Searching the cabin he found that all of Abby's personal belongings were missing. He was puzzled momentarily why his clothes were also missing until he realized that his things and his horse had disappeared to help Abby think he'd run out on her.

"Wow! That jerk had really thought this thing through. By now, Abby will be convinced that I left her willingly." In five large strides he crossed to the corner of the room where the unmade bed remained as he had last lain in it. Roughly he jerked at the plank on the floor in front of the bed. He lifted the board he had pried loose before he fell asleep that last night he was at the cabin. "Thank goodness it is still here," again he spoke aloud to himself as he lifted the small but very heavy bundle wrapped in burlap that he had hidden under the floor joists. Hefting the small but heavy object in his hand he quickly put it in his pocket and left the cabin to saddle Abby's mare. He headed the horse back to Shabby Shacks. He decided his next stop was to see if Abby was still at the Reverends. He rather doubted it but prayed that he wouldn't be too late to find her.

An hour later he was pounding the front door of the rectory heavily. Joseph shocked both the Reverend and his wife to see him standing at their door. They both truly believed that he had taken off and would never be heard from again. They were so used to the many men who and came and left just as quickly in their little settlement. They figured Joseph was just one more who left when things didn't go his way.

"Where is she?" He demanded rudely!

"Why Mr. Jordan! Where have you been? Why did you leave without telling us?" The Reverend blamed Joseph for what had happened to Abby.

"Leave her?" I didn't leave her! That dandy man friend of hers came to the cabin, hit me on the head and then tried to have me killed, but instead I was sold as an indentured sailor! However I managed to escape. Now would you please tell me what's happened to the only woman I will ever love?"

He told his story so fast, the Reverend's head was spinning, but what he did gather, was that he and his wife had made a grave mistake in believing Jeffrey's story. And now they were responsible for the young woman's safety who was currently in his custody.

The Reverend and his wife looked at each other in shocked disbelief. "You better come in and sit down." The Reverend invited him in and closed the door quietly behind Joseph.

Before the Reverend could finish speaking, Joseph interrupted. "Please is she here? Oh! Please tell me she is!" he pleaded.

"No son, I'm afraid she is no longer in Shanty Shacks." Reverend Martin's wife spoke up.

"Well, where is she then?" he queried anxiously.

"Well, slow down son, let's figure this out," the reverend interrupted him, "Tell me again what you said at the door so we can determine what needs to be done. I need a moment to digest what has happened to you," he requested. He needed to stall for time so he could pray for the right words to use to inform Jeffrey where Abby had gone and why. He was also praying that God would forgive them both.

Jeffrey was exasperated! Taking a deep breath he tried to slow down his anxiety level. He figured it might help them to help him, if he calmed down a bit and let them come to believe in him again. He knew they were upset with him for trying to marry a woman that he didn't even know was or wasn't married to begin with, but if that wasn't bad enough now these good folks were under the impression that he had "up and left Abby" all on his own. He knew that if he was to get their much needed help, he needed to regain their confidence in him.

Running his anxious fingers through his mussed up hair, he quickly retold his story. "So that's it, that's what this man Jeffrey did to me and now from what I gather she must be in his company as well." He ruefully submitted wishing against all hope that he was wrong.

"Are you serious?" Marion asked him in disbelief.

"Yea, I mean that jerk and his buddy hit me on the head knocking me unconscious and paid two sailors to dump my body into the sea." But instead, the sailor's sold me to a sea captain to become an indentured slave instead. I reckon it was lucky for me that they were a couple of crooks who were smart enough to double the money those two paid them to get rid of me. Lucky for me I came to and freed myself just before the ship set sail for China. I barely got off that ship before she pulled anchor and sailed away."

His audience was looking at him appalled. The story moved so fast, it was hard to believe, but looking at his bruises and hastily wrapped head bandage they never doubted a word he said.

They both stared at him silently for a few moments. His patience was wearing and he nearly got up and left in his anxiety and determination to find Abby, but he knew that being patient and giving them time to digest their shock at his story would be his best course of action at the moment. So he sat there and willed himself to be patient.

Finally, Marion, raised her hands to her face and said, "Oh no! Joseph I' fear we have done you a tremendous wrong. Please find it in your heart to forgive us for we truly believed that Jeffrey was telling the truth. He told us all that you said you did not want to fight for her. So after the story of all you had done for your dear little woman, we thought maybe you had tired and just wanted to get away from all the trouble being with her had caused you. So we helped convince Abby…,

Joseph had been patient enough, He cut her off and anxiously asked, "So, Where is Lydia, Abby, or whatever her real name is?" He anxiously prompted them for an answer. He just didn't have the time to be polite to the Reverend and his wife right now. All he could think was where was Abby and how could he get to her before it was too late! Joseph was so angry he was barely refraining from resorting to foul language in front of the pastor and his wife.

"Son, I'm so sorry to tell you this, but we thought they were gentlemen. The big man informed us that your young woman was officially and legally engaged to the younger man. They told us that you had kidnapped her. We thought they were telling us the truth. We urged your little lady to return to Savannah, Georgia with them." The Reverend confessed as he paced the floor putting distance between himself and Joseph.

He fully expected Joseph to hit him as he nervously confessed the innocent but shameful part he and his wife had played in Abby's disappearance. We searched everywhere for you, but you and your horse and your belongings were nowhere to be found." He added.

"Oh my dear! We are so very sorry," his wife interjected. We truly thought you'd left her. If it's any comfort to you, she was broken hearted. She said she loved you deeply and she refused to believe you had run out on her." Marion tried her best to console him and give him confidence that all was not lost.

"Thanks for that Mrs. Martin. I definitely needed to hear that she loves me still." I was so afraid she might have made the decision to pick Jeffrey over me." Joseph relaxed slightly. "Now at least, I know I have a chance to find her and bring her back. So do you know when they left and how they planned to get to, where was it…, Savannah, Georgia again, you said?"

"Yes, dear, they booked passage on a ship out of San Francisco," the reverend's wife volunteered. And yes, it's Savannah Georgia where they were headed. Your young miss told me of her amnesia and the horrifying events she had been through. She said you didn't even know her real name. So if it helps, her name is Abigail Anderson. Her father is Charles Anderson. I'm sure you will find her in Georgia if you hurry. She implored him.

Joseph grabbed his hat and bolted for the door, "Thanks for the info, I'm heading for the first ship to Savannah!" He called to them along with his thanks for their information.

"God go with you young man! We will pray for a successful journey for you. That's the least we can do to try to right the wrong we have done." The Reverend and his wife called to him as he mounted Abby's mare and rode out of sight.

"Oh dear, we may have unwittingly put that young lady in harm's way. The Reverend looked painfully at his wife.

"We'll pray that he gets to her as quickly as possible." Marion consoled him. Together they closed the door of the rectory and went into their bedroom and fell upon their knees. They sincerely begged God to forgive them for the ill part they had innocently played and they prayed for God's grace that he would allow Joseph to catch up with Abby before it was too late."

Completely upset, Joseph rode away formulating his plan in his mind as he rode to the Assayer's office. "Thank god, I found this huge nugget of gold! He said to himself as he put his hand into his pocket to enclose it safely into his palm. I'm cashing it in and then heading straight back to San Francisco to book myself on the first ship to Savannah. There was no need to return to the cabin. His things were gone. Afraid a delay would cause him to miss the next ship to Savannah, he decided to make the long trip to San Francisco without having any sleep. He was determined to catch the very next ship to Savannah and if luck was with him hopefully the love of his life would be on it and he would have her back in his arms where she belonged.

Arriving in San Francisco, dead tired and in need of sleep, he headed straight for the ticket booking office to inquire on the next ship out to Ga. His heart plummeted at hearing that he had just missed the ship that was headed to Georgia. He was devastated to learn that the next ship to the southern coast of the United States was a full three weeks away. Having no other choice, he decided to get some rest and wait for the next scheduled ship. It was a huge delay and he feared that it would cost him his beautiful bride, but he reasoned he had no other choice.

To try to get to her on horseback this time of year was foolish indeed as the fall season was upon them and the snow would soon be falling heavy and blocking the Rocky Mountain passes before he could get through. Having no choice, he booked a room for three weeks, shopped for a couple of outfits of clothing to replace his stolen items and then he found himself standing in front of a small church chapel. He stood outside staring at it for a few moments.

Suddenly he found himself walking through the door and going to the front pew. Slowly he fell to his knees and found his way and his future by conversing with God, the almighty. He put all his faith and trust into God's hands. And then he gave his worry and fears to God for his control of the situation. Then to his amazement he felt a tremendous feeling of peace entered his soul. The anxiety he was feeling left him and the ability to be patient fell upon his shoulders. He somehow knew that he was going to get there in time. His faith in God had been renewed and all he had to do was be patient, listen and trust in God as he let go of his own need to control. He found peace in the knowledge that God would handle this huge mess in his own way and in his own timing.

Resigned and at peace with himself. He walked the streets of San Francisco. He found an up and coming affluent neighborhood that was growing quickly with the building of many new homes. He selected a lot, and over the next three weeks, while he waited for his ship to sail, he assigned a crew and began building the new home that he planned to bring his wife Abby home too. He knew his faith in God had to be strong for it to work. So he did everything he could to show his maker that he fully believed that God would make his dreams come true.

Chapter Twenty-Three

Christmas Eve morning came way too quickly for Abby. Her knees were shaking as she allowed her father to walk her down the aisle to become Jeffrey's bride.

"Whatever am I doing?" She asked herself for the umpteenth time. "You are doing what you are supposed to be doing!" Her conscious answered her again for the umpteenth time. "Joseph left you, Abigail Anderson, and you now have no other choice than to gratefully accept the life you have been blessed to be allowed to return to!" She chastised herself strongly, but as her stomach knotted up she knew she was sorely failing to convince herself that she was doing the right thing.

Charles Anderson was beaming as he walked his beautiful daughter down the aisle and handed her over to Jeffrey Browning. He was so relieved that everything had worked out after all. Now all he had to do was get Abby through this ceremony and everything would return to normal. His Savannah cohorts had reassured him that his social status and his daughter's reputation would not be hurt any further once she became Mrs. Jeffrey Browning.

"Nothing can go wrong now." He whispered to his daughter attempting to reassure her that their reputations would remain in tack as he handed her over to Jeffrey. She looked incredulously at him! "Could he really be that daft?" she wondered.

Her horrified expression was not lost on him. However he attributed it to her nerves and decided that it was normal in every marriage to feel somewhat nervous.

"Who gives this woman to this man in holy matrimony?" the Reverend's booming voice scared Abby tremendously gaining her immediate attention.

"Here it is!" her conscious told her. She watched her hand in slow motion being given by her supposed father into Jeffrey Browning's strong, lean perfectly manicured hand that seemed so alien to her.

She panicked and looked at Charles anxiously begging him not to do this. It was her last hope! But she felt her father release his hand from hers as he passed it to Jeffrey. She felt that she needed to choke and might even lose her breakfast! "But I haven't eaten anything," she reminded herself and somewhat calmed momentarily at the strangely timed thought!

"Her father replied to the Reverend loudly so that the congregation could all hear him, "I do!" Bowing slightly, Charles turned and left his frightened to death daughter standing with weakened knees in a full state of panic, staring at him fearfully as he backed away from the Alter and returned to his assigned seat smiling broadly.

"Oh happy day!" he was thinking to himself oblivious to the horror his daughter was feeling!

Abby jumped and stared in horror at Jeffrey's long fingers as they closed around her dainty white gloved hand. She wanted desperately to pull away from him and run from the room. Instead, she was shocked to realize that her body had a mind of its own. She watched herself obediently turn to face the Alter and the Reverend standing tall before them holding his bible preparing for them to tie their lives permanently together.

"I didn't tell you to turn towards the alter, so who did?" her mind chastised herself as she listened obediently to the Reverend as he began his long speech regarding marriage and the responsibilities of the union of two people together.

"We are gathered here…" Abby listened to the voice of her lifelong pastor as he began her wedding ceremony. His voice echoed deep in her ears. It sounded so far away. As if she were in a dream, and at any moment she prayed the dream would end.

Startled back to reality, she heard the words, "Is there anyone present who has a legal or moral reason to object to the union of these two young adults to prevent them from being united in holy matrimony?" The Reverend loudly inquired.

The congregation became strangely silent. Everyone looked at everyone else, all wanting to know if anyone had the courage or the reason to stop this all highly exciting and long awaited wedding ceremony. Some even looked directly at Elizabeth Whatley and her mother.

She was momentarily hopeful. "Please someone speak up!" she prayed silently. "What about you Elizabeth, the one time I need you to be your pushy self, you sit there silently keeping that big mouth of yours shut!" Her thoughts were running rampant with ridiculous hope and accusations. "Come on anyone, anything! Get me out of this mess!" she implored silently to the entire congregation. She was appalled to see all the silent smiling faces of her friends all sitting there just waiting for her to hang herself. She couldn't believe that for once, Elizabeth and her mother remained sitting there silently looking downward at their own hands resting in their laps, saying nothing! Nothing at all that would save her!

She nearly found her own courage to stop the wedding! She tried to command her mouth to open and voice the words, "Just forget it, Jeffrey! *I DON'T WANT TO BE YOUR WIFE!*" But the image of her future, living as a rejected and constantly humiliated spinster in the city of Savannah prevented her from doing so. She knew that unless she went through with this marriage her life in Savannah would become totally intolerable. So her legs stood firmly rooted to the spot and her mouth refused to open and voice her true feelings. She felt doomed and locked in imprisonment for the remainder of her life. She couldn't even ask God to carry her through this horrible marriage ceremony. She was simply a puppet on a string and she knew it!

"Do you, Jeffrey Browning, take this woman, Abigail Anderson to be your lawful wedded wife to have and to hold, from this day forward…," On and on, the Reverend's monotone droned! Abby found herself to be listening from somewhere far away. She tried to focus on Jeffrey but the only face she could see through the tears that began to stream down her face was Joseph's. Suddenly she jerked her hand away from Jeffrey as he spoke his answer loud and clear for all to hear.

"I do!" Jeffrey's booming voice declared vehemently!" He quickly grabbed her hand back, squeezing it tightly.

He wasn't about to give her the chance to run and leave him stranded at the Alter. And he knew how very real that possibility was. He and he alone, knew that he was forcing her to do what her entire soul was dead set against. But he had her trapped. There was no escape for her now. He made certain that he saw to that!

Standing next to her he could hear her soul screaming "NO! Let me go free!" And if that wasn't enough he had seen her imploring him with her eyes not to do this to her. He jerked her tightly squeezing her small hand a little tighter to warn her to obey him! He wasn't taking any chances on destroying his political career and besides, she had thought she was in love with him once upon a time. So he would simply teach her to love him again, he reasoned in order to justify his bad actions.

Abby winced at the pain in her hand as he squeezed it tightly in warning, she looked up at him absolutely hating him at that moment. He saw her hatred for him, but only squeezed her hand again even tighter in warning. "Don't disobey me! Abby!" His eyes warned her.

"And do you, Abigail Anderson,"

"Oh God, what am I to do? Here it is the moment of truth! And I am trapped! Oh so trapped God! Why? Why? Are you putting me through this?" Panic filled her and she instantly implored her savior in heaven to help her. Her eyes widened in even greater fear as she awaited the moment she knew she was going to hear her own voice betray her and say *'I do!'* to that which *she absolutely didn't want to do!*

"Take this man…," the Reverend continued nonstop robbing her of precious time, "Jeffrey Browning to be your lawful wedded husband? To have and to hold…, etc..etc., she heard him continue to drone out her wedding vows. She almost wished he would hurry and she could get this awful thing behind her. Then as she blankly stared at the pastor she became unable to discern his words.

The Reverend finished with his tirade. The congregation waited tensely for her to reply. She stood there staring at the Reverend unable to move. A full minute passed and she stood there transfixed.

"Well, do you?" asked the Reverend attempting to shake her out of her reverie.

She could hear him and his request. She attempted to force herself to respond. She shook her head strongly to clear her thinking. Nervously, the Pastor began to repeat his question to Abby a third time. Again she listened to her Pastor clearly ask her again if she would take this man to be her lawful wedded husband.

"However am I going to answer yes to this? She squirmed, panicking. "Oh please floor, can't you just open up and allow me to disappear forever?" the ridiculous request went through her mind unbidden. Again she looked toward Jeffery. Her eyes beseeched him to stop forcing her to do this. She saw his refusal to free her in his dark brown eyes commanding her to simply comply.

The Reverend suddenly coughed to clear his throat. "Ah hem!" he voiced and then he slightly laughed, a little embarrassingly directed at the congregation.

"I believe we have a case of marriage nerves here!" he attempted to stall for time to allow Abby to recover and answer him and also to cover the embarrassment of her failure to answer him. He also hoped that his minor little bit of humor would help the congregation to laugh. Usually unexpected humor could turn a very nervous congregation to feeling at ease again.

"*SHE MOST CERTAINLY DOES NOT!*" Came the unexpected booming denial for her from the back of the church! All eyes pivoted to the rear of the church to stare in shock at the tall blond haired strange man, who entered wearing a red checkered shirt, his jeans stuffed in cowboy boots. He grabbed his funny looking Stetson hat off of his head, marched through the double doors and interrupted their wedding just in the nick of time!

The spell of momentary silence suddenly engulfed the entire church and just as suddenly it was broken by the loud banging of the church vestibule doors against the back walls as the stranger burst through them and made his way down the red carpeted center aisle straight towards the bride and groom standing at the altar. The loud bang made them all jump nervously in their seats. A huge buzz of confused chattering instantly ensued amongst the congregation all of whom were questioning each other as to who this stranger was and what did he think he was doing. They watched him hastily advance down the long red carpeted aisle between the polished mahogany pews.

Abby's knees froze as she instantly recognized Joseph's voice. Her eyes rose upward and she uttered a momentary prayer "Oh thank you GOD!"

"Nooooo…, NO! He's right! I certainly do not!" She vehemently answered the Pastor.

Jerking her fingers from Jeffrey's suddenly gone limp clasp in his surprise at seeing a supposed *dead man* stop his wedding ceremony. She grabbed the front of her lace layered wedding gown above her knees shocking the congregation as once again she ran oblivious to them. She ran away from the Alter, down the very aisle she had just sedately marched down in the opposite direction and threw herself into Joseph's arms.

"I knew you would come and save me! I knew you hadn't left me!" She sobbed heavily into his chest. All her depression and fears dissolved instantly. She sobbed loudly in her happiness that he had come for her! "And just in time!" she noted.

He mumbled her name as he finally held the love of his life in his arms once again but only for just a second. Then he immediately shifted her from his arms and without another single word he lifted the heavy wedding gown out of his way and with his other arm he lifted her legs. Ignoring the entire congregation, the Reverend and Jeffrey, he pivoted carrying her with him out of the church doors he had just entered so unceremoniously.

Again the double doors slammed in the face of the now entirely immobile congregation as they watched the bride being willingly kidnapped right before their very eyes!

Stunned from the unexpected drama that just occurred before their eyes, the congregation was silent and momentarily paralyzed. After a moment the entire congregation returned their eyes in unison to rest on Jeffery? "Well? What now?" the many pairs of eyes questioned him?

Their demanding gaze tore into him, but he stood motionless still trying to determine how a *dead man* had suddenly become a *living man* and that *living man* had just kidnapped his bride and destroyed his life *AGAIN!*

"Lydia, I mean, Abby girl, whom ever you are, did you really think I would leave you?" Joseph blurted out to her panting for breath from carrying her weight and moving at the same time. "You of all people should know how very much I love you!" He reprimanded her with all the love he felt for her in his panting words. He still carried her in his arms as he cleared the vestibule and kicked open the heavy front doors of the church and descended the many front marble steps straight to the waiting buggy without ever missing his step.

He placed the now ecstatically happy girl with flowing tears of joy streaming down her face, carefully into the carriage seat. Throwing all the yards of while lace and ruffles in beside her, he quickly hopped into the carriage and crossed in front of her to sit beside her. In one quick continuous moment he grabbed the reigns gave them a flick and they were off.

While driving the buggy he bent down and kissed the now exuberantly happy woman beside him. Without missing a beat he managed to keep on kissing her as he deftly turned the carriage team at the corner and headed away from the church.

She pulled away from his kiss only long enough to declare softly, "I absolutely love you Joseph Alan Jordan!" Then she hugged him as he replied,

"And I love you too! My darling precious Lydia, I Mean, *ABBY!*" he laughed as he corrected himself! Hysterically they laughed together happily! He placed one arm around her shoulders holding her as close as he possibly could while the horses proceeded to take them towards their new life at last!

Inside the church, Jeffrey stood stock still. Shocked into silence for a moment as everyone, including himself watched this strange man walk off with his intended bride to be. Her answer refusing to marry him was echoing in his head repeatedly. He turned to stare at the shocked face of his Pastor who was standing with his mouth hanging open and his arms up in the air silently questioning him as to tell them all what had just happened?

Turning four shades of red, a very embarrassed Jeffrey cleared his throat loudly. He pivoted to stare at the incredulous looks of his wedding guests. True to his political nature, he heard himself declare to the hundreds of wedding guests in attendance.

"Excuse me, but as your future Governor, of this great state of Georgia, I gave you my word that there was to be a wedding here today!" he blurted out stupidly. "Just give me a moment to retrieve my bride and we will continue with the ceremony." Laughing nervously he nodded to the silent congregation as he purposefully strode down the aisle himself and disappeared out of the wedding Chapel's double doors fully intending to retrieve his bride.

Standing at the top of the marble steps of the church, he cocked his head slightly in disbelief as he watched his bride throwing kisses and more kisses upon the man who had interrupted his wedding. He stood glued to the steps unable to move as dumbfounded, he watched the ecstatically happy couple ride off in the hired barouche. It was the longest five minutes of his life. He just stood on the concrete steps and stared after the retreating buggy as his almost bride and her lover rode out of his line of sight.

Jeffrey suddenly snapped back to attention. He turned, slamming his forehead with his outstretched palm in disbelief, his hand continued upward to run his fingers through his newly styled cropped head in bewilderment.

"Now what!" dazed he questioned himself as he turned to re-enter the church. Still in shock, his hair standing straight up in spikes from his hand movements through it, he strode ceremoniously, back into the church and down the long now intimidating red carpeted aisle.

Suddenly he stopped before Elizabeth Whatley and her mother. He rudely reached past Mrs. Whatley and roughly grabbed Elizabeth's hand and violently pulled her from the pew. Practically dragging the shocked girl who was trying to run to keep up with his long strides, he proceeded back to the waiting Reverend at the Alter who was watching the scene unfold before him in amazement.

Turning to face his invited guests, he said, "I promised you a wedding today! And my dear guests, a wedding you shall have!" he declared convincingly! "May it be known to all here today that as your future Governor of this great state of Georgia, that you may always count on me to keep my word to you!" he vowed his loyalty to them all

Elizabeth stared at him dumbly for a moment. "But I don't have on a wedding gown?" she stupidly told him. He frowned and glared at her. Suddenly she realized that special wedding gown or not, she may never have another chance to become Mrs. Jeffrey Browning! She pulled herself together and turned to face the stunned Pastor.

"You may begin again, Pastor Fredrickson," she ordered him and declared her acceptance of Jeffrey's impromptu and inappropriately given proposal at the same time.

The guests in the church remained eerily silent. Their eyes bulging from their sockets as they watched and accepted this unexpected turn of events. Charles Anderson never heard the ceremony that made Elizabeth Watkins and Jeffrey Browning man and wife. He simply sat in his seat, dazed, unable to think or hear anything around him. His daughter had just destroyed him again he was sorrowfully thinking.

Poor Jim Tucker, stared silently in shock as he lost his chance for the woman he had spent courting for over four years now. He was stunned into disbelief.

But Both Jeffrey's little sister, Bernadette Browning and Elizabeth's mother, Jewell Whatley were grinning ear to ear! Suddenly new doors had opened to them both and it appeared they were going to get their wish after all. Jewell was about to become the next mother-in-law to the future Governor of Georgia and Bernadette Browning congratulated herself gleefully as Jim Tucker was now free and she could begin working on turning her attentions onto him immediately! She gazed upon the unsuspecting man in open adoration and totally ignored Jeffery and Elizabeth's impromptu "I do's!"

Chapter Twenty-Four

Abby's tears of joy continued rolling down her face as she kissed Joseph again and again. You came for me, you really came! She voiced softly to him again and again.

"Of course I did!" Joseph told her laughing as he pulled her into his arms, "and even though I almost didn't make it in time. I would have killed that man with my own two hands if I had to in order to take you back to California with me! Don't you know how very much I love you?" He asked her again as he smothered her to his chest. Relief flooded through his now shaking body as he realized that he had barely made it to the church on time.

"Oh Joseph, I don't know what to say. I didn't want to marry him. Only I didn't have any idea what else I could do! Everyone said you had left me. I insisted on going to the cabin after you, but you and all your belongings and your horse were gone. I was so heartbroken, she sobbed into his arms. But you are here now and I am in your arms. Oh Joseph, don't let them take me away from you again! She begged him as the horrifying thought went through her head that Jeffrey might try again to stop her from being with her Joseph.

"You don't ever have to worry about that again!" he assured her reassuringly in his Texas brawl. "Baby girl, we are headed straight back to the ship I just arrived on. The captain is waiting for us. He is going to perform our marriage ceremony immediately! Then I am going to take you to the cabin I have purchased for our return journey to California!" He spoke the dreamed of words to the anxious girl.

"Then, after I have made mad passionate love to you, making you my *legal* wife in every sense of the word for ever more, then and only then, if you want we can return to your father's home to gather your belongings and anything else you want. But in two days, we are heading back to California on the same ship I just arrived to Savannah in!" He was triumphant in his jubilation of his plan's successful conclusion. "No one, not now or ever is going to separate us from each other again," he pulled her tighter and reassured her softly!

"But Joseph, how can we afford the fare for the ships journey back? I'm not so certain that my so called father will be willing to help me financially anymore?" She informed him of her concerns.

"Oh yea! My dearest Love! I nearly forgot to tell you," he pulled her away from him slightly so that he could stare directly into her questioning eyes. "Honey, we are rich!" he announced!

Her eyes questioned him if she had heard him correctly, "Whatever are you talking about?" she questioned him. In her mind they were returning to their little cabin near Shanty Shacks and she was going to have another chance at becoming the town's teacher.

"Well now!" he declared! "Here's the best part of it all. On the day of our interrupted wedding I was so doggoned angry n' all at being sent away and not being allowed to stay with you, that I started panning for gold to pass the time while I waited for the preacher to call for me to come visit with you. Baby girl! I found gold the night of our almost wedding!" he excitedly declared his good luck to her! "And honey bunches, you're not going to believe this, but I found the biggest gold nugget you ever did see!" He smiled at her as he showed her the money that over filled his wallet. And this isn't even but a drop in the bucket of it!" he assured her. "Oh and sweetheart, them hands of yurn r never gonna be rough or calloused again, cause right now we have a brand spanking new home being built for the two of us right smack in the middle of the very best new neighborhood of San Francisco!" He was so proud he grinned ear to ear as his wife's eyes got bigger and bigger in her shock at his surprising news!

She stared at the money in disbelief. "You mean you never ever really left me?" She asked him, "I thought you had walked out on me but then when you showed up in the church just now, well, I just thought you had changed your mind and decided to come after me after all." She confessed her thoughts to his surprised ears!

"Gosh no, darling, I never left you. I found the gold and hid it under the floor and then I was so tired after the beating your so called betrothed and I endured, I returned to the cabin, prospected a little and then went in and laid down on the bed and passed out. The next thing I knew, I awoke in a ships hold severely tied up with a huge lump on my head."

"Apparently your Jeffrey had tried to have me killed but instead my unconscious body was sold to a rotten scoundrel of a ship's captain. He intended me to become his newest indentured slave and then he was going to sell me as a permanent slave to anyone in China who would pay a handsome price for my skinny butt!" He told her the story as he burst into laughter! "But I fooled them all! Baby girl! Each and every one of them!" he bragged.

Her face became red with anger and her heart hardened even more against Jeffrey as Joseph related the story of how he had been kidnapped and ordered to be murdered but had been sold into slavery instead.

She finally came to the realization of what a horrible dishonest man Jeffrey Browning actually was capable of being. She had almost married a dangerous man whom she realized wouldn't stop at murder if it was in his best interests. She shuddered in tremendous relief that fate had intervened for her and saved her.

Closing her eyes, she quickly thanked her heavenly father again for his second intervention that saved her from evil. She asked for forgiveness for her rash behavior that had led to all the drama she'd recently endured. And she silently promised him that she had learned her lesson and vowed to him to do her best to allow him to take control of her life from this moment on.

She came to the understanding that her father in heaven was magnificent beyond her comprehension. Even with all the damage done by her to herself due to her own rash decisions, God had found the way and the timing to save her from her own destructive behavior.

"Oh Joseph, I'm so sorry I ever doubted you." She told him. "The truth is that I love you so very, very much. I have been unable to face life without you at my side." Grabbing his head she kissed his lips softly.

Joseph groaned as his desire for her took immediate control of him. He pulled the buggy to a stop in front of the gang plank of the ship they were to return to California in. He turned and grabbed Abby in his arms and began returning her kisses passionately. Finally all his dreams had come true and he was the luckiest man alive. They continued kissing each other passionately oblivious to those around them.

"Harrumph!" came the loud sound from the top of the gang plank. "Are you two coming aboard so that I can perform your marriage ceremony or are you going to consummate this marriage before I can actually marry you?" Jovially, the ship's captain demanded of them as he stood on board smiling broadly with a twinkle in his eye.

"Laughing, Joseph reluctantly let go of Abby only long enough to drag her up the wooden gang plank and onto the gorgeous sailing vessel. Once there standing before all the hired hands as witness, the Captain of the *Good Golly Molly* performed the long awaited ceremony and finally he *legally declared them Man and Wife!*

A Note From The Author, Judon Gray

I began writing Abby's birthright many years ago but life has a way of disrupting ones desires. I never forgot about the fictitious girl who came alive in my heart. It was many years before I was driven to return to her story. Then, my fingers flew across the keyboard as the adventurous unbelievable story of our young heroine quickly appeared on paper from the confines of my mind and heart. Her story needed to be told and I hope you have enjoyed sharing her adventures.

But stay tuned, because in *Abby's Legacy*, now nearing completion, our heroine and her love return to give you much more excitement as you enjoy their continual adventures. You will not be able to put either book down as the two lovers find themselves in one unbelievable and unexpected predicament after another! Will they choose their own destinies or will fate intervene for them again?